PRAISE FOR R. MORGAN

"A police procedural set in one of the snazziest fantasy settings ever."

— RACHEL NEUMEIER, AUTHOR OF *THE FLOATING ISLANDS*

"A fun fantasy mystery featuring a vibrant, inclusive world and a deep friendship between the protagonist and her partner sleuth. If you'd like a diverting escape to lift your spirits, Rocío and Hala have just the adventure for you."

— COURTNEY SCHAFER, AUTHOR OF THE SHATTERED SIGIL TRILOGY

"A fun, sometimes serious novel that blends humor, mystery and magic beautifully."

— A. T. GREENBLATT, NEBULA AWARD-WINNING AUTHOR OF "GIVE THE FAMILY MY LOVE"

SHADOW OF THE CITY

SHADOW OF THE CITY

R. MORGAN

Copyright © 2021 by R. Morgan

All rights reserved.

No part of this book may be reproduced in any form or by any electronic or mechanical means, including information storage and retrieval systems, without written permission from the author, except for the use of brief quotations in a book review.

The views expressed herein are those of the author and do not reflect the views of any other agency, organization, employer or company.

www.rafmorgan.com

Cover design by Jenny Zemanek

Version 1

ISBN 978-1-948516-05-1

The Fourth Gorgon press

New York, NY

To Cari, Ignacio, Gökhan, Jill, Kamma, Katie, Natasha and Yuko, for helping me through a terrible year. This book is all about friendship and nothing about divorce.

And to Martha Wells, whose books have provided solace, enjoyment and inspiration since I discovered CITY OF BONES in the sun-speckled fiction room of the Brooklyn Public Library, circa 1999.

CHAPTER 1

Detective Rocío Díaz Rossi had investigated a lot of crimes in her seven years with Miraflores Community Justice Center, but none had ever involved an underground access tunnel to the subte, a disappearing wall, and an empty room that resembled a crypt.

"Hala, we're supposed to be determining how the wall could be removed without anyone noticing, not investigating the room that appeared once the wall was gone," Rocío reminded her partner, Detective Hala Haddad Sosa. "Not that disappearing walls or empty rooms are crimes. I'm not even sure what we're doing here."

Her voice rang overloud off the close, pitted brick walls and vaulted ceiling, betraying her nerves. Behind her, electric bulbs, retrofitted into wrought-iron brackets for gaslights, lit the access tunnel for the subte—the subterranean train. Even here, twenty meters below the city, the lights had amber-tinted glass shades.

Only Rocío's flashlight lit the room before her, small and dusty and claustrophobic. Clearly it was not part of the subte—even further out of their jurisdiction than she had thought. And creepier. She hated anything having to do with old burials, long-dead bodies or strange funeral practices, a legacy of her nonna, who had liked bloodcurdling cautionary tales, especially ones about the Ghost Years. The low platform in the middle of the room was perfect for a coffin and made Rocío think of all those stories. Luckily the few bodies she saw as a detective were generally recently dead.

The flashlight in her hand flickered and died, and Rocio's breath hitched.

"The empty room might logically have something to do with the missing wall. The light, please," Hala said, steady and reassuring as always.

Rocío shook the flashlight to see if the connection was loose. "It's dead, just a sec."

She recharged the battery with the innate magic every Benerex had, a process a bit like pushing a button that existed only in her mind. The flashlight flickered back to life, and she pointed it over Hala's shoulder, catching her cropped black hair and dark skin in its jittery beam before sweeping it across the nonexistent, noncriminal contents.

"Go back to the plinth in the center," Hala said.

Rocío made a face but obeyed. "What do you see?" She steadied the light. The plinth was about four centimeters high, dust-grimed blue, unadorned and empty. "I see the tracks of at least two people besides us, though I can't tell if they were here this morning or two centuries ago."

The air smelled of machine oil and magic—like ozone and burnt sugar—most likely from the batteries powering the lights in the tunnel. They'd passed the battery room on the way here, one of the many 'landmarks' Old Nico had mentioned in his directions to supplement the signage on the walls. Old Nico was a neighborhood institution and had been the superintendent for this section of the Miraflores subte line for almost as long as it had been here, through flooding, strikes and storms. A few months ago, he had tipped them off about tainted cacao beans being smuggled through the subte tunnels, so when he had flagged them down from his booth and asked for help, they had agreed to check out the missing wall and apply their expertise to the mystery.

"Not two centuries." Hala crouched for a better view of the floor, and Rocío adjusted the flashlight. After seven years of working together, some things were second nature. "A little more to the right.

Look how the footprints smudge this thicker dust on the threshold. They entered and exited from this tunnel, which was only possible sometime in the last week or so, according to Old Nico."

She didn't say anything about Rocío missing the obvious. For one thing, what was obvious to Hala was not always obvious to anyone else. And after seven years of friendship, she knew a thing or two about Rocío, including the fear of ghosts that was distracting her now. Instead Hala reached up and guided Rocío's hand and the flashlight beam to the opposite wall, revealing a bricked-up doorway in the stone. Her hand was warm and dry on Rocío's. She stopped at a maker's stamp on one of the bricks. The upside-down logo wasn't familiar to Rocío.

"Ah, that's González and González, an Iberex brickwork that went out of business two hundred years ago. The brick must have been ballast in a trading ship, which means it's likely that other door, and this room, predate the subte by at least as long."

Of course Hala knew that. "Unless someone reused old bricks."

"Yes." Hala pointed Rocío's flashlight at the other two walls, each with its own bricked-up doorway, and then at the wall immediately to their left. "Look at that."

In Rocío's imagination, the darkness immediately populated itself with ghosts and bogeymen. She squelched those thoughts firmly. "With everything you carry in your pockets, I don't understand why you refuse to carry a flashlight."

Hala always wore sturdy broadcloth trousers covered in pockets of disparate sizes, widths and uses, from which she routinely extracted astonishingly varied things, such as mosquito repellant or samples of first-century silk from Jeen. The invariable trousers necessitated a thick leather belt to hold them up, but she varied her tops; today it was a flannel work shirt in her favorite green and a woolen overcoat. Rocío's trousers had a more normal number of pockets, and her alpaca wool sweater and camel hair coat would have done a good job of keeping her warm if the chill hadn't originated from inside her. With her long dark hair wound up and pinned, the nape of her neck felt exposed. She should have worn a scarf.

"You barely carry anything—it's only fair. Look." Hala pointed to a dark patch on the newly exposed stone.

"You still haven't answered my question. What are we doing here?"

"Hold the light steady." Hala used tweezers to free a splinter, dropped it into an evidence bag and returned everything to yet another pocket. "This room wasn't empty. The corner of one of the tiles is chipped, and whoever was here removed something wooden. I want forensics." She stood, dusted off her knees and pushed her bangs to the side. They were long for Hala, and she would no doubt raze them back to infinitesimal soon.

"Property crimes," Rocío said dubiously, "are not our office. And are too bougie for your interest even if they were. We should have told Old Nico to contact POPA." POPA was the disordered acronym for Property Offenses Against the People.

"And let him down? You wouldn't."

Rocío blew out her breath in surrender. "Okay, I wouldn't. But we should get someone from POPA here instead. That should satisfy Old Nico. I don't want to come back down here with forensics." She shuddered theatrically. "I think we deserve pastries from Benito's after this."

"I'm surprised at you," Hala said, removing her spectacles and stowing them in a case in another pocket. "Old Nico deserves better from us. If he hadn't told us the last time he saw something strange, we never would have found out who was smuggling those cacao beans. And what's stranger than almost two hundred kilos of stone going missing without anyone noticing?"

Rocío refused to be distracted by Hala's off-the-cuff estimation. Sudden suspicion stabbed through her. "Let me guess." She swung the light to shine on Hala's face.

Hala blinked back at her, her expression completely blank, a definite sign of no good.

"'Anything interesting, you tell me, Old Nico, and we'll investigate for you,'" Rocío said, imitating Hala's even voice. "That's what you told him, isn't it? Seres celestiales—you and your curiosity. Fine. Let's go talk to Old Nico about when this could have happened, and then tube forensics. Just let me out of here."

Consulting with Old Nico again revealed that the window, so to speak, for his disappearing wall had to be between Saturday, 4 April and today, Tuesday, 14 April. The old man extracted a willing promise from Hala to follow up with the Department of Transportation about work orders while he investigated whether anyone had lost a key to the maintenance entrances; those were the least conspicuous ways to remove such a quantity of rock.

Leaving Old Nico's office, Rocío and Hala traversed the bowels of the city via more access tunnels and very civilized stairs, neither of which resembled actual bowels, thank the seres celestiales, and emerged, blinking, outside. Rocío opened her umbrella and took a deep breath of leaf mold and horse manure. The muscles in her back relaxed, and thoughts of ghosts receded to where they belonged, the dim recesses of her mind.

In mid-autumn, the city of La Beneficia de nuestros vecinos y los seres celestiales (La Bene for short) was not at her most attractive, but the rain pattered softly, comfortingly, and birds cheeped slightly frantically, as if they had stayed out late partying instead of doing their housekeeping chores for the winter and now realized how unprepared they were. On the median, the brightly colored umbrellas of pedestrians waiting for a horse-drawn trolley to pass made a pleasant picture against the bare branches of the Tipa trees lining the broad avenue.

Hala turned left on 15 de agosto instead of right towards the tube office. Rocío ambled after her and popped a piece of gum into her mouth, waiting to see if Hala was going to tell her where they were going now. Rocío absently greeted a street cleaner she knew and a neighbor from her apartment building, which was only a few blocks away, where the neighborhood changed from swank to merely chic.

"I wish someone had invented recording more than ten years ago so we had an idea what the really old accents sounded like." Hala turned left on Calle ch'eju'ut, one of the oldest streets in the city, where families who traced their ancestry to the first refugees to arrive in La Bene lived in mansions behind more trees, whitewashed walls and wrought-iron gates.

Rocío accepted this non sequitur with the ease of practice. "Like Old Nico's? My grandparents sounded like him, except for my nonna, of course. Are you thinking of doing a linguistic analysis?"

"I'd love to track how fast each immigrant group adapts to and changes the dominant accent."

"So where are we going?" Rocío finally gave in and asked.

Hala stopped abruptly at the entrance to the biggest house on the street. The black gates were worked in the shape of mountain peaks tipped with gold. Rocío tilted her umbrella back to get a better look at the grounds and the mansion, though she could see only a slice of dark green manicured oleander bushes and a white portico and columns.

"Montenegro House," Hala said. "If it's not above the underground room, I'll eat my socks."

"Don't do that. You're still wearing yesterday's."

Hala turned her intense stare from the house to Rocío. "How do you know that?"

It was a game they played; their minds worked so differently that they often came to the same conclusion by wildly different routes. But that didn't mean Rocío couldn't get back at Hala a bit for luring her underground and not telling her where they were going after.

"Really, Hala? I *am* a detective. A bona fide member of the Miraflores Community Justice Center. And I happen to know you only have one pair of $E=mc^2$ socks. Which you also wore yesterday. And laundry day is Sunday in your house."

"Umphf. I ran out of clean socks because of the rain on Tuesday."

"Hala, it *is* Tuesday."

"Last Tuesday. I missed laundry entirely this week." She turned back to the house. "Rocío, the empty room is there. What's more, it must be within their wards."

"You're sure?" Rocío asked, straightening.

"Dirty socks sure."

"About the wards, too? Because opening up an unused room in the subte is one thing, but getting through expensive wards like the Montenegros must have is another."

"Yes."

Her flat tone increased Rocío's worry. "Surely we'd have heard if someone had tampered with their wards."

Then again, the Montenegros, one of the wealthiest and most important families in the city, had their fingers in most political pies. So maybe not.

"They might not know yet." Hala marched up to the gate.

"Wait."

Hala had people skills; she just didn't always use them. She showed her ID booklet to the gatekeeper.

"Let me do the talking," Rocío whispered. "They're not going to like this."

"I usually do."

The gatekeeper gave them a nod and allowed them in, revealing the house at the end of the drive. Black gate, white shell drive, white house, black angular details around the door and windows. It reminded Rocío of the Kaellic dance troupe that had come through last year, their bodies stiff straight lines imposed on the world, emphasized by the stark white costumes printed with black knotwork designs.

As they approached, the door opened, disgorging the Ministrx of External Relations—an imposing older man with silver hair—and two women in their early thirties, who looked enough alike to be cousins and were probably assistants. All three were most likely related, because that's how politics worked in La Bene. The pins in their elaborately arranged hair were no doubt real gold and silver with real gemstones, unlike Rocío's enameled silver-plated steel. The woman with the lighter brown hair whispered to the others, recognition and interest flaring in her eyes, and Rocío braced herself.

Ministrx O'Higgins nodded courteously. "Detectives, is there a problem?"

"Nothing to worry about," Rocío said blithely.

"I'm Ministrx O'Higgins Cruz, and these are my assistants,

Gumersinda de Herrera Nuñes and Críspula de Herrera Carmona. Should we be concerned for Ministrx Montenegro?"

As a stratagem to extract Rocío's and Hala's names, it was fairly obvious.

"Not at all, ministrx," Hala said. "Have a good day."

Rocío guessed that as soon as the group stepped past the gate, they would begin to speculate wildly. That wouldn't endear them to Ministrx Montenegro when she learned of it.

When they were out of earshot, Rocío said, "Those are unfortunate names."

"Very old Benerex names. The twenty-fourth of November and the thirteenth of March in the old almanac," Hala said, reprising her role as human repository of mostly forgotten facts.

"Ah, of course," Rocío said dryly, used to Hala's habit of spouting obscure information.

The Montenegros' majordomo held the door open without communicating any welcome. She was middle-aged, with the straight nose and sharp cheekbones of Disi ancestry. The laugh lines around her eyes hinted at a sense of humor that was not in evidence at the moment. She didn't blink when Hala introduced them, and she didn't offer to take their coats or umbrellas.

"Ministrx Montenegro is not available at the moment."

Rocío nudged Hala out of the way. "We understand the ministrx is a busy woman," she said, balancing courtesy and authority. "We only need a moment to speak with her. It is important and sensitive. I'm sure she would like to hear what we have to say."

"The ministrx is unable to see you at this time."

"Tell her—"

Rocío stepped on Hala's foot and spoke over her. "We would like to leave her a note."

"Of course." The majordomo extracted the necessary tools from the table in the foyer and continued to block further entry to the house, so Rocío penned her note in situ, summing up the situation, and folded it.

"We'll wait, just in case," Rocío said.

The majordomo withdrew up the stairs and left them dripping on the black-and-white mosaic inlay.

"I don't see how that was more effective than what I was going to say," Hala said. She flicked a nail against the cobalt vase on the silver-mounted demilune table, and it pinged.

"Don't do that," Rocío said. "It's worth your yearly salary."

Hala hesitated with her hand still raised and gave Rocío an incredulous look.

"Seriously. It depends on what your goal is," Rocío said. "Mine is primarily to not offend the ministrx so much she decides to get us fired and only secondarily to let her know she might have a problem."

Hala snorted. The majordomo's return precluded any further response, for which Rocío was grateful.

"The ministrx is not available."

"Thank you." Rocío nodded to her and pulled Hala out the door by her arm. At least it had stopped raining. Hala didn't speak as they crunched down the drive to the street.

"What do you think?" Hala asked, turning the right way for the tube office.

"You know as well as I do that interpreting body language depends on each individual's patterns, and changes to the pattern—"

"Rocío."

"If you'd let me finish, I was going to say that the majordomo seemed more surprised on her return than she was to see us knocking on the door, so you could extrapolate that she read the note or passed it on to the ministrx, with the same result in either case."

"Will the ministrx call us back?"

Rocío's parents had spent decades aspiring to leave the ranks of the well heeled and well bred to join the highest ranks of the political elite of La Bene, and had ... bestowed ... upon Rocío all the education and exposure money could buy in an effort to achieve that goal. At seventeen, Rocío had run away to join the theater. At thirty-four, she had joined the CJC. In neither career had she been able to prove her parents entirely wrong; knowledge of the elite was useful.

"I think she will. Eventually."

〜

Plaza de los mártires, a trapezoid-shaped plaza left from when the city was part of the Ka Empire, was deserted because of the recent rain, except for a man feeding quail next to the DON'T FEED THE BIRDS sign. Rocío felt free to ignore the violation of the public good, especially as no one had complained about it to her. On the west side, the tube office stood two doors down from the Community Justice Center in a row of shops, cafes and homes, the buildings low shapes that at any other time of the year emphasized the largeness of the sky; in autumn they seemed to barely hold it up.

This pneumatic tube office wasn't open to the general public but was reserved for the use of public servants such as bona fide members of the Miraflores Community Justice Center. Such as them. Also, firefighters and emergency workers of all types. Rocío pushed open the heavy wooden door. Gustavo, the big, dark-skinned magicker in charge of the office, had his feet up and a cup of cafe con leche cradled in his lap. It smelled heavenly and was probably from Benito's. Rocío shot an accusing look at Hala, who ignored her.

Gustavo lowered his feet with a thump and rubbed the back of his hand against his tightly curling beard. "This doesn't look like an emergency. I barely recognize you, Rocío, in this state of calm."

"I'm calm."

"She's calm." He turned his thumb at Hala.

"She's dead inside," Rocío joked.

"I'm rational, which both of you could be if you only tried," Hala said.

When Rocío had joined the CJC, it had taken almost six months to figure out if Hala had a sense of humor and how to tell when she was joking. The answer was yes, and the corner of her left eye crinkled a bit. It barely crinkled now. Only a few other masters of the human face and a retired actor turned detective who had received conditional love from her parents would have noticed.

"What is it this time?" Gustavo asked. "I haven't recovered from the outbreak of malarial mosquito fairies four months ago."

"Technically you'd be dead if you hadn't recovered from the MMFs," Hala said. "We all would be."

Rocío shuddered at the memory of the demented fairy faces on mosquitos the size of cicada wasps. She had scars on her hands from their bites, and quick-onset malaria hadn't been fun either, but they'd caught the man responsible. The city adjudicator had found no signs of remorse in him, and the people of La Bene had almost unanimously asked for transportation, and so he had been sent to the Ka Empire to the south. Because magic was geographic in nature—the manipulation of electrical energy in La Bene or the manipulation of fairies in Enkladt, to name just two—he would have to relearn how to use magic, which the Ka shamans would prevent.

"Not an emergency," Rocío said. "Just a message. A routine, unimportant message."

"Uh-huh." Gustavo didn't look like he believed her. She didn't believe herself, either. Hala had a talent for discovering the strange, and Rocío was developing a talent for the dangerous. The combination often had unnerving results.

They trooped down into the bowels of the earth again—though compared to the subte, these bowels were too short for viability for a living organism—and entered a well-lit, civilized office. Or rather a well-lit cross between the office of a low-level bureaucrat and a child's idea of a mad scientist magicker's den constructed by a master artisan, which it kind of was.

Bins marked with dates lined the bottom edges of all four walls, logbooks peeking out of the tops of a few. Above them were the end points of the pneumatic tubes through which messages in rocket-shaped capsules hurtled across La Bene in minutes to each district's community justice center, public tube office, fire station, or the House of Refugees, La Bene's seat of government. In the center of the room was the power apparatus, made of gleaming steel and copper and bearing more than a passing resemblance to a grasshopper as long as Rocío's arm. It needed a level-three magicker to operate, hence Gustavo.

Hala seized a pad of very thin paper and a pen from Gustavo's desk, pushed aside machine parts and more pads, and started scribbling.

"They'll never be able to read that," Rocío said, looking over Hala's shoulder. Hala crumpled her first effort and started again. "Better ask if there was any work done that Old Nico might not know about."

Hala stopped writing to give her an incredulous look.

"Okay, probably not, but just ask."

"Where to?" Gustavo asked.

"Department of Transportation," Rocío and Hala said at the same time.

"Well, as long as you're sure." Gustavo winked at Rocío. "Don't forget to date it."

Hala dated it in the three calendars—La Bene's: 14 April, year 449; the Ya Empire's: 12.14.15.14.13 / 2 Ben / 11 kumk'u / Lord of the Night G5; and the Ka Empire's: Year 17 of the Divine Emperor Lloque.

"Show-off," Rocío said. Most people needed a calendar converter for the Ya Empire's system.

Hala's eye crinkled a bit more.

Gustavo rummaged in yet another bin, producing one of the dull brown rocket capsules, since it wasn't an emergency. Those got red capsules for fire, green for medical assistance, yellow for community justice advocates, et cetera. In spite of all the emergencies Rocío had dealt with, she still occasionally had the impulse to manufacture one so she could enjoy launching the shiny capsules into the tubes.

Hala jammed her now-legible note inside the capsule, and Gustavo flipped the switch on the grasshopper machine, keeping his other hand on the contact panel on its back to power it with his magic. The machine purred, a disconcertingly catlike sound to come from a hard-edged, shiny grasshopper-like machine, powering the hidden pump that sucked air through the tubes.

In La Bene magic manifested as electrical energy, an extension of the body's electric field beyond its bounds and under conscious control. In school everyone learned to warm their tea and not give others accidental electrical shocks. Those who went to the University for magic learned more. The CJC's basic certificate program ensured advocates learned to detect residual magical fields and work some specialized machinery. Rocío had passed, barely, because magical foundational theory was hard, and you couldn't practice more advanced magic without it. Others, like Gustavo, went to the University and became bureaucrats or teachers or engineers who developed new machines. Anyone could, just like anyone could become a plumber, but not everyone wanted to become a magicker, just like not everyone wanted to be a plumber.

Gustavo cocked his head, his gaze turned inward, barely looking at the gauge that measured magical input into the machine. He didn't need to; he'd been the tube magicker here for longer than Rocío had been a detective.

"Tube fifty-two," he said, which wasn't magic at all but mechanics.

Hala opened the cap on the indicated tube and tossed the capsule inside. The vacuum sucked it away.

CHAPTER 2

THE COMMUNITY JUSTICE CENTER was a graceful old house that had
been donated to the CJC around the same time the subte had been
built. It dated back almost to the founding of La Bene and the arrival
of the first refugees more than four hundred years ago. The previous
owner still maintained the pristine white façade, the crisp molded
scrolls and seashells above the door and windows, and the polished
brass doorknob. The wooden shutters in the deep-set windows were
open, allowing in as much light as possible on such a dim day and
letting out the sounds of yelling.

Rocío and Hala exchanged a glance and stepped inside, into a
raucous wave of sound.

Three teenagers in the rumpled school sarongs and sweaters of
the Hakaara Polytechnic School sullenly kicked their heels against
the legs of the bench on the left, waiting for a counselor to help them
sort out their problem. A woman in a Ya-style indigo huipil with a
long-sleeved black shirt underneath and a man in a black house
servant cap and an unseasonable kilt stood at the desk across from
the door, loudly arguing about who had arrived first.

Chief Maurata Martínez, in a sadly precedented display, was
babbling about a hole puncher and blocking the stairs, while at the
bottom, Deputy Chief Oshinsky bas Rifke huddled with her assistant
and two jurisprudence adjudicators. And two chaskis—teenaged

message runners serving vocational apprenticeships with the CJC in the hopes of getting adult jobs there as advocates, support staff, counselors, magickers or forensic techs—were betting on the reason for Maurata's upset.

Advocate Espinoza Onyeneme, who should have been at the desk, pounced on Rocío and Hala before the door even closed behind them. "Someone to see you," she shouted, her next words lost as the teenagers erupted in an argument about who had sabotaged whom in the mathematics competition.

Chief Maurata, who should have asserted control in the CJC, had never really twigged to the fact that it was part of his responsibilities. Deputy Chief Oshinsky usually did his job as well as her own, but her discussion seemed serious. Which left Maurata's job, as usual, to anyone who stepped into his vacuum.

"Enough!" Rocío's stage-trained shout stunned everyone into silence. "Chief Maurata, the hole puncher is in the second office on the left on the third floor."

He bolted up the stairs as if the future of the CJC depended on it.

"You"—she pointed her finger at the three kids—"will shut up, or we'll tell the adjudicator you should all get double community service sorting garbage."

One of the girls said, "That's not—"

The other one pinched her, and she stopped talking.

Rocío folded her arms and stared them down. They ducked their heads, whispering, and gave her dirty looks, but since they had quieted, Rocío ignored them.

Now that Maurata was no longer blocking the way, Deputy Chief Oshinsky hustled her group up the stairs.

Hala took over. "Officer Espinoza, Ministrx Montenegro may be contacting us soon about a crime. I want to hear about it when she does. And we're expecting a return message from the Department of Transportation."

"Are you predicting crimes now?" Espinoza asked incredulously. "Never mind. Detective Díaz, thank you for getting them to listen."

Espinoza was the shortest person Rocío had ever known, though she compensated by staying extremely fit, taking up more room than could be accounted for physically, and sporting a serious expression, but she probably hadn't loomed over the teenagers convincingly enough. She saved that for adults who should have known better than to do whatever had landed them at the CJC. Also, she was still recovering from gender-affirming surgery, which was why she was on desk duty on a Tuesday, a time that generally didn't require much looming.

"There's a chaski for you in interview three. She has a message from your mother," Espinoza said.

Hala had started to turn away, but she stopped to listen.

Stiffening, Rocío fiddled with a hairpin that didn't need fixing. An automatic soothing habit. She forced her hand down. "I could just ignore her."

"You could," Hala said.

"I was *joking*," Rocío said, half offended Hala could think she was serious.

"Sadly, I knew that."

Rocío caught Espinoza's eye and tilted her head at the teenagers, who were muttering again. Espinoza nodded and pointed the woman in the huipil to a seat; she huffed and plopped into it with as much attitude as the teenagers. Espinoza rolled her eyes and herded the kids to a counselor's office.

Hala trailed Rocío to interview three, which was the nicest, the one with the comfortable furniture and watercolor paintings of fishing boats. The chaski, a young woman in loose pants and a tight jacket, jumped up when Rocío entered the room. Hala leaned against the doorway, radiating disapproval.

"Are you Rocío Díaz Rossi?" the chaski asked. At Rocío's nod, the chaski tapped the badge of the tube office pinned to her jacket. "Message for you from Analicía Rossi Dey." She handed Rocío an elaborately folded and sealed letter.

Rocío cracked the seal over the table to catch the pieces of wax. It was the usual summons. She stifled a disgusted sigh. It would just give Hala ammunition she didn't need.

"No response," she told the chaski, who bobbed her head and scampered out of the room.

"You're going?" Hala asked, so studiously neutral it called to mind every comment she'd ever made on the subject of Rocío's inconsiderate, exhausting mother.

"She said it's urgent." Rocío matched Hala's tone to avoid discussion. Hala couldn't understand; her family was different. Lucky, lucky Hala.

"Just once, you could not go," Hala said.

"I know you don't like her, but she's my mother," Rocío explained, gesturing inadequately. "I'll be back soon."

On her way back to the CJC, Rocío wrote summonses for a woman scalping opera tickets and a food vendor whose health inspection sticker had expired, but it didn't make her feel better. She wanted to arrest a bad guy, preferably someone who mugged little old ladies or a corrupt politician or her mother, for the crime of terminal delusion. She'd invent the category just for her. If she slipped the paperwork into Maurata's expense reports, he might sign it without noticing.

Assistant. That's what she thinks I'm worth. The summons had been an ambush, her mother's minor politician friend offering her a job as an assistant. As if she didn't already have a job, and one she liked.

"Don't be silly—that job doesn't matter, darling. The CJC is just the district government. It isn't real government," her mother had said, making *darling* sound more like an epithet than an endearment. And then she had claimed Rocío had embarrassed *her* in front of her friend by turning down a position she had never asked for.

A perdido assistant position in a politician's office. It was a time-honored system of political apprenticeships, generally reserved for family members and close family associates. Rocío was neither, and in that position, she would either have to fight viciously for every opportunity or beg for crumbs. *That's what my mother wants for me? Her jaw ached from clenching it so hard. Why do I let her do this to me every time?*

Her own response had been less than satisfying. She had told her mother she'd stop responding to her messages if she kept doing this, but they both knew it for an empty threat.

The sight of a friend's strained, gray face abruptly pulled Rocío out of her thoughts. María Paz looked straight through Rocío, her eyes shocky. Her teeth worried her bloodless bottom lip.

"Maipa?" Rocío reached for her arm. "What's wrong? Can I help?"

María Paz focused on her and jerked back. "Rocío, I can't—excuse me." She rushed away, careening off a chaski, sending his stack of newspapers fluttering to the ground. The boy shouted a curse after her, and Rocío bent to help him collect the papers.

After he hurried away, Rocío unwrapped a piece of gum and surveyed the street. On one side, the sign for the gossip rag *Oye* glittered in gold script. On the other, an accountant's somber font read BETEN AND DAUGHTERS. Had Maipa just exited one their offices?

A brief conversation with the accountant established that Maipa had not visited their establishment. That left the gossip rag, a disturbing prospect. Inquiries there might get Rocío or the CJC on its front page; she wanted that about as much as an actor wanted to forget her lines on opening night.

Back at the CJC, Espinoza pounced on Rocío as soon as she walked in. It was much quieter than it had been an hour ago. "Chief Oshinsky wants to see you."

"Right now? Just me?" Rocío asked.

"Yup."

"Do you know what about?"

"She didn't say." Espinoza shrugged.

Rocío left her coat in the locker room and took the stairs to Oshinsky's office. Her assistant, Paloma Faro Otxandabaratz, gestured her in, perhaps a tad more gracefully than usual. Rocío wasn't sure what that meant.

"Close the door, please," Oshinsky said. She had fine graying brown hair pulled into an unadorned bun that Rocío's mother would have frowned at and calloused hands her father would have lifted his eyebrows at ever so slightly, had they ever met Oshinsky. They would have noticed the intelligence in her blue eyes, but without the outward packaging cared for to their standards, they would have dismissed it. And they'd have failed to see the humor in them entirely.

"What's up?" Rocío slung herself into the armchair on her side of the desk and glanced at the altar to Oshinsky's ancestors on top of the bookcase. Sometimes it held a clue to her concerns, but today it was the usual marigolds, candles and photos of her parents.

"I want you to do something for me."

"Of course." Rocío sat up straight and reached for her notepad and pencil. The last time Oshinsky had asked her to do something with that tone of voice, it had involved a tacata music contest, embezzlement and black market turkeys. In other words, it hadn't been boring.

"Not like that." Oshinsky steepled her fingers, the paleness of her eyes, a rarity in this city full of brown-eyed citizens, still disconcerting after all these years. "Paloma is smart and quick thinking but also methodical."

"Yes?" Rocío asked, confused but willing to go along.

"She also wants to be an advocate and eventually a detective."

"She'd be a good one—she's sharp, like you said," Rocío said, finding her place in the conversation. "Doesn't miss a lot."

"Which is why I want her to start field training with you."

And she lost it again. An annoyed flush heated Rocío, and she shifted, wishing she hadn't worn a wool sweater. The image of Paloma's perfectly coifed hair and perfectly composed face rose in Rocío's mind. Her pulse pounded in her ears. Unlike Oshinsky, Paloma was perfectly smooth, perfectly elite. She was exactly what Rocío's parents wanted Rocío to be, exactly what she didn't *want* to be. Every model her parents wanted her to emulate looked like Paloma. Rocío could and did deal with people like her every day, but at a distance. Then she came back to the CJC and got away from them. Training Paloma meant she would never get away. It would be like having her mother hanging over her shoulder.

Seres celestiales, Paloma was probably angling to be chief after Maurata and be Oshinsky's boss. Her family was closer to the top of the social hierarchy than Rocío's, but only just. In that position— their shared position—it was your duty to improve the status of your family. Rocío's refusal to do so was the main source of the friction between her and her family.

Being the chief of an important community justice center like Miraflores, which lay at the heart of La Bene's government district, was a prime stepping stone into politics. Those positions went to the people with connections, not the ones who did the hard work, like Deputy Chief Oshinsky; she would never be chief, because she was third-generation Benerex with no ties to the founding families. She had worked her way up to the rank of deputy chief. And what had Paloma done to deserve a promotion? Been born to the right family, that's all. Didn't Oshinsky see that?

"Oh. Are you," Rocío cleared her throat, "sure about her?" That sounded sincere, right? Not passive-aggressive? Or just aggressive?

"If she wanted to stay my assistant, I would keep her forever, but that's not what she wants."

And Oshinsky helped her people get what they wanted. Look at Rocío, one of Oshinsky's many protégés; look at half the forensic techs and chaskis who had become a regular staff member at the CJC. And now Oshinsky wanted to nurture a social climber into a position of authority over her and the whole CJC, never mind sticking her in the middle of Rocío and Hala's partnership. It made her feel sick.

But there were some things you didn't say right out to the boss, not even the best boss. Like, *I think you're being hoodwinked by someone you trust.* That took finesse that Rocío currently didn't have. Planning.

"I don't think I'm the best choice for this." There, that sounded reasonable, although it didn't actually address the problem. "I haven't trained a new advocate before, not from start to finish."

"It's time you did," Oshinsky said cheerfully, with no sign that Rocío's hints had landed. "Hala will help you. And I'm here to answer questions and support you. You're one of my best, Rocío."

Usually Oshinsky's hard-earned praise made Rocío proud, but now she just felt resentful. "But maybe not the best for *this*." And then she stalled, because who would be the best at protecting Oshinsky from herself? Not the other Díaz. Not Fede or Leo or Felix or Julia, the other detectives. "You could ask Hala." Even as she said it, she knew Hala's abilities lined up with Rocío's priorities, not Oshinsky's. So it wasn't likely she would say yes. And Paloma would still be right there.

"Paloma's strengths are similar to yours. She's good with people, and she's good at reading them. I want you to do it."

Rocío blinked and looked away from Oshinsky's direct gaze. She wanted to say no. But what reason could she give? *I don't like her* didn't hold water. You didn't have to like someone to work with them. And Rocío wasn't, quite, willing to have a tantrum and lose Oshinsky's good opinion. But she didn't want to train Paloma, work with her every day for months, give her advice, bring her into her metaphorical family and then watch Paloma destroy that family. *Get a grip, Chío,* she told herself. *This isn't a play.*

The desk didn't hold an answer. Neither did the framed photograph of Oshinsky's son and daughter. "Chief..."

"Good." Oshinsky rapped her knuckles on her desk and startled Rocío into looking at her. "I want her to start immediately."

Rocío tried to resign herself to her fate. "Right. Anything else?"

"Just my thanks."

Paloma wasn't at her desk when Rocío left Oshinsky's office. *Reprieve.*

Rocío rushed down the back stairs. She found Hala with Yaco Tuz, a forensic tech, in one of the labs, explaining something about wood.

"There you are," Hala said. "I was wondering if I needed to send in the rescue team."

"Very funny."

"The Department of Transportation—"

"We have to go," Rocío said, snagging Hala's sleeve. "Sorry, Yaco."

He half lifted his hand to wave, but Rocío steered Hala to the back exit before he could finish.

Hala twitched out of Rocío's grasp and eyed her thoughtfully. "I need my coat, and so do you. It's raining again."

"Fine." Rocío reversed direction, but rather than cutting through the internal courtyard, where they'd be more visible, she led Hala the longer way around the back of the building, past the labs and along the edge of the big open office where the advocates worked.

She scanned the room and spotted Paloma facing away from them, next to Hala's and her desks. Rocío focused on the locker room door, blocking out everything else on the theory that if she didn't look at Paloma, Paloma wouldn't look at her. Once inside, she hustled them both into coats, used a small spark of magic to short-circuit the alarm on the emergency exit and pushed Hala out. She took the time to make sure the door closed tightly, which would reset the alarm, then hustled Hala down the alley.

"What did Oshinsky want?" Hala asked.

Rocío turned up her collar against the drizzle and didn't speak until they had reached the main street. "I hate this part of autumn. Hola, Señorx Romero," she called to the older woman sweeping leaves off the doorstep of Café Storia. "Is your son sick again?"

"He is, but how did you guess?" Señorx Romero leaned on her broom, brows arched in question.

"He usually does the sweeping," Rocío obliged her. "And also the doctor's assistant has been gossiping again. He's trying to impress one of the chaskis at the CJC."

"You hear everything, don't you? I've never seen such a talent for keeping gossip straight."

"Ouch. That's a little harsh."

"No, no," Señorx Romero said. "It's a good thing in a detective. Come for lunch. Ravioli with squash and walnuts."

"Are we having lunch? You never did explain where we're going," Hala said, sliding a look at Rocío.

"We're—"

"Detective Díaz," Paloma called. "Detective Haddad." She practically bounced up to them, smiling pleasantly.

"Hello, Paloma, what are you doing here?" Hala asked.

That was the thing about Paloma—she was always pleasant. The expensive gold and red silk wrappings in her shiny black hair were always evenly spaced and studded with gold or silver pins inlaid with lapis or amethyst. Her face was a perfect oval; even her earlobes were perfect. She reeked of privilege and pleasantness and she was a very good assistant. Rocío had always admired her competence until now. From an uninvolved distance. She really didn't want all that pleasantness up close and personal.

"Deputy Chief Oshinsky sent me. She says I'm ready for field training in support of my request to become an advocate, like you. I'm excited to be working with you. Thank you so much." She exuded sincerity and eagerness.

Rocío studied her, looking for signs that Paloma knew she'd been purposefully left behind. The elite of La Bene had grace and body control drilled into them, through years of etiquette classes, to mask their emotions, but Rocío had attended the same classes at her parents' insistence. Paloma's chin might be a little too high, her voice a little too forceful, but that could be nervousness.

"I'm excited for this opportunity," Paloma gushed.

"How wonderful," Rocío said more flatly than she intended, and then winced internally at her own lack of grace in comparison to Paloma. But Rocío was determined not to be taken in by her. If Oshinsky wasn't going to be careful, Rocío would be careful for her.

Paloma's smile faltered, and Rocío became aware of Señorx Romero still leaning on her broom, watching them.

"Well done," Hala said, with all the warmth Rocío hadn't been able to summon. "I didn't expect you to break with your family's expectations for another four months. Rocío is an excellent choice of mentor. You have a lot in common."

Rocío and Paloma broke off their staring contest to stare at Hala instead.

"What? I have people skills, even if Rocío always gets all the credit."

When Hala did use her people skills, they were often aimed at preventing Rocío from saying things she shouldn't. Like now.

"So where are we going?" Hala asked. "I assume the chief sent you."

"Right." Paloma almost visibly pulled herself back on topic. "The manager of La Valle reported a theft, and Chief Oshinsky is sending you. Us."

"Señorx Romero, will you save some of that ravioli for us?" Rocío asked.

"Of course. Anytime." Señorx Romero resumed sweeping.

"Ready?" Hala asked. "Rocío?"

"I'm ready," Paloma said with more peppiness than the situation warranted.

I'm not. "Let's go." Even to her own ears, Rocío sounded as sullen as the teenagers that morning. An annoyed detective, an overeager, unwanted advocate-in-training and the volatile world of one of the most famous performance spaces in La Bene. What could possibly go wrong?

CHAPTER 3

Paloma was mercifully unintrusive on the trolley, the clop of the horse's hooves on the cobblestones was soothing and Rocío recovered some of her equanimity. *I can out-pleasant even Paloma while I figure out what to do.*

"Yaco was telling me about the splinter I found when you interrupted us," Hala said.

Rocío winced. "Sorry."

"It's too small to identify on it's own, but it might be enough to match to a larger piece, if we find one."

Rocío didn't say anything about needles and haystacks and letting creepy crypts lie. Besides, with the Montenegros' wardstones involved, that wasn't an option.

Paloma glanced curiously from Hala to Rocío. "We'll explain later," Rocío said. "Not here."

"And the Department of Transportation confirmed that no work of any type was authorized in that subte tunnel," Hala said. "They're inventorying keys and will let us know if any are missing, though they said there are dozens."

The trolley slowed at the corner of La Quinta and Bulevar Sascahuama. "We're getting off here," Rocío told Paloma, trying to fulfill her vow of pleasantness, and the three of them jumped down from the still-moving trolley with four other passengers.

Going to La Quinta was like stepping into the past and going home. To a nice home, not like the one Rocío's parents had made. She had spent most of her twenties here in bars and performance spaces. Her parents had spent most of their forties trying to get her out while Rocío fell in love with theater, found mentors, got her first part, got a better part, danced and acted across the neighborhood's stages, mentored others. Her parents hadn't stood a chance.

By daylight, La Quinta looked shabby but not seedy. By lamplight, it was alluring—this strip was home to some of the best poetry, dance and music venues and small theater productions in the city.

La Valle was still the uncontested leader for tacata and dance performances and had been for almost two decades, equivalent to two centuries in show business time. The exterior was covered in handbills layers deep. A forensic historian could excavate and maybe never find the walls underneath. The top layer was yellow with a stylized woman in blue jumping or dancing in profile, announcing the opening of *La Ingenue* on Wednesday.

The door was propped open. Rocío pushed aside the red velvet curtain and paused. Even compared to the gray afternoon, it was too dark inside for her eyes to adjust immediately.

"Aleksandr would not do such thing," yelled a thickly accented Rusic voice. "He is my brother. I tell you is not him. Something happened to him!"

"Something happened!" shouted another voice with a north Bene accent. "Something happened, all right. Your thieving brother sold my show, took the money and is halfway to Jeen by now."

Rocío's eyes adjusted. Chairs were upended on small tables scattered throughout the room, and the smell of lemon cleaner and beeswax polish hung in the air. Underneath was the tang of spoiled yeast and old alcohol, most likely chicha, the fermented maize or potato beer everyone drank. It smelled like home.

Onstage, two men leaned in, shouting in each other's faces. The Rus was about 190 centimeters and sixty-five kilos. Rocío judged he was constitutionally thin rather than undernourished from poverty. In spite of the chill, he wasn't wearing a coat, only the white linen blouse with full sleeves gathered at the wrists that Rocío associated with people from the Rus. The flowers embroidered on the front were red, the left cuff was ink-stained and his trousers had more ink on one knee. Something about his clothes shouted *recent arrival*, though his compatriots who had lived longer in La Bene wore almost the same thing.

The owner of the establishment, René Sahakian Quispe, called Pepe by everyone who knew him, looked like a brawler with his broad shoulders, flattened nose and beetling eyebrows. In Rocío's experience he was mild mannered even in the midst of theater people's crises, which was saying a lot. It was bad for a show to be stolen, but it wasn't *that* uncommon, so she couldn't imagine why ... oh, wait, she could.

"My show—my brother—JEEN!" the Rus spluttered, apparently unsure which accusation upset him the most.

"All yours," Hala said sotto voce to Rocío.

"Pepe," Rocío called, but he was already vaulting from the stage to embrace her and kiss her cheeks four times. The ornate tupu pin holding his serape closed caught on her coat. "You know I hate that," she said, extracting herself.

The Rus about toppled over without the weight of Pepe's anger to hold him up.

"Mi amor, my savior, I need you, I'm courting you," Pepe declared.

"This, this—" the Rus yelled.

Hala helpfully handed up her ID booklet.

"This is police, so obviously in your bags? This man has done something to my brother. I need help, not minion."

Rocío put a restraining hand on Pepe's shoulder. "We're not in anyone's pockets, señorx ...?"

"Piotr Arkadyevich Prokofiev," he said, drawing himself up, his nostrils flaring. He had a sharp nose, high cheekbones and pale eyes. "How do I know?"

"Señorx Prokofiev, we do community justice here in the Miraflores district of La Bene, which means we know the people who live and work here well. It looks strange to outsiders, but we serve everyone equally, including new arrivals." It was her standard explanation, used hundreds if not thousands of times a year.

La Bene was a port, and the city welcomed refugees and immigrants, one of the mandates given by its refugee and immigrant founders. For people who had left or fled places without community justice, with police who protected only certain segments of society or a military used against its citizenry, the explanation wasn't enough. Only actions sometimes reached across that breach.

"I'm Detective Rocío Díaz Rossi, this is Detective Hala Haddad Sosa, and this is Advocate Paloma Faro Otxandabaratz."

"Oxtand ..."

"Advocate Faro is fine."

"We're here to help," Rocío said. "Please tell us what happened."

Piotr Prokofiev looked to Pepe for help, never mind they had been screaming at each other moments ago. At least he knew Pepe. Rocío had watched a thousand recent immigrants make the same calculus of trust.

"Go on, tell them," Pepe said.

"My brother. He is missing." Prokofiev gulped for air and stalled as if saying the words to strangers had been too much.

After a moment, Rocío coaxed him. "What were you yelling about when we came in?"

"Last night, The Legionnaire—you know?" Prokofiev asked.

Rocío nodded, her suspicion confirmed. The Legionnaire was Pepe's main rival and had to be involved for him to lose his legendary calm.

"They premiered my dance."

"*My* dance," Pepe muttered. Rocío squeezed his shoulder, and he shut up.

"*La Ingenue*. It is wonderful." Prokofiev shifted his head, shoulders and hips, and suddenly he was a young woman admiring someone. "The ingenue, she falls in love, is seduced, abandoned"—another shift, and he was dejected and demoralized—"but she persists, she prevails, she unleashes the inner strength of a fox." Another shift, and he was triumphant and proud.

Rocío massaged her forehead, more suspicions aroused.

"It's better than he's making it sound," Pepe said. "There are only so many plots—it's all in the execution, and the Prokofiev brothers are top choreographers. New and fresh from the Rus. And I got La Zorra."

Of course he had. La Zorra was La Bene's premier tacata dancer. If she was involved, the production was everything Prokofiev claimed and the accusation of theft serious.

"Then the La Zorra comes this morning screaming about The Legionnaire and he"—Prokofiev stabbed a finger at Pepe—"he comes screaming that Aleksandr is gone, he must be responsible for missing master dance score. It is gone almost a month, but now he is screaming my brother is responsible.

"But not Aleksandr, not my brother, he would not do this. Something has happened, and we are wasting his time talking, talking.

"I fear for him." He clasped his hands. "You must help. The La Zorra, she call you, and Pepe call you about ... how do you say ... theft of property. But I say only one thing can have happened to my dear brother. Murder."

The word dropped into the late-afternoon quiet of the bar, tightening Rocío's muscles. This was her neighborhood, and the bar owners, actors, dancers and musicians were her people to protect, her home as much as anything or anyone was.

Get a grip, Rocío. Bad things happen everywhere. La Quinta isn't exempt.

Hala cleared her throat and said, "Let's rule out all the other possibilities first, Señorx Prokofiev. We'll do everything we can to find your brother. Can you show me his room and tell me more about him?" She herded Prokofiev towards the stairs behind the bar.

"You know the drill, Pepe," Rocío said quietly, aware Paloma was watching for posterity. "Not that different from a bar fight, except we'll be looking for proof of ownership. Get the dancers and the musicians in so they can make statements. Have them bring their contracts and any letters or tubes you sent them about the production. The tube office will have the dates or the stamps for postal letters. Do you have backers? They'll have to give statements, too, show the paper trail for the money. We'll do the same with The Legionnaire, and then you'll go before the adjudicator."

The familiar words felt newly awkward in her mouth with Paloma at her shoulder.

"I know," Pepe growled. "I keep my paperwork. We all remember the Rose–Mirage feud," he said, naming two bars that had battled each other into bankruptcy. "He's melodramatic"—he jerked his chin after Prokofiev—"but a good choreographer. A good team, the two of them."

"You don't think the brother was murdered."

"They're always fighting, throwing things, making up. My spouse complains that they keep her from sleeping and she doesn't want any more artistic types as lodgers. Keep the business and the house separate, she says. Two is enough. She means me and her. But who else is going to live above a bar? Artists!"

"Do they usually stay mad for this long?"

"No." He scratched his chin. "They're more of the summer thunderstorm types: flash and bang and lots of rain, and then it's over." He squeezed his chin harder as he realized what he'd said. "You don't really think ... that kind of thing doesn't happen here—I gotta check my cast." He ducked out from under her hand and yelled for his chaskis.

"What do we do if it's a murder?" Paloma asked as they climbed the stairs.

Rocío sighed and checked her pockets for gum. "The same thing we do if it's not: we investigate."

Aleksandr's room was a thin slice of the corner, one of five, despite what Pepe's spouse had threatened about not taking boarders. The window faced the back, there was a small sink but no bathroom —that was at the end of the hall—and all the furniture was sturdy and painted deep blues and greens, the work of Pepe's spouse. The open doors of the built-in wardrobe revealed empty hangers and a forgotten handkerchief crumpled at the bottom. The rest of the room was as devoid of personal objects and seemed strangely neglected.

It was the dust, Rocío realized. A thin layer covered the wood plank floor, the embroidered cushion on the chair, even the inside of the wardrobe and the wavy glass in the mullioned window. Pepe was too good a housekeeper to have let the room get into such a state.

Only one set of footsteps marred the dust: Hala's, who was currently crouched to look under the bed. She palpated the mattress and then felt along its sides. Prokofiev stood in the doorway, wringing his hands.

"How much stuff does your brother have?" Rocío asked, capturing his attention. "Would it fit in one bag?"

"Nyet. He collect many things, is given many gifts. Postcards, coasters, seashells, those blue bottles you make here, with dried and fresh flowers—he had a bundle of those ones with many petals. They are gone, too, and they are not in garbage jars outside. Even my razor is gone. I left it here yesterday. It is as if he never is here. He would not take my razor. He hates shaving." Prokofiev waved his arms for emphasis. "He always goes to barber. In same way, he would not take my recorder. I use to compose. Someone takes things to make look same he is gone, but takes my things too."

"A voice recorder?" Paloma asked.

Rocío startled. She had managed to forget Paloma was there.

"No, we do not have in Rus. Instrument." He mimed piping.

"We need you to make a list of everything that is missing," Rocío said.

"Not exactly everything," Hala said, pushing herself up with a hand on the bed frame. She displayed a piece of paper folded to hold dust that glittered an odd silvery blue gray.

Rocío lifted her hand to check if it was magic residue, and Hala pulled it out of reach. "It stings, and it moves away from your fingers. I had a hard enough time collecting it the first time." She withdrew an evidence envelope from one of her pockets, folded the paper into it and returned it to the pocket.

"What does this mean?" Prokofiev asked.

"It's magic residue," Hala said. "It's not from something you did?"

He was already shaking his head. "In Rus I ask birds to come sing. Here maybe I can warm my tea, but easier to walk downstairs."

"And your brother?"

"Same. Although in Rus he never get birds. Bats. He say they sing, too, but we can't hear." He wrapped his arms around himself, his face crumpling. "Something bad happened."

"I have to agree," Hala said, patting his arm, "but that doesn't mean we won't find him. Have you received a note or anything that indicates he was abducted? No? We will do everything we can to find him. We just need to ask you a few more questions."

Prokofiev moaned and collapsed into the chair at the top of the stairs.

"Paloma, can you get Señorx Prokofiev a cup of tea?" Rocío asked.

"Sugar? Milk?" Paloma prompted. She seemed to decipher some answer from his gesture and padded gracefully away and down the stairs. Prokofiev covered his face with his hands and sniffed wetly.

Hala drifted to the window and examined the view while Rocío peeped into Piotr Prokofiev's room. A red jacket with black trim was draped over the edge of the neatly made bed. One of those painted wooden dolls that had a series of smaller dolls inside sat atop a folder thick with paper on a small table under the window. Any other belongings were tidied out of sight. The wooden furniture, painted yellow and green, and the windowpanes gleamed with cleanliness.

At the slight rattle of a teacup in its saucer, Rocío returned to the hallway. Paloma patted Prokofiev's arm, and he raised his head, his face calmer. He accepted the cup and sipped.

"I am, excuse ... What are your questions?"

"When did you and your brother come to La Bene?" Hala asked conversationally.

"Eight months since. September."

"Why did you come to La Bene?"

"An invitation from the lieutenant governor. We make the dance for the year-end festival last year. You see? No? Then we stay to study this tacata and bring back to Rus. They will love." He faltered, looking towards the empty room.

"Did you do any other training besides dance and music? Lights, magic, scenery, that sort of thing?" Rocío asked, keeping her tone light and sympathetic.

"Just dance. No time."

"When did you last see your brother?"

"Yesterday night. We ate with the dancers here, I think at eight. I play a card game. I not notice what he does after dinner. I go to another bar. This morning is when I realize he isn't here and his room is ..." He waved helplessly.

"Who did he spend time with?"

"Who not? The troupe, the bar staff, the backers, the audience, the—what do you call the message children? Chaskis. Sasha likes everyone, wants to know everyone. He says he puts in dance. Our choreography."

"Did he have a lover?" Rocío asked.

Prokofiev shrugged, his whole body participating in the movement. "No one special."

"Do you have a lover, someone who might be jealous of the time you spent with your brother?"

"Someone who would harm our dance by harming him? No, I do not know anyone like this. Everyone understands dance is most important thing. I cannot believe it. It must be stranger who does this thing." He covered his mouth and spoke through his hand. "You have to find my brother."

"We'll do everything we can, Señorx Prokofiev," Rocío said, although she doubted everyone did understand that the dance was the most important thing. Getting ahead, doing better than your rivals, hurting your rivals because they did better ... artists were not known for being immune to human jealousies and competition.

"Here's my card with the address of the Community Justice Center," Rocío said. "If you think of anything or hear from your brother or anyone else with information, come to the Center or get one of the chaskis to bring us a message. If you don't want to do that, you can send a tube—a message by pneumatic tube. You'll have to pay for that, though. Ask Pepe if you need help. Are you staying here?"

"Yes." He folded his hand around the card.

"We'll be in touch to keep you informed, and we may have more questions," Hala added.

"Yes. Of course. Yes."

They left him, looking lost and forlorn in the bare hallway.

Downstairs, Pepe was scribbling messages and handing them out to the flock of chaskis waiting around him. About half probably wanted to work in or run a bar when they grew up, and the other half wanted to be performers. This was the first step on that road.

"Pepe," Rocío said, "do you have any idea who did the actual stealing or when? Someone who works at The Legionnaire?"

"If I knew, don't you think I would have told you?" He flung his hands out. The nearest chaskis ducked. "I've been tearing my hair out trying to remember, but it's been almost a month. I just assumed one of us had mislaid the score. How could I be so complacent?" He moaned. "It's no good trying to remember if anyone suspicious was here. Everyone in entertainment is suspicious."

"We'll look into it," Rocío said soothingly. Something about one of Piotr Prokofiev's responses was bothering her. "Pepe, did Aleksandr Prokofiev have a lover?"

"Oh, well." He reached for another piece of paper, and when he looked up again, his face was too composed.

"Come on, Pepe," Rocío said. "We've heard it all"—though maybe Paloma hadn't heard it all yet—"and this is a possible kidnapping."

"He was spending a lot of time with"—he cleared his throat— "Isis Soler Ibáñez."

Rocío felt a little shock run through her at hearing her long-time friend and sometimes lover's name.

Pepe looked at her. Hala looked at her. Piérdalo, even Paloma looked at her.

"Were you trying to protect me, her or yourself, Pepe?" Rocío asked. "Not that it matters. Was she here last night? No? Is there anything else you haven't told us?"

"No, no, no. I'm sure Isis wouldn't ... that is ... nothing else."

"What time will your cast be here?" Hala asked.

"I told them to come right away, but you know ..." He flipped one hand palm up, palm down. "They're performers. Not before six at the earliest."

"And when did you last see Aleksandr Prokofiev?" Hala asked.

"Last night. The troupe had dinner here after rehearsal. I didn't notice when he left."

"Who was he with?"

"No one in particular. Everyone. He's friendly."

"We'll send more advocates to interview everyone at seven," Rocío said.

He clutched the table at this confirmation of foul play, looked at the children watching him, and didn't say anything.

Outside, the neighborhood was gearing up for the evening's performances. A delivery boy on a bicycle wobbled to a stop, the eggs racked between the handlebars miraculously staying balanced. A gray cat twitched her tail, watching. The smells of cooking drifted out of newly opened windows: sweet corn and chicken roasting, garlic frying in olive oil and sugar caramelizing. By unspoken agreement Rocío, Hala and Paloma began walking down La Quinta towards The Legionnaire.

"Rocío," Hala said.

Rocío waved her away. "I'll keep an open mind, but you know she didn't do anything to him. We'd all know if she had." Isis was not the quiet, sneaky type. She was the denounce-you-in-the-House-of-Refugees-so-everyone-knew-she-was-responsible-for-your-destruction type.

"I'm relieved you're keeping such an open mind," Hala said dryly.

"Can I ask a question?" Paloma asked.

"Of course," Hala said with a sharp look at Rocío. "It's a requirement."

"What do you really think about the dust? The magic residue, I mean."

"Good question. A normal amount of magic use gone wrong does not produce that much residue," Hala said. "Other than that, I'm not qualified to say."

"Really?" Rocío asked.

"Yes, really. I haven't come across this texture or color before. It's very fine."

"You didn't taste it, did you?" Rocío asked, stopping short. "You remember what happ—"

"I didn't, and I was fine last time."

"You were in the University Hospital for two weeks."

"Because they wanted to study me, not because there was anything wrong with me."

Rocío threw up her hands in the gesture she had used in *Mathilde* when Mathilde discovers her oldest daughter has eloped with the ne'er-do-well who is after the family money. It was a good gesture.

Paloma scratched her nose. It was possible she was hiding a smile. With anyone else, Rocío would know whether they were hiding a smile. It was annoying.

Hala stopped at the alley that led to the nearest tube office. "I'll send a message to Oshinsky to send more advocates and question the entertainers at La Valle."

"Paloma and I will talk to the people at The Legionnaire, especially the owner, and then the people on the street back towards La Valle, but we'll leave the bars and the businesses to the other advocates. The west side is going to need more than two, what with the shrine, the park and the open-air theater. And the Andretti Opera alone is going to need two advocates."

"I agree. I'll coordinate," Hala said for Paloma's benefit, as she almost always coordinated. "We'll start with a search radius of a kilometer, centered on La Valle. Have you seen any dogs?"

"Hmm?" Even Paloma's monosyllabic vocalizations sounded polite.

Rocío was less thrown by the non sequitur from years of experience. "Two cats, a rat, several yellow-winged blackbirds and green parakeets and a tanager. No dogs."

"Me neither." Hala disappeared down the alley.

"Why did she ask about dogs?" Paloma asked, mystified.

"No idea. She'll probably tell us at length at some point. Let's go."

In stark contrast to La Valle, the outside of The Legionnaire gleamed the soft cream of recently cleaned stone, and the curling decorations around the door and windows had been painted an inviting peach color. The only poster on the façade was framed and under glass to the right of the door. It was burgundy and black, proclaiming THE REDEMPTION OF A WOMAN: A NEW DANCE IN THREE ACTS. TICKETS ONE PESO. The sound of a piano playing a tacata filtered through the door.

"Hmm," Rocío said.

"These renovations are recent. I can smell the paint," Paloma said.

Rocío opened the door, and they entered.

"We're closed," said a bored teenager without raising her eyes from her book.

Paloma stalled, and Rocío made a show of taking out her ID booklet. Paloma fumbled hers out of her sleeve, but she was ready when the girl finally realized they weren't leaving and looked up.

"We're from the Miraflores Community Justice Center. Is Señorx Legionnaire here?"

"Inside," the girl said, already turning back to her book.

Rocío pushed through the curtain at the end of the vestibule, and the full force of the music hit her. The pianist pounded out Rodrigo's "Apasionado," and the two dancers on the stage seemed united with the music. The woman stalked and circled the man, who drew himself up under her regard and then exploded into motion. The finale was half dance, half battle, the muscles in their arms and legs flexing, their hands caressing, their feet entangling but never tripping. Rocío found herself holding her breath and then clapping so hard her palms stung when the dancers stilled.

They bowed, and Pepe's archnemesis, of the same name as his club, pushed away from the far wall where he had been leaning.

"Is that from *The Redemption of a Woman*?" Rocío asked. "I'd say it was mistitled if so. That looked like redemption for both of them."

The male dancer grinned at her, and the woman winked. Rocío flushed for reasons having nothing to do with crime.

"No," Señorx Legionnaire growled. "You owe me two pesos. Now leave." He made shooing gestures.

Rocío tore her gaze away from the dancers to examine him. He was an unprepossessing man who had probably had gender-affirming surgery half a century ago; the Ya shamans had gotten better at throats in that time. He was thin, wrinkled and dark skinned, with rheumy eyes and an incongruously lovely contralto profundo.

The inside of the club had also been refurbished since the last time Rocío had been there years ago; as Paloma had said, it looked and smelled new. The faux pillars along the walls had been remolded to look like palm trees with glass "leaves" set in the ceiling. Rocío suspected the lights behind them were soft greens and blues to complement the peach cushions on the chairs and tablecloth borders. She was also fairly certain that the piano was a brand-new Vogl and Daughters. Expensive.

"We're from the Miraflores Community Justice Center," Rocío said, showing her ID booklet again. Paloma copied her more smoothly this time.

The pianist leaned against the piano, and Rocío had a feeling she was anticipating a good show. The dancers didn't even pretend they weren't listening.

Rocío introduced herself and Paloma and said, "We're looking for Aleksandr Prokofiev. Have you seen him?"

"Prokofiev, eh? No. Go away." He glared at them from under lowered eyebrows.

"Were you named after the club?" Paloma asked, and then clasped her hands behind her back. "Or is the club named after you?"

It was the first sign of nervousness she had shown. *Finally—she's not nerveless after all.*

"My parents started it, if you must know, when they came to La Bene, and they took the name for themselves and for me."

Many immigrants who came from cultures that did not use surnames the way Benerex did took a place name or a noun or adjective that had meaning to them.

"Paloma," Rocío said in a low tone, "go ask the dancers and the pianist if they've seen Prokofiev. They might not want to say anything in front of him."

"What are you whispering about?" Señorx Legionnaire demanded.

Paloma mounted the stairs to the stage and drew the dancers closer to the piano.

"Don't think I don't know what you're doing," he grumped. "I told you I don't know anything about him. They don't mix, you know, people from La Valle and The Legionnaire. It's like the Ka and the Ya. Like water and oil. I haven't seen him."

"You know who he is, though."

"Oh, yes. I keep my eye on that pretentious upstart at La Valle."

Rocío parsed that to mean Pepe, not Prokofiev. "He's not here, then?"

"Who, Prokofiev? I just told you."

"Then you won't mind if I look around," Rocío said, abandoning any hope of coaxing him into conversation.

"Look around? Look around? No, you can't look around."

"Señorx Legionnaire, did you know Aleksandr Prokofiev is missing?"

His mouth slackened, and Rocío read it as surprise. The thing about reading body language was that it wasn't mind reading. He could be honestly surprised Aleksandr Prokofiev was missing, or nefariously surprised they'd connected it to him, or surprised that his gamble on *La Ingenue* was going to be more successful than he had hoped because one of the choreographers was missing. Body language merely guided her questions.

When new advocates asked how Rocío could see emotions they couldn't, she showed them her photo series and explained about microexpressions, the feelings people revealed in the split seconds before they could control their faces. She told them to study the expressions people made when they were lying or tense or hiding things or relieved, and that they would learn with time. Or they wouldn't, but she never added that out loud. Some people were better at it than others. For Rocío, reading faces was so automatic that she could no longer summon the process up to the conscious level.

Señorx Legionnaire recovered his belligerence quickly and said, "What's it to me?"

"You've been accused of stealing his choreography."

"Take it to the adjudicators, then," he spat out.

"We will." She let the words hang in the air as she moved closer. "But meanwhile, you're putting on a new dance, and I've been told it very closely resembles the Prokofievs' piece. Maybe you're keeping Aleksandr Prokofiev out of the way for a few days while you perform his show and get it established."

"Where do you get off, coming in here and spouting that bullshit?" Señorx Legionnaire's chest puffed belligerently. "Get outta here!"

"That's not possible," Rocío said, her tone level and her arms loose at her sides. "I want to see for myself that he isn't here. And the adjudicators will take your cooperation into consideration when you go before them for theft."

He spun around and yelled "Go away!" at the stage. Paloma reared back in surprise. He stomped up the steps. Rocío followed, hoping he wasn't going to punch Paloma on her first day as an advocate-in-training. That would be bad. *Though slightly satisfying.* No, she didn't really think that.

"Señorx Legionnaire," Rocío said warningly.

He banged the piano's fallboard down, almost smashing his pianist's fingers. The woman snatched them free just in time. "I don't need you until eight," Señorx Legionnaire shouted in her face. "All of you, go away."

"Ancestors forget you, too, old man," the pianist said. She gathered her portfolio of music and left. Rocío let her. Paloma had talked to all three long enough to get the important information, and anyway, Rocío suspected she would be returning to The Legionnaire for the dancers, which would also give her a chance to talk to the pianist if needed.

The male dancer snorted and rolled his shoulders, while the woman ignored Señorx Legionnaire long enough to stretch one leg straight up next to her ear and then the other.

Señorx Legionnaire clenched his fists and leaned forward but didn't advance on her. Rocío relaxed a little at this sign of self-control.

The dancer's point made, she brushed past him, saying, "You're going to give yourself a heart attack one day, and then what will happen to your precious club?" The two dancers left the stage together.

Señorx Legionnaire stomped in a circle, his boots thudding on the wooden stage, and Paloma shifted to stand next to Rocío. He whirled to face them. "I'm in *entertainment*, not kidnapping. I've nothing to hide."

Rocío snorted. "I was in entertainment, you know. Entertainers are always hiding something."

He examined her. "You're *that* Rocío Díaz. Your Agatha was much better than Nerina Rebassa Fonollet's." He crossed his arms and blew a fluttering breath through his lips. "Fine. You can search my place, but not without me. And if you smash things, I'll take you to the adjudicators."

Paloma shifted, probably ready to protest that community justice advocates didn't smash things.

Rocío spoke before Paloma could, deliberately mild. "Fair enough."

Rocío let Señorx Legionnaire draw ahead of them. "How is your eye for measurements?" she asked Paloma, low-voiced. "We need to be on the lookout for hidden cabinets or rooms, that sort of thing." Hala had a terrific spatial sense, but she wasn't here.

"Do you really think he's here?" Paloma asked, bouncing on her toes. "The dancers and the pianist said they haven't seen him. They said—"

"Try not to jump to conclusions at this point." That came out sounding harsher than she had intended, and she tried to modulate her voice. "Just keep your eyes open and tell me what they said later."

Señorx Legionnaire led them backstage, where they pushed through racks of costumes to tap on walls while he alternately scolded them for ruining things and expounded on the history of a costume or a prop.

"And that dress with the glass beading was for a production of *Die Wilde Dame*—"

"Do you have a basement?" Rocío asked.

"Do I have a basement? Of course I have a basement, and it's full of chicha, both maize and potato, and aguardiente, not lost Rus. It's not a dungeon. I'm not hiding anything. This is a place of business, you know."

They trooped down the stairs. To Rocío's relief, the well-lit room with whitewashed stone walls was filled with barrels and bottles and admitted no possibilities of ghosts, ghost stories or other horrors. The barrels could have been hiding a crawlspace and Aleksandr Prokofiev, but they would need dogs to sniff him out or heavily muscled minions to shift the barrels.

"So who are your backers for this new show?" Rocío asked, pretend idly.

"Don't need 'em."

"Really? The Legionnaire must be doing astoundingly well."

He grunted.

"I don't think I know of any other venue in La Quinta that could put on such a large piece without backers, especially after extensive remodeling."

"Shows what you know."

At the end of two hours, they had determined that Señorx Legionnaire did not have Aleksandr Prokofiev stashed in a closet or a hidden room. This proved only that he was smart enough not to keep a kidnapping victim in a club that hundreds of people passed through every day. He did have a collection of tacata vinyls that would make Hala's mother jealous, and an otherwise-tidy office with piles of sheet music, choreography notes and scripts on the floor and desk. A quick perusal did not unearth the dance score for *La Ingenue*.

Rocío's stomach growled. "Okay, we're done here."

Both Paloma and Señorx Legionnaire looked relieved.

Outside, the sky had cleared to a high weak blue with emaciated clouds shredding ever thinner. Rocío turned up her collar against the wind. "I want a torta de milanesa."

Paloma turned towards a vendor with a faded green stall, but Rocío hooked her elbow and steered her away. "Not that one."

"Shouldn't we start at one end of the street and work our way down?"

"After we eat. It's not far." Rocío chose a stall decorated with rows and rows of open scissors glued to the front. Rust streaked the clapboard, and the three-legged wooden stools were splintery and crooked, but the smell of pan-fried chicken made her mouth water. "One combination, Señorx Lila," Rocío told the woman at the counter. "Paloma?"

"I'll have the same."

"Only the best for you, monito." Señorx Lila dropped two breaded chicken fillets in the pan, rolled two chiles rellenos in batter and slid them into a deeper frying pan. The oil spat, and the smells of cooking cheese and pepper filled the air.

They chatted for a few minutes about Señorx Lila's mother before Rocío asked, "Have you seen Aleksandr Prokofiev? One of the choreographers at La Valle?"

"Is he the thin one or the thinner one?"

"The thinner one." Rocío showed her the photo of Aleksandr Prokofiev provided by his brother.

"Let me think." Señorx Lila cut two day loaves, layered in lettuce, tomato and avocado, added the milanesa, the chiles rellenos and the tops of the bread, wrapped them in unbleached napkins, and handed them across her counter. "Not lately. Not this week. I heard his dance is opening soon, so maybe he's taking care of last-minute details." She added pastelitos de banana to a brown paper bag and handed it to Paloma.

Rocío tried to pay her two pesos and forty centavos, but Señorx Lila picked out the pesos, leaving the centavos.

"The treats are my treat for seeing your face. I miss your performances."

"Thank you."

They chose a table. Rocío balanced on her stool, blew on her sandwich and took a careful bite. The skin of the chile relleno resisted her teeth, but the inside was soft and gooey with melted cheese, and the milanesa was slightly crunchy and firm. Saliva flooded her mouth, and she almost moaned at the taste.

Paloma bit into her sandwich and then looked down at it with surprise. "Seres celestiales, this is good."

"What did you learn from the dancers and the pianist?" Rocío asked.

Paloma swallowed hastily and wiped cheese off her perfect chin. "They said that Señorx Legionnaire hates Señorx Sahakian—Pepe— and has for as long as anyone can remember. They also said everyone who works at The Legionnaire is gossiping about where he got all this money. He started fixing the club about a month ago, but no one knows where the funds are coming from."

"A month ago—that's when Pepe said the dance score went missing. Good work," Rocío said. *There, that didn't sound grudging.*

"At first everyone was nervous about working on a show with no backers, but it seemed like Señorx Legionnaire's pockets were bottomless."

Paloma peeked at her through her eyelashes, as if gauging Rocío's reaction, and Rocío's tolerance crumbled away at that calculated expression, reminding her of exactly why Paloma was here. Rocío took a large bite of her sandwich. She didn't like being reminded of her childhood.

"I'm fairly sure they knew the score was stolen, but I got the impression they didn't care they were receiving stolen goods," Paloma said.

"What makes you say that?"

"I can't pin it down. Something about the way they stood or moved closer together?"

Rocío licked grease off her fingers and wiped them on the crumpled napkin. "Pay attention to that instinct." She chose a pastelito and blew on it.

"You were on the stage," Paloma said.

"You knew that." Rocío savored her first bite, the creamy banana inside the crisp fried dough.

"I didn't know you were famous."

Rocío shrugged. "Just because that old man and Señorx Lila know me doesn't make me famous. You know how neighborhoods are, as bad as the CJC. You knew enough to look at me when Isis's name came up, and you probably know my favorite color and what time I was born, too. Yours is lilac, and you were born in the afternoon."

"But Agatha is a big role. You have to be good to play her."

"Why, thank you," Rocío said.

Paloma flushed.

Rocío *had* had to be good; her parents had wanted her to fail so she'd go crawling back to them and be the little society girl they'd tried to force her to be to advance their family's interests. Her parents' interests—they had never been Rocío's.

They ate in silence for a few minutes. "Was Hala right? Did you go against your family to become an advocate?" Rocío asked, not in retaliation for the Agatha comment. Really.

Paloma took a large bite of the pastelito and chewed and swallowed too rapidly to appreciate it, in Rocío's opinion. She waited to see if Paloma would answer.

"I have been going against them," Paloma finally said.

"Being the assistant to someone middling important like Oshinsky is one thing; that could be a ticket into politics. But aiming to be a detective and mixing with the masses is another."

Paloma was too well trained to hunch, but she crushed the paper bag with quite a lot of force. "Shouldn't we return to asking if anyone has seen Aleksandr Prokofiev?"

"Sure." Rocío now knew exactly as much about Paloma's motivations as she had before. She plucked the bag from Paloma's hands and deposited it in the trash. "You coming?"

CHAPTER 4

By SEVEN THIRTY it was dark. They had spoken to residents, shop-keepers and vendors all up and down La Quinta between the two venues and hadn't found anyone who had seen Aleksandr Prokofiev after ten p.m. on Monday. Even Paloma's polite façade was sagging, and Rocío felt drained from splitting her attention between doing her real job, teaching Paloma and keeping her emotions under wraps. The younger woman had been remarkably subdued all afternoon, with none of the ruthless industry she exhibited as an assistant.

"Time to call it quits for the day," Rocío said and turned towards the corner where the trolley car passed.

"But we haven't found anything."

"Other people are looking." They had crossed paths with the advocates from the CJC that Hala had arranged, and they would keep working, asking the bartenders, waitstaff and hundreds of people who filled the bars, clubs and street in the evening. "We're in this for the season, day after day, until we succeed. We can't afford to burn ourselves out on the first afternoon, and we need to sleep and eat and find ways to replace the emotional energy we use."

A trolley stopped, and people dressed for a night out streamed off. Rocío caught the handrail and swung aboard, Paloma following a moment later. They squeezed in between the evening commuters, and Rocío thought maybe they should have walked.

Paloma averted her face so she wasn't breathing right into Rocío's. "But isn't it strange that no one saw him?"

"Not necessarily. There's more than one way out of La Valle and La Quinta, and the daytime crowd and the nighttime crowd are different."

A woman with too many bags pushed between them, almost losing a tomato. Rocío tipped it back in, and they couldn't talk for a few minutes while people boarded and got off and adjusted to the new shape of the crowd.

"We just haven't found the right people to talk to yet," Rocío finished.

"So what do we do now?"

"We write our reports. Tomorrow we'll go to the immigration office and see if any other Rus came to La Bene recently." Fairness demanded Rocío say, "Good job today, Paloma."

Paloma's face lit up with a real smile, and Rocío kind of hated that she couldn't take it at face value.

Rocío looked up from a tube message to find Yaco, the forensic magicker, standing next to her desk. He had an alpaca wool hat pulled down over his ears so just his bushy black eyebrows showed, and Rocío realized how cold it was in the CJC. Technically they were inside, but with only thin doors separating them from the interior courtyard, they might as well have been outside. She sent a pulse of magic into the metal coils in the back and seat of her chair, practiced enough to not burn herself. The resulting warmth seeped into her muscles.

"I told you Isis didn't have anything to do with this." Rocío waved the message at him. "She's in El Ombú Ya and has been for days."

"You know I don't have any idea what you're talking about, right?" Yaco asked.

"Right, of course." Rocío sipped her coffee and spit it back into the cup. It was cold and oily and too far gone to reheat, magically or otherwise. "Ugh. Do you have something for me?"

"Not yet. Hala gave me the dust she found in Aleksandr Prokofiev's room. I'm running five simultaneous tests: the omni-essence test, the copper test, the hocus pocus test—"

"Yaco, stop. I only know what the hocus pocus test is, and that's because it's not its real name."

"Oh, right. It's the Bernabé-Caswallawn-Fumagalli-Quiroga test."

She gave him a Look.

"What I'm saying is, it will take a few days. If it even works." He frowned and folded his arms, then unfolded them.

"Spit it out."

He sighed. "I have a funny feeling about this," he said, folding his arms again. He looked embarrassed.

"Hala always says that intuition is just observations that haven't risen to the conscious level yet."

"Does she?" His expression lightened. "You know, that makes me think of the third law of magical dynamics, that magic is a closed system with differences based on geographic location and teaching tradition and—"

"Yaco, what kind of funny feeling?"

"A bad one. Look, it's nothing, and you're going to be late for dinner."

Hala waved from the front door, her coat already on. Rocío's coat was bunched in her hands, never mind the fact it had been in her locker and she'd changed the combination again this week in a symbolic expression of her wish for privacy and an unwrinkled Celiz scarf, which was expensive and not designed to be treated like a used hanky.

"Piérdalo." She didn't question how Yaco knew where she was going. She went to dinner with Hala and her family every Tuesday. As she'd told Paloma, the first law of community justice was that everyone learned everything about everyone if they didn't know it already. The CJC tended to attract nosy do-gooders, after all.

"Keep me posted," she called after Yaco. "About either. Or both!"

He lifted a hand in the air to show he'd heard.

Rocío grabbed her keys and wallet and threaded her way through the desks.

"Sorry," she said to Hala, who shrugged.

"Did you tell Paloma your expectations for tomorrow?"

Rocío stared at her blankly. "Piérdalo. I told her we were going to immigration but not what time." She scanned the office.

Maurata was talking at Paloma next to the back hallway. Her face was arranged in an artful facsimile of interest that only the most self-interested could fail to identify. "Double piérdalo. Let's go."

"You're going to abandon her to Maurata?"

"I'm not abandoning anyone. She's still Oshinsky's assistant. It's her job to deal with Maurata. Besides, she's trained all her life for facile interactions with the bores of the elite. She can take care of herself."

Hala raised her eyebrows. "Rocío, do you want to talk about why this is bothering you?"

Rocío started to walk away. Over her shoulder she said, "I don't know what you're talking about. I don't—"

The evening desk advocate interrupted. "Haddad, Oshinsky wants you to lead the briefing tomorrow morning."

"Do you know why?" Hala asked.

"Just that something big is happening," he said with the instincts of a veteran who'd seen it all before. "Goes all the way up."

"And will no doubt fall all the way down on us," Rocío said.

His laughter followed them out of the station and allowed Rocío to pretend she didn't feel Hala's disapproval pushing her down the street to their bicycles.

The ride to Albaicín, the immigrant section of Miraflores on its border with Arabasca, was chilly but not wet. The air bit Rocío's cheeks and woke her up and made the warm lights, the music of bandoneóns and ouds, and the smell of cooking lamb spilling from the restaurants and homes even more welcoming.

After a few blocks, Hala asked, "Did Yaco say something about the forensics from my underground room?" It was a peace offering, and Rocío accepted it as such.

"It's your room now, is it?" Her coat flapped around her hips as she made the turn onto Hala's street. "He didn't say anything about it. We talked about the dust from Aleksandr Prokofiev's room."

Hala's house was a limewashed green between a light blue house and a dark purple one. Every house on the block had blue windowsills and lintels. In their homeland it would have kept away evil spirits and the evil eye; in La Bene, people said, it kept away ghosts. As far as Rocío knew, it hadn't been tested.

Hala's father, Tamim, opened the door just as they arrived. "There you are." He swept Hala into a hug. There was no mistaking their relationship; both were slight, dark skinned and black haired. Then it was Rocío's turn, and she let herself relax into his welcome.

"Your mamá has been waiting for you," Tamim said.

Experience told Rocío that this meant music before food. Good music before good food.

She took off her boots, the pale blue tiles cool under her feet before she slipped on the house shoes Hala's family kept for her. The red-and-black embroidery and gold beads always cheered her up. Hala's were green and black and curved up at the toe.

Hala detoured to her family's altar, decorated with hyacinths and a single candle and kissed her thumb to the drawings and photos of her family. Rocío wondered if Hala's ancestors had anything to say tonight other than the usual *You don't eat enough* and *When are you going to have children?* At least that's what Hala reported they said; people heard only their own ancestors. Rocío knew Hala's paternal grandfather often gave good advice, but a good amount of time praying was required first.

Hala's mother, Giaconda, plump and unprepossessing, beckoned them into the living room from her place balanced on the arm of a chair. Tamim resettled himself and his guitar next to her. Rocío barely had time to greet Hala's youngest sister and settle on the blue-and-cream-patterned sofa before Tamim launched them into "Paciencia." Giaconda's usual softness was shed like a coat, and her intense, immense presence filled the house. Rocío imagined the neighbors holding their breath to not miss a single note.

The warmth in the house, from the space heaters and from Hala's family's easy affection, and Giaconda's voice propelled the day's worries out of Rocío's head: her own mother, Maurata's incompetence, the missing Aleksandr Prokofiev, Piotr Prokofiev's despair,

Paloma. Some of the thoughts might even reassemble themselves in a pattern after. One of Hala's older sister's cats settled in Rocío's lap, a comforting purring weight. The warmth and closeness was the antithesis of Rocío's parents' home. *Why wasn't I born into a family like this?* In her memory she heard her nonna's voice: *Family is family, and you never turn your back on them.* It had been easier when nonna was alive.

They sang four more songs, and then Hala's cousin Khaled appeared in the doorway and announced that supper wouldn't wait any longer and he would eat it all without them if they didn't come immediately. Tamim put down his guitar and ushered them into the next room, his arm around Giaconda, who leaned into him, still humming the last song into his ear. The kitchen was warm and steamy and smelled of cardamom and lemon.

"Where is everyone?" Hala asked. Usually they ate in the living room; the kitchen was too small to contain Hala's brother and sisters and their spouses and children and her other cousin and his spouses and children.

Rocío let the discussion of their whereabouts wash over her as she set the table with mismatched earthenware plates. Khaled nudged her out of the way to deposit a bowl of lamb tagine on the table.

"Sit," Tamim said. "In the Holy Ones' names, eat."

Rocío took a seat between Hala and her younger sister, Salwa. Giaconda passed Rocío a bowl of rice studded with pistachios and parsley. For a few minutes they ate in appreciative silence. Giaconda even stopped humming. Rocío relaxed back in her chair, content to be surrounded by people who accepted her and each other and weren't talking about crime. Khaled's foot tapped hers, and she met his eyes briefly for a private smile.

"Any murders today, Hala?" asked Salwa. She had been Giaconda's perimenopause surprise, more than twenty years after Hala's birth.

Rocío hid a sigh and spooned up a large bite of lamb. So much for no crime talk.

"Not today, and hopefully not tomorrow," Hala said around a

mouthful of tomato salad. "There aren't many murders in Miraflores."

"But there are in La Bene. Khaled has a book."

Hala raised her eyebrows at him.

"*Nefarious Murders in Our City, La Beneficia*—whole name—*in the Last Century, Mainly Concerning Multiple Murders and Some Merely Sensational Ones.*"

"Imagine if they wrote song titles like that," Giaconda said.

"Well, there you go—last century," Hala said.

"But your first case as a detective was a murder, wasn't it?" Salwa asked.

"'I Lost My Job and My Children Hate Me But Chicha Will Always Save Me,'" Giaconda said, rolling the words out.

"Do you want to be a detective?" Rocío asked. She didn't say *this week*, but it was implied.

"I want to be a forensic magicker." Salwa stabbed her fork into a tomato.

"'Lo Siento,'" Khaled said, naming a popular song that fit Giaconda's description.

"Or 'El Vagabondo,'" Tamim said.

"Who was the most nefarious of the nefarious, according to your book?" Hala asked.

"Guess," Khaled said.

"Diego Raya Silveira," Tamim said, frowning.

"Eugenio Fernández Suárez," Rocío said.

"Mario Trujillo Casallac," Hala said. "Papa, you just think it's Diego Raya because he murdered refugees who'd paid him to get them out of Laena during their civil war."

"He was a monster. He murdered dozens of refugees. By anyone's calculations he must be the worst. Do we really want to talk about this over dinner?" Tamim asked.

Giaconda pursed her lips and shrugged. "'My Daughters Hate Me But I Just Want Them To Do Better Than Their Old Man.'"

"'If You Leave,'" Salwa guessed.

"'The Road I Walked,'" Hala contradicted her, and Rocío resisted the urge to kick her.

"That's my girl." Giaconda passed the artichokes to Hala as a prize.

"That's not fair," Salwa said, "I thought we were doing ballads."

"'If You Leave' fits, too," Rocío assured her.

"Diego Raya wasn't arrested or tried in La Bene," Hala said, "so he doesn't count. It's Trujillo. His assassination of the governor and lieutenant governor led to ten years of political chaos and indirectly to the deaths of hundreds of people. He almost invalidated the peace accords between us and the Ya and Ka Empires."

"But he didn't. It's Fernández," Rocío argued, drawn in in spite of herself. "He created necromancy out of Ka death magic. A whole method of magic based on pain and killing to find out secrets and extend his own life. Not to mention he murdered fifteen people."

"A defunct magic system. Necromancy hysteria was not responsible for as many riot-related deaths and food shortages as Trujillo." Hala pointed a finger at Rocío. "There hasn't been another necromancer since Fernández, but the political unrest Trujillo planted keeps coming back."

"Don't point, mi amor," Giaconda said.

"Fernández wasn't smart enough to be the worst murderer," Khaled said.

"What does that mean?" Salwa asked. "The people he killed were still dead."

"He murdered newly arrived immigrants, whom he thought no one would miss," Khaled said.

Salwa made a rude noise. Giaconda snorted. Even Tamim put down his fork and said, "Really?"

"He didn't know immigrants," Giaconda said, looking over her family fondly.

Tamim had immigrated to La Bene when he was fifteen with his brother, Khaled's father, and two cousins and had immediately taken rooms at the Ysen Association, which was run by the sister of the headman of their old village in Ysen Arat. Most immigrants were embedded in similar networks, and disappearing in La Bene wasn't easy, even if you wanted to.

"The riots weren't something Fernández planned," Khaled said.

"So I don't think they should count. Trujillo wanted civil unrest and helped instigate riots."

"But he didn't torture people," Rocío said.

"Why can't we talk about something pleasant, like Salwa's new girlfriend?" Tamim asked plaintively.

"Salwa's slurpy girlfriend." Khaled made a sappy face.

"Ha ha," Salwa said. She threw a piece of bread at him, and it bounced off his forehead. He grinned at her.

"What happened to the murderers?" Salwa asked. "Were they caught?"

"Sort of," Khaled said. "Diego Raya escaped custody and fled to the Ka Empire. While everyone was arguing about whether they were going to extradite him, he died in that big cholera epidemic they had. Obviously they couldn't send his body back after that, but a Ka shaman showed up with a femur and said it was proof Raya was dead."

"But the shaman couldn't use magic here," Salwa said. "So what did that prove?"

"They had to take her word for it," Hala said.

"Oh."

"Eugenio Fernández was caught, tried, hanged and burned, and Mario Trujillo was caught in one of the riots he started and killed," Khaled said.

"Why are you reading such morbid stuff, mi amor?" Giaconda asked.

"I wanted to see if Hala's fascination with crime would rub off on me."

"I'm not interested in sensationalism," Hala said, "I'm interested in the science of solving crimes. You might as well be reading *Oye*."

Oye was the main gossip rag in La Bene and ran stories about everything from wardrobe malfunctions to exposés about corruption, bribery and nepotism, though admittedly they scooped the latter less often.

"While Hala is reading *La Bene Journal of Science*," Rocío said.

"I like *Oye*," Salwa said.

"Of course you do," Khaled said.

"Do you have today's *Oye*?" Rocío asked, breaking into the incipient family argument, which was about to prove that families never let you mature beyond fifteen in some respects.

"Yes!" Salwa said. "It's so good. There's a piece about the jewelry the governor wore at the ten-year anniversary party for the entrance pavilion of the House of Refugees and a letter from the Ka empress about the convict exchange program." She bolted from the table in her enthusiasm, ignoring her mother's command to wait until she had finished eating.

The conversation turned to Ka politics until the plates were empty and the sugar cookies devoured. Rocío escaped clean-up and Giaconda's invitation to stay the night with the excuse that she and Hala had an early meeting and promises that she would pick up the slack next week.

Hala walked her to the door. Rocío changed her shoes and waited for whatever Hala wanted to say.

"*Oye*?" Hala asked.

"Just something I want to check," Rocío said, thinking of María Paz Belli's strained face. Rocío still hadn't thought of any good reasons for Maipa to have been at *Oye*'s office.

"Habibti, have dinner with us on Thursday, not your parents."

"I have dinner with my parents every Thursday," Rocío said.

"You don't have to."

"Of course I do."

"You don't, actually," Hala said.

Rocío frowned. "Don't be silly."

"Just think about the fact that maybe you don't." Hala took Rocío's forgotten coat from her hand and helped her into it, pausing to hug her as she tugged it closed. "Just remember I said it."

Rocío walked slowly home. She was not at all surprised when a tall shadow detached itself from a jacaranda tree and fell into step beside her, and she gratefully forgot Hala's odd comment.

Khaled's warm hand slid down her arm. He interlaced his fingers with hers. "What made you want to work in community justice?"

"Not getting domestic on me, are you?"

"Why all these accusations tonight? I like my life the way it is.

Next week I'll be out of the city and on a ship, watching the sun set over an entirely new place each night for months."

She squeezed his hand. She very much liked her life the way it was, too. She and Khaled were friends and sometimes lovers and didn't expect a marriage contract of each other. She knew whose bed she wanted to be in next week, but that was for then; she didn't mix past or future lovers with present ones. "I didn't choose community justice work because of murder," she said, answering his original question.

The apartment buildings on this block were all Ka built, made of sand-colored stone fit so perfectly together a hair couldn't be inserted in the seams. The bodega on the corner was doing brisk business in chicha and cigarettes. A bunch of kids sat under the trees bordering the street, playing guitars and singing a song about early death that only those who didn't believe their lives would end could sing.

Rocío pushed open the front door of her building, exchanged greetings with the concierge and led Khaled to the second floor. The neighbor's baby was crying, and the hall smelled like green corn tortillas and roasting poblanos. She unlocked the door and walked through the front room without turning on the lights.

In the bedroom she said, "I like putting things right," not the glib answer she often gave to the merely curious who asked about her job.

"Justice." The crystals on the shade tinkled as Khaled turned on the lamp on top of the dresser. It glowed peach and amber without shedding much light on the rest of the room.

"Not really, or not only. Justice is big and abstract and cold." She folded her coat over a chair and turned so he could take the pins out of her hair. "When I left home, strangers took me in and became another family to me. I do the same for them, just on a different scale. I give individuals some of what they need to put their lives back together—or keep them together. It might be justice, but more often it's making the world knowable and controllable again so they can go on with their lives."

"Also," Khaled said, and then she muffled the rest of his words with a kiss.

Rocío woke to pounding on her door. Khaled sat up, his eyebrows arching in a question. Rocío pulled a dressing gown around her and grabbed the baton she almost never used.

Through the door she heard the concierge pleading, "Señorx, please, you're waking everyone up. The Montero-Cohns have a young child—" On cue a baby started to wail.

"Rocío, open your perdido door before your neighbors riot and kick you out on the street!" Isis shouted.

"Ancestros perdidos," Rocío swore, wrenching the door open. "Shut up." She dragged Isis inside, apologized to the concierge and Señorx Montero, who had just opened his door, and shut her own.

"I thought you were in El Ombú Ya with an *alibi*." Rocío dropped the baton so she could use both hands to hold Isis in place.

In the light coming through the windows, Rocío could see that Isis's eyes were feverish, her blouse was on backwards, and she had on a scarf but no coat or poncho. Her skin was cold under Rocío's hands.

"Then it's true," Isis said flatly. "He's dead."

"Isis, we don't know that," Rocío said. "He's missing." Isis stared at her blankly, and Rocío shook her once. "Isis, as far as we know he's not dead."

Isis tried to push past her into the living room, but Rocío held her in place. "Shoes," she said.

"Shoes, shoes, how can you—I don't know what's happening to him!" Isis's voice got louder and shriller with each word.

The lights bloomed behind Rocío, and Khaled coughed. Isis snapped her mouth closed. The light reflected off the light catchers and deepened the rose tint of the limewashed walls. Rocío had chosen the color for its soothing quality, though she didn't think it would have much effect on Isis.

Khaled had gotten dressed except for his socks. He had lovely feet, high arched with straight toes. Next to them, the electric heater started chugging out warmth. It wasn't just his feet that were lovely, but clearly that portion of Rocío's night was over.

"I put out some things for tea," he said. "Isis, Rocío will do her best for you. She always does. I'll give you some privacy." He dropped a kiss on Rocío's head and patted Isis's shoulder as he squeezed past them in the small entryway.

"Thank you," Rocío said.

The door clicked shut behind him, and Isis said, "Right, shoes," in a more controlled voice. She stiffly shucked her muddy boots, leaving them askew in front of the door, and moved to the center of the living room. "I *was* in El Ombú Ya. I received a message."

"A ransom note?"

"No." Isis retrieved a wooden document case from her satchel, two thin sheaves of wood used by government offices to preserve paper files, and handed it to Rocío. "The case is mine."

Rocío fished gloves out of a kitchen drawer and opened the case. The note was three lines in block letters.

YOU TOOK SOMETHING FROM ME, AND NOW I'M TAKING SOMETHING FROM YOU.
SAY GOODBYE TO YOUR PET RUS.
OOPS, IT'S TOO LATE.

Rocío's fingers went cold with dread, and she kept staring at the note, buying time to think. There was no way Isis was going to calmly step into the background and let the CJC take care of this. *I thought I had more time to figure out how to keep her from interfering in the investigation. What am I going to do?*

"Someone is hurting him to get to me," Isis ground out. "This is unacceptable. I need you to find out who is responsible."

"I'm already on the case," Rocío said reasonably. "You knew—" And then reason caught up with her. She stepped forward, just barely managing to put the note on the coffee table before grabbing Isis by the arms. "You didn't know that, did you? You didn't come here to give me information, you came to get it from me and start some sort of rampage across La Bene. Isis ..."

Isis glared back at her. "I need to know who's responsible."

"You will. But *I* will find out, and I will take care of it. The CJC will. You will not ruin yourself over this. You will not play into their hands like that. Someone who knows you sent this note, expecting you to do just that."

Rocío held her gaze. She'd seen Isis in the grip of rage like this before. Isis might see the sense in what Rocío said, but that didn't mean she would be able to stop herself. "I will lock you up so fast your head will spin if you do anything, Isis. And not house arrest—I'll put you in the holding rooms for people we think are an immediate danger to others."

"I know."

And she had come here anyway. "Piérdalo, Isis, if I have to watch you, I can't give my full attention to Prokofiev."

Isis flinched in her grip. "I won't endanger Sasha. I don't think there's another promise I can make that you'd believe. Now, can I tell you about this note?"

"Seres celestiales." Rocío let go and ran her hands through her hair, twisting it into a tail to keep it off her face. She rifled through the detritus on her counter, found a stick of gum and pointed her thoughts in the right direction. "Tell me about the note. When did you get it? Have you warned your spouses?" *Or was one of Isis's spouses warning her?* Open marriage contracts were not a panacea against jealousy. Not that Rocío could picture either of Isis's mild-mannered spouses as kidnappers, but it had to be admitted as a possibility.

"Of course I have," Isis said. "As soon as I got it on Monday."

"Monday? That's before Aleksandr was kidnapped."

"What? No." Isis started to pace, her feet thumping in spite of the layered throw rugs. *Thank the seres celestiales and Ka builders for thick floors.*

"That can't be—I sent him a message—I thought it was already too late, but I sent him a warning to be careful, just in case. And now you're telling me it wasn't too late, but something happened to him anyway!"

Isis meant she'd sent the warning by semaphore, the system of towers that transmitted visual messages in alphabetic code throughout the Ya and Ka Empires and from the empires to La Bene. Only government officials like Isis and Rocío could use it for official purposes, but only politicians like Isis got away with using it for personal reasons.

"And who gave you the note?" Rocío closed the case and stripped her gloves off.

"A messenger service brought it to the house where I was staying with friends. I left my assistant there to try to track down who sent it, but it wasn't a secret that I was in El Ombú Ya."

"Do you have any idea who sent it? Or what they mean that you've taken something away from them?" *Does this mean we're looking for a group of people? Or one person who planned in advance?*

"I'm in politics." Isis flung her arms out. "We take away with one hand and give with the other. It could be anyone. Do you have any leads? Know anything?"

"Who knew you were in El Ombú Ya?"

"Any number of people. Possibly dozens."

"Did anyone follow you from El Ombú Ya?"

"You haven't answered my questions," Isis said.

"Answer mine first."

"Fine. They couldn't have. I changed horses at tambos"—government way stations along the road—"and then I went to La Valle. Pepe told me what had happened. I came here."

Isis had known all along that Rocío was handling this case. "Isis."

"Would it have stopped your rant?"

"No."

Isis smirked at her.

It was actually comforting, in a twisted sort of way. Same old Isis. "You're a piece of work. Okay. Did you go home? Did you notice anyone following you or watching you?"

"I went home. I made sure everyone there was okay. Then I went to La Valle."

"And had your spouses received your warning?"

Isis stopped pacing. "I didn't ask. I don't know. You think ..."

"I think if we find out whether only your message to Aleksandr Prokofiev went astray or if all your messages did, that might tell us something."

"Where is he, Chío?"

"Did Pepe say anything? Like if Piotr Prokofiev had received a ransom note since we talked to him?"

"No, he didn't. Because they don't want a ransom, they want to hurt me. When I find out what coward did this—attacking me through Sasha! He's an artist. He should be nurtured, not ..." She looked around wildly.

"Do not throw things," Rocío warned.

Isis gave a stifled scream. She tore her scarf off, threw it to the floor and stomped on it. "That didn't help," she said in an oddly normal voice and then burst into tears. She sank to the floor.

Rocío crouched beside her and hugged her. This time Isis leaned all her weight onto Rocío. The force of her sobs shook them both. "How could you do this to me?" Isis sobbed. "How could you make me cry?" The last word dissolved into a wail.

"I know it hurts," Rocío murmured, holding her tightly. "It's okay to cry when it hurts."

Eventually Isis's sobs calmed, and she rested her head on Rocío's shoulder with a sigh. She wiped snot on the backs of her hands and hiccupped a laugh. "That's disgusting. I need a handkerchief."

"I have to get up to get one." Rocío kept her arms tight around her.

"No, don't." Isis mopped her face with her scarf and blew her nose. "It's an ugly scarf, anyway. How am I going to find him?"

"I'm doing everything I can. So is Hala. So are half the advocates at Miraflores CJC."

"But sometimes it's not enough."

"No." They were both silent. Rocío was contemplating what that meant, as was Isis, probably. "Do you want a drink?"

"No."

"Do you want to sit on the sofa?"

"No." Isis dropped her head to Rocío's shoulder again.

"Okay. Can you answer some more questions for me?" she asked gently.

"Do you think he's dead?" Isis asked, her voice muffled against Rocío's arm. "You can tell me the truth."

Rocío stroked Isis's hair. "I think it's too soon to give up hope," she said.

Isis rubbed her nose. "What are your questions?"

"When did you last see Sasha?"

"Last Friday. He was putting the finishing touches on his dance, holding rehearsals. He was consumed. Everything was going so well." She scrubbed her hands over her red and splotchy cheeks. "What happened between then and now?" She didn't wait for an answer. "We had dinner and saw an appalling modernist play, but Sasha made me stay to the end. He said they were doing interesting things with space. I couldn't see it." She named the playwrights, two theater world staples. "Sasha is the kind of person you want to feed."

"Speaking of, I have a new tisane from Hala's sister that's supposed to be warming and energizing without caffeine. You still look cold. Come on." Rocío levered Isis to her feet and led her to the small kitchen. Isis stood in the center, blocking Rocío's path to the cabinet, until Rocío sat her down on one of the stools.

"Here." Rocío gave her the tin of tea and two infusers, one shaped like a whale, its tail designed to curve over the lip of the mug and hold it in place, and the other shaped like a dinosaur, its long neck serving the same purpose. Isis had given them to her years ago. "One scoop." She used a small bit of magic to heat water in two mugs. "How did Sasha seem that night?"

"Normal. Animated." Isis's voice was anything but. "That's why he's such fun. La Bene is new to him."

"What about his brother, Piotr?"

"You don't suspect him, do you? They're like two drops of water." She frowned, took the mugs from Rocío and dunked the infusers. "Inseparable. Dinosaur or whale?"

"Whale." Rocío wrapped her hands around her mug and drew the smells of the cacao, pepper and cardamom tisane into her lungs. "Don't get mad. I have to ask: Do you think Sasha could have left and not told anyone?"

"No." Isis didn't sound angry; she sounded sure. "I really don't. Everything was going well for him. He said being in La Bene woke up his creativity. He has a new performance about to debut, he has his brother, he has me. My spouses like him and Petya, you know, Piotr. They're like us, nicknames for everyone. I just don't see him leaving."

"If Sasha did go off on his own without notifying Petya, where would he go?"

"Music venues. Dance halls. Bars. The docks. The ships fascinate him. Anywhere in La Bene, really. It's"—she choked on a sob—"it's endearing how fascinated he is by everything."

Rocío sipped her tisane and waited for Isis to recover her composure. "And when did you leave La Bene?" she asked.

"I know you know by now that I left on Sunday. It's one of the first questions you must have asked as part of your investigation. So why are you asking me questions you know the answer to?"

Maybe the energizing tisane had been a mistake.

"Do you think Sasha could be involved in something shady?"

"On purpose? No. But he's, you know. Fresh off the boat. Naïve about some things." Isis turned her mug in a circle. "You know who was hanging around? That anarchist. You know the one I mean."

Rocío hurriedly extracted a notebook from the pile of mail on the counter. "Shen? I wasn't informed that he was back from community service."

"That one. And there was this guy who kept propositioning Sasha, wouldn't take no for an answer. Pepe would know who it is."

Rocío scribbled a note and rolled her tight shoulders, bracing herself for Isis's reaction. "I'm going to tell you something, and you need to control yourself."

Isis twisted to look at Rocío, preemptively angry.

"Did you know that the Prokofievs' dance score was stolen—"

Isis slammed her mug down, and it cracked in half, spilling tisane across the counter.

"—and The Legionnaire performed it on Monday?" Rocío finished quietly.

Isis slammed her fists on the counter, smashing the metal dinosaur flat. Blood seeped into the puddle of tisane, bright red against its muddy brown.

"I guess not." Rocío dropped a towel on top of the puddle and got up to find a clean one for Isis's hand. "I liked that infuser." Still, Isis's reaction could have been worse.

"I'll get you another one. Right after I make Señorx Legionnaire wish he'd never been born."

"And then I'll have to arrest you, which would make me very upset. Here." She dabbed at the blood on Isis's hand, made sure none of the little metal wires were stuck in it, and wrapped it. "I didn't tell you so you could threaten Señorx Legionnaire. He's already on the adjudicators' calendar for May first. I told you so I could ask if you thought Sasha had anything to do with it." Although for the life of her, she couldn't see how. Aleksandr didn't seem to have the kind of money Señorx Legionnaire was throwing around.

"No. Definitely not. He would never betray his brother."

Rocío grunted, dipped a tea bag of chamomile flowers in a new mug and pushed it towards Isis.

"But meanwhile that pisscup is performing our show. Isn't he?" Isis growled.

"Isis."

"Let me have this." She turned burning eyes on Rocío.

Rocío gestured denial. "You know I can't. Stay away from Señorx Legionnaire and The Legionnaire. Promise me."

"Rocío Adele Díaz Rossi, don't make me promise."

"Isis Cecelia Soler Ibáñez," she said in a hard, uncompromising voice.

Isis huffed. "Fine. But only about Señorx Legionnaire. You can't keep me out of the search for Sasha."

"If you step one toe over the line—and I mean the spirit of the law, not just the letter—I will lock you up." Rocío imprisoned Isis's wrist for emphasis.

"Fine, I promise. I'll stay away from Señorx Legionnaire. And your warning is noted." Isis shook her off, and Rocío let her.

"It had better be." It was enough for now. Keeping Isis's vigilante tendencies under control would have to be tomorrow's problem.

CHAPTER 5

THE NEXT MORNING, the CJC buzzed with energy. Everyone seemed to know something big was going on, but no one knew what. Chief Maurata had barricaded himself in his office, and Deputy Chief Oshinsky had taken a few advocates, all of them older and as close-mouthed as doorknobs, to an undisclosed location.

"She took the automobile?" Rocío asked Hala, scratching her head. It was too early for puzzles after too late a night. "Why would she do that?"

There were about twenty cars in all of La Bene—Hala would know exactly how many, but Rocío didn't want to—and they were unwieldy, slow and tended to blow up. Why Miraflores precinct had rated one was a mystery not even Hala had been able to solve.

"Shush," Hala said, and called everyone into the meeting room for the morning briefing. Besides Paloma, who looked annoyingly fresh, like she'd gotten a full night's sleep, about twenty advocates and tech staff crowded into the windowless room and took seats or leaned against the walls.

"Listen up, everyone. There have been developments in the Aleksandr Prokofiev kidnapping," Hala said, and all the movement and chatting died down as everyone in the room gave her their full attention.

"Developments?" Rocío asked under her breath.

"I want everyone thinking about this case, even if you're not assigned to it. We'll do announcements at the end." Hala steepled her fingers and swept the room with a measured look. "It's possible that the kidnapping was intended to harm Ministrx Soler Ibáñez, Aleksandr Prokofiev's lover."

She paused for a reaction. Someone cursed politicians, and a murmur ran through the room.

"This does not rule out Piotr Prokofiev as a suspect, either for unknown reasons or as a way to harm Ministrx Soler, and we'll continue those inquiries."

Piotr Prokofiev might be a victim, or he might have killed his brother. Maybe Piotr was jealous of his brother and Isis. Ancestros, maybe Aleksandr Prokofiev wasn't even missing and the Prokofiev brothers were targeting Isis together, or maybe Aleksandr had already left La Bene and Piotr was taking advantage of his departure. Or Aleksandr was planning on extorting money from Isis. Or both of them were. The permutations were endless. Rocío clutched her coffee and drank deeply.

"However, we'll need to expand our investigation now that we know Ministrx Soler could be the target," Hala said. "Detective Díaz, would you tell everyone what you learned last night?"

Before Isis had fallen asleep on Rocío's couch, she had made a list of people who might want to harm her. The lieutenant governor was at the top, followed by other ministrx and their staffs and several people Rocío recognized as backers for shows. It ended, to Rocío's surprise, with one of Isis's spouse's brothers. It was a long list.

Rocío summarized Isis's visit and the list and handed off the threatening note to Yaco for forensics to look at.

"This paper is too coarse to get good fingerprints from," he said, "but we might be able to tell whether the ink was made in La Bene or in the Ya Empire."

"Yaco, please share the results of the tests on the magic residue we found in Aleksandr Prokofiev's room," Hala said.

Yaco pulled on one of his bushy eyebrows. "Ha—Detective, it's magic, not science. I'll know more in another day or three." He looked at her like he wasn't sure he should say more, and Hala gestured for him to keep going.

"Fine." He turned to face the room and raised his voice. "The main tests are still running, but we found more magic residue in Tili Alley. Not the alley behind La Valle, but the next one over. It dead-ends in a covered cul-de-sac, which is why the dust was preserved and not washed away by the rain. It was a match for the residue in Prokofiev's room."

Viernes, Yaco's youngest tech, said, "The alley is sheltered enough for someone to perform magic without being observed. So something happened in his room, and then something else happened in the alley that's probably connected to Prokofiev."

"Yaco." Hala gestured for him to continue.

He glowered at her, almost visibly willing her to change her mind. She stared back neutrally. Anticipating something interesting, people sat up straighter and leaned forward. Rocío noticed Viernes biting her lip and glancing between Yaco and Hala.

"Please tell everyone the rest of what you told me this morning," Hala ordered.

Yaco closed his eyes for a long moment, visibly bracing himself. "We have no idea what they were doing with all that magic energy. We don't have enough data yet. But I don't like it. And the residue isn't reacting to the tests as it should. So, we need to consider ..." He stopped and wet his lips. "That we might have a problem like the one in January. That we might have a copycat."

Rocío slapped her forehead. "Way to get to the point, Yaco."

Viernes snapped her pencil in half. More than a few people muttered uncomfortably and rubbed their scars from the mutant malarial fairies. Rocío caught herself doing the same and forced her hands to relax.

Fistfights, embezzlement, even murder and local magic they could deal with. Imported magic, like the magic that had created the MMFs, was something else, even though it quickly lost its potency when it was transplanted to a new country. It just didn't lose it quickly enough sometimes.

"You can see why I want everyone thinking about this case," Hala said, raising her voice. "We can't ignore the fact that foreign magic was used to devastating effect earlier this year."

"This doesn't sound anything like the MMFs," someone called from the back.

"Maybe it's not a copycat, but someone who learned more than we'd care for," Hala said.

"So we might be looking for a recent immigrant in a city of immigrants," Rocío said. "Seres celestiales, how much imported magic is running around this city?" She didn't rub her scars again, but it was close. "I never thought I'd say this, but I'm seriously considering petitioning my district council member for stronger immigration controls at the port."

"It could be a Benerex citizen who has been away and returned, to account for the possible La Bene and Ka elements," Yaco said.

"This is all speculative at the moment," Hala said. "Keep your minds open."

"Magicker Aapo Chuquisengo Camal from Cempol is coming today to consult," Yaco said, talking faster than before. "Hopefully we'll know more then."

Cempol stood for Central Municipal Police. They handled cross-district cases and had ties to the University and better specialists. They also always thought they were in charge.

"Cempol's involvement notwithstanding, Deputy Chief Oshinsky and I expect you all to be vigilant."

That was incredibly diplomatic of Hala, considering she had to mean "Cempol will definitely try to cut us out." People sat up straighter and exchanged looks full of meaning, like *Cempol's not taking it away from us this time*. Nothing like a little foreign magic and interagency rivalry to make people pay attention. Or possibly Hala was being strategic, making everyone focus on proving themselves instead of panicking about imported magic.

"Moving on to the list of possible suspects provided by Ministrx Soler," Hala said, "I don't have to tell you how sensitive this is."

"Shouldn't you remove Detective Díaz from the case?" the other Díaz asked, tipping his chair back on two legs. He had hated Rocío since she'd started at the CJC for reasons known only to him, though Rocío suspected it was insecurity heightened by the coincidence of them sharing a surname and Rocío's quicker-than-usual promotion to detective four years ago. He was also good-looking in a rangy kind of way, and he knew it and had a certain expectation of being the center of attention that Rocío just naturally seemed to foil.

"Seeing as how she and the ministrx are known lovers," Díaz drawled.

"I spoke to Ministrx Soler's housekeeper yesterday," Advocate Zhou spoke up. He was quiet, competent and solidly built. Rocío liked what she knew of him. "She says Soler was in El Ombú Ya and had been for four days prior to receiving the note. She was expected to return this coming Friday. The spouses' alibis checked out. If one of them did it, they had someone's help. It's possible the ministrx kidnapped Prokofiev, but not likely."

"We're not crossing Ministrx Soler off the list of suspects just yet," Hala said, "but we'll concentrate on this new information.

"As I was going to say before you interrupted, Detective Díaz, I'll be assigning different advocates to speak with the people on this list. I'll speak to Deputy Chief Oshinsky about the lieutenant governor myself," Hala said, tapping Isis's list, "and I'll bring up your concerns with her, but unless she says otherwise, Detective Rocío Díaz will continue working on the case.

"Now, did anyone find someone who saw Aleksandr Prokofiev after ten p.m. Monday night?"

"It's like he disappeared into thin air," the other Díaz said. "Do we have any proof that the owner of La Valle isn't the type to kill him and bury him in his basement? Besides Detective Díaz's *feelings*."

Rocío hid a frown. She had years of practice ignoring Díaz, since he had seemed to relish the times she'd confronted him about his behavior. Maybe it was time to revive the tradition of boxing competitions at the CJC so she could pay someone to kick his ass legally. Sort of legally.

"If Pepe—that's René Sahakian Quispe, the owner of La Valle— did kill someone, it would be the owner of The Legionnaire, not his favored choreographer," Rocío said quellingly.

"Not even if the Prokofiev brothers threatened to leave?" Díaz asked. A few people shifted uncomfortably at his challenging tone.

"Of course it's a possibility, but Pepe would still have the rights to the dance. And why would he bury only one Prokofiev brother and not both?" Rocío asked.

"We don't know, do we?" Díaz asked. "That's my point. But we haven't found anyone who saw Prokofiev leaving La Quinta. Isn't that right, Detective Haddad?"

"I returned to La Quinta last night," Hala said, "to speak to performers on the late shift. Or the early shift, as the case may be." Hala tapped her fingers on her chin. "I talked to waiters, singers, dancers, musicians and audience members, and no one saw him. Then I talked to the street cleaners, insomniacs and bakers, and none of them saw him either. But I didn't speak to the garbage collectors; they went on strike yesterday."

There were bars and restaurants all up and down La Quinta and the neighboring streets, and they usually had two sets, with the second starting at eleven. And the Andretti Opera had rehearsals most nights it didn't have actual performances.

"Detective Díaz," Hala said, "I want you to go check the basement of La Valle and then talk to the garbage collectors, see if anyone saw Prokofiev. They're picketing outside the Office of Public Services."

Hala settled her spectacles on her nose and consulted a clipboard. "Detective Zhou, take—Advocate Espinoza, you're off desk duty today? Go back to The Legionnaire. The owner's story about the dance doesn't make sense, and he couldn't produce any evidence of backers, but he suddenly has a lot of money. Find out if he stole the dance score himself or if someone else did it for him or just sold it to him after the fact."

Hala assigned an advocate to Tili Alley to recheck statements in case they had missed an eyewitness there and told another advocate to put an announcement in the papers, asking anyone who was at a show on Monday and had knowledge about Aleksandr Prokofiev to come forward. She handed out the rest of the assignments, including Rocío's to question a handful of theater people from Isis's list and some people in the neighborhood, and then quickly went through the other outstanding cases.

Hala ended with, "Everyone, please welcome Paloma Faro. She's starting training to be an advocate."

There was a friendly chorus of welcomes, and Espinoza clapped Paloma on the back so enthusiastically she almost tipped out of her chair.

"You're with Detective Díaz today." Hala nodded to Rocío to indicate which Díaz she meant, as if the chief would trust the other Díaz to train anyone.

There goes any chance to ditch Paloma. Rocío sighed. *Yesterday wasn't so bad, right?*

"Dismissed," Hala said, ending the meeting.

"Paloma, will you give me a minute with Hala?" Rocío asked.

Paloma nodded and filed out of the room with the rest, except for Yaco, who stopped next to Hala, his heavy brows drawn down.

"I'm sorry, Yaco," Hala said, putting up a hand to forestall an outburst. "I know you think it was too soon to bring up MMFs, but we need to be prepared."

"There's not enough evidence. You understand science." He rubbed his eyebrow. "I thought you'd agree with me. Now they're all riled up, and who knows what they'll do."

"Public safety can't always wait for solid evidence, and our advocates need to know all the possibilities. I need to think about their safety, too."

Rocío rubbed at her scars again, and Hala caught one of her hands and turned the back towards Yaco.

Yaco stared at it with a frown. "I guess you can't be premature with this. I got the preliminary report from my junior techs on your underground room. They did not like that assignment at all. They said it was creepy and scared themselves silly with stories about grave robbers. However, they did their job. Something large was removed from the room by three people. My techs also found blood. I'll tell you more when they finish running tests and I've reviewed their work."

"Okay." Hala rubbed her forehead. "Thank you. I do listen to your advice. Please don't withhold information from me."

He grunted and stumped away, muttering under his breath.

Hala pressed her hands over her eyes.

Rocío leaned back in her chair and squinted up at her partner. "He'll forgive you. So, you didn't sleep last night." That explained the dark circles under Hala's eyes. "And aren't planning on sleeping tonight."

"I slept." Hala waved away Rocío's concern.

"For how long?"

"A few hours."

"Tell Oshinsky you need two advocates on La Quinta between ten p.m. and three a.m. tonight," Rocío said. "Or I will."

"I won't sleep anyway."

"You will, because you'll have that very nice valerian tea your sister makes."

Hala made a face at her, and Rocío took it as surrender.

"Do you need help with Díaz?" Hala asked. "The chief will tell him to back off if you ask."

"I can deal with him. He thinks our success rate is due to the cases we pull and that if he had our cases, he'd have our success rate."

"Did you know scientists think the human capacity for denial is because one hemisphere of our brain can hide things from the other?"

Now, why did that statement seem so pointed?

"Do not forget Paloma," Hala added.

Right. That's why. "Will you send her to me on your way out?"

"No."

"Hala ..."

"You need to take responsibility for this, Chío."

"Fine," Rocío said to Hala's back.

Paloma looked up from a stack of paperwork with a transparently eager expression, making Rocío doubt herself. *Maybe I'm wrong. Maybe she does want to be an advocate.*

"I've read so many reports I thought writing them would be easy, but it's different trying to do it yourself, isn't it?" Paloma said.

"Here, let me take a look. Sorry I had to leave in a rush for dinner last night." Rocío scanned the report. It was better than those of some detectives she could mention. "This is good. Sign it and leave it with the others. Are you ready to go?"

"To immigration?"

"Change of plans. I sent a chaski to copy the list of immigrants who arrived within a month before and after the Prokofiev brothers. We're going back to La Quinta. Besides the portion of the list Hala assigned to us, there are the people the advocates missed yesterday. And Isis mentioned an anarchist."

"I'm ready." Paloma scribbled her name on her report and downed her coffee in one enthusiastic gulp.

I should be happy *to have such a smart, eager trainee.* "How long have you wanted to be an advocate?" Rocío asked, testing.

"I've been thinking about it for a long time, but really the MMFs decided me." Paloma glanced sidelong at Rocío. "You and Hala and the chief—you saved so many lives." Her eyes shone. "And the ceremony after was so moving."

Where Maurata and Oshinsky had been awarded medals for outstanding service. *Oh, yes, Paloma has her sights set high,* Rocío thought sourly. *But not if I have anything to say about it.*

By late afternoon the clouds had parted enough to let a bit of pale blue sky show, and weak sunlight illuminated Parque Dolores, the big park at the northern edge of La Quinta. Children playing pelota-ya shouted on the ball court, and people strolling in blue coats and colorful wool hats were bright spots against the browning grass and the gray trees. The woman Rocío and Paloma were looking for was making good time on the path around the park.

They had spoken to everyone on their portion of the list, collected alibis and one memorable diatribe, but so far no one stood out as a suspect. They had also spoken to the owners of the flower shop that had been closed yesterday, the butcher's delivery girl and half a dozen other people who'd been missed during the first sweep of La Quinta, none of whom had seen Aleksandr Prokofiev on Monday night. Señorx Safavi was the last one on their list. Rocío hoped someone else was having better luck.

"Señorx Safavi?" Rocío asked, falling into step with her. On Rocío's suggestion, Paloma was on Rocío's other side to avoid making the señorx feel boxed in.

"And you are?" Señorx Safavi asked, not breaking her stride, her mane of gray hair bouncing and the distinctive dragonfly pin on her coat lapel flashing. It was definitely the woman who rented the floor above the flower shop.

"Detective Rocío Díaz Rossi and Advocate Paloma Faro Otxand-abaratz from Miraflores Community Justice Center. One of our other advocates spoke to your daughter about a missing person, but you weren't home at the time."

"Walking is the only thing that keeps the insomnia away. And sometimes not even that," Señorx Safavi said.

"Do you mean you walk late at night?" Rocío asked, feeling a slight surge of hope. "Were you out Monday night or early Tuesday morning? Did you see this man?" Rocío handed her Aleksandr Prokofiev's picture.

Señorx Safavi sighed to a stop. She moved the photo back and forth in front of her face, searching for a point of focus with the gesture of someone whose near and far sight were both betraying her. "Is this the man that disappeared? You'd be surprised how many people are out at one a.m."

"Any dogs?" Rocío asked, thinking of Hala's cryptic comment outside of La Valle the day before.

"Not that night, come to think of it. Usually there are a few. You know, I might have seen him, not in La Quinta, but in this park."

"Where was that?" Rocío kept her voice interested but not urgent.

"By the lake, looking rather tweedy and despondent. I thought about speaking to him—there was a suicide here three years ago. I saw that man, and I will never forgive myself for not talking to him. But a woman was with this one. They seemed to be arguing, and I thought he couldn't be suicidal if he had that much spark in him, so I kept on."

"Do you mean tweedy as in wearing a tweed suit?" Paloma asked.

"Yes, very different from what he's wearing here," Señorx Safavi said, tapping the black-and-white photo. "This makes him stand out, and I bet it's colorful. In the tweed he looked like that common sort you don't notice much."

"And you're sure it was one a.m.?" Paloma asked. She had easily caught the rhythm of interviewing, which, Rocío had to admit, wasn't always that different from making small talk at a party. A lot of it involved getting the other person to feel comfortable enough to just keep talking.

"Thereabouts. I could tell it was going to be a bad night for me. They tell you to not watch the clock, but I'd have to get someone to hide the clocks. I left my house around midnight and walked my usual circuit, up La Quinta to Dienne's Fountain and back to the park. That takes close to an hour, and I was in bed again by two, as usual. Didn't help, though."

"Did you get a good look at the woman?" Rocío asked.

"She had her back to me and was all wrapped up in a dark coat. I'm not even sure why I thought it was a woman, but I did."

"Señorx Safavi, excuse me, but with your eyesight, how sure are you that you saw this man?"

"Sure." She handed the photograph back. "I was wearing my spectacles. I always do at night, and during the day if it's not raining." She fished them out of a pocket and planted them on her face. "That's better. I hope the rain has stopped for a while. You don't think he's in the lake, do you?"

"Do you?"

"Well, I was wrong before, and he did look very down."

"Could you show us where exactly you saw him?"

"I don't see why not." Señorx Safavi resumed her ground-eating stride, and they quickly reached the south side of the lake. Lago Dolores, as it was officially named, or Lago Nicolás, as everyone called it, for the infamous highwayman who had faked his own death by drowning shortly after the park opened, was bordered on this side with sand-colored paving stones and a matching thigh-high balustrade.

On one end stood a bronze statue of Patricia O'Higgins on horseback, a Galish woman with an outsized legacy as one of the founders of La Bene. On the other was a stele inscribed in Ya, Ka and Iberex with the peace accords between the first two, predicated on ceding the disputed city that became La Bene to the Iberex refugees as long as they maintained it as a buffer between the two empires.

A plaque in Benerex provided an explanation for those who couldn't decipher Iberex, which was anyone without an education in languages, and the date in the three calendars: 9 July, Year 1; 11.12.0.9.15 / 8 Men / 18 K'ayab / Lord of the Night G5; and Year 3 of the Divine Emperor Cápac.

"They were under that tree." Señorx Safavi pointed to the first bench at the end of the balustraded area. A wrought-iron lamppost stood next to it, close enough that identifying someone at night wouldn't be hard.

I'll have to check whether it's working. Even during the day, the towering cypresses with their feathery bright green needles threw a lot of shade. At night, without the lamp, the darkness would be impenetrable.

"Is that all?" Señorx Safavi asked. "I have to walk another three kilometers if I'm to have any hope of sleeping tonight."

"That's all. Thank you for your help."

Señorx Safavi strode off, and Rocío led Paloma to the spot for a closer look. The cypresses hugged the edge of the lake, their roots like knobby knees buckling through the pedestrian paths, and the bank was thickly padded with their brown needles. They didn't look disturbed, like someone had trudged through on the way to their last breath, but it had also been almost two days.

Rocío walked along the lake's edge, hands clasped behind her back. Paloma trailed behind.

Isis was impulsive, hot-tempered, loved being in the spotlight and didn't mind making enemies, as evidenced by the long list she had given Rocío. She had called politics 'long-form theater for the in-est of the in-crowd that reaches into the stomachs and pockets of millions.' But even Isis had admitted that no one on the list stood out as a kidnapper/possible murderer. Her rivals were more likely to outbid her on a show or business interest, pull strings in government or block one of Isis's pet policies in the House of Refugees. Stealing a dance score and selling it to a competitor wasn't beyond them, but most had the connections to use the machinery of government to pressure someone if they wanted. Ancestros, people with those connections could have gotten the Prokofiev brothers deported, though deportation was usually reserved for foreigners who committed crimes.

So what are we missing?

"Paloma, what do we know about Monday night?"

Paloma jogged a bit to come even with Rocío. "What people told us, or what was in the reports?"

"Everything we know so far."

"Aleksandr Prokofiev bought a round at about ten for the owner of La Valle, the bartender, La Zorra and two of the other dancers, though the dancers were only drinking chicha de mora, not fermented. Piotr Prokofiev wasn't in La Valle. He was at another bar with a few of the musicians. I can't remember the name."

"That's fine, keep going."

"Everyone agrees that La Zorra started dancing around then, so no one in La Valle noticed when or how Aleksandr Prokofiev left, just that sometime after that he wasn't there anymore. Do you believe that, about La Zorra? Is she that good?"

"I take it you've never seen her dance. She sucks up all the air in the room, and you feel like you have to watch her or you'll stop breathing."

"But probably not everyone feels that way," Paloma said.

"True, though she's been known to hit people if she thinks they're not paying enough attention." Rocío had seen her do it. And sympathized with the reaction.

"And she didn't hit anyone that night, which might mean he didn't leave during her dance," Paloma said, skirting a puddle.

"Also true."

"I was thinking ..." Paloma clasped her hands behind her back.

Rocío should break her of that nervous habit, but it was a convenient way of knowing how she felt. "Go on."

"About the magic residue we found in Aleksandr Prokofiev's room. I did some research into who gets advanced magic training even if they don't go to the University for it. If we ignore imported magic—I don't mean *ignore*, just set to the side for a minute"—she looked an appeal at Rocío and continued at her nod—"and consider people who could generate that much residue. It didn't help, though. I didn't realize how many people get magic training as part of their jobs."

"Like us," Rocío said. "It's a good thought. Keep thinking it; maybe we'll find a way to make it useful. We still have too many suspects. What we need is a motive." Rocío left the path and slid down the bank to the edge of the water, startling the ducks into paddling furiously into the questionable safety of the open lake.

From this little spur of land, Rocío had a good view of the spot Señorx Safavi had pointed out. Unfortunately, it didn't tell her anything.

"What else? Just thinking out loud here," Rocío said, even though she'd done nothing of the sort herself.

"Do you think he might be in the lake?" Paloma asked.

"I think it's worth looking into. But first there's a certain anarchist I want to find."

Pedestrians at the end of their workday clogged the sidewalks and streets, with the occasional omnibus or cart nosing through like an earthworm. The shutters were open on the cheap bars and food stalls that consisted of little more than outside counters and stools, and the doors of the more permanent establishments were open as well, letting air and patrons in and smoke and noise out. Rocío's second stop was La Grande, an outside bar that was anything but in size.

"Would you look at that," Rocío said, and pointed to a shaggy-haired man. "That's our anarchist. Paloma, it's better if I talk to him alone."

She left Paloma stranded on the curb. At the bar Rocío bought a melon agua fresca for herself and chicha for him. "Hello, Shen," she said, settling herself next to him at the rough counter. If she wasn't careful, she was going to get splinters in her butt.

He was a slight small man with dark hair and eyes who could have been pure Ya, Ka, Jeen or from any of the Poly Poly Islands. Rocío couldn't tell, and he had never said.

"What do you want?" He stared at her without blinking. Even though he was an infamous anarchist criminal and she represented the rule of law, he wasn't afraid of her, probably because he really believed the dogma he spouted.

She placed the chicha in front of him. "Would you know anything about the theft of a dance from La Valle?"

"Intellectual property can't be stolen—it wants to be free," he said automatically. Apparently free chicha was also the best chicha, given the way he slugged half the glass down.

"So you shouldn't have any problem telling me about it." Rocío took a more considered sip of her drink.

"You're right. It's a conspiracy of the elite to keep the people down. I'll go on a hunger strike if you arrest me. The people won't stand for it."

"I'm after bigger fish, Shen."

"Yeah?"

"Did you know the choreographer disappeared?"

"You don't think I'd harm an artist, do you, Rocío? That would be a crime against humanity." He knocked on the counter and pointed at her. "I don't harm people."

"I know. That's why we're having this friendly chat here over chicha instead of at the CJC. Come on, Shen. Tell me."

He swigged his chicha and swished it around in his mouth. "You should have stuck with theater, not this bougie upholding of a false law that oppresses us. But you've always been straight with me. I liberated the dance," he said, not even bothering to lower his voice. She kind of admired his dedication to his lifestyle. "But it wasn't my idea. It was Emma's," he said, naming a fellow anarchist.

"When exactly was this?"

He tilted his empty glass at her, and she signaled to the barkeep for another.

"Last month. Give or take."

"What did you do with the dance score after you stole it?"

A waitress deposited his chicha in front of him. It rocked a little on the uneven counter, and he grabbed it to steady it. "If you try to bring me before the adjudicators for this, I'll say you beat me and forced an untrue confession."

"I'm from Miraflores Community Justice Center, Shen, not Cempol."

"All the same."

"Bigger fish, remember?"

"I gave it to Señorx Legionnaire, and he paid me."

She didn't point out his participation in the system he claimed to despise; he had a rant on that about subverting the system from within. She'd heard it already. Several times. "Did he arrange the theft?"

"Him?" Shen snorted. "No way. He's been brainwashed, just like you, into believing your capitalist overlords. He had a real wrestle with his conscience before he took it. If it hadn't been La Valle's show, I don't think he would have. He wasn't expecting it."

"Really?" she asked. *That's interesting. And strange.* "Have you seen Aleksandr Prokofiev lately? Notice anything unusual around here?"

"Not unless you think entertainers partying it up is unusual."

"No." She dug in her pocket for a few coins. No use asking Shen about Emma's whereabouts; that kind of information wasn't free from him. "Enjoy the chicha, Shen."

"Emma said good things would happen to us," he said, surprising her. She settled back on her stool.

"And have they?"

He gulped the rest of his drink. "Can't say as they have. Emma was convicted of defacing government property."

"Graffiti?"

"Now, that would be like her. Mutilated rats on the front steps of the House of Refuges. She was framed. She's in Campeche Ka now. Labor exchange program. I went with her, just to see what capitalist oppression really looks like." He shuddered. "It's all dust and rock. No tacata. No chicha. No nothing. Just holes in the ground that people go into and don't come out of."

"Wow." Forced labor in Campeche Ka was to community service as the "Battle Hymn on the Eve of War" was to the song "Twinkle Toes Comes to Town." "Dead rats doesn't sound like her. And what about you? Anything good or bad happen lately?"

"You bought me a chicha. Not what I was expecting, though."

Were the theft of the dance score and Prokofiev's disappearance connected? She hadn't thought so before. While outright theft of an entire performance wasn't common, the line between influence and stealing was blurred in the creative community of La Quinta. But if Isis was the target, ruining a show she had invested in could be an additional method of revenge.

Shouting drew Rocío's attention. The evening edition of the papers had come out, and the newspaper chaskis were waging a war for clientele. That wasn't unusual, but the size of the crowd around them was.

"Stay out of trouble, Shen," Rocío said. Not that he would.

As she crossed the street, Paloma appeared and grabbed Rocío's arm. Her eyes were wide, and she had a copy of *Oye* crumpled in her other hand. "The chief arrested the lieutenant governor."

The shill for *Oye* shouted, "Scandal scalds Sabato! Lieutenant governor sold out La Bene!" The chaski for *El Universo* had the more sedate "Lieutenant governor sole treason arrest!" but a much louder voice. And the chaski for *La Ciudad* was losing out with less volume and the rather bland "Government roots out corruption!"

"Ancestros perdidos, that's where she was this morning?" Rocío tugged the copy of *Oye* from Paloma's hand, her thoughts whirling, and scanned it. Deputy Chief Oshinsky was mentioned by name. "Reporters are going to be swarming the CJC."

"She's going to need my help. We have to go."

"Yes, of course," Rocío said, but she had an entirely different reason for returning to the CJC.

CHAPTER 6

REPORTERS SPILLED off the sidewalk in front of the CJC and into the plaza. As soon as they spotted Rocío and Paloma approaching, the reporters mobbed them, shouting questions and shoving cameras and recorders in their faces.

"Is it true that Sabato sold Iberon the info two years ago that almost started the war?" a reporter called, nearly catching Rocío in the mouth with a recorder.

"You know more than I do," Rocío said, muscling her way forward.

"Can you comment on the fact that Sabato seemed to expect someone higher in the government to protect him?"

"Don't quote me, but the lieutenant governor thought there was someone higher in government than him?"

They laughed, and Rocío was able to push through to the door. Or almost to the door, because two Cempol officers blocked her way. Rocío recognized one of them and groaned. "Officer Smith, let us through, please."

"Authorized personnel only," Smith said. She was a light-skinned woman with a rather square face, a slight Enkladt accent and inflexible ideas about, well, everything.

"We are authorized personnel," Rocío said. "You know I'm a

Miraflores detective, and this woman works with ... me." Better not to mention Paloma's connection to the chief in front of the press.

"What's the matter, detective? They won't let you into your own building?" one of the reporters asked.

"Cempol wouldn't know a detective if one bit them in the ass," another reporter said, and Smith frowned and settled into an even wider-legged stance.

The other Cempol officer glanced at Smith uncertainly. "The reporters seem to recognize them," he said. "And she seems to know you."

"Well, I don't know them," Smith said.

Rocío didn't bother to argue that they'd met on the job at least three times before. "And now?" She opened her ID booklet and gestured for Paloma to do the same. She should have started with that, but she always forgot how infuriating Smith was because it didn't seem humanly possible to be so attached to the letter of the law. Except there was Smith, every time.

Smith scrutinized the ID booklets while a couple of reporters heckled her about her ability to read. "Detective Díaz, Señorx Faro, you're free to enter." Smith stepped aside, and Rocío squeezed through behind Paloma. The reporters probably wouldn't print her name and comment with so much else to report. Probably.

It was relatively quiet inside, though the sound of a heated discussion floated down the stairs from Oshinsky's office.

Paloma said, "I have to—"

"Go," Rocío said, and Paloma dashed up the stairs. Rocío took a deep breath, free of Paloma's presence for at least a little while. Now to see what Hala thought of Rocío's theory.

She found Hala at her desk. "Hala, I have—"

"Oshinsky submitted a request to search Lago Nicolás. Divers are necessary, as at its deepest points, the lake is four point one five meters deep—"

"Hala, later."

Díaz came into the room with two other advocates, arguing loudly, and Rocío changed her mind about what she was going to say. "Not here," she said. "Let's go out the back again."

Hala stood and shrugged on her coat. "You found something? Wait, where's Paloma?"

"Helping Oshinsky." At least Rocío could ditch Paloma with a clear conscience this time.

"That's good. Cempol didn't manage to keep all the reporters out, and there's at least one ministrx upstairs accusing the chief of leaking the news and someone from Cempol saying the same thing."

"Oh, seres celestiales, that's as likely as Oshinsky committing treason."

"Don't say that too loudly."

No reporters lurked by the back door. Rocío made sure it latched closed behind them. She squinted against the glare of the setting sun. "I haven't found anything. Yet. I need to confirm something before we go charging back to Ministrx Montenegro, and I want to know what you think." She set off walking, slipping on soggy leaves smelling of leaf mold and standing water.

Hala jogged to catch up. "Ministrx Montenegro, huh? You decided I'm right?"

"Fine, you were right, the empty room is important. I think there might be a connection to Aleksandr Prokofiev. Or rather, to Isis. It's clear he was kidnapped—"

"Or worse."

"Or worse, to get at Isis."

"You think my empty room is a crime." Hala stopped walking and grinned at Rocío.

Rocío snagged her arm and pulled her along. "Don't just stand there—the reporters might spot us. Yes, yes, you were right, and I was wrong. Are you going to gloat or listen?"

"I don't gloat—"

"Ha."

"I'm thinking. The fact that both Isis and Ministrx Montenegro are politicians wouldn't get you this excited. Kick over a rock in Miraflores and you find ministrx."

Rocío splashed through the edge of a puddle. "Not just two ministrx, Hala. What do Isis Soler, Sofía Montenegro and María Paz Belli have in common? Wait, don't answer. I saw María Paz outside

Oye's offices yesterday. She wouldn't tell me what was going on, but I've been checking *Oye* for any scandal notices that mention her."

"Ah, your sudden interest in my sister's favorite gossip rag. You haven't found any?"

"Not yet."

"Of course, the absence of evidence isn't evidence of absence." Hala clicked her tongue thoughtfully. "So, scandal and María Paz Belli, destroyed wardstones and Sofía Montenegro, and a missing Aleksandr Prokofiev and Isis Soler. Have you found a connection?"

"How about this," Rocío said, turning her collar up against the chill evening air; "What do Isis Soler Ibáñez, Sofía Montenegro Dhavale, María Paz Belli Chambi and the lieutenant governor's spouse, Ana Valdivia Áquila, have in common?"

"The lieutenant governor?" Hala stopped walking again. "Rocío, you think the lieutenant governor's arrest today was part of this?"

Rocío turned to her, watching the emotions washing over Hala's face settle into shock.

"They're all ministrx, they're all on the Sub-Committee on Legal Affairs and I think they're all being threatened."

Rocío was a familiar enough presence in María Paz's house that the majordomo directed them to the bedroom without an escort. Rocío led Hala to the second floor, aware that her partner was taking everything in, from the Adergie oil painting of a storm above the cordillera, glimpsed through an open door, to the magnificent Tymoteusz, more sculpture than timepiece, of a magpie perched on a clock with a large tanzanite gleaming blue violet in its beak. The house was quiet, the rest of the family out, none of the other servants visible. Rocío knocked on the bedroom door and opened it without waiting for a response.

María Paz looked up, her brown eyes wide and red-rimmed. Her face crumpled, tears leaking down her cheeks. She untangled herself from her bed linens and threw herself at Rocío.

"Chío," María Paz sobbed into Rocío's neck, only the top of her head and her glossy chestnut hair visible, "we're ruined." She was a limp weight in Rocío's arms.

Hala closed the bedroom door behind her.

"Shh, Maipa." *I was hoping I wasn't right.*

Rocío maneuvered María Paz to the four-poster bed and lowered them both to sitting, batting the blue and purple brocade bed curtains out of the way. Clinging to Rocío, María Paz stuttered incoherently through her sobs.

Hala's eyebrows had almost reached her hairline, less impressive than it should have been because her bangs were so long. *Wait,* Rocío mouthed. Hala leaned against the door, her eyes sharp as she scanned the patterned Laenish carpet, polished rosewood furniture and portraits on the walls.

"Talk to me," Rocío said, bracing herself. If they were dealing with the same person who had kidnapped Aleksandr Prokofiev, what had they done to Maipa? "Come on Maipa, tell me what's wrong. I can't help you until you do."

"You shouldn't have come," she wailed.

Rocío rocked her. "You knew when I saw you outside *Oye*'s offices that I would I know something was wrong. No one goes there for a good reason. I'm worried, as your friend and as an advocate. Tell me what's going on."

Shaking, María Paz sat up and wiped her face. Her cheeks were chapped from weeping and her clothes askew, though they generally were unless someone dressed her. "I can't tell you. No one else can find out."

"Maipa, *Oye* is going to print something, aren't they? What could be so terrible?"

María Paz stuck out her chin and didn't answer.

"I presume that her son is not her spouse's biological child," Hala said.

Rocío gaped at her. María Paz had broken her marriage contract and deceived her spouse?

María Paz wailed and collapsed on the bed again. "You know already. We're ruined."

"You're not helping, Hala," Rocío snapped. "Tell María Paz"—*and me*—"why you'd say that. That is not common knowledge, Maipa. Hala just knows things." She gestured for Hala to get on with it.

"Ministrx Belli, I assure you I haven't shared my theory with anyone. Your son's eyes are blue, as are yours, but your spouse's are not. Nor are anyone's in his family, as I had ample opportunity to observe last year at the gala at the House of Refugees. While this alone isn't enough to conclude anything about his biological relationship to your spouse, your son also has freckles, while neither of you does."

María Paz raised a hand to her unfreckled cheek.

"Given what we know about the laws of heredity—which I admit is still limited, as the science of genetics is in its infancy—"

"Hala."

"—and combined with your repeated glances at the photo of your son, I concluded there was a ninety-five percent chance that he wasn't your spouse's child. Your reaction confirmed it."

Not helpful, Rocío mouthed at Hala. But María Paz had exchanged crying for hiccupping and staring at Hala.

"I'm sure there aren't more than a few people in all of La Bene and the Ka and Ya Empires who could make that deduction, or care to. Although you shouldn't have chosen a lover with blue eyes. Brown would have been safer."

As ever, Hala's sum-up needed work.

"What ... how ..." María Paz trailed off, her mouth open.

"And someone told *Oye*?" Hala prompted. "But how did you find out?"

"And what did you threaten the editor with?" Rocío asked. "There wasn't a hint of the story in yesterday's edition."

María Paz sat up, withdrew a scrap of paper from a hidden pocket in one of the bed pillows and thrust it at Rocío. "I didn't threaten him exactly."

Rocío glimpsed familiar block letters and let the note drop into her lap. She pulled on gloves and picked it up. The light, thin paper used by the tubists clung to Rocío's fingers as she smoothed it open.

Rocío handed the message to Hala.

María Paz made a frustrated gesture. "You can't tell. No one knew, and now everyone will, no matter what I do."

"Who knew before yesterday? You did get this yesterday?" Rocío asked.

"Yes." María Paz pressed her hands to her cheeks. "No one. Only the three of us knew."

"The three of you?"

"An—my friend, and Entienne, my spouse."

"Entienne knows?" Rocío asked, surprised.

"It was his idea, and it will all be wasted if this comes out. And poor Phillippe. We were waiting until he was older to tell him. He won't understand."

Rocío and Hala exchanged a look, and Rocío tried not to make any more assumptions that would no doubt be overturned immediately.

"Your friend is the biological father? Could he have told *Oye*?" Rocío asked.

"Never."

"Maipa, someone else got a note like this. You're not the only one being threatened. I need to know his name."

María Paz's expression turned mulish. "I can't tell you, and he wouldn't do this. I know he wouldn't."

"Maipa—"

"We swore we'd go to the grave rather than tell anyone besides my son."

"Did—" Rocío stopped, struck by a thought. "Could your ancestors have told someone in your family?" The dead knew things the living did not. Very rarely, they revealed secrets to their descendants that shook a family.

"I, how would I know?" María Paz crossed her arms. "But even if

88

they did, no one in my family would try to hurt us like this. They'd guess why we did it."

Rocío bit her lip. "It's not something we can investigate, anyway."

"Ministrx," Hala said, "the person who threatened you may have also kidnapped someone. His life is in danger. You really need to tell us who the father is. You must see that."

María Paz sat up straight. "He didn't tell, and he didn't kidnap anyone. I'll tell you what I told the odious editor of *Oye*: I will make you regret it if you pursue this."

"Maipa," Rocío said helplessly, "you can't go around threatening people."

"I meant with lawyers, Chío. But I'm telling you, neither Entienne nor my friend would hurt anyone. But if I find out who told that edacious editor in the first place, I'll make a ghost of them, and that is a threat."

"Maipa, that's a serious crime."

"So arrest me."

"I'm not going to arrest you."

"Then go out there and find out who is committing crimes that actually matter."

She answered all their other questions about the sub-committee, suspicious persons and threats to her and the other ministrx, but they didn't get any more out of her about her secret, no matter how Rocío tried.

"Khadija." Hala beckoned to the chaski sitting on the front desk.

Khadija stopped drumming her heels against its side and slid to the floor, looking guilty. "I'm sorry, Detective."

"Never mind that. Get Yaco. Tell him to meet us in Oshinsky's office and bring the report on the underground room."

Khadija darted off.

The lines around Oshinsky's eyes were deeper than yesterday, but her bun was savagely neat. It wasn't every day that she had to help arrest the lieutenant governor, even if Cempol had done the actual arresting, and then hear that two of her detectives suspected a plot against some of the most prominent ministrx in La Bene. Rocío had just finished summarizing when Khadija knocked and entered.

"Message from Cempol, Chief." Khadija thrust a slip of paper at Oshinsky. "And Señorx Yaco is on his way. He's just slow." She backed against the wall, trying to make herself invisible so she wouldn't be dismissed before they discussed anything interesting. Sliding a glance at Hala, she laced her fingers together. It wasn't quite an imitation of Hala's straight-fingered pose, but it was close. In spite of herself, Rocío smiled, the girl's hero worship of Hala a bright spot in a disturbing day.

"Cempol has taken our warning to heart," Oshinsky reported, her tight voice loosening. "They'll question Ministrx Valdivia and leave the others to us, as we're closer, but they'll be here in the morning to coordinate. That reminds me, Rocío—I'm sorry, but I told Paloma she should go home. I should have left that to you."

"That's okay," Rocío said, as if she hadn't forgotten about Paloma as completely as the waves smoothed footprints from the sand. What had Hala said? Denial? "I'll catch her up in the morning."

Hala stirred in her chair as if she was going to say something but didn't speak.

At another rap on the door, Oshinsky squinted through the cloudy glass panel and called, "Yaco, come in."

"Chief." Yaco planted himself in front of Oshinsky's desk. "I told Detective Haddad that I haven't had time to look at this report. She saw fit to tell the whole CJC we might have imported magic loose in the city again, and the advocates are bringing in every unfamiliar plant, food and small animal, asking my techs if it's imported magic—"

"Any dogs?" Hala asked, leaning forward.

Rocío winced.

"No dogs! And no time!" he shouted, shaking the rolled-up report at Hala. "And it's your fault."

Khadija scowled, her hands closing into fists.

"Yaco, I am sorry," Hala said.

"Please, Yaco." Oshinsky gestured for calm. "I'll have a word with the advocates tomorrow morning. Will you please sit? Is that your report on the empty room in the subte? New information suggests a connection with Prokofiev's kidnapping."

"Not my report," he grumbled, but sank into a chair. "The junior techs'. It wasn't supposed to be important. Wait, a connection?"

"Unfortunately," Oshinsky said.

Yaco flipped open the report and started reading. "That can't be right." His lips moved as he flipped to the next page and then back. "Approximately two hundred and ten centimeters long." The blood drained from his face, and his jaw dropped. "K-Khadija." He cleared his throat. "You had better leave. And don't listen at the door."

Shrugging, Khadija glanced at Hala again and then slipped out of the room.

"Yaco?" Oshinsky prompted.

"Why do you think there's a connection?" he asked, clearly stalling.

"Another ministrx has been threatened," Rocío said, attempting to hand him the evidence envelope with María Paz's note inside. When he didn't take it, she placed it on Oshinsky's desk in front of him.

"I should have paid more attention when they talked about grave robbers," Yaco said. "And I complain about the kids not thinking."

Hala raised her eyebrows. A cold chill slid down Rocío's spine.

"Yaco, talk," Oshinsky ordered.

"Well." He closed the report and squared it on the desk before looking up. "Can you think of a good reason to steal a coffin?"

There was no good reason to steal a coffin.

Sometimes burial sites were desecrated, but that was done publicly, to shock, offend and horrify. This would have to be an old coffin that wasn't well remembered. In the Ka Empire, burning a dead body destroyed the living's connection to their ancestors and the afterlife and was the ultimate crime, except when ordered by the empress.

In the Ghost Years, the period after the Founding when Iberex burial practices had interacted with the magic of a city that had changed hands between the Ya and Ka multiple times over the centuries, uninterred ghosts had stoked chaos. Those years were the stuff of nonna's favorite stories. The city had imposed strict burial regulations, and now ghosts were limited to those poor souls whose bodies were not found quickly enough for a decent burial in a cemetery.

Oshinsky kissed her thumb in the direction of her family altar and said a prayer under her breath.

"I knew that room reminded me of a crypt," Rocío said, shuddering.

"The wood splinters are pine. The object that was removed is the exact dimensions of a coffin. The techs wrote all that data down and didn't draw any conclusions," Yaco said, slapping the desk. "They also collected a lot of dust, possibly magic residue, but it hasn't been tested yet."

"None of us guessed it was urgent. Test it for a match with the residue in Prokofiev's room," Oshinsky said, rubbing her forehead. "That's your top priority. Along with all your other top priorities."

Yaco pulled on his eyebrow. "Well? Do any of you know why someone would steal a coffin? You seem to know more than I do."

"It's been illegal to inter the dead anywhere besides cemeteries since the Ghost Years," Hala said, the very neutrality of her voice broadcasting her concern.

Oshinsky sat back in her chair and steepled her fingers. "We don't know, but there's no reason to sit here speculating when you can go ask the owner of the coffin. According to Cempol, Ministrx O'Higgins, Soler and Montenegro are at the latter's house having an emergency meeting. Go on. You can warn them that we think the members of the sub-com are being targeted and question Ministrx Montenegro at the same time. *Gently.* And don't come back here tonight for anything besides another disaster."

Rocío didn't want to think about coffins and long-dead bodies, so she asked Hala about something else as they walked to Ministrx Montenegro's house. "Are you going to explain your dog fixation?"

"I've learned there are at least three street dogs that call La Quinta home."

"But no one has seen any dogs."

"Exactly—not since the night of Prokofiev's disappearance, when one of the neighbors heard a dogfight. Street dogs have an approximate territory of 0.259 of a square kilometer to 0.155 of a square kilometer—that's a generalization as well as an approximation, you understand—and it's unlikely they would change territories."

"Okay. So?"

"Their disappearance is an anomaly. As is the magic residue from Prokofiev's room."

"And a stolen coffin," Rocío said dryly, brought full circle to the thoughts she'd been avoiding.

"Correct, but it's an anomaly I can pursue, independent of ministrx and forensics."

This time when the Montenegros' majordomo tried to put them off, they insisted on entering, and after a few moments she gave up on out-stubborning them. Rocío and Hala followed closely on her heels. The house was as luxurious and impeccable in taste as promised by the foyer, but far different from María Paz's newer wealth and status. The wood furniture was dark and ponderous, glowing rosy with polish, the floors marble with mosaicked edges, and the paintings executed by old masters from Iberon. In other words, a match for the stern black-and-white exterior.

At the top of the stairs, the majordomo knocked on a set of ornately carved wooden doors before opening them. "These detectives from the Miraflores Community Justice Center insisted on seeing you, ministrx. They were here yesterday."

Ten people looked up at the announcement and stared at Rocío and Hala with varying degrees of interest. Seven were assistants, the next generation of politicians, all of a type: sleek, well bred and well dressed, ranging in age from early twenties to early thirties. Four had dark hair, two had lighter brown, and one young man had sleek blond hair. All seemed unformed; life hadn't yet made an impression on them with any distinguishing marks or wrinkles. Curiosity flashed across their faces and disappeared as quickly.

Ministrx Montenegro appraised them from the head of the glossy wooden table in the center of the room. She wore a gorgeous Paolo Cordano red-and-orange jewel-toned shawl of silk and wool with the distinctive short fringe. Her brown eyes and cheekbones were as sharp as they must have been when she first became a politician at least forty years earlier, though her skin was soft and crêpey.

Ministrx O'Higgins twisted in his chair to look at them, the worry lines on his face strangely apparent for such an experienced politician. The pins in his hair were subdued, in the manner affected by sober elderly men asserting the wisdom of their age and place. He had at least fifteen years on Ministrx Montenegro, and his cotton shirt, long jacket, sash and trousers were an order of magnitude more expensive than hers.

Isis's mask was even less well maintained. Hope briefly surfaced in her eyes and then submerged again as Rocío met her glance.

"Well?" Ministrx Montenegro asked unwelcomingly.

"I'm Detective Rocío Díaz Rossi, and this is Detective Hala Haddad Sosa. We're from Miraflores Community Justice Center. We wouldn't have interrupted if it wasn't urgent. We need to speak with you alone for a few minutes, Ministrx Montenegro, O'Higgins and Soler."

"Leave us," Ministrx Montenegro said. One raised fingertip indicated the assistants.

Pique tightened the corners of the youngest woman's mouth— one of O'Higgins's assistants. The blond man didn't like it either. The others didn't react, just filed out decorously, except Isis's assistant, who paused to touch her hand before gathering his things. The majordomo closed the door behind them, leaving them enclosed in the black-and-gold room. It was not a restful room for Rocío, but maybe evidence of all her wealth was restful to Ministrx Montenegro.

"What is this about?" Ministrx Montenegro demanded.

"This week three of the five members of the Sub-Committee on Legal Affairs have experienced harm or attempted harm, either personally or to someone close to them. You're aware of the recent threat against Ministrx Soler and the subsequent disappearance of the choreographer of a show she had invested in?" Rocío paused, watching their reactions. "Today we learned that Ministrx Belli has been threatened. This makes the timing of the lieutenant governor's arrest seem suspicious. Have you received any threatening notes, Ministrx O'Higgins, Ministrx Montenegro?"

"You think—" Ministrx Montenegro began, but Ministrx O'Higgins lurched to his feet, knocking his glass tumbler across the table. The sweet smell of rum flooded the room. His face paled to gray.

"You think we're being targeted. My spouse and my grandson are home alone. I have to—Juan Pablo, Críspula, Gumersinda!" he barked through the closed door. "We're leaving!"

The door opened, revealing the uncertain face of the blond man.

"William," Ministrx Montenegro said, detaining O'Higgins with a hand on his arm.

"Later, Sofía. Send Cempol," he said, shaking her off, and strode out, gathering his assistants to follow like ducklings in his wake.

"Did he come on foot?" Hala asked.

"I'll send servants with him and tell his household to be alert," Ministrx Montenegro said and called through the doorway to one of her assistants.

While they spoke, Rocío turned to Isis. "Any news?"

"No," Isis said, her voice rough. She had dark circles under her eyes, and the skin on her face was dry from her long ride back to La Bene, or more crying.

"Then you should go home, too. We need to speak to Ministrx Montenegro privately."

"Yes."

"But don't go alone."

"I brought some people with me."

Isis was too quiescent, and her ready agreement made Rocío uneasy. She considered the possibility that life had finally knocked the vim out of Isis and just as quickly discarded it. *What is she planning?* "Remember, this is my job, not yours."

Ministrx Montenegro finished her conversation, and Isis stood. "Sofía, I'm leaving, too."

"Take care." Ministrx Montenegro squeezed Isis's arm. Isis raised her hand to cover Ministrx Montenegro's and then left.

"Well," Ministrx Montenegro said in a very different tone from before. "I was about to ask if you really thought the incidents were related, but it seems that William does. What is it you want to tell me?"

"Ministrx O'Higgins did seem very disturbed," Rocío said. "Do you know if he's been threatened?"

"I don't." Ministrx Montenegro folded her hands on the glossy table top.

It felt like Ministrx Montenegro was interviewing them rather than the other way around. But Rocío was used to powerful people who thought they were in charge of everything. "Have you received any threatening notes?"

"Not this week. It happens from time to time."

"Did you check your wardstones? We left a note about that yesterday," Hala said.

"My majordomo did. She reported that everything was as expected."

"You should check them yourself," Hala said, leaning forward. "I believe it is quite likely they have been compromised, maybe in some subtle way only you would notice."

"That's ridiculous, Singh would—" She checked herself and said in a considering voice, "No, given your news, I'm not going to stand on pride." She stood and tugged on the bellpull. "That will summon Singh. Come on, don't just sit there."

They met Singh at the top of the stairs. "Do you have your keys?" Ministrx Montenegro asked. "Good. We're checking the wardstones. I know you checked yesterday, but we will do so again."

Singh's lips tightened, but she led the way without demur. They descended three levels, past the ground floor, where kitchen noises and talking were audible, to the cellar. They passed through several rooms, all well lit and clean, with shelves stocked with jars of compote and smoked hams and extra furniture covered in protective cloths lining the whitewashed walls.

"Your cellars seem larger than your house," Rocío said. She thought they had passed below the front wall of the house at least two rooms back.

"It was common at the time this house was built, soon after the Founding," Ministrx Montenegro said.

"You knew that?" Rocío asked Hala.

"Of course."

Singh led them to the left and used her keys to unlock the last room in the corner. She unhooked a lantern from the wall and lit it.

"There are no electric lights in the room?" Hala asked.

"I never saw the need," Ministrx Montenegro said. "There's no reason for anyone to spend time in here."

Rocío took out her flashlight. It was getting a lot of use this week. They crowded into the small room.

Singh held the lamp high, and the shadows retreated grudgingly, revealing the room's only contents: a wooden chest about as tall as Rocío's knees, set close to the far wall but not touching it. The deep carvings of half moons and triangles were stained a dark brown and free of dust.

Rocío had learned about house wards in the magic certification course, but she had never grasped how they worked, apart from the fact that the objects used to create them, usually stones, were "tricked" into thinking they were an extension of the body's electric field, not just of one person but of all the people who "belonged" inside the field, either permanently or temporarily. People who didn't belong activated an alarm or worse. It went without saying that only the rich could afford them.

As she stepped closer, Rocío could feel the current of an active wardstone. The hairs on her arms stood up as if she'd rubbed a wool blanket against them. Still, Ministrx Montenegro gestured for Singh to unlock the chest, and she heaved the thick lid open.

Ministrx Montenegro stared down at the wardstone. "This one is active."

She glared at Hala, and Rocío was sure the ministrx's canny political mind was imagining connivances and schemes. *It's a good thing I think Hala is right; I do not want this woman as an enemy.* Ministrx Montenegro didn't invite them to examine the wardstone.

They moved to the southeast corner of the cellar. Singh repeated the ritual. Ministrx Montenegro stepped into the room.

Her mouth tightened, and she gestured for Rocío to use her flashlight.

Rocío entered. The difference was obvious. There was no charge to the air, no sense of a current pulling at her skin. She pointed the flashlight at the chest.

From this angle, Rocío could see that the back was caved in. The front seemed undamaged, and from the doorway the chest had looked whole. Ministrx Montenegro opened it without a key, and the lid swung farther than it should have. Wood splintered, and the lid fell to the floor with a bang. Dust swirled up.

Singh sucked in a sharp breath.

"Ancestros perdidos." Ministrx Montenegro stifled a sneeze. "Singh."

"Ministrx." Singh's voice cracked. "I'm so sorry. I didn't enter the room yesterday. I didn't believe them, and I didn't perform my task as I should have. I failed you."

Hala cocked an eyebrow at Rocío, who pursed her lips in return. Either Singh was an open book and knew nothing about the sabotaged wardstone, or she was a very good actor.

Ministrx Montenegro rubbed her lips with one finger. "I should have come myself. I don't hold you responsible."

Singh clutched the wall and bent her head.

"Look, then." Ministrx Montenegro gestured Hala and Rocío closer.

Inside the chest a fragment of white rock about as big as Rocío's palm lay in a bed of white dust speckled with gray. From a few other smaller pieces she could tell it had once been a sphere.

"Before yesterday, when was this last checked?" Ministrx Montenegro asked.

"I did it, on Wednesday the eighth. Nine days ago," Singh said unsteadily. "I opened the chest as I always do, except yesterday. The wardstone was undamaged and active."

"But what could do this? And why?" Ministrx Montenegro asked.

"The eighth is within the window we're looking at: Friday the third to yesterday, the fourteenth," Hala said. She removed a loupe from her pocket and peered at the dust. "There are no signs of either

98

water or acid, though I don't see how either could be the method of destruction in this case. They would leave obvious signs of their use."

"Is that how a wardstone is destroyed?" Rocío asked, trying to reach back into her memories of the magic certification course. The instructor had had a melodious voice, which should have made it easier for Rocío to retain the information but hadn't.

"There are four ways a wardstone, or any magical device, can be destroyed: prolonged submersion in water, the application of acid, the application of brute force—really not recommended unless you want to die—and consumption."

Wait, isn't consumption only theoretical? The instructor's voice came back to Rocío: *Very few things eat stone, and that is why stone is the medium of choice for wards.*

The missing wall in the subte tunnel had been stone.

Hala met Rocío's eyes, and Rocío was sure they were thinking the same thing. She wanted to discuss it, *right now*, but it had to wait.

Hala retrieved a pair of tweezers and evidence envelopes from her pocket. "Hold this." She gave Rocío one envelope and picked up a gray filament from the dust. Rocío kept an eye on the ministrx and Singh.

"What did you find?" Ministrx Montenegro demanded.

"I'm not sure. On first inspection it seems vegetal. Is that unexpected?"

Ministrx Montenegro shook her head with what looked like genuine confusion. "That's ridiculous—there shouldn't be anything in the chest besides the wardstone. Alexa?"

"I checked the wardstones, I swear, ministrx. There wasn't anything wrong with them or different about them." Singh leaned forward. "If there was something growing in there, I would have told you. If I had seen the damage, I would have told you."

"I believe you, Alexa," Ministrx Montenegro said. Singh's lips parted in relief before she quickly pressed them together again. Ministrx Montenegro pretended not to notice.

Rocío believed her, too, though ultimately a case had to be built on facts, not on her feelings about other people's feelings. "Who else has access to these rooms?"

"They're kept locked. Singh has one set of keys, and the other is locked in my desk. Only my daughter Verra and I have keys to that."

"Rocío, the envelope," Hala said, and Rocío held it out so Hala could deposit the filament in it. Hala collected dust in another envelope.

"Señorx Singh, where do you keep your keys?"

Singh gestured restlessly. "I have them with me at all times, either in my pocket or locked in my nightstand while I'm asleep. I swear."

Ministrx Montenegro patted Singh on the shoulder, a surprising gesture from such a formal, elderly woman. Singh looked like she didn't know how to react, though her posture eased.

"Ministrx, what effect would destroying one stone have?" Rocío asked.

"It leaves a weak spot in the defense. Someone could enter the house without triggering an alarm. But the front of the house is the most securely guarded. There's a doorman who doubles as a guard at the gate, and all the servants who answer the door have security training. Detectives, are you done here? I'll go with you to the other two rooms. Alexa, we need to check the house. Start organizing the staff. I want to know if anything has been taken—"

"Or added," Rocío said.

"Or added, and if anyone knows anything about the wardstone."

Hala took Rocío's flashlight and directed it at the lock on the chest and then the matching piece on the floor. "It looks as if the lock was forced." Hala said. "It's possible that the damage to the back of the chest is a result of whatever pulverized the wardstone. I hope you don't object to us taking the lid for further examination?"

Ministrx Montenegro hesitated and then waved a hand. "Very well."

"I'd also like to check the rest of your cellars," Hala said.

"The cellars." Ministrx Montenegro's eyes narrowed, and she tapped two fingers against her thigh. Rocío had a sudden memory of her nonna banging her cane on the floor during her fights with Rocío's mother. Nonna had usually won those fights.

"You haven't told me why you suspected my wardstones were compromised. What are you looking for?"

"On Tuesday a subte worker on the Miraflores line reported that part of the wall in one of the access tunnels had been demolished, revealing an empty room. We have reason to believe the room was once part of your house and is within your wards. We also believe a coffin was removed."

Ministrx Montenegro's lips parted slightly. Rocío thought it might be equivalent to gape-mouthed astonishment on anyone else. Singh actually gasped this time.

"A coffin? There are no coffins in my cellars."

"The room had been bricked up, probably a very long time ago. Can you recall anything about your house that might be pertinent?"

"You're saying you believe someone destroyed one of my wardstones to enter a room I didn't know existed? To steal a coffin I didn't know existed? And that it's linked to this kidnapping, the lieutenant governor's arrest and whatever has William so upset?"

So Ministrx Montenegro had also thought Ministrx O'Higgins's reaction had been extreme.

"It's a possibility we can't ignore," Hala said.

"You seem to know so much about my house, Detective," Ministrx Montenegro said in a voice that could freeze water. "Where is this secret room? I want to see it."

"I assure you, this is inference only, based on what I know about the construction of the subterranean railway and the old houses of La Bene."

"But you can find the room from here?"

"Yes. Or more specifically the entrance to it."

"Alexa, you check the other wardstones first, then organize the staff." Ministrx Montenegro marched out of the room, sucking everyone up in her wake to trail after her.

In the end they had to enlist the help of several brawny servants to move two cabinets and enough china for a dinner party with all the ministrx in the House of Refuges, but Hala found the room with only half a meter of error. Most of the cellar walls were whitewashed stone blocks about as big as both of Rocío's feet together, but the section of the wall that Hala uncovered held the shape of a bricked-up doorway.

Hala was not going to need to eat her socks, because she was right. Again.

Someone had destroyed Ministrx Montenegro's wardstone so they could enter a forgotten room in her cellars and steal a forgotten coffin.

"Ah," Hala said, the only sign of satisfaction she would allow herself in front of these witnesses. "This is old." She reached up to touch the center stone in the arch. "You can tell by the width of the keystone. I suspect there's a row of rooms on the other side and that the wardstone rooms at either end are the only ones still in use. The bricked-up doorways in those rooms are likely hidden behind thicker plaster."

Ministrx Montenegro's lips were pressed so tightly together they almost disappeared.

"It wouldn't be a good idea to unblock this doorway," Rocío said quickly. "It's open to the subte on the other side."

The servants exchanged incredulous looks, though Rocío wasn't sure if it was because of the existence of hidden entrances to secret rooms in the cellar of such a respectable house or because Rocío had suggested that a course of action the ministrx might be contemplating wasn't wise.

"And it's a crime scene until everything is resolved," Hala put in, "but afterwards I'm sure the superintendent would be amenable to closing it up again from the other side."

Ministrx Montenegro stared at the bricks for a long moment. "Very well. You were right about this. You can question everyone in this house. Roust them out of their beds." She took out a pocket watch. "You'll have to—it's almost midnight. Singh?"

The majordomo stepped forward. "The other wardstones are intact, ministrx." Her tone implied cautious approval of the situation.

"You can examine those if you want," Ministrx Montenegro said to Hala. "You will keep me informed."

"Of course. If I may suggest ... if you have any architectural plans of the house that could tell us what was in that room, that would be very helpful."

That Hala hadn't said *who was in that room* demonstrated an extreme level of tact. Rocio wasn't sure what had brought it on or if it was warranted. "You really don't know whose coffin was in there?" she asked.

"If I had known it was there, I would have done something about it," Ministrx Montenegro said, flicking her fingers as if brushing away something distasteful. "Interred it legally and far from here, for one."

"Um, yes," Rocío said, suppressing a shudder. "If you could just give us a moment, I need to speak to Detective Haddad."

Ministrx Montenegro barked a laugh. "No doubt. I'm not going to make you stay in the cellars for privacy. I don't believe in punishing the messengers. You can meet in the servants' hall. Singh will take care of it."

Rocío shivered in spite of herself. Not that she thought there were ghosts down here. Ministrx Montenegro's house was too well kept for a haunting to have gone unnoticed. But she had had enough of cellars and underground tunnels all the same.

"Hala, do you know what that was? In with the wardstone?" Rocío asked in a low voice, hoping the words wouldn't carry.

They stood in the middle of the brightly lit servants' hall between a long dining table and display cabinets full of white stoneware. A grandmother clock ticked against the far wall.

Hala bounced on her toes. "A possible connection to the subte excavation. Yaco will double-check for me, but I believe it's a fragment of lichen. My theory is that foreign magic was used to accelerate its normal growth to rapidly reduce the stone to dust."

"Imported magic?"

Hala sobered. "It looks that way, but only scientific analysis will give us that answer."

"Great. So you're saying you found a magicked lichen that eats stone fast," Rocío said.

"Quite." Hala smiled at Rocío with satisfaction. "A lichen that could eat a magic wardstone would have no trouble with a nonmagical stone wall, don't you think? And voila, a room appears where there was never a room before."

"Answering the question of how someone could have removed that much stone from the subte without anyone noticing."

"Revealing not just the room but its connection to two serious crimes. The ministrx didn't know about the coffin, did she? My empty room *is* a crime

"I'm impressed you managed to restrain yourself from saying that for so long," Rocío said dryly. "I already said you were right and I was wrong. I really don't like the amount of planning this implies."

"A fast-growing lichen is only fast compared to geologic time, I assume. However, I agree. The fact that someone was able to remove Prokofiev from La Quinta and leave no witnesses implies a certain amount of planning, but the magic involved, coupled with the amount of knowledge needed to attack Montenegro and Belli and possibly Valdivia through Lieutenant Governor Sabato, implies exponentially more planning."

"And insider knowledge."

"We need to change our focus from immigrants and anarchists to politicians. Stricter immigration controls won't affect them."

"I'll sleep better at night knowing that," Rocío said. "Oh wait, I won't, because now we're officially investigating unidentified magic, crypts and stolen coffins."

CHAPTER 7

THE NEXT MORNING Rocío was knee-deep in garbage with only Paloma and the other Díaz for company and mentally cursing Isis, who was directly responsible for this new malodorous low point of Rocío's life.

When she had walked into the CJC earlier that morning, Oshinsky had slapped a newspaper into her hands. "Did you know about this?"

REWARD FOR NEWS OF ALEKSANDR PROKOFIEV'S WHEREABOUTS was emblazoned across the whole front page of *El Universo* in two-centimeter-high letters.

Ancestros perdidos. "No, of course I didn't," Rocío said cautiously. Forty-five hundred pesos. You could buy a house with that, or a quarter share in a factory.

"I'm holding you responsible anyway," Oshinsky said with uncharacteristic sharpness. "You said you talked to her, convinced her not to do anything rash."

The pressure from the ministrx and Cempol must be tremendous; making an example of someone was not usual behavior for Oshinsky. Everyone in the office had suddenly developed an intense interest in whatever they were doing and kept their heads down or turned away. Everyone except the other Díaz, who was clearly enjoying the fact that Rocío was on the receiving end of the chief's ire for a change.

"Chief, no one is responsible for Isis," Rocío said. "I told her last night to let us do our jobs."

"Do you know how many resources this is going to tie up? It's a good thing Cempol is involved. They're putting a whole team on it. Nine people who could be otherwise employed looking for whoever is threatening ministrx in this city. And I don't have an assistant in the middle of all this."

So take her back. Rocío barely bit back the words in time. Oshinsky wasn't being reasonable about Paloma, but now was not the time to convince her of that.

"We cannot afford to mess this up," Oshinsky said, raising her voice to address everyone. "This situation is bigger and more complex than we thought, and the stakes are higher. It's not just one man's life in danger anymore. We need to be alert and smart and solve this fast."

And then after the morning briefing, Oshinsky had sent Rocío to Tili Alley, site of the additional magic residue Yaco's team had found. They had identified it as a match for the residue in Aleksandr Prokofiev's room. In addition, businesses in the alley had complained about the smell of something dead in the garbage bins that had gone unemptied because of the garbage collectors' strike. It had seemed possible that Prokofiev hadn't made it out of the alley. The cadaver dogs hadn't signaled for human remains, but there was definitely something dead there, and Oshinsky had chosen her least favorite people of the day to check it out. Which was why Rocío was sorting four-day old garbage from a big blue dumpster into smaller evidence boxes in case forensics had to process it further.

From genius detective to punishment detail in less than twelve hours—that must be a new record. Hala would know, but Hala was off doing something that smelled much better. Rocío knew that because everything smelled better than where she was now. The narrow street trapped the heat from the back of the falafel joint, overlaying the stench of garbage with the smell of cooking oil, and dark grease and effluvium stained the cobblestones a permanent black.

"You shouldn't have pissed off all those actors, Díaz," Rocío couldn't help saying as she lifted a soggy bundle of newspaper and unwrapped it to expose rotting cabbage and chicken bones. *Are my gloves leaking? It feels like my gloves are leaking and this putrid sludge is seeping into my skin.* She couldn't even take a deep breath to calm herself. She'd made that mistake once and almost puked into her mask. Only the thought of the humiliation of vomiting in front of Paloma on the third day of training her had enabled her to fight her gag reflex.

"Kick that closer to me, Paloma? We're going to need another evidence box for just garbage soon."

"Well, you shouldn't have pissed off the chief," Díaz said. "And you brought Paloma down with you, so in my book that's worse."

If anything, his body language was more aggressive without anyone else around: feet spread wide, arms outstretched to claim more space. Claim more garbage. Rocío snorted to herself and got her spitefulness back under control. He could have it.

"I don't mind," Paloma said.

Both Rocío and Díaz lifted their heads to look at her. Paloma had half a rotten pumpkin rind in one hand and a smear of unidentifiable brown stuff down the front of her protective coveralls.

"I mean, of course I mind, but someone has to do it, right?" Paloma said.

Rocío had to grudgingly admit that Paloma was throwing herself into the job to an extent Rocío had never expected.

"Rookies," Díaz muttered, his voice muffled by his mask and his position head-down in the dumpster. "What have you ever done to deserve her admiration, Rocío?" He straightened and dropped what looked like a handful of feces into the box labeled HAZARDOUS BIOLOGICAL WASTE.

Paloma said, "I—"

"Shut up, Díaz," Rocío said. "She just wants to learn how to do the job." *Admiration? No, that's just Díaz being sour.*

They worked in silence for a few minutes until Paloma said, "Rocío?"

"Hm?"

"Isn't it a good thing that Ministrx Soler offered a reward?" Paloma asked.

"It brings out the nutters," Díaz said.

"Díaz. Do you want me to report you to the chief? Remember the memo on respectful language for people of all levels of mental health and abilities? Paloma, Díaz is a good example of what not to do at the CJC."

"Ancestors forget you, too, Díaz," he said.

"What he means is a reward brings out opportunists and people who might not have a firm grasp on reality."

"But shouldn't it help?" Paloma asked.

"Keep working while you talk," Díaz snapped.

"You weren't at the CJC when the diplomat from Iberon offered a reward for his missing son. It was absolute chaos, and ninety-nine percent of the information was useless. We already have too many leads, too many details."

She counted them off to illustrate. "Five members of the sub-committee, all with their own enemies. Seven assistants, and a new third secretary to the sub-committee whose appointment was contentious." That was the unhappy blond man from Ministrx Montenegro's last night.

"The sub-committee meets twice a week at Ministrx Montenegro's house, so they all theoretically had access to the wardstones.

"Plus there are the individual dramas. For example, the spouse and only child of Ministrx Montenegro's daughter, Verra Montenegro, died two years ago. Two years isn't too long to wait for revenge for a son and a grandson." Rocío raised her arm to wipe sweat from her forehead and then thought better of it. Who knew garbage put out this much heat? Well, that and all the protective gear. Thank the seres celestiales it was autumn.

"Then, moving away from Ministrx Montenegro: only the seres celestiales know what Ministrx O'Higgins knows, because he's only talking to them and Cempol, who won't talk to us; Ministrx María Paz Belli isn't talking about the threat against her; and the editor of *Oye* says he destroyed the note he received and that any information it contained is confidential because of the laws protecting journalists."

"Like he's a journalist," Díaz said, snorting.

Rocío seemed to have come to the end of a layer of restaurant refuse and moved into discards from the paint store. Old newspapers, a broken paintbrush, empty sample jars of paint. Her sense of smell was now pretty well gone, but at least the solid refuse didn't feel as squishy and revolting as the food waste.

"Is that where Hala is today? At *Oye*?" Díaz asked.

"No, the adjudicator already agreed with the editor. She said we didn't have enough evidence to link Prokofiev's disappearance to the editor's information."

"Because he destroyed the note," Díaz said, slapping the dumpster in outrage. It boomed hollowly. "If he hadn't, forensics could have tried to match the handwriting and the paper to the two notes the ministrx received. The editor probably has something on the adjudicator. Everyone in this city knows each other or does business with each other or is sleeping with each other." He sneered at Rocío as he said it.

And she'd been momentarily sympathetic to him for his outrage about the adjudicator's questionable judgement. "I don't know where Hala is."

"She went to the Government Archives for something," Paloma said.

Rocío's mildly charitable feelings about Paloma, inspired by her willingness to work, swung back towards annoyance. Clearly dumpster diving was not conducive to emotional equilibrium.

"So to sum up, we already have too much information and not enough staff to process it. Finding anything helpful in the dubious tips brought to us by the well-meaning, the greedy, and the deluded is as likely as us finding a lead in this—oh no."

Rocío really looked at what she held. At first glance it had seemed to be some kind of paint roller, about twelve centimeters long and covered in black cloth. On closer examination, the cloth was short black hair, matted and crusted with blood. The solid inner part was bone, sawed through on both ends. Hair? Or animal fur? Nausea that had nothing to do with garbage roiled through Rocío's stomach.

"What is that?" Paloma asked, sounding baffled and disgusted.

"I think it's a dog leg."

A maggot dropped onto Rocío's foot. "This is what stinks." It was strong enough to wake up her sense of smell, coating the inside of her mouth even through the mask. She knew from experience she'd be smelling and feeling the film of it on her teeth for a week, long after it should have dissipated from repeated brushing and gargling and washing.

"I have one, too," Díaz said.

Rocío turned. He held what looked like a fuzzy roll of cloth. It was a good six centimeters shorter than the one Rocío held and brownish red.

"At least I'm pretty sure this is a dog's leg," Díaz said, "Not that I'm an expert."

They met each other's eyes, for once in perfect accord. Dead mutilated animals elevated an already-bad situation to new levels of bad. Rocío tried to think of a non-ableist word. *Creepy. Scary. Dangerous. Serial killers* also came to mind. She saw the same thoughts on Díaz's face, though neither of them was ready to speak them aloud in front of Paloma just yet.

"Do you think those are the dogs Hala has been looking for?" Paloma asked, looking from Rocío to Díaz.

"I have a very bad feeling that they are," Rocío said.

Back at the CJC, Rocío scrunched her wet hair in her towel and reveled in being clean and having a moment to herself in the locker room. The smell of garbage was still a not-distant-enough memory, but at least it was a memory. Forensics had taken the dog bones and boxes of garbage, and she finally had time to think. Something about the dog bones was bothering her, something more than the obvious. It wasn't as if she were trying to recall a fact, exactly; it had more emotional weight to it, like simultaneously trying to remember and forget a bad dream upon waking. She tried to trace the thought back. It had risen to the surface when she had looked at the exposed bone of the dog's leg.

The door banged against the wall, letting in the smell of coffee, a gust of cold air and the sound of a lot of people arguing. "Hey, close that," Rocío said, swiveling around on her bench.

Espinoza staggered in and grabbed the nearest locker to stay upright.

Rocío surged to her feet, scattering hairpins off her lap. "What's going on?"

"They arrested Ministrx Soler and a bunch of anarchists."

Another advocate staggered past the open door, grappling with a short woman bellowing obscenities.

"Seres celestiales, are they rioting in the CJC?"

"Yes, you could say that." Espinoza lunged for the door, Rocío on her heels. The other woman disappeared into a knot of brawling anarchists. She bellowed, "Order! Desist!"

They shouted back, "One solution: revolution!"

Rocío punched an anarchist armed with a stapler and jumped on top of a desk, scanning the room. In one corner Viernes and another young forensic tech had barricaded themselves behind a desk. An anarchist climbed over a spill of chairs towards them.

"Viernes! Look out!" More shouting drowned out Rocío's warning.

Paloma surged forward, grabbed the encroaching anarchist by his waistband and boxed his ears. The man next to her—was that the bandoneónista from La Valle?—clubbed him over the head with two clenched fists. The anarchist wavered, raised his hands to his head and collapsed to his knees. The bandoneónista said something to Paloma and threw himself on the back of another passing anarchist. Paloma stayed to guard Viernes.

Attracted by Rocío's shout, an anarchist lunged for her feet. She kicked him. The meaty thunk of her boot against his chest vibrated up her leg. He flew backwards into the crowd. She shook off a shudder from the violence.

"I'm going to kill her." There was no doubt in her mind Isis was responsible for this somehow.

From her vantage point she could see there were about ten anarchists, five musicians from La Valle and more advocates and staff piling into the office every moment. And there was Isis, circling Shen the anarchist in one corner. She favored her left side, but Shen's nose dripped blood over his lips and down his chin, and one arm hung useless.

Rocío jumped to the floor, shoving anarchists and musicians out of her way. A woman snagged her arm, staggering drunkenly, and breathed chicha fumes in her face. Rocío pushed her off just as the other Díaz shouted, "Ware!" A canister glinted in his upraised hand —a smoke grenade.

Rocío sucked in a deep breath, half closed her eyes and flung herself towards Isis.

The smoke grenade clattered against the floor and popped. A billow of thick white smoke erupted into the room. A few of the more experienced anarchists kept fighting, but most people fled for the exits.

Rocío ran across the room, pushing anyone who got close out of her way. "Díaz!" She shoved Shen at him, grabbed Isis's arm and slung her into interview three. She slammed the door behind them and threw the lock. A cough tore her throat, and she bent over, supporting herself on her knees.

"What—" Her voice cracked, and she sucked in a few more breaths. "Piérdate, Isis! What are you doing?" She pushed her damp hair off her face and straightened.

Isis eyed Rocío warily and for once didn't say anything. Lacerations slashed through one eyebrow and across the arch of one cheekbone, and she had cuts on her knuckles.

"Isis. What did you do?"

"It was just a little bar fight," Isis said lightly. Falsely. So falsely.

"That was a riot," Rocío ground out. "In the CJC. Tell me what you did."

"I found Shen."

Rocío didn't allow any expression to cross her face. If there was any chance Isis didn't know Shen's connection to the stolen dance score, Rocío wasn't going to be the one to tell her.

"I expressed my feelings about the arts to him," Isis said.

Clearly Isis knew. Rocío groaned. "Of all the reckless, ill-advised ... wait, you said a bar fight. You didn't go to the General Strike? You did, didn't you. You walked into an anarchist meeting place and attacked him?"

"I didn't go alone."

"No, you didn't, did you?" Rocío swept her hair off her face again and twisted it into a haphazard knot. "How badly hurt are you?"

"A few bruised ribs, I suspect."

Rocío leaned against the door, her knees loose with relief. It was easier than standing. "Serves you right. You're like a perdido cat—you knock a vase over, and you're the only one who doesn't get wet. Seres celestiales, Isis. Who told you about Shen?"

Someone pounded on the door, sending vibrations through Rocío's chest.

Isis pressed her lips together, tried to fold her arms, winced and let them fall back to her sides.

"Rocío! I know you're in there." Díaz pounded on the door again. "If you're not dead, the chief wants to see you."

"Isis, answer me."

"Now, Rocío." Díaz pounded on the door so hard it shook.

"Píerdalo. This is not over," Rocío told Isis. "Díaz," she shouted, "I'm opening the door." She wrenched it open. He held a baton half raised. Blood smeared his arm. He looked pissed. Behind him the room was clear of anarchists, musicians, anarchist musicians and smoke.

Díaz dropped his arm. "Right. I thought you had her. You're going to a holding room, Ministrx." He glared at Rocío as if he expected her to protest.

"No argument from me. She's all yours."

Rocío stabbed some pins into her hair before knocking on Oshinsky's door. The chief's voice was neutral when she called for Rocío to enter.

Rocío glanced quickly at the extra candles burning in front of Oshinsky's altar. There were also asters for patience. *Right—I need some of that myself.* A chaski would probably be by any moment with violets, the traditional flower for riots.

Oshinsky had on her stressed face, the corners of her mouth turned down. That was actually a good sign; when she controlled her expression more fully, it was bad. She pressed her palms flat on the desk as she looked Rocío over, like she was holding back a lot of emotion.

"You wanted to see me, Chief." Rocío made sure all the inflections were in the right place to convey respectful attention.

"Detective Haddad assures me you didn't tell Ministrx Soler who sold the dance score to The Legionnaire. Is that true?"

"Yes, Chief, it's true. I didn't so much as hint at it." Rocío bit back further explanations.

Oshinsky tapped her fingers on the desk, and her frown got deeper.

"You don't look relieved, Chief."

"Sit down."

Another good sign for Rocío, if not for the whole situation. She took a seat and wished she had a prop to occupy her hands. If she wasn't going to get yelled at, that meant she was going to be asked to clean up the mess. And considering the mess was Isis, it would be a doozy. There was no way Rocío could serve the CJC and her fellow advocates and protect Isis at the same time.

"I didn't think it was you," Oshinsky said, and Rocío felt some more tension release from her shoulders. "But that means someone else told her."

"Yes." It was a hard truth that had to be said.

"This means we have to start looking at our own for divided loyalties, vulnerabilities that would make someone take a bribe or resentments that would make someone want to hurt the CJC."

"I think if someone in the CJC were really out to hurt us, we'd know about it. But I don't even have a guess who it could be at this point. I'll keep my eyes open," Rocío said, not just because she would —of course she would—but because Oshinsky needed to hear that offer of solidarity. Though there was no way she was going to offer to talk to Isis until the chief suggested it.

"I know you will." Oshinsky's hands relaxed to a more natural position on the desk. "I told you to keep a lid on Soler."

Rocío waited.

"I know, that's like keeping a lid on a boiling pot of water. I want you to talk to her. Try to make her see sense and tell us who her source is."

"Yes, Chief. I'm glad you're trusting me with this." *Because I sure as ancestors was going to do it anyway.*

"The adjudicator issued an order confining her to her home to avoid further public disorder. She has to stay there."

"It's possible she found out through the reward she posted."

"I can only hope so. Try to find out from her. And Detective Díaz, don't do anything to make me put you on probation, demote you or dock your pay."

The *Detective Díaz* stung more than the warning. "I won't."

"How is Paloma doing?"

"Fine," Rocío said, off balance. She hadn't expected the conversation to go in this direction and wasn't prepared. "She learns quickly. She'll be a great interviewer one day." *If she commits herself to that and not just to social climbing.*

Now was not the time to try to make Oshinsky see what Paloma was. Rocío knew it was a mistake even as she said, "Are you sure, though, that this is a good idea?"

The small movements of Oshinsky's hands stopped. One of the first things Rocío had learned in her parents' house about reading body language was that the sudden cessation of movement was either a sign you were on to something or a sign of danger. Rocío knew which this was.

Pierdalo, why did I open my mouth without something specific to tell her?

Oshinsky glanced at her altar and rubbed the back of her hand. "This is a tough case to start training a rookie." Her voice was even. Compassionate. "My door is always open to you, Rocío. But here's my advice: don't let your prejudices get in the way. Think about it. I know you can do this and do it well."

Rocío barely kept herself from flinching backwards in her chair. Each one of Oshinsky's words felt like a dart piercing her skin. Rocío linked her hands in her lap and clenched them hard. *Prejudices?* She wanted to ask what Oshinsky meant, but she felt frozen in place.

Oshinsky kept talking. "I think Paloma can be as good as you one day, and that's why I put her with you. I need you to do this. For me. For you. For Paloma. Can you do it?"

Rocío had given up caring about her parents' approval a long time ago, but they had never believed she could do something when she doubted it herself. Realizing that she was skating close to losing Oshinsky's approval shook Rocío. No, it was realizing how much she didn't want to lose her approval and how visceral that felt, just as it had when she was a child and had wanted to please her parents. Rocío couldn't find any words.

For once she didn't know what expression was on her face, but Oshinsky seemed to read everything she needed to see there. "Go talk to Ministrx Soler."

Rocío took the long way to the holding rooms, stopping in the locker room to splash water on her hot eyes and check the pins in her hair. *Prejudices? What did Oshinsky mean? I'm not prejudiced.* She ignored the small mental voice that told her every human had prejudices and leaned on the sink, meeting her own eyes in the mirror.

Her reflection knocked the uncomfortable thoughts out of her head. Uncertain—that's how she looked. Hunched against a blow. She forced herself to straighten and relaxed her face, smoothing out the worried wrinkle between her eyebrows. *Did I look like this in Oshinsky's office?*

No. She'd sat straight, torso towards Oshinsky and open, feet slightly apart to convey confidence but not aggression. But maybe at the end ... She tried to remember what her face had felt like. Closed her eyes. Felt the lurch in her chest, like all the organs in her body were trying to shrink. She opened her eyes, took one look at herself, and snapped them shut again, appalled. *I looked like that in my parents' house. No, no, no. I have a place here, and it is mine. I won't lose it. Think about something else. Think about the case.*

Aleksandr Prokofiev still missing … Isis fighting anarchists … a possible leak in the CJC … threats against ministrx … the lieutenant governor's arrest … dismembered dogs. *Dogs.* What did that make her think of? Not Hala; something else. Nonna? Why would she be thinking of her grandmother? She tried to chase the thought back, ran into the memory of Oshinsky's office instead and flinched away.

"Pull yourself together, Chío," she said aloud, copying the voice of her first teacher in the theater. That was a good memory. She'd done really well in the theater, and she'd left because she'd found another passion, not because she couldn't stay, like when she'd left her parents' house. "You're a good detective. You've got this."

She fluttered her lips and ran through some vocal exercises, and by the time she left the bathroom she felt better and had the beginning of a plan for Paloma.

Isis, though, was the same perdido plan as always.

More shouting, from the back of the building this time, was audible as soon as Rocío left the locker room. *That's Oshinsky.* The chief almost never yelled. Rocío's stomach tried to crawl up her throat. *This day.* She sucked in two deep breaths to calm herself and wound through the desks to Hala.

Oshinsky yelled, "—speak to Commander Dhavale about this—" Her voice dropped in volume.

"What now?" Rocío asked Hala. Everyone was standing around, not even pretending not to listen, though the words weren't clear anymore.

"Officer Smith."

"You're kidding. She's never made me yell like that, though I've wanted to."

"She's the Cempol liaison, and she's here to take the dogs' bodies you found," Hala said in a low voice. "Thanks for that, by the way."

Rocío searched her pockets for a stick of gum. "Someone put Smith in charge of something? Does that mean Cempol thinks the dogs are linked to Prokofiev's disappearance? Or that they're not?" She gave up on her pockets.

"Listen." Hala grabbed Rocío's elbow and pulled her towards the holding rooms. She stopped in the hallway. "I assume Oshinsky believed that you didn't tip Isis off about the dance score?"

"Of course she did." Rocío waved away Hala's concern with a lightness she didn't feel. "Thank you for that."

Hala pursed her lips like she wasn't buying it. "She asked you to talk to Isis again? Then you don't have much time. Oshinsky expedited the request for the divers to search the lake for Prokofiev's body. Another witness came forward to say he saw Prokofiev heading towards Parque Dolores the night he disappeared."

"He couldn't have spoken up *before* I spent my morning sorting garbage?"

"Prokofiev was with a woman. And Oshinsky hasn't told Cempol about the divers. We need to be there in forty minutes."

Oshinsky shouted something in the back that sounded like "—paperwork!"

After a pause while they waited for more shouting, Rocío asked, "What about the dogs?"

"I don't know if they think they're related. But the dogs were not just dismembered; there are pieces missing."

Rocío swallowed down gorge. "Pieces?"

"There are no paws. And one is missing a tail, though it's possible that happened antemortem."

"Animal sacrifice? Serial killer?"

"I'm sure they're thinking along those lines and that they're afraid of public panic if other people start thinking it, too."

"Oshinsky—"

"No one besides the techs know. Oshinsky thinks if the CJC keeps the dogs' bodies, it will limit the pool of people who know. Now go on, talk to Isis."

"Seres celestiales."

"At least you talked to Oshinsky before Smith got to her."

"Right." Rocío took another deep breath, pushed all thoughts of Cempol and dismembered dogs to the back of her mind. "What are the charges against Isis?"

"Incitement to riot. That was just for the bar fight, though. I don't know if they'll add charges for the fight here."

"Right."

Holding room one didn't look that different from interview three, with some comfortable furniture, worn leather-bound books and unremarkable landscape art, except the divan was longer in case someone needed to be held overnight. Isis leaned against the wall, unusually still, the cuts on her face cleaned and bandaged.

"Your hair is coming down on the side," Isis said.

"Who did you bribe for the information?" Rocío asked, skipping the chitchat and going with her instincts.

Isis's eyes flickered closed just a second longer than usual when Rocío said *bribe. And there it is.*

"Chío, my dear, why would you say that?" Isis said with false brightness.

"Cut it out, Isis. It's me. We will find out, but the time we spend doing that is time people aren't working to find Sasha."

Isis grimaced, all her teeth visible. "And be accused of bribing an officer of the city? I don't think so."

"That wasn't so hard, was it? See how much progress we're making already? Was it an advocate?"

"I know your tricks," Isis said, turning her face away from Rocío's gaze.

That was okay; Rocío knew Isis so well she didn't need to see her face. "Support staff? Forensics?"

The tendons in Isis's neck stood out and relaxed, as if she had suppressed the impulse to cross her arms. She had to be in a lot of pain to have let that slip. Unless it was a ploy.

"Isis." Rocío moved to stand in front of her and cupped Isis's chin in her hands, not something she would do with just anyone held in this room. Isis's skin felt too cool under her fingers, and the urge to comfort her rose up. Rocío squelched it. Isis had gotten herself into trouble, as usual, and this time she'd gotten Rocío into it, too. "Was it forensics?"

"You are so annoying," Isis said, but her eyelids had flinched again, and Rocío was sure.

"So are you." She smoothed her finger across Isis's cheek, under the cut, and dropped her hand. "You have to stay out of this. Why can't you understand that and let us do our jobs?"

"You know I can't do that."

"And that's why you're being confined to your house by the adjudicator. Incitement to riot, Isis. You could have been killed. Or gotten someone else killed."

Isis sucked in a breath but said lightly, "The squeaky wheel gets the grease."

"You're not a squeaky wheel, you're a shrieking banshee of a wrench in the gears. Just ... be careful. I don't know what I'd do if something happened to you. You and Hala are the most important people in the world to me. Apart from my parents and brother, of course."

Isis leaned forward and rested her forehead against Rocío's. "I can't hug you because of my ribs. But you're important to me, too." Just as Rocío let herself relax a bit, Isis added, "And Sasha is important to me."

"You are directly responsible for the rotten day I'm having. Literally rotten."

"And I'll take the comment about your family in the spirit in which it's meant."

"I'm not arguing with you about family today."

"Neither am I."

Rocío let herself absorb the comfort of Isis's presence—and yes, there was quite a bit of irony there—for another moment before pulling away.

"Have you changed your mind about telling me which officer of the CJC you bribed?"

"Nope."

"Why can't you be more biddable?" Rocío asked.

"Why can't you?"

"Fine. But I'm going to say this again: have you considered that you're doing exactly what the kidnapper wants? Blowing up all over town, creating trouble for yourself and for us so we can't do our job and find Sasha?"

Isis's face froze. "I'm not."

But Rocío had scared her, or at least made her think about something she didn't want to think about, and that was going to have to be enough for now.

"Do not dump your escort when they take you home, Isis. There is someone out there threatening ministrx." Rocío refused to feel guilty for using whatever tactics were at hand.

"I know. I won't." Isis's said, and Rocío believed her, at least on this one narrow issue. That was one problem taken care of for now. Too bad there seemed to be a never-ending lineup of problems to be fixed.

CHAPTER 8

Rocío and Hala didn't have a chance to catch each other up further on the way to Lago Nicolás or while they stood at its edge with Piotr Prokofiev on one side and spectators on the other. The routine of directing the public and coordinating with the divers steadied Rocío's emotions, and she was glad to be outside in the cold and not in another small office, facing off against people she cared about.

"What did you do to your hair?" she asked Hala in a further effort to restore normalcy. It was short again, back to her usual cut, standing up in spikes and making her look like a curious porcupine, but more uneven.

"I did it myself. It was getting in the way."

"Hmm."

The odd haircut suited her. Luckily the same could be said of the chaski who had copied her, one of the younger ones with a serious case of hero worship. Rocío had been worried about what the girl's family would say, but luckily the chaski's mom had laughed and said those kinds of crushes were healthy for a young girl. Hala had shrugged and pretended not to notice, but Rocío thought she was secretly pleased.

Beside her, Piotr Prokofiev shivered in spite of the garish orange-and-purple scarf wrapped around his neck as five divers waded into the water, their wool wet suits covering every part of their bodies except their faces, which were fitted with chunky glass-and-rubber masks. The dive coordinator stood on the bank, where a tent and braziers had been set up as the divers' relief station. It was cold enough that they wouldn't be able to stay in the water for long, though "diving" was a bit of an overstatement. At this end, the water was mostly waist high at its deepest.

"He would not do suicide," Piotr Prokofiev insisted again.

"It's not just suicide we're concerned about, Señorx Prokofiev," Rocío said. "A witness saw him here fighting with a woman. Can you think of who that might have been?"

"Anyone." He shrugged. "Who knows. He talk to many women. He fight with the La Zorra, but this is art, not ..." He gestured uncertainly to the lake. "She has vision, he has vision, I have vision, we fight and make better vision."

"Was there anyone in the troupe who had problems with him?"

"The dancers?" He looked surprised. "They love us."

Hala had said almost the same thing after questioning the dancers. Aleksandr Prokofiev had been living the blessed life of an artist whose career was on the upswing. The usual megalomania of entertainers had been focused on making sure the Prokofiev brothers would take them along as they rose. Until Isis came along and ruined it.

That's not fair. This is not Isis's fault. It just feels like it right now.

The divers were halfway across the lake, using a combination of underwater lights and rakes to probe the bottom. The water was murky and smelled heavy with stirred-up vegetable decay. The ducks had fled, though a few crows watched from the cypresses, occasionally commenting sardonically in their rough voices, and a small crowd of onlookers had gathered at one end of the paved area. A vendor had appeared, informed by that sixth sense they all had—otherwise known as a very well-developed gossip network—and was selling tea and churros. At least it wasn't chicha.

"Why didn't you tell us your brother and Isis Soler Ibáñez were lovers?" Hala asked with that clinical detachment she did so well, as if the speaker could tell her he'd crowned himself king and started a war with the Ka Empire and she wouldn't turn a hair.

Paloma shifted like she might protest and then stilled, hopefully remembering that Piotr Prokofiev might be a victim or he might be a murderer.

"Isis?" He raised his eyebrows. "They were ... infatuated? More interested in making love than fighting."

"Any—"

One of the divers exclaimed in surprise and gestured a colleague over. Rocío squinted at the muddy water but couldn't see what they had found. Prokofiev clutched his head.

The divers discussed something in low voices, and the second diver splashed away and returned with two crowbars. They levered them into place around the unseen object and strained. Rocío shrugged her shoulders, trying to ease her tension. Two more divers joined them and reached into the water. A familiar-looking blue dumpster rose into view, and Rocío's stomach sank. Another garbage bin. Just great. It was more than big enough for a body, especially if it had been hacked up like the dogs had been. Rocío reached for her own clinical detachment.

The divers maneuvered the bin to the bank. Prokofiev's teeth chattered.

"Stay here, please," Rocío said. Hala said something to Paloma too low for Rocío to hear, but it was probably "A dead body hidden in a garbage bin will be in an advanced state of decomposition and a seething mass of insects is not the best choice for your first body."

In any case, no one followed Rocío as she strode towards the divers. They maneuvered the dumpster out of the lake. Rust streaked the blue metal. If necessary, Hala or the techs could estimate how long it had been in the water from that.

"Can you open it?"

The divers fixed the crowbars in place and pried at the dented lid. It groaned and warped but didn't open.

"Do we have more pry bars?" Rocío asked.

"Hold your horses, Detective," one of the divers panted, and leaned on her bar.

"Just give them a minute," the dive coordinator said. One corner popped up, and then the three others followed in quick succession. "See?"

"I didn't doubt you."

"Hmm. All yours now."

Rocío pulled on leather gloves and steeled herself, glad her hands didn't shake. She lifted the lid.

The putrid smell of old trapped garbage rolled out. Not, thankfully, the sweet rotten smell of a decomposing body or the sound of a lot of maggots. The two divers gagged and stepped back. Rocío breathed shallowly through her nose. The smell was bad, but the taste if she breathed through her mouth would be worse. From what she could see, the bin was full of food scraps and newspapers. Still, the cold water could have inhibited both putrefaction and insect development. *I've been working with Hala so long even my thoughts sound like her sometimes.*

Rocío put out her hand for a pry bar and flipped the top layer of newspapers back. More refuse. Chaskis ran up with a smock and evidence bins. Rocío turned to beckon to Paloma, but she was leading a shaky Piotr to one of the benches with a hand under his elbow. She guided his head to his knees.

Rocío frowned. Paloma was taking on a helper role in a way she didn't like. Hala came over, tying her smock.

"I need to talk to you about Paloma," Rocío said.

"Thank the Mother of the Holy Ones, finally. Yes, you do."

Rocío transferred her frown to Hala, taken aback by the fervency of her response.

"But this is not the appropriate time or place. Quick and dirty?" Hala asked, gesturing at the garbage bin.

Rocío turned her attention back where it belonged. "Yes."

The top layer was squishy even through the thick gloves. *Not again.* She groped for something solid. Her hand closed on something long and cylindrical. Bones? *It could be anything*, she admonished herself. She lifted it, squinting as if that would protect her. *Typical shielding behavior*. Analyzing her own body language helped with the detachment.

"Furniture." It looked like a chair leg. Strangely, her muscles tightened with renewed tension.

"Me too," Hala said.

That layer went quickly. Rocío got more tense instead of less. If they were going to find anything, it would be soon. The noise from the crowd was louder now, and the cold air chilled the sweat on the back of her neck. Hala's arm brushed against Rocío's as she reached into the bin.

The next layer was mostly newspaper. Rocío had to stand on one of the empty boxes to reach. Her hand skimmed across something hard and round wrapped in paper. Adrenaline surged through her. Her pulse pounded in her palms. If she hadn't already been holding her breath against the smell, she would have now.

She picked it up but kept it out of sight, below the rim. As she unwrapped it, she exposed the soft white of bone, and her hands shook. She peeled back the last layer of paper, exposing the elongated skull of a pig.

"Oh, seres celestiales," Rocío said.

"*S. domesticus*," Hala said, looking over her shoulder. "Someone's lunch?"

"Great. I'm not going to be able to eat pork for a long time."

"That's the last of it. No dead bodies."

"Gracias a las diosas de mis madres. Señorx Prokofiev"—Rocío raised her voice—"it's not him. We didn't find anything."

Piotr Prokofiev collapsed.

They stepped away from the garbage bin, and Rocío took a deep breath. The air smelled of fried bread and sugar and wet soil. For the moment no one was near enough to overhear them.

"Where were you this morning?" Rocío asked.

"Mostly trying to get Cempol to let me talk to Ministrx Valdivia. Futilely, I might add. I didn't manage to talk to Ministrx O'Higgins, either. I spent most of the morning trying to catch up to him."

The dive coordinator joined them. "I have to say I'm relieved it's just garbage."

"Someone avoiding their garbage fees," Rocío said. "And we get to clean it up."

"We'll do that; it's our site. You've probably had enough garbage today."

"You have no idea," Rocío said. "Thank you."

"It might have been a prank. I'm surprised we haven't found anything else in there so far—besides the pram and the chandelier, I mean."

Rocío sighed. The adrenaline was draining out of her. "He's still out there somewhere."

"Not too much longer," the dive coordinator called, already heading back to the edge of the lake. Rocío startled, thinking the diver was pronouncing on Aleksandr Prokofiev's chances of survival. "He—" Then she snapped her mouth closed, realizing the diver meant the search wouldn't take much longer. *Where are you, Aleksandr Prokofiev? Are you still alive?*

Back at the CJC, the desks and chairs were upright and in their places again, all evidence of the earlier mini-riot erased, except for a broken light fixture on one wall and the smell of burnt sage over smoke grenade. Maurata pounced on Paloma at the door and herded her upstairs, ranting nonstop about the incompetence of all of his underlings. Rocío looked around guiltily, expecting Hala's condemnation for not trying to extricate Paloma, but Hala was talking to Espinoza at the front desk. *Piérdalo. Paloma's an adult.*

Rocío threw herself into her chair. It creaked. Her back twinged. The chair she could replace; the back not so much. *Time to exercise,* she promised herself. Ice skating maybe, except the rink wasn't open yet. Swimming, then. The ocean was probably still warm enough, if barely. *I could go to Balneario Solís.* For a moment she allowed herself to think longingly of the little beachside resort, the wide expanse of white sand, and the bracing chill of the surf. *Ugh, no, it's Thursday. I have dinner with my parents.*

"Look at that," Hala said, dropping a tube message on Rocío's desk.

The note from the Department of Transportation said all keys to the subte had been accounted for, no evidence had been found of any break-ins or unauthorized entries and the DOT would be very obliged if the CJC had any theories they could share.

Rocío stared at the note longer than necessary. She really hadn't wanted Hala to be right about the imported magic. It took effort not to rub the scars on her hands. "That's a fairly firm confirmation. Did you talk to Yaco?"

"I did. He concurs with my hasty examination at Ministrx Montenegro's house. Mixed in with the powdered remains of her defunct wardstone was a vegetal fragment, and to be more precise, a lichen."

Rocío rubbed her forehead. "Are you going to tell me it matched the magic residue in Aleksandr Prokofiev's room?"

"It didn't."

"Oh. That's … worse? Is it imported?"

"Yaco doesn't know yet. He's—"

"Running more tests?" Rocío finished for her.

"Yes. Where's Paloma?"

"Uh. Maurata wanted to talk to her."

"And you couldn't tell him she was busy, that she had an appointment to interview witnesses or collate reports or something? What is wrong with you?" Hala frowned at her.

Rocío slid the photograph on her desk two centimeters to the left. Her nonna also seemed to frown at her from within its frame. *Everyone thinks I'm messing this up.* She flinched away from the memory of Oshinsky telling Rocío to not let her prejudices get in the way.

"Chío, do you think this is about your parents?" Hala leaned on the edge of Rocío's desk, her strong dark brows drawn down and clearly visible with her hair newly mowed back.

"What, are you apprenticing with that quack alienist now? What's his name? Frisk? Frond? Fred?" She sounded truculent even to herself. *This wasn't the plan. I was going to ask Hala for help.* Then she argued with herself, *Yeah, to get Paloma to reveal what she really is to Oshinsky.* That had been the beginning of the plan, anyway; the rest hadn't really been sketched in. But Rocío didn't want Hala's help, not if Hala was going to talk to her like this and take Paloma's side.

"Are you going to tell me I want to sleep with my mother and kill my father?"

Hala didn't smile. "You obviously don't have a problem with your friend María Paz Belli. I don't see the difference between her and Paloma."

"Leave Maipa out of it. That's different." The unreasonable words kept gushing out of her, seemingly bypassing any control Rocío had. Her conscience asked, *Isn't Hala right? Maipa is privileged and ambitious, too, and I don't have a problem with her. Is it because I met her at the theater, not in an office?*

"Paloma makes you uncomfortable because you look at her and see what your parents are always pushing you to be. You don't see *her* at all."

Rocío pushed her chair back, the legs screeching on the wood floor. "Hala, stop. You said you wanted to talk about training Paloma, not that you were going to attack me."

"That is what we're talking about."

"I don't have to listen to this."

Before Rocío could stand, Hala leaned on the arms of her chair, blocking her in. "You said it yourself. You're worried."

Hala was so close Rocío could see the lighter flecks in her dark, very serious eyes. "What? I didn't."

"At the park. That's why you wanted to talk to me, correct? You're worried about your ability to train her."

"That's ridiculous." Rocío pressed herself into the back of the chair, wishing she had a piece of gum. "That's not what I'm worried about. She—" She started to tell Hala about her concerns, but Hala didn't let her.

"Well, you should be, Rocío. You need to take a hard look at yourself."

First Oshinsky and now Hala? "I'm not listening to this." She knocked Hala's arms aside and lurched to her feet, knocking her mug over and spilling the morning's coffee across the reports on her desk. "Ancestros perdidos."

"Here." Hala swiped an ink-stained rag used for blotting pens from the next desk. It was immediately soaked through. "I'll get a sponge."

Rocío swallowed against the tightness in her throat and rifled through her desk for something else to use, coming up with a stick of gum instead. She crammed it into her mouth.

Hala came back with a sponge, a towel and a Paloma, cutting off any chance to argue further.

Which is good, right? Rocío would have to figure out what to do on her own. Meanwhile, she'd keep doing everything she was supposed to as an instructor and prove Hala wrong. Rocío was a good teacher, a good colleague. Paloma was just the wrong trainee. She would show her true colors eventually. Hala *was* wrong.

"Just think about what I said, Chío." Hala said, swabbing the reports delicately before moving to her desk. "Now, I know you have dinner with your parents, but let's coordinate for tomorrow."

"I do have to go soon," Rocío said, glaring at her. *When did the world get so topsy-turvy that I'm considering my parents as an escape from Hala?*

"Here, Palomita." Hala moved an extra chair next to her desk.

And since when does Hala use a nickname for Paloma?

"Thank you." Paloma sat, her legs arranged neatly, and opened her notebook on the edge of Rocío's desk. She looked very eager. "What did you find out this morning?"

"Chío, are you going to sit, or are you going to loom?"

That was exactly what Rocío's nonna used to say. Hala was manipulating Rocío with her memories of Nonna while also suggesting that her body language was aggressive. Rocío recognized what she was doing, and it still worked. She forced down her anger and—yes— guilt and dropped back into her chair. At least *it* didn't betray her. Not that Hala was betraying her.

Hala sat. Neither she nor the chair creaked. Unfair.

"I wasn't able to speak to Ministrx O'Higgins, but Officer Smith told me that he did not receive a threatening note," Hala said.

Rocío snorted.

"I agree—he certainly acted as if he had been threatened, but there were several other Cempol officers there who corroborated her information."

"Okay." Rocío leaned back, trying to focus on the case and not all the random emotions careening around inside her and messing her up.

"If Ministrx Valdivia didn't receive a threatening note either, it could be because the person sending them didn't want to throw doubt on the treason charges against her spouse," Hala said.

"And if Ministrx O'Higgins didn't receive a note ... he also committed treason? And Ministrx Montenegro?" Rocío asked. "That's a bit much, isn't it?"

"But Ministrx Montenegro's wardstone was destroyed. If she had received a threatening note, she might have checked her security, including her wardstones," Paloma said.

"I'm not saying they all committed treason, just that we need to prioritize speaking to Ministrx O'Higgins and Valdivia tomorrow," Hala said. "They're hiding something."

"They're politicians; of course they're hiding something," Rocío said. "We need some kind of leverage to get them to speak to us. Or some way to trick them. Any ideas? No? Let's think about it overnight." Thinking about the case was much better than thinking about Paloma. "What happened with the dog bones?"

"The chief managed to retain custody." Hala smiled thinly. "So that avenue of investigation is still open to us. Espinoza is going to find someone in La Quinta with a strong stomach who might be able to tell us if they are the La Quinta street dogs."

"Try Pepe's spouse," Rocío suggested. "Paloma, didn't you say in your report that she was painting upstairs in La Valle and that she heard a dogfight?"

"Yes, on Monday night around ten, the same time Aleksandr Prokofiev seems to have disappeared. She thought the dogs were right under her window, but when she looked out she didn't see them."

"Or two alleys over? What if it wasn't a dogfight? What if they were being killed?" Rocío asked.

Paloma shuddered.

"I'll suggest it to Espinoza," Hala said. "What about the clothes?"

"What clothes?" Rocío asked.

"Since our witness from the park, Señorx Safavi, said she saw Prokofiev in a tweed suit, I sent Pérez to La Valle to search through the costumes for Prokofiev's usual clothes," Hala said.

"He didn't find them," Paloma said.

"Is it possible they were hidden among Piotr Prokofiev's things?" Rocío asked. "They're close enough in height."

"I thought of that and found a seamstress to go with Pérez," Paloma said.

"Good thinking," Hala said.

Paloma smiled at the compliment. Rocío clenched her jaw, realized she was jealous that Paloma felt more comfortable with Hala than with her, and gave herself a mental slap on the head. *This is not going to be a problem forever.*

"She said no, all the clothes were the same measurements."

"Anything useful from the newspaper announcement or Isis's reward?" Rocío asked.

"Don't let Oshinsky hear you asking about that," Hala said. "I've never seen her so angry."

"No," Rocío said, "me neither."

"Cempol is sifting through all the responses and hasn't passed anything on to us yet." Hala dragged her fingers across her scalp, making her hair stick up in spikes and half curls. "The results have been less than helpful."

"Which is why we don't usually offer rewards." Rocío leaned farther back in her chair and examined the cracks and whorls in the plaster ceiling. There was one that looked like a jaguar and another that looked like a bearded man with a secret. If the secret was what had happened to Aleksandr Prokofiev on Monday night, he wasn't telling.

"So what do we do now?" Paloma asked.

"Now we take a break," Hala said, "and let our unconscious minds work on the problem while we take care of our physical needs. See you tomorrow."

Hala picked up her coat and left, and Rocío knew exactly why.

She was giving Rocío the chance to try again with Paloma, and Rocío would, though not for the reasons Hala thought. She would be the best perdido instructor, and Paloma would still show everyone what a social climbing mercenary she was, and everything would go back to the way it was before.

"Did she just tell us to have sex? Not with each other, I mean," Paloma added hastily. "Just in general."

"Hala does consider sex a physical need. But she meant food, exercise, rest, *or* sex, or whatever else helps you get ready to come back tomorrow and do this all again."

And I probably need some rest and perspective before I talk to Paloma about ... anything. It just makes sense to do it tomorrow instead. It does. Rocío had an uneasy feeling that she might be proving Hala right. *No, I just need to plan my approach. That's all.*

"Are you sure it's okay for us to leave? What if someone needs us?" Paloma asked.

"I'll tell you what Oshinsky said to me in a similar situation," Rocío said, willing to be sidetracked. "She's probably said it to you, too: then they'll need us. Either they'll figure it out on their own, or they'll wait. And there are other advocates here, doing their jobs, looking for leads to follow. Listen, you need to be able to leave the job at the door."

"That seems so ... callous." Paloma slanted a glance at her as if she were assessing whether Rocío was offended by her choice of words.

"Suffering because Prokofiev is suffering is not going to help him. The opposite, in fact. We need to be at our best when we or any of our colleagues find a lead. That's how we'll help him."

"Oh. How do you make sure you're ready?"

"Normally I exercise. Hala recites poetry in front of strangers. What's the thing that knocks everything else out of your head?"

"I don't know," Paloma said, tracing a line on the desk.

"I suggest you find out. You need activities that give you back yourself when you spend all day giving yourself to others." *That was instructor-like, right?*

Rocío put one hand on the desk and uncrossed her legs,

mirroring Paloma's posture to establish more of a rapport. She stopped herself from leaning forward; that could signal intimacy, but it could also be taken as dominance. "Let's talk tomorrow, okay? I think I could ..." *Do better as an instructor? Use your help to figure this out?* The words stuck in her throat. "... benefit from your feedback. What areas you need help with, that kind of thing." Rocío hid a cringe. *That was pitiful.*

But Paloma's face lit up. "Great. There are a lot of things I want to ask you."

"Great. Tomorrow is another day." *And spending the evening with my parents will no doubt equip me to meet the challenge of Paloma with grace and cheer. Of course it will.*

CHAPTER 9

Khaled lounged on Rocío's bed, watching her dress for dinner. In fact, Rocío had taken care of her physical needs and was feeling better for it. Khaled was always fun. His hair was unpinned and fell in a shiny dark wave across the peach-colored sheets, and he hadn't dressed yet. And she had to leave him and his warmth and go sit in her parents' chilly dining room instead.

"Those owls are your favorite, aren't they?" Khaled asked, referring to the particularly fine embroidery on her huipil.

"Yes?" She smoothed her top and checked her earrings, necklace and hair.

"You always wear something you really like when you have dinner with them."

He was too observant. "I've kept you around too long," she said with mock horror. He stretched, showing off the long strong lines of his body. "Oh, now I remember why."

"Sure you don't want to stay?"

"Obviously I want to stay."

"You'd rather attend an autopsy, I think, so I'm not flattered. But it's true, isn't it? Last week it was the jade earrings, and before that the silver armbands."

She frowned at him. *Do I invite him over every time I go to my parents'? No, the armbands were two months ago.* She hadn't added him as a coping mechanism.

"Why don't you ask Hala to go with you? Or me? We're friends, Rocío."

"And subject you to that ordeal?"

"You mean allow your friends to support you?"

"Ha," Rocío scoffed.

"You don't have to go."

"Ha-ha. Don't be ridiculous. What kind of person deserts their family? Especially at the last minute."

"Is it desertion to skip a family dinner?"

She turned away from him, unwilling to see the expression in his eyes. "Family is family. I owe them my existence and at the very least my presence at Thursday dinner. You should know that."

"Have you ever thought of doing something different?"

"It doesn't matter. I can't switch my parents for someone else's. I'm lucky they're alive and well off and healthy. Others aren't so lucky."

"I meant—"

"Khaled, I don't want to talk about it." She banged the lid of her jewelry box closed and checked her necklace a second time. Temper in hand again, she turned back towards him. He was right in front of her. He kissed her cheek, and she leaned away, wary of more importuning.

"If you won't take someone with you, at least take the memory of what we just did."

She relaxed into his embrace and let out a huff of laughter. "Not even that is enough, Khaled."

Rocío followed the majordomo to her parents' living room. Her mother and father were posed under the painting by Adergie of the Cordillera, which was slashing, gorgeous and powerful and her mother's prize possession, not because she particularly admired landscapes but because owning an Adergie was a coup that she never tired of showing off.

"Darling," her mother trilled without moving towards Rocío, "how lovely to see you." Their dog, Eva, a papillon, small and ferociously cute, sniffed Rocío's feet, not having received the memo that Rocío was the supplicant and must make all approaches.

"Good evening, Rocío. I'm glad to see you made an effort with your clothing this time," her father said.

It's Vervain, as he probably knows. And before that it was Xoc. Not couture, but not burlap bags, either. She couldn't hover in the doorway all evening, as much as she might want to. She presented herself for their kisses. Her father gave her air-kisses; her mother briefly pressed one cool cheek and then the other against Rocío's.

"Where's Miguel?" Her brother, the dutiful, golden child, and his spouse and children lived with their parents and occasionally served as a buffer, much as La Bene did between the Ya and Ka Empires, but not as reliably.

"Miguel and Sebastián were invited to dinner by the Ministrx of the Environment and Natural Resources. They had to go, of course," her mother said.

"Of course," Rocío echoed.

"Have a drink," her father said, offering her a mojito. She accepted it even though she didn't drink rum, had never drunk rum, had told him a million times that she didn't like rum. Eva cocked her head at Rocío as if in commiseration.

When Rocío was younger she had fought them on every single thing, but she didn't have the energy anymore and she saved it for the biggest things. Mojitos weren't even on the list.

She launched into small talk, hoping this time she'd succeed at steering the topic. "Have you had any luck getting a portrait done by Zsolt?" she asked, naming the fashionable painter of the moment.

"Really, Rocío," her father said, "luck has nothing to do with it, as you'd know if you'd listened to anything we taught you while you lived under our roof."

"It's a figure of speech, Father."

"We've spoken to Thisbe"—her mother named the master Zsolt worked under—"and she has assured us that Zsolt would adore us as subjects for a painting. I'm sure we'll be, oh, if not next, then very soon. It's all very traditional and proper. None of this newfangled 'gallery' system some of the younger artists are experimenting with."

"Did you speak to Elif, like I suggested?" her father asked. "It's a chance to get in on the ground floor on this joint venture with the Ya on mining. The prospects are very good, you know."

"No, Father."

A maid appeared in the doorway and announced, "Dinner is ready."

"Stay, Eva," her father said. Eva lay down with her legs stretched out in front of her, looking desolate but obedient.

A little like me. "Excuse me a moment," Rocío said, stopping at the altar to the family's ancestors. Not even her mother could protest, though she looked like she wanted to.

Hello, Nonna.

Chío, don't let her get to you. Her nonna's presence enfolded her like a hug with the smells of anisette and coffee and the powdery scent of her perfume, except it was in Rocío's mind, not tickling her nose.

"Rocío," her mother called.

I miss you, Nonna.

"This looks lovely," Rocío said, entering the dining room, and winced at her choice of word. The table glittered with crystal and new china, off-white with a gold band around the edge and, *seres celestiales,* that was their monogram in the center. That was new. "What's on the menu? Do you still have Andreas?" If she could get them talking about their chef and food, maybe they wouldn't follow the well-worn grooves of their favorite topic of conversation: how Rocío had failed them as a daughter.

"Of course we do," her mother said. "Answer your father, dear."

Bracing herself, Rocío sat opposite her parents and took a sip of her mojito, forgetting until too late what it was. At least its bad taste was a distraction. "I have a job. You know that, Mother. We discussed it earlier in the week."

"It's not a real job," her father said, signaling for the maid to start serving.

"It is a real job." *Why do I bother?* "I made detective in four years instead of seven. I'm very proud of that fact." *Why can't they be proud, too?* twelve-year-old Rocío asked forty-three-year-old Rocío. She suppressed the question, knowing that was an even more fruitless avenue of conversation. "I make a difference in this city, I help people. All sorts of people."

"But you have to associate with such low types." Her mother smoothed her finger over the heavy silver stem of her soupspoon. "I'm not sure it's worth it. I really don't understand why they paired you with that daughter of immigrants. Can't you ask for someone else?"

Rocío picked one of several possible answers to that. She'd tried them all in rotation. "I like Hala, and I like working with her."

"But—"

"And you're the daughter of an immigrant yourself."

"Not that kind. Mamma was a very important person in the Falmali States."

Rocío ate a bite of fish to avoid answering that self-serving statement. Nonna had been the youngest daughter of a consigliere in the small town of Leccetto in one of the smaller Falmali States. "The fish is very good," she said, even though all she could taste was the rum, heavy in the back of her throat, like her parents' inability to accept her life. She shoved the thought down.

"Of course it is. And my father's family came over on the first boat to La Bene and helped establish this city."

"He was a sailor, not that there's anything wrong with that."

"Don't talk to your mother like that."

"He was an advisor," her mother said, cutting into her fish with a knife. She looked down, realized her gaffe and picked up her fork. "He helped make La Bene the city it is today."

For a few minutes her mother and father congratulated each other on being foresighted enough to have illustrious ancestors who had made La Bene the jewel of the south, and Rocío didn't have to talk at all. The empty fish plates were replaced with bowls of delicate walnut soup, one of her favorites. Rocío attributed that to Andreas the chef rather than her parents.

"We heard you're working closely with Leire Otxandabaratz Montero's daughter. How lovely."

"This is a good opportunity for you," her father added. "What are you doing to solidify the relationship?"

The walnut soup suddenly sat too heavily in her stomach. She put down her spoon. Of course her parents' house was no refuge from Paloma. How had she even thought it could be? Paloma's mother was a prominent developer who occasionally socialized with Rocío's parents. Rocío hadn't anticipated this offensive, and she should have.

"Do try to make it a permanent attachment. Any child of Leire's is going to go far; you should make sure she takes you with her."

Rocío didn't recognize the undertone in her mother's voice at first, and she felt almost dizzy with disorientation when she did. It had been so long since her mother had approved of anything Rocío had done.

She wrapped her ankles around the legs of her chair. Knowing it was a freeze response indicating discomfort did nothing to alleviate the feelings. She wished her parents weren't so Benerex and so fond of shoes in the house. She wanted to feel the floor beneath her feet and know something was stable. Really, wearing shoes in the house was a dirty habit if you thought about it. The tangential thoughts gave her enough room to recognize her knee-jerk responses and not act on them.

Approval from her parents felt worse than disapproval from Oshinsky.

"Mother." Rocío stopped. She didn't know what to say.

A social climber recognized another social climber, and Rocío's parents excelled at their chosen sport. But that meant Rocío agreed with her parents' assessment of Paloma, and disagreed with Hala and Oshinsky, two people she trusted more than anyone in the world. Certainly more than she trusted her parents and their instincts. *Is this what Hala and Oshinsky meant? Am I carrying around my own version of my parents' prejudices? Am I seeing Paloma as they see her?*

Am I wrong?

"Think how far you could go with her," her mother said with an expansive gesture encompassing the heavens. Or just a high political office.

"Much farther than without her, since you don't exert yourself," her father said.

"She could be head of your little center in just a few years. Then Cempol, and possibly even the governor's office. Just think."

Rocío felt a little sick at the thought of all the people her mother was blithely shoving out of their jobs, even just mentally. No, she just felt sick. They'd always been like this, and Rocío had never wanted any part of it. She didn't want to be like them, didn't want to treat Paloma the way they would, didn't want even a distorted reflection of their responses controlling her actions and reactions.

Oh, seres celestiales. I think Oshinsky was right. Oh no. She swallowed hard.

"If you help her now, darling, she'll help you later," her mother said.

Focus, Rocío. Tomorrow you can figure out Paloma. Right now you need to survive this dinner. "Please stop. That is not going to happen," Rocío said. "None of it."

"Don't be ridiculous," her mother said. "All you have to do is let it happen."

"You don't even have to do anything," said her father.

"It's not what I want." Rocío struggled to hold on to her emotions. She was not going to fight with them. She was not going to let them control how she acted. She was not going to reenact every childhood dinner she'd endured in this house. She was an adult, and she had coping skills now.

She unhooked her feet, set them flat on the floor and pressed down, grounding herself. "I—"

"Dessert," the maid announced, flourishing, appropriately enough, a platter of bananas flambé.

The flames were blue-hot, and the smell of burning brandy and sugar filled the air. The maid offered the silver cover to Rocío's father so he could extinguish the flames.

There's a metaphor in there, somewhere.

"Excellent." Her father did the honors, and the maid slid the platter onto the table while another removed the remains of their meal. "Tell Andreas he continues to be a master of his profession."

While the maids were there, her parents talked lightly about the interior designer a friend had hired. Appearances must be kept up, although Rocío was sure the maids had heard everything said while they were out of the room. And whatever Rocío's declaration might have been stayed a mystery, even to herself. Now that the moment had passed, she wasn't even sure what she would have said.

She concentrated on her bananas flambé, which was creamy with just the right amount of brandy to cut through the sweetness. She scraped her spoon around the edge of her bowl to capture every last drop, and her mother said, "Really, Rocío."

Shortly after that, Rocío left.

She paused in the hallway outside her dark, empty apartment and leaned her head against the door. She didn't really want to be alone. She was always welcome at Hala's, even when they were fighting. Though they'd never fought like this before. But one of Hala's sister's therapy cats sounded like an excellent idea just now. A soft warm presence that didn't expect anything from her except mutual comfort.

The door opened from the inside, and Rocío jumped back, swallowing a surprised shout. Her apartment was not dark, empty or locked, because there was Hala.

"What did I tell you about picking my lock?" Rocío growled. Just a moment before she'd wanted to see Hala, but *really*. "You don't have any manners." She pushed inside.

"You should get a better lock."

"Please. You'd just pick that one, too."

The lights were on, and Rocío's swimsuit, a towel and a blanket were folded neatly on the settee.

Hala held up her own bag with a towel and a thermos visible inside. "This is probably your last chance to swim until the spring. They're predicting a cold snap tomorrow."

"You don't like to swim."

"But you do. Come on, I borrowed the automobile."

"Why would you do that?"

"To give you something you don't feel bad about fighting."

"Oh, joy." But Rocío followed her out of the apartment.

~

The auto wallowed around the turn into Balneario Solís like a drunken whale. Rocío practically had to stand on the clutch to shift optimistically into second. Good thing the streets were clear at this time of year, as the auto drifted to the right without any prompting from Rocío. She hauled it back on course, holding the steering wheel at five degrees to the left of straight.

Ancestors forsake Hala, but she was right. The miasma of self-doubt and anger was already peeling away like a sticky adhesive yielding to lemon juice. And Hala was the lemon. In the best way possible, of course. Unless the auto's engine exploded again, in which case Hala would be downgraded to a regular lemon. Under the unspoken terms of their temporary truce, they didn't discuss Paloma, work or families.

Most of the businesses along Balneario Solís's one road were already shuttered for the winter, with the exception of one café with lights shining through the steamed-up windows. A couple opened the door, letting out music. It was Hala's mother's most famous recording, and Hala sang along: "... Perfecto distingo, lo negro del blanco ..."

They reached the end of the road, and the smells of the sea and sun-warmed grasses washed over them. Rocío pumped the brakes, and when that had no noticeable effect, shifted into neutral and used the hand brake. The auto drifted to a stop just before the dunes, and Rocío climbed out. Overhead the stars glittered in the deep black of the sky, just like in the song.

"This was a good idea," Rocío said.

"We aren't even in the water yet."

"You don't have to swim. I know it's not your favorite pastime."

"Don't be ridiculous." Hala pulled a portable heater from the back seat. "I'm going to beat you."

"I wasn't aware we were racing."

"I'm not going to dignify that with a reply." Hala turned on a flashlight, swung it in an arc and located the path to the beach.

"You brought your own flashlight. I'm touched."

The first shock of water stole Rocío's breath. She flung herself under. For a moment her limbs wouldn't obey her, and she hung, suspended. The salt stung the delicate skin around her nose and mouth, and then Hala splashed past her. Rocío surfaced and took off after her.

They swam until there were no thoughts left in Rocío's head and the bones in her feet ached with the cold. They dragged each other from the surf, shed their suits and wrapped up in blankets. Hala turned on the heater with a surge of magic. For a while they sat without talking. Slowly Rocío stopped shivering, and thoughts seeped back into her head, but they were softer, with fewer sharp edges. The front of her body was almost too hot from the heater, while the night air was too cool on her back and her damp hair. A nightjar chirred from the grassy edge of the beach.

"I was thinking about Cempol," Hala said at the same time that Rocío said, "Something has been bothering me all day."

"Just one thing?" Hala asked.

"Ha. No. Since we found the dogs. What about Cempol?"

"Why were they so keen to take the dog bones?"

"So both of us are worrying about dogs now," Rocío said. She dug her toes into the cool sand. "Does Cempol know something they're not telling us?"

Hala snorted. "Do you even have to ask? What's bothering you?"

"I can't quite catch the thought. Something to do with my nonna."

Hala put down the thermos she'd just picked up. "Nonna Antonetta? Did she tell you something?"

"No, nothing like that. It's a memory."

"Nonna Antonetta was most famous for stories about ghosts and other spectral occurrences."

Rocío pictured her nonna, in her housedress with a kerchief over her hair, smelling of talc and perfume, her arm warm around Rocío's shoulders, the way they'd always sat when nonna told stories. But they hadn't been just stories; they were folktales about all the things that had gone wrong when the Iberex refugees had brought their funeral practices to La Bene, which had been Ka and Ya in alternation for centuries, their magic touching on death in a way Iberex magic never had.

A chill chased down Rocío's spine. There was one story Nonna had told only once, when one of Nonna's friends had come to them with a black eye, a broken rib and her dead cat. The thought that had been nagging at Rocío since she'd found the dog bones blossomed in her mind like an algae bloom strangling a pond.

"Hala." Rocío pulled the blanket tighter around her shoulders. The night suddenly felt very big and dark, and she wished they were in a cozy sitting room with lights and all the comforting objects of everyday life around them. "Nonna told me about Eugenio Fernández once, and how he cut off the paws of dogs. She was warning me, that people who hurt animals would hurt people, too, because they like causing pain."

Hala made an inarticulate noise in her throat and hugged her knees.

"I almost forgot," Rocío said. "Shen the anarchist told me something. His friend Emma was convicted of mutilating rats and leaving them in the House of Refuges." She didn't say any more, waiting to see if Hala would make the same connections she had or if she would laugh and say Rocío was imagining things.

"You don't know the details?" Hala's breathing was too quick.

"No."

"Mutilated rats, mutilated dogs, unexplained magic use." Hala's voice was strained as she traced the same mental path as Rocío. "Secrets revealed."

"María Paz said no one else knew that her spouse wasn't her son's biological father," Rocío said unwillingly. "Surely there would be more signs if it's ..." She couldn't force herself to say it. "Say we're wrong."

"We haven't found Aleksandr Prokofiev yet."

"Imported magic could still be responsible, couldn't it?"

"One explanation is simplest. We could theorize multiple

imported artifacts such as the lichen and the magic residue in Prokofiev's room. Or we could look to our own history."

Benerex magic hadn't touched on death the way Ka and Ya magic had until Eugenio Fernández Suárez, the monster of La Bene, the city's worst murderer, created a whole new method of magic out of that mix, designed around pain and killing.

Hala saw it, too.

One explanation for all the unexplained occurrences.

Necromancy.

CHAPTER 10

"THIS IS A TERRIBLE IDEA," Rocío whispered.

"This is the least terrible of all our terrible ideas tonight. Hold the flashlight steady," Hala said.

Rocío gripped the flashlight harder and made sure it was pointed at the lock Hala was attempting to pick. The lock to the vault at the University where all the restricted books were kept chained to the wall, away from the public and anyone sick enough to try to revive the practice of necromancy.

They had gathered their stuff on the beach, packed the automobile and driven back to La Bene, arguing all the way. Not about what to do; they both agreed they needed more information before bringing their dubious proto-theory to anyone, even Oshinsky. The dispute was over how to get that information.

Rocío was in favor of rousting one of the Cempol magickers from their bed. Hala had pointed out that that avenue of inquiry was likely to be blocked by any number of factors, such as an extremely irate level-ten magicker arresting Rocío and Hala for even suggesting necromancy could be an issue, all in the name of protecting the public good. So here they were instead, taking the most direct and most felonious route.

"That's it." Hala turned the knob and gently pushed open the thick wooden door. Rocío swept the room with her flashlight, revealing a gray stone floor and walls, five shelves crammed with books and codices, and a whirring electric air purifier. Nothing jumped out at them, though Rocío was willing to admit it was only her overactive nerves that made that seem likely. After all, the only things chained up in the vault were books. *I think.*

"Hala, are you sure the university doesn't have wardstones here?"

"Yes." Hala stepped into the room. "Ninety-five percent sure."

"If I'm fried to a cinder, I will hold you personally responsible."

"Nonsense. The university would not be so incautious. We'd merely be incapacitated. Though I admit it would likely be painful. And there is an elevated possibility of heart attack if you have a weak heart. Do you?"

"Just at this moment I might."

They passed the stacks holding the less virulently restricted books, heading to the back, Rocío leading the way since she had been here more recently than Hala. At the end of the required magic certification course for civil servants, the instructor had brought the class here and told them they'd never need to know anything in these books but that he was required to impress upon them their responsibility to use magic ethically.

"It's impossible to learn necromancy because it isn't taught," Rocío said, repeating the argument they'd had in the auto. It was getting slightly easier to say the word as if it were part of their world and not one of Nonna's horror stories. Rocío did not like that effect.

Hala pointed her flashlight at her face and raised an eyebrow.

Rocío jumped. "Seres celestiales, don't do that. You'll give me a weak heart if I don't have one already."

"It's a circular argument. There they are." Hala pointed her flashlight at the back.

This part of the University had been built by Benerex, not recycled from an older Ya building, so there were no stern visages of past rulers carved into the walls or repeating motifs of skulls. Rocío wasn't sure her nerves could've taken that. The steel girder in the wall was exposed, and chains as thick as two of Rocío's fingers ran from it to five books on a chest-high shelf. One was small and bound in brown leather; one was long and narrow with the word FORBIDDEN tooled into the red cover; and the other three were the sort of beige ledgers still used to record adjudicators' decisions, though they lacked the usual date and jurisdiction information on the covers.

"The ledgers?" Rocío asked.

"Yes." Hala casually opened the one on the right and flipped through the first pages. The chain rang against the metal girder.

Rocío took a deep breath when neither Hala nor the book burst into flames. If there was an alarm, it wasn't audible in the room.

"This one is labeled 'three,' but that's it," Hala said. "I can't even find the adjudicator's name."

Rocío picked up another. "This one is the same." The old paper was slightly rough under her fingers and smelled sweet, like vanilla and almond.

"The handwriting is legible, at least."

"'On 11 November, year 347 of the founding of the city La Beneficia de nuestros vecinos y los seres celestiales, the accused, Eugenio Fernández Suárez, was brought before me,'" Rocío read.

"You'll have to skim if we're going to find out what necromantic magic could actually do besides kill people in extremely painful ways."

"Hala, I thought you would be the one to appreciate the history of this moment. How many people have turned these pages since this adjudicator wrote on them?"

"Yes, yes. I'm merely appreciating it while also reading. We have a deadline. Not to mention we're breaking several laws and our oath of office."

"I'd managed to forget that, thank you."

It was hard to skim handwriting. Rocío's elbow grew sore from propping up her flashlight, her eyes were dry and itchy and the legalese for the most nefarious trial in the history of La Bene was getting harder and harder to decipher when she found something that made her skin crawl.

"Hey." Her voice came out rough. She cleared her throat and started again. "Fernández did amputate his victims' feet and hands. That's not urban legend. Yay. And he disemboweled them as well, though the adjudicator says Fernández didn't confess to that."

"Ah. Our dogs' paws were amputated, but they weren't disemboweled."

"Oh. Good?"

"Does it say anything about animals?"

"Not yet."

"I don't know if that's encouraging or terrifying. On the one hand, it could mean we're starting at shadows. On the other hand, it could mean we not only have a necromancer on the loose, we have an innovative one." Hala rubbed her nose. "No one we've interviewed has struck me as a fiend."

"You know it's not that easy to tell. The worst humans often seem innocuous. Personable, even. They've learned camouflage. It helps them succeed at their crimes."

"I know." Hala turned another page.

Sometime later Hala straightened, keeping her finger in the book to hold her place, and rolled her shoulders. "This is it."

"What?"

"'Fernández claimed his greatest achievement was finding the secret to eternal life, in the death and decay of his victims. But necromancy also revealed what was hidden and hid what should otherwise be revealed. The accused boasted that he could speak to all of the dead, not just his own ancestors, and that there was a great clamoring in the afterlife. The accused convinced this adjudicator of the truth of his claims with a barbaric show, that on its own would be enough to merit the most extreme punishment available in our civilized city.'"

"Wow."

"Yeah. The adjudicator says Fernández was shrouded in darkness and strange lights and a loathsome smell. 'Panic and fear palpably emanated from him,' and they had to break for two days so everyone in the chamber could recover."

"I think the university needs to improve their security. Or burn these books." Rocío rubbed her palms on her legs. "I'm going to have nightmares."

"They can't burn them. They never found Fernández's own records."

"Do you think it's what we're dealing with now?" Rocío closed her book and squared it on the shelf. The chain jangled faintly.

"I think we have to leave. It's almost three in the morning."

"Surely there would be more signs if ..." Rocío's voice sounded strained even to her.

Hala ran her hands through her hair, mouth pinched. "We're scientists. We formed a hypothesis, we gathered information. We have insufficient data at this time. We need to continue to observe."

"It's not possible," Rocío said. "No one knows how to practice necromancy, Hala, it's interdicted. I know." She raised a hand to stop Hala from interrupting. "But even if someone else broke in here like we did, there's nothing in these books about how to go about becoming a necromancer."

Hala rubbed her forehead tiredly, sliding her fingers under her spectacles and over her eyes. "We need to look in the other two books," she conceded.

"Diosas de mis madres. Why did I open my mouth?" But Rocío knew they needed to do it.

"I'll take the forbidden one."

"Good. That one looks more gruesome."

The small brown one was gruesome enough, as it was a compilation of the reports of the advocates who had been involved in the investigation into Fernández. Rocío was able to flip through it fairly quickly; advocate reports hadn't changed that much in the last hundred years.

"Hala, listen to this. 'Intermixed with the human remains, we found the incomplete skeletons of dogs, cats and rabbits.'" Rocío shivered. She skimmed over a few pages. "Here's the forensics report. Two dozen animal skeletons were removed from Luken's Folly, 'that foul den where he murdered innocents.' Due to their location under the human remains, it seems that they were killed first. The hind and front paws of the dogs and cats were not recovered. The rabbit skeletons were incomplete with no pattern identified."

Hala pushed up her spectacles. "Nonna is right again. You owe her a good dinner."

"Yeah. But you know what I didn't find in here?"

"Anything about long-dead bodies and coffins?"

"Did you? What's in that book?"

"The medical coroners' reports," Hala said, her voice ironed flat of all emotion. "No long-dead bodies. Fernández's victims were alive when he disemboweled them."

Rocío shuddered. "Are you okay?"

"Can I sleep at your place tonight?" Hala asked. "If I have screaming nightmares, I'd rather not wake my family."

Rocío slung her arm around Hala's shoulders. "Oh, but it's okay to wake me?"

Hala leaned into her, smelling of salt water and fresh air and scared sweat. "You'll probably be awake already from your own nightmares."

"Are you kidding? I'm not planning on sleeping ever again."

"Rocío."

"Yeah?"

"Theoretically, if we have a necromancer on our hands ... why? Why would someone do something so horrible? Is it someone who wants to live forever?" Hala sounded shaken. Hala never sounded shaken.

Rocío pursed her lips and stared into the darkness. "Maybe," she said, picking her way through her own reactions to the case.

The notes Isis and Maipa had received that spoke of humiliation and deprivation. The proximity to real power of the ministrx involved. The slyness of getting the lieutenant governor arrested to hurt his spouse, Ministrx Valdivia. The cunningness needed to survive without power among those who had it. Rocío recognized that; her childhood had been that. Manipulation and avoidance when pandering, flattery and appeasement didn't work. With time, distance and good examples from people who didn't use love as a weapon, Rocío had grown up and developed better coping methods. And, yes, a measure of power to protect herself.

"But I don't think so," Rocío said to Hala. "I think it's someone who doesn't have power, desperately wants it and is prepared to do almost anything to get it."

In the morning Rocío felt hungover, her head packed with gruesome details she'd rather not remember and her body heavy from lack of sleep. She hadn't had nightmares, but Hala had, and it was almost more disturbing to see her usually unflappable partner upset.

Dinner with her parents felt like it had happened years ago, until Paloma walked in and brought it all back. The likelihood of finding Aleksandr Prokofiev alive felt dim and far away, and Paloma was too bright and right there, wearing designer clothes and entitlement, humming under her breath with no regard for anyone else as she sorted through reports from the Cempol team assigned to Isis's reward. Rocío's insight from the night before was still there, too, but good intentions were hard to focus on with everything else that had happened.

An hour into reading reports, Rocío finally unclenched her teeth and asked, "What are you humming?"

"I did what you said, and I went to the opera." Paloma fanned her stack of reports and smiled into the distance. "You were right—I feel so much better. Nerina Rebassa Fonollet was amazing. Have you seen her?"

"Of course I have."

Seemingly oblivious to Rocío's precarious mood, Paloma hummed another bar. "I heard her in my dreams all night. I wanted to run away and join the opera."

"And give up such a good place here?" The words spewed out of her mouth as if she were channeling her mother's nastiest sentiments and tones. Her posture was her father's: aggressive, dominating. Horrified, she recoiled.

Diosas de mis madres, Hala was right. Oshinsky was right. What do I do?

She clapped her hand over her mouth and let her eyes go wide, not acting, not even exaggerating, just letting everything show in a way she never had with Paloma. "Ancestors protect me, Paloma, I'm sorry." Rocío deliberately dropped her shoulders. "I'm in a rotten mood, but that's no excuse for taking it out on you."

"Oh."

Rocío saw it in Paloma's eyes as she decided not to trust her instincts, decided Rocío couldn't have been as contemptuous as she'd thought, decided to let it slide, and it only made Rocío feel worse.

"It's all right."

"I'm sorry," Rocío said again, shame crumpling up the words. *Now I hate myself more than I hate her. I do not hate her. I hate my parents, and I hate myself for acting like my parents. I thought I had left them behind. I think I'm so good with people, but I'm still messing up the thing everyone told me not to mess up in exactly the way they told me not to. Was Hala right about* everything? "It's not all right."

"I'll just get us some tea."

Paloma walked away, and Hala came up behind Rocío and clamped her hand on Rocío's biceps.

"What is wrong with you?" Hala whispered, but they both knew she wanted to shout.

The temporary truce was over. Because Rocío had broken it, in spite of her best intentions, because she couldn't help it, because of a bad mood and a short temper. Because she wasn't the person she had thought she was, that Oshinsky or Hala thought she was. And because maybe her coping methods weren't as good as she had hoped. How was she any different from her parents, except in scale? Intentions didn't count.

Rocío wrenched away from Hala. Why did she have to be there to see this version of Rocío, one she hadn't known was living in her? She would reject Rocío as Rocío had rejected her parents. Rightly so.

"Rocío, this isn't like you. You are kind, supportive, encouraging—a good teacher."

Rocío couldn't stand to look Hala in the eyes, so she looked past her, blanking her own expression.

"If you go on like this, you'll never forgive yourself. You need to find a better way to address this situation."

Rocío hid a cringe. Hala never talked to her like this. Hala was right; she had to get this out into the open. Rocío ground out, "Am I wrong, Hala? Paloma is using us to get to the top."

"What are you talking about?"

Hala sounded so surprised that Rocío finally looked at her. "She wants Oshinsky's job?"

"Rocío." Hala ran her hand through her hair, a dumbfounded expression on her face. "Have you even talked to her? Have you asked her why she wants to be an advocate?"

"I don't need to." The fault lines seeded last night expanded into cracks running through Rocío's certainty. She heard her own words as if someone else had said them. When had she ever thought she didn't need to talk to someone to understand them? She was all tangled up, and she wasn't sure how she'd gotten to this point.

"I never thought I'd see the day you let your prejudices get the better of you. You need to—"

"I brought tea," Paloma said uncertainly.

Rocío wanted to know what Hala thought she needed to do. Just as urgently, she didn't want to know. Belief in Hala's judgement won out. *I have to get rid of Paloma. I mean, get her out of the way. I mean ... piérdalo, I need to talk to Hala.*

"I think—"

"Detective Hala!" A chaski paused in the entrance to the office, spotted Hala and made a beeline for her. "There's a Cempol officer here to talk to you. It's about Ministrx O'Higgins!"

Everyone turned to look at the chaski. He tried not to grin, but having a legitimate reason to shout inside the CJC clearly pleased him, as did bearing such important news. No one, and certainly not the chaskis who had their ears at every door, could fail to know that the advocates wanted to speak to Ministrx O'Higgins.

"We're not done talking about this," Hala whispered to Rocío. "You haven't done anything irreparable. Yet."

Cempol, always there when you don't want them. But Hala was right about one thing: Rocío never talked to people like she had to Paloma. Bitter. Closed-minded. Prejudiced? Was Oshinsky right about her? Was Rocío wrong about Paloma? And did that make how she was acting even worse?

Officer Smith strode into the room trailing Espinoza, who was saying, "Officer Smith, if you could just wait a moment, I'll bring the detectives to you."

"It's okay, Advocate Espinoza," Hala said.

"She just walked in," Espinoza said.

"I can see that," Hala said. "Officer Smith, you seem to have news."

"Ministrx O'Higgins wants to see you, but he only has a short window of time between appointments."

"Then we shall not inconvenience him," Hala said equably, as if she hadn't spent most of yesterday trying to chase down the ministrx.

"Do we have time for tea?" Paloma put the three cups on the desk.

Rocío looked at her watch: eleven a.m. already. "It looks like it's going to be a long day," Rocío said. "I vote yes. Thank you."

Paloma tried out a smile and looked relieved when Rocío smiled back.

Rocío drank her too-hot tea. *Not irreparable yet for Paloma, but what about me?*

Ministrx O'Higgins was not at home.

"What do you mean he isn't home?" Smith asked. "He sent a message telling us to come meet him."

Seres celestiales, she sounded officious. The young blond man didn't like that at all. He had introduced himself as Señorx Juan Pablo Ricci Cartier, the third secretary to the sub-com. Rocío recognized him from Ministrx Montenegro's house on Wednesday. He didn't look much happier now.

"No one here sent a message," he said. "Are you *quite* sure you read it correctly? Why don't we read it together and see what it says?"

Behind him, the two assistants with the old-fashioned names looked less annoyed and more confused, and like they'd been on the receiving end of his disdain before and were glad it was directed at someone else this time. It was almost worth the trip to watch Smith get snubbed. Of course, Rocío, Hala and Paloma were also getting snubbed; they were still standing in the magnificent marble foyer and hadn't been invited farther into the house.

"Of course I don't—young man, it is your obligation to tell me who sent the note and where the ministrx is now," Smith said. The soles of her shoes clicked against the black-and-ecru floor as she stepped forward as if she were going to throw open the glossy black interior doors and search for the ministrx herself.

"Oh, really?" He folded his arms and planted his feet.

The two assistants exchanged a glance, and the older one with the darker hair and an air of confidence, Gumersinda, stepped forward. "There really has been some mix-up; no one would have scheduled an appointment with you just now. The ministrx is at his grandson's school, and the visit was planned weeks ago."

"Well, I intend to get to the bottom of this," Smith said loudly.

"It was probably Críspula—she's always messing up," Juan Pablo said with calculated carelessness.

The younger assistant stiffened, and her lips tucked in at the corners. Rocío's dislike for Juan Pablo abruptly crystalized. She hated it when people used their power to bully others, like her parents had done to her. *Like I've been doing to Paloma, intentionally or not? She doesn't know I'm wrestling with my feelings; she just knows that sometimes I'm nice to her and sometimes I'm not, and it doesn't have much to do with how she acts.* The thought was deeply shaming.

"Young lady—" Smith began.

"Let's focus on the essentials," Rocío said, her voice cutting through Smith's bluster easily. "It doesn't matter who is to blame. Did Ministrx O'Higgins intend to make an appointment to speak with us, and do you know when?"

"He hasn't made an appointment," Juan Pablo said.

"But he said it was important that he do so," Gumersinda said quickly, her gaze bouncing between Juan Pablo and the advocates in front of her.

"You could make an appointment for him," Paloma suggested.

"I don't think that would be wise." Juan Pablo shifted like he was about to usher them out the door.

"Oh, but surely they could speak to him before the sub-com meeting today," Críspula said to Juan Pablo, the thread of malice in her voice not quite masked. "That would be entirely appropriate, seeing as how this concerns the whole sub-com."

"I—" Juan Pablo said.

Críspula kept talking. "You do know, don't you, that they're meeting at four today at Ministrx Soler's house, because of her house arrest? All the ministrx will be there."

Juan Pablo glared at Críspula. She lowered her eyes. Mostly, Rocío suspected, so he couldn't see the expression in them.

"There are some papers Ministrx O'Higgins wanted to show you," Gumersinda said quickly. "Críspula, why don't you get them?"

Críspula practically skipped down the hallway, no doubt counting this as a win in the power games clearly happening in this house. Rocío would have stood there in intentionally awkward silence while they waited, not even admiring the stone sculpture of a piper on the table, but Smith bumbled on about custody and chain of evidence and receipts. Rocío tried not to roll her eyes.

After a few minutes Gumersinda said, "I'll see if she needs any help."

"Congratulations on your recent appointment as third secretary," Hala said after Gumersinda padded away. "Was there much competition?"

Rocío bent to examine the sculpture to hide her interest; Hala did not make idle chitchat.

"Of course. It's an important post." Juan Pablo puffed out his chest. "I was the clear choice. It's not as if Críspula had a chance," he said, raising his voice slightly. "She's too young and inexperienced." He smiled as if to invite them to agree with his assessment.

Rocío stared back without expression. He failed to notice.

"There were other candidates." He was expounding on their shortcomings when Gumersinda returned with a stack of paper, looking worried. Críspula's expression was completely blank.

"Is everything okay?" Rocío asked.

"These were clearly marked to be sent to the CJC," Gumersinda told Juan Pablo.

Paloma slipped between Gumersinda and Smith to capture the papers. Críspula detained Paloma with a hand on her arm. Smith kept blustering on, but Rocío heard Críspula say, "Palomita, your mother told my mother you were training to be an advocate, but I didn't believe it. If you wanted a job, why didn't you ask me or one of your other friends?"

"This is what I want," Paloma said flatly.

"That's good, then. I didn't realize." Crískula smiled up at her. Paloma nodded. Juan Pablo reached for the papers, and Paloma gracefully slid away from them both and resumed her position at the back of their little crowd.

Hala ushered them out of O'Higgins's house before Juan Pablo could come up with a reason to keep the papers or Rocío could button her coat against the cold. She then mentioned a regulation that sent Smith bounding back to Cempol, and the other three walked the half block to 15 de agosto and stopped on the median to look at what Crískula had given them.

"It's notes and a list of people Ministrx O'Higgins thought might harbor more than the usual hard feelings against him and the sub-com," Hala said. "More people to interview. Though"—she flipped to the next page—"there is some overlap with the lists the other ministrx gave us."

"That Juan Pablo was something," Rocío said, rubbing her hands on her pants like she could remove the residue of his presence. Or her own bad behavior?

"He's always been like that," Paloma said. "Any of the others would have been a better choice for third secretary or for politics in general, even Crískula, even if she is young."

"When we questioned Ministrx Montenegro's staff, one of her assistants mentioned there was some disagreement over his appointment," Hala said.

Rocío nodded, trying to remember what else they had learned about Juan Pablo on Wednesday night. "Did you go to school with him, Paloma?"

"And University. Most people think he's charming."

"Do you think Ministrx Soler and Belli opposed his appointment?" Hala asked.

"That's a thought." Rocío tipped her head back to stare at the bare branches stippling the gray sky. Bullies often bullied because they felt powerless. Juan Pablo could fit, as a suspect.

"If this is about revenge, that could account for the lack of threats against Ministrx O'Higgins and Montenegro, if they voted for him."

"But it doesn't explain Ministrx Valdivia," Rocío said. "Appointments are a simple majority—three against two. Paloma, what do you think?"

"Is he nasty enough to attack someone who tried to get in his way? I'd say yes. But on this scale? Threatening Ministrx Belli with a scandal, I can see that. But kidnapping or murder? And what about the—" She lowered her voice and looked around. The latest flock of pedestrians had crossed the street, leaving them alone on the little strip of grass. "—imported magic? I don't know."

Rocío and Hala exchanged a glance. They had decided to wait for more evidence before bringing Oshinsky any alternate theories about magic. Hala had decided they shouldn't tell Paloma either, and Rocío had agreed. It didn't change the investigative angle ... much. And there was no use bringing everyone else up to the level of panic Rocío experienced whenever she thought the word *necromancy*.

"He could have help. Willing or unwilling," Rocío said. "Though you'd think Isis's reward would have shaken something loose there."

"He'd have to be very sure he could get away with it if he did any of it," Paloma said. "He's one of those people who ... hides his malice."

"We should pursue this. Good thing we know where the entire sub-com will be this afternoon," Hala said. She checked her pocket watch. "We have plenty of time to get there."

CHAPTER 11

"We're almost to the House of Refugees," Paloma said. Even with the portable heater imparting some warmth along with a strong burnt dust smell, it was cold enough in the carriage that afternoon to require blankets, hats and gloves.

"Are you going to tell us why we're stopping here?" Rocío asked Hala, tapping her watch and resisting the urge to shove it in Hala's face. "It's five thirty. We should go straight to Isis's house. We might be able to catch the ministrx and the end of the meeting."

"It's unlikely, so does it really matter what time we arrive? Ministrx Soler will still be there," Hala said.

"I can't believe those protestors opened all the hydrants," Paloma said.

"I can't believe it's cold enough the water froze." Rocío adjusted her scarf. "It's only mid-April." She could barely believe they'd gone swimming last night.

"I can believe Maurata made us wait for hours while he sent messages to Cempol," Hala deadpanned.

The sound of the carriage wheels changed as they turned onto the cobblestone street behind the House of Refugees. Rocío opened her door and leaned out, the cold air a slap to the face. Pedestrians surged across the street and down the sidewalks, shoulders hunched against the unseasonable cold in their too-light coats. She scanned the crowds for the chaski Hala had sent on her mysterious errand. Paco spotted the carriage first and ran towards them, waving a large document tube.

"Hey, are you ever late!" he gasped out, his breath steaming. "I got them, Detective. The clerk said she's holding me personally responsible for them as well as you. If anything happens to them she said she's removing our houses from La Bene's public services maps. Can she do that?"

Hala leaned over Rocío's shoulder and captured the document tube. "Let's assume she can and exercise all due care. In or out?"

"Out."

"Hold on." Rocío passed a basket to Paco. "We saved you some empanadas."

"I'm starving." Paco pulled back the cloth. "Fugazetta and choriempas! Those are my favorite." He hopped onto the driver's bench.

"I know. Tomás," Rocío called to the driver, "some of those are for you if you want them."

"I'll fight to the death for a good empanada."

Rocío closed the door and took her seat on the cracked cushions. Tomás snapped the reins, and the carriage jerked forward, then settled into a smoother motion, though it still jostled over the cobblestones.

"Well?" Paloma asked, and she sounded enough like Paco that Rocío was reminded of how young Paloma was.

"I believe the carriage lamps may not be sufficient for this task." Hala fished a flashlight from the carriage's side pocket and opened the mystery tube. She pulled out several large sheets of paper about the size of an occasional table and spread them over her knees.

The one on top was a line drawing labeled in chalky blue: c/ CH'EJU'UT, 2, MIRAFLORES, LA BENE. CELLARS. The architectural plan for Ministrx Montenegro's house. Rocío craned her neck until her mental image of the layout of the house matched the drawing.

"Are these originals from the Government Archives?" Rocío asked. "The clerk probably will remove your house from La Bene maps if you damage them."

"So *we* shall be careful." Hala leaned back so Paloma could see the drawings better. "According to her note, this is the most recent rendering." She pointed to the date on the bottom.

"Year 360. Still a hundred years ago," Paloma said.

"Hold this." Hala passed the flashlight to Rocío and took a loupe from her pocket. "These are not the most conducive circumstances for this task." As she examined the drawing, Rocío followed Hala's finger with the flashlight.

"Not this one," Hala said. The three of them maneuvered the sheet to the bottom on the pile. "Ah, she's arranged them in reverse chronological order. This one is a mere fifty years before the other. And she has included the subte plans. I had planned to buy her dinner, but this deserves dinner and a play."

"Why don't you look at the oldest one first?" Paloma asked.

"I prefer to be methodical when I have the luxury," Hala said, her voice muffled as she bent lower.

Rocío's and Paloma's eyes met over Hala's head, and for once Rocío thought they were in perfect accord. "Hala, you have a hitherto unexpected flare for the dramatic. Can you please skip to the oldest house plan?"

"What?" Hala straightened and stared at Rocío through the loupe, her eye magnified, until she remembered to lower it.

"We're in an agony of suspense. Will the mystery of the empty room be revealed?" Rocío imitated the plummy voice of a popular puppeteer. "Or will we have to wait a week for the next installation in the newspaper?"

"Oh. Oh, very well. It wasn't on this one either." Hala thumbed through the remaining sheets. "This one is from 106 post-Founding."

They rearranged the plans, and Hala went through her routine again. Rocío leaned forward to check nothing was touching the heater, horrified at the thought of accidentally setting three-hundred-year-old architectural plans on fire.

"Hmm."

"What?" Paloma asked.

"We should have stuck to my method," Hala said. "Look." She

pointed to a line of boxes that weren't on the more-recent plans. "They're here, but they're merely identified as family crypts."

"Were you really expecting *x* marks the spot? Or a name?" Rocío asked.

"I am occasionally optimistic. Help me."

They reshuffled the papers, but the crypts appeared only on the earliest plans. "They're not on the subte plans, as is to be expected." Hala pointed to a heavy red line. "This is Avenida de los pueblos and the subte tunnel." She placed her thumb on the empty place on the map where the ministrx's house would be and her forefinger on the red line, measuring the distance. "Underground it's actually less than one street away from Calle ch'eju'ut, and the access tunnels abut the property boundary." She pointed to the straight lines of the subte tunnel, the access tunnel and the message tubes running parallel to them. "This is where we entered the subte." She tapped a square crossed by three bars and traced their route along the tunnel, an unbroken line. "No rooms, empty or otherwise."

"So we didn't discover anything?" Paloma asked plaintively.

"We discovered that the empty room belongs to Ministrx Montenegro, and we need to ask her if she has uncovered any more about her family history and what might have been in there," Hala said.

"Should we do that? Instead of going to Ministrx Soler's house?" Paloma asked.

Rocío eyed Hala, who cocked an eyebrow in return.

"No," Rocío said. "It's still worth going. Isis's party—"

"I can't believe she's having a party," Paloma said. It was one of the things they had found out during this very frustrating day of literally getting nowhere.

"That's Isis for you." She was the type of person who would rather be surrounded by a hundred people than be alone. Rocío ticked off reasons for going on her fingers. "The party is a chance to talk to the ministrx's assistants again about Juan Pablo and the whole situation without the ministrx leaning over their shoulders, so to speak. Plus I want to know if Isis has any information she hasn't shared with us."

Paloma looked blank.

"As a result of the reward," Hala explained. "Someone could have gone to her directly, bypassing us."

The sound of the wheels changed again, and Rocío twitched aside the window curtain. The glass radiated cold, numbing her nose. "We're almost out of the city."

The smooth bulk of the old Ka wall that marked the northern border of La Bene blocked out the wintry blue sky. And then they were in its shadow, and Tomás slowed for the approach to the gate. One side of the carriage rubbed against the stones, set long before the Iberex brought horses to the Ka and Ya Empires, when the largest beast of burden was the llama. Then the carriage was through, and the sky opened up, huge and impersonal without the clutter of city buildings. The pampas stretched out before them, sere and rolling and vast—short brown grass, longer silvery-brown grass and the occasional bare tree.

As much as Rocío usually loved the open space, today its desolation called up all her worries about necromancy and poor Aleksandr Prokofiev and her own missteps with Paloma and Hala. She snapped the curtain closed and turned back to the others. "Let's go over what we know again."

Forty minutes later the carriage crunched over gravel and stopped, rocking slightly. "We're here," Hala said, and Tomás opened the door.

In front of the sprawling, yellow plastered house, festive torches blazed almost the same color as the start of the sunset. A servant escorted them without question to the internal courtyard. The temporary canvas roof trapped the warmth from the paraffin heaters, and the guests had discarded their coats to dance, eat and talk. A very good tacata band played in one corner.

Rocío spotted the entertainment people first: dancers, actors, assorted theater people and most of the cast of *La Ingenue*. They were partying with an edge Rocío would have recognized even if she hadn't known about Prokofiev's disappearance; voices were a little too loud, drinks gulped a little too fast, the dancing a little too frenetic, without care for one's own limbs or those belonging to others, never mind the blue flowers bordering the patio. Everyone was focused on now now now to blot out thoughts of yesterday and tomorrow, indulging in anything that would dampen concerns about what was happening or had happened to Prokofiev. Isis had most likely locked the doors of unused rooms to limit the damage to her house.

In another corner La Zorra gestured emphatically, her presence so commanding Rocío imagined the bracelets on her arms jingling, though she could not hear them over the noise of the party at that distance. Her conversation partner was one of the backers of *La Ingenue.*

The other guests were in government, either elected officials or staffers. The comptroller and the ministrx of wreck were sharing a bottle of imported mezcal with O'Higgins's assistants with the unfortunate names and Juan Pablo. Rocío spotted Ministrx Montenegro's three assistants and a woman who fit the description of Ministrx Valdivia's assistant. Some of the tension in Rocío's shoulders eased at this sign that their information had been correct and they might actually accomplish something this evening.

A server tried to offer them refreshments. Hala asked for Isis, but Rocío had already spotted her under a fig tree, wearing white. One of her spouses spoke rapidly and intently while their other spouse hung onto Isis's arm.

"Over there," Rocío said and led Hala and Paloma through the throng.

"There's something wrong with this party," Hala said.

"The strange mix of political staffers and theater people? It is extreme, even for Isis." Rocío dodged a woman waving a drink.

"I meant the way they're standing."

"I think you're right." Rocío scanned the party again, this time paying attention to her twanging nerves. Usually at a party of this size, people gathered in fairly regular clumps, more thickly around food or alcohol and the edges of the dance floor. Here there was a gap at the center, as if people were avoiding someone or something, but Rocío couldn't identify who or what that might be.

Isis spotted Rocío and untangled herself from her spouses. Hala paused, hands on her hips and a frown on her face. Rocío moved to meet Isis, Paloma following.

"Chío, darling." Isis kissed Rocío's cheeks.

"I don't think this is what the adjudicator had in mind when he put you on house arrest."

"It's the opening week of *La Ingenue*. We always have a party, and I won't let this time be any different. The show is doing well." Her smile showed too many teeth. "Señorx Legionnaire can be forgotten by his ancestors."

"Why isn't there a show tonight?" Paloma asked.

"It's superstition," Isis said. "The—"

A woman screamed, and then a man. Another woman shouted.

"Isis, stay here. I mean it. Paloma, follow me." Rocío shouldered her way through the partygoers who had become a crowd, some jostling to get closer to whatever was happening in the center of the courtyard, others fleeing. Juan Pablo stumbled away and vomited a thin stream of alcohol and bile onto his shoes.

"Step back, please step back," Hala said calmly and authoritatively, patting people on the shoulders and arms as much to calm them as to get them to move.

Two bodies were staged in the exact center of the courtyard. A man and a woman, their skin waxy not just from lack of blood circulating under it, but from a lack of blood, period.

The reason: their hands and feet were missing. Like the poor dogs. Like Fernández's victims. Rocío's hands went cold, and sweat sprang up along her spine.

The descriptions from the forbidden books flashed through her mind. Amputation and disembowelment. Torture. Perversion. Except there wasn't any gore. No blood, no bloodstains on their clothing. No smell of death or the sickly sweet smell of blood.

She looked at their faces. They were in the middle of their lives, so much unlived life taken from them. They had died in fear and violence. No last kiss to a mother or a daughter, the soft press of lips and the comforting smell of a relative's skin. No ordering of accounts, no goodbyes, no actions. No more choices, good or bad. It didn't matter how they had died, if some depraved person had used them for twisted magic. The living had to act for them now and close their lives with justice to meet and repudiate the injustice of their deaths.

Calm settled over Rocío. It was like the moment of going on stage, when all the anxiety and anticipation fell away and there was just the role and the play. She knew exactly what she needed to do and in what order without having to think about it.

Paloma gasped, covering her mouth with her hand, and Rocío spared her a glance to see if she was going to faint, but instead she saw recognition written clearly across Paloma's face.

"Who are they?" Rocío asked.

"Martine Carter de Herrera and her brother Loeis." Paloma's voice was weak, but it didn't waver.

"They're de Herreras?" Rocío asked sharply. "Two of Ministrx Montenegro's assistants are de Herreras."

"Yes, they're related to her and Ministrx O'Higgins. They're cousins." Paloma swallowed thickly. "I know them, Rocío. I used to play Labyrinths with them. A lot of people here did."

"I'm so sorry." Rocío took Paloma's hand and squeezed it. "And I'm sorry, but I need you to work. Can you do that?"

"Yes." Paloma dragged her gaze away from her childhood friends. Her face was creased with pain, but her pupils constricted as Rocío watched, and she tightened her lips and straightened.

"Tell our driver to make sure no one leaves and to send Paco to Villalta CJC. He has to be fast if they're going to be able to use the semaphore before sunset to send messages to Miraflores CJC, Cempol and the other ministrx that the crimes are escalating. Get Isis's majordomo to give him a horse. Paloma?"

"Oh, yes. I understand. The chief at Villalta needs to know, too." She slipped away through the crowd.

Thank the seres celestiales, Paloma was able to master herself. If she could do it in this situation, they would make a detective of her yet, and Rocío would be grateful to have been wrong.

Villalta CJC covered the entire eastern half of the area outside La Bene's walls. It was slightly closer than La Bene, but it wasn't close. It would take time for additional help to arrive.

Preventing anyone from leaving was unlikely to net them the

murderer, but surely someone must have seen something? *Almost no one saw Prokofiev. Is this what the long-ago adjudicator meant when they wrote that necromancy hid what should otherwise be revealed?* She pushed the thought away and turned back to the bodies.

The woman, Martine, looked to be in her late thirties, with lightish skin and a birthmark on her chin. She was average height, though it was actually hard to be sure without her feet. Her hair was still coiffed and up, with most of the pins and cords in place, even around the bloody gash on the left side of her head. Had she been taken by surprise? She was dressed in merino wool trousers and a classic pullover blouse, suitable for the office.

The Carter de Herreras family exported sheep's wool to Enkladt and the northern duchies across the ocean. It was a well-off family. Judging by the fine grain of the skin on the dead woman's forehead, the bridge of her nose and around her eyes, she had never worked outside in the sun and the wind. The hands would have told even more of the woman's story. Rocío's stomach turned over. *Not now, Rocío.*

The man, Loeis, was younger and even paler, with light brown hair similarly arranged and no visible injuries. He was of average height, with the same caveat, and attired equally well, though his shirt was cut more casually, as if for a day out with friends rather than work. Neither wore a coat. There was something wrong with the lines of their clothes. They were lumpy and distorted instead of flat and smooth, as well-tailored clothes ought to be. As if something were hidden under them.

At that grim thought Rocío looked up to scan the faces of the guests, looking for recognition and guilt. Isis's spouse Tano shook, their face gray. Their other spouse, Jacinta, kept Tano upright with an arm around their shoulders. Isis's face was gray except for two patches of red high on her cheekbones. Fury, Rocío diagnosed.

Críspula was staring motionless, shocked, at the bodies, only her lips moving. She seemed to be saying, "How did this happen?" repeatedly. Gumersinda dropped her glass, and it shattered at her feet, spraying wine on the hem of her robe and the dead woman's shoulder, contaminating the crime scene. Several people leaned on trees and chairs with vomit near their feet. A few people sobbed. La Zorra drew her scarf around her shoulders and stood straight like a soldier.

Hala touched Rocío's arm. "Amputated hands and feet, Rocío," she said in a very low voice. It was a measure of her shock that she said anything at all. "I fear our late-night excursion was more pertinent than we hoped."

"Seres celestiales," Rocío said. "Priorities, Hala."

Secure the scene, the situation and the witnesses first. Deep thinking second. Thoughts about necromancy definitely second, or third, or Rocío wouldn't be able to do her job.

"That's what was wrong with the party. These people were here all along, but we couldn't see them. He 'hid what should otherwise be revealed,'" Hala said, quoting the adjudicator's words about Fernández.

"Hala, we can't think about that right now. Focus." If Hala lost it, Rocío might not be far behind.

"Yes, of course. Sorry." Hala sucked in a deep breath.

"Right." Rocío adjusted a hairpin that didn't need it. "Paloma recognized them. They're related to Ministrx Montenegro and O'Higgins."

"Holy names. We need to get this under control." Hala tilted her head at the guests, indicating she would be discreet while Rocío made herself the center of attention. These were roles they often played.

"Okay, everyone," Rocío said loudly enough for her voice to echo off the stone walls of the house. "I'm Detective Rocío Díaz Rossi, and I'm here to handle this. Please take a few steps back. Yes, thank you." Stunned and drunk or on the edge of it, most of the guests obeyed her, but she needed to get their attention off the bodies. "I will need your help"—Paloma pushed through the crowd and signaled to Rocío that her task was done—"to keep this area clear so we can look for evidence. We'll need to talk to you, too. You may have information vital to discovering what has happened here. Advocate Paloma Faro Otxandabaratz will take your statements. Anything you say could be extremely important. You could hold the key to bringing justice to these poor people. We're counting on you." That should work on the egos of the politicians and performers alike. "If anyone recognizes them, please go—"

"To the dining room," Isis said loudly from behind Rocío. "They're de Herreras," she added softly for Rocío's ears only. "They weren't invited."

"Please go to the dining room and tell Advocate Faro, here." Rocío gestured Paloma to her side. Paloma's closed expression could hide serenity or panicked control; it was that good. "Isis, where should I put everyone else?" Rocío asked.

"The music room. It's big enough."

"Everyone else, please follow Isis to the music room."

A few people rushed to the house. They would be the ones eager to tell all they knew. Those who were too shocked to act milled aimlessly. The majority followed Rocío's directions, though who knew how long that would last with this group.

"Paloma." Rocío caught her arm and drew her close. "I'm sorry to do this to you so early in your training, but I know you can do it. You're good with people, and you're smart. You read every report that crosses Oshinsky's desk, don't you?"

Paloma hesitated and then nodded.

"So you know all the questions to ask: when did you arrive, did you see anything, how do you know the victims, when did you last see them. Get a recorder from the carriage, use a notepad as a prop, and talk to each person individually. Get one of Isis's servants to write down their names on a list and talk to them in that order."

Paloma's lips moved soundlessly like she was repeating Rocío's instructions.

"We'll ask Tomás to search the carriages and grounds. When he says it's okay, let the unimportant guests leave. Hala and I will question the ones you think have important information."

"I don't ..."

"You do. The same way you know who to let into Oshinsky's office and who to keep out, whose request is urgent and whose isn't."

"No, that's experience with Oshinsky, not with murder."

"It's experience with people. You had that before Oshinsky hired you. Trust yourself." *Seres celestiales, she looks young.* "I trust you," she said firmly. "You can do this." She debated saying, *You* have *to do this,* but in the end she just said, "You know these people; you said it yourself. Use that. And Hala and I are here if something comes up that you can't handle. Send someone for us if you need to." She held Paloma's eyes until the other woman nodded, her lips pressed tight and her chin firm. "Go on, then. Shit-stomp 'em." The traditional theater expression slipped out before she could think better of it, but Paloma almost cracked a smile, and when she turned away, she looked less like she was going to her own interrogation.

Isis chivvied the last of her guests inside, hopefully not destroying any more of the crime scene, though Rocío knew that was a forlorn hope. She would bet her beaded Ik-ho shoes that the Carter de Herreras hadn't been murdered here, anyway.

Hala returned from the carriage with the camera and began taking pictures. "Isis's driver is with Tomás, keeping people from leaving as best they can," she said. "Tomás blocked the drive with our carriage, but someone on foot could get by him in any number of ways. I'd bet my Mamalluca microscope they weren't killed here."

Rocío nodded at the echo of her own thought but didn't bother to respond otherwise. She let her eyes unfocus, a trick she used that often brought previously unnoticed details to her attention.

The victims had definitely been staged, not just dumped in a hurry. Their shoulders were lined up, their knees bent and legs tilted towards each other's. It could be an imprecise copy of the Ka burial position or just a space-saving measure, given their placement in the middle of a party. Their eyes were closed, which could mean remorse or that the killer couldn't stand the accusation of open blank eyes or any number of other things.

Hala finished the roll of film and knelt next to the dead woman. "Ready?" She handed Rocío evidence envelopes and gloves, pulled hers on and started to examine the woman. Rocío took the man. She untucked his shirt and pulled it up, trying not to anticipate gore and disfigurement.

A dozen bright orange flowers fell from the folds of his shirt. Marigolds. Fresh, crisp blossoms with neatly trimmed stems.

"What *is* this?" Rocío said at the same time Hala exclaimed in surprise.

More marigolds nestled on the woman's unmarred stomach. Both victims had firm, young skin. Whole skin, without a cut or scrape or exposed organ.

"They were in her shirt," Hala said.

"These as well." Rocío readjusted her expectations. "We keep going?"

"We keep going."

Rocío pushed the man's shirt up as far as it would go. Here were the savage marks of injury: gaping stab wounds, seven—no, eight, from his chest up to the base of his neck. Any one of them could have killed him. Even if he'd had immediate medical help, he wouldn't have survived. Rocío stretched out the shirt, trying to see the inside without removing it. A few faint smudges of blood corresponded to the wounds, but it should have been saturated, not to mention slashed and torn, if Loeis had been wearing it when he was killed. She pulled the shirt down and smoothed it carefully back into place.

"The killer dressed him after he was dead," Rocío said. "No head wound, though."

"Five knife wounds to the chest and neck in addition to the head wound."

"You think it was a knife?"

"I believe so."

The man's pockets yielded nothing but some lint, a few coins and a matchbook from a popular bar. Rocío dropped them into an evidence envelope. The clothes were definitely bespoke, but she didn't want to move him to search for a tailor mark before the forensic techs got there.

Hala lifted a flower for Rocío's inspection. "It's barely withered. It must have been cut today." She sealed her evidence envelope. "At least fifty people have walked around them in the last few hours, but I don't see any footprints next to them. Or dropped food except this wine."

"That happened after they appeared."

"Did you feel anything when they became visible?"

"Maybe ... cooler," Rocío said uneasily, edging up to the topic neither of them wanted to discuss. If she started thinking about necromancy she'd scream just like some of the guests, and that wouldn't help anyone, least of all Martine and Loeis.

They stared at the dead man and woman.

"Let's stick to science," Rocío said.

"I think that's my line."

"Come on, we have to do it." Rocío settled her professional distance around herself like a poncho.

She rolled up the man's sleeves, a mockery of a living man's habit. Blood smudged the cuffs, but not nearly as much as there should have been. She took a deep breath of eucalyptus-and-paraffin-scented air before looking at the stumps.

Her breath hitched even though she'd expected the shock of seeing those smooth limbs ending in nothing. Or rather in exposed muscle and bone, moist and so, so organic looking. She moved so she couldn't see his face. The dark hair on his forearms curled intimately.

The cuts through skin, muscle and bone were clean, uniform and slightly ragged. Not unlike what you'd see on a cut of meat in a butcher shop.

"This was done with a saw," Hala said. "I can't say for sure without a microscope, but I think these are hesitation marks."

"Their killer knew them," Rocío said, several things coming together at once.

Hala sat back on her heels, raised her hands to run them through her hair and then stopped, probably remembering she was gloved and had just been touching a dead body. "Why do you say so?"

Rocío knew from the faint emphasis on *you* that Hala agreed. "You put marigolds on your loved ones' graves and your ancestors' altars so they can smell them in the afterlife. You don't do that for a stranger. Their eyes have been closed. Coupled with the way they're laid out—carefully, respectfully—I think the killer knew them."

"I have to agree. Especially if these are hesitation marks. Still, the amputation ..." It wasn't like Hala to not finish a sentence.

Rocío knew Hala was thinking the same thing she was and swallowed against the acid bile rising in her throat. "Hala, are we seeing what we expect because of what we did last night, or are we seeing what's here?"

"Or does someone want us to think what we're thinking?"

Rocío interlaced her fingers and frowned down at them. "If so, they still know more than I'm comfortable with. Though that could narrow the list of suspects." Her voice sounded strained even to herself. "Surely there would be more signs if it's ..." She couldn't force herself to say *necromancy*. It wasn't a comfort that Hala also seemed unable or unwilling to say it.

"On the other side of that argument, I'm not familiar with any other magic system that could achieve the disparate effects we've witnessed or theorized." Hala squeezed her hands together as if to keep them out of her hair, mouth pinched. "It might be time to turn from science to art."

Rocío laughed humorlessly. "Art says what we dare not?" That was from one of Hala's favorite poems. "If it looks like a duck and quacks like a duck, it is a duck?"

"Apropos, but not what I had in mind."

Rocío bit her lip. She didn't need to search her memory for the line from the play *The Necromancer Dies Last*. Her thoughts had circled around it since her first glimpse of the victims. "'It's necromancy, Father, can't you see that?'" Her voice throbbed with intensity, though she left out the shriek. Quoting made it easier to get the words out, though this situation felt less real than the play. "I still think it's a stretch," Rocío said in a more normal voice. "No one knows how to become a necromancer."

"This could be someone's attempt to reach that state."

"Ugh. That's preferable. In a disgusting sort of way." It also meant Aleksandr Prokofiev was probably dead, and she didn't want him to be.

"It is a bleak thing to hope for." Hala didn't sound hopeful; she sounded grim. She was probably calculating the statistical probability of finding a magicker in La Bene, the Ka or Ya Empires or the Tolec Principalities capable of counteracting a necromancer. If Rocío calculated statistical odds, they would be about whether they would have their own personal riot at the

CJC when Maurata found out about this. *Maybe we don't have to tell him?*

She shook off the ridiculous thought, and the normal sounds of an evening in the countryside impinged on her awareness.

"Listen." The sun had set while they'd examined the bodies, and crickets whirred. A black-crowned night heron barked, and a sheepdog answered it.

"Regardless of the condition of the bodies, if necromancy was done nearby, everything would be dead or in hiding. At least that's what the plays and urban legends say. Did you read anything about that last night?"

"No." Hala smoothed the dead woman's blouse down. "I concur that those are not reliable sources, but in any case the physical evidence makes it extremely unlikely that these two were killed here."

"We need to find out where this murderer is operating from," Rocío said.

"And why they staged the bodies here. Did they choose to reveal them when we walked in? Is the perpetrator here? Was that a coincidence?"

Paco ran into the courtyard and flailed to a stop, his eyes huge. Isis's spouse Tano rushed in behind him. They stopped when they saw it was too late to shield him, a resigned expression on their face. Rocío moved to block his view of the dead bodies.

"Detectives," he panted, white faced and sweating, "I made it. I have an answer from Miraflores CJC and a message from Villalta CJC."

The boy's eyes repeatedly darted to the bodies. It wouldn't be a kindness to turn so his back was to them. Instead Rocío pulled off her gloves and put her hand on his shoulder. "Is the medical coroner coming?"

"Y-yes." He steadied. "But not ours. The one from Villalta. He should be right behind me. Miraflores said no one was available."

Rocío stifled a curse. "Okay. Go tell Señorx Tano that I said you need a cup of their best chocatl."

"Yes!" He ran off, the bodies forgotten for now. She'd have to make sure the staff therapist and his parents were briefed.

Tano met her eyes across the patio and nodded. No stranger to crises or working children, they steered Paco to the kitchen. Good— that would give the kitchen staff something to rally around. If they hadn't started already, Tano would get them to serve coffee and tea to everyone, as much to steady the staff's nerves as the guests'.

"We need to speak to everyone here," Rocío said.

Hala inserted her pen into the woman's shirt cuff and lifted the arm for closer inspection. "Hmm."

Note to self: do not borrow Hala's pen. "We can't leave them alone."

"No." Hala shook herself and gently set the arm down. "There are too many people here. I'll wait for the coroner. You start questioning people."

"If he's not here in twenty minutes, I'll relieve you."

"No need."

"Uh-huh." Rocío pressed Hala's shoulder and walked away before Hala could work herself up to support an argument she didn't believe. Rocío pushed up her sleeve to look at her watch, and an image of the woman's severed wrist flashed through her mind. She set the thought aside. Only five minutes to seven. It felt much later.

CHAPTER 12

Rocío asked Isis's majordomo to extract a willing Isis from the music room so Rocío could avoid being seen by the guests and having to respond to questions she didn't have answers to. *I'm not shirking my responsibilities to Paloma,* she told herself, pretty sure she was shirking her responsibilities to Paloma. The problem was she didn't know how to meet all her responsibilities without a staff of at least seven more advocates. *Just Espinoza would be nice. I'd even take Díaz.*

"I need a place to question people," Rocío told Isis. "Intimate."

Isis led her into an elegantly furnished sitting room. It was too big, but it had an inlaid table that Rocío could repurpose once she got rid of the large vase of autumn lilies it currently supported.

"Who is doing this, Rocío? First Sasha, and now dead de Herreras in my garden?"

"Do you think you're being targeted? Does it feel personal?" Rocío watched Isis carefully.

Isis gave a bark of laughter. "Chío, does it feel *personal*? There are dead people in my house."

Rocío flicked her hand like she was waving something away. "Beyond that. Something about where they were placed? The timing?" She didn't want to lead Isis more than she already had, but that meant asking vague questions.

"No," Isis said, frowning, "but it does feel malicious. Do you have a suspect? Is that why you're here?"

"What time did your staff start preparing for the party? Did you hold the sub-com meeting here as planned?" Rocío asked, well aware of the dangers of thwarting Isis by not answering her questions even though it was her job right now. She stepped to the left, away from a porcelain vase she had always liked and closer to the ormolu clock she never had. The tactics she had used in her own home would not work here.

"When could someone have put them there, you mean? They started setting up this afternoon before the sub-com meeting. That started at two and went until just after four. Now answer my question."

"Was everyone there?" Rocío mentally cursed Maurata, the weather and the protesters who had made them miss that meeting.

"All the ministrx."

"And?"

"The three secretaries and all the personal assistants. Everyone you saw at Ministrx Montenegro's house on Wednesday." Isis fiddled with a figurine of a woman. "You think it was one of them? But it couldn't be, because we were all together."

"Isis, you know I can't answer your questions right now."

Isis growled and started pacing. "But you think someone I know is doing this. To me. Not to Sasha, not to poor Martine or Loeis, though they're the ones who are dead." She whirled to face Rocío. "I hate feeling helpless. What can I do?"

"You gave us a list of people who might want to hurt you. Have any of them acted differently recently? Has anyone been aggressive or more nervous or excited than usual?" She didn't want to mention Juan Pablo while they were all stuck in Isis's house. Ancestors only knew what Isis would do.

"You want me to stand here and *think*, while people are being murdered?" Isis yelled in Rocío's face.

Rocío stood still, not flinching. "You *are* good at it when you bother," she deadpanned. It didn't help.

"I hate this! Sasha might be dead and I can't do anything!" A flush flared up her neck, turning her face almost purple. She whirled and hurled the ormolu clock at the floor. The glass case shattered, the bronze horse's legs bent and a corner of parquet flooring flew across the room. Isis stared at the ruined clock, her chest heaving.

From the doorway Hala said, "That was a Tymoteusz."

Isis turned her back to Rocío, braced her hands on the wall and breathed deeply.

"I need Rocío," Hala said. "The advocates from Villalta CJC are here."

"Okay," Isis said. "Okay. But I will make whoever is responsible regret it, past death into the afterlife. Ask my majordomo for another room."

Rocío blew out a breath. She had really been hoping Isis would conjure a name—Juan Pablo's?—out of the convoluted recesses of her brain so they could end this. She should have known it wouldn't be so simple. She watched Isis for a moment, wondering if she should offer her a hug. But an ormolu clock wasn't the only thing that could break.

Rocío slipped out of the room and closed the door behind her.

Hala rubbed her forehead. "Well?"

"The meeting lasted from two to four, and everyone was in attendance."

"Without knowing when the de Herreras were killed, that doesn't tell us much."

Rocío sighed. "I didn't realize I was hoping she could point at someone and say, 'They did it.'"

"Understandable." Hala slung her arm around Rocío, and they leaned into each other. "Advocate Cetz is in charge of the Villalta advocates. I told them about our theory. She doesn't believe me, but she's not letting it interfere with her work.

"The coroner is examining the bodies. It's the young one, so he isn't drunk, but he's terrified. He did believe me. Advocate Cetz and another advocate are questioning the theater people, and a third advocate is outside with Tomás, doing the best they can without lighting. The lights in our carriage weren't powered recently and need a level-four magicker to do it. Villalta doesn't have a magicker at all. Or lights. They don't have many big investigations out here. People solve their own problems."

"And if they solve them with murder, it's generally pretty obvious."

"Paloma identified a few people to send home. The problem is most everyone here knows the victims. Cetz asked if you would interview the political staffers. I told her they're not that different from theater people, and she said they're all different from sheep herders and she's not messing up the first murder in Villalta on her watch."

Rocío rolled her head against the wall to try to relieve some of the tension in her neck. She needed coffee before she did any more interviews. "Wait, staffers?"

"The ministrx browbeat Paloma into letting them leave. They're at our disposal tomorrow in their offices, et cetera, et cetera."

"Piérdalo." Rocío banged her head against the wall. Her temples throbbed with sudden rage. She breathed deeply, trying to control it. *I shouldn't have trusted her. I should have known she couldn't do it.* She reminded herself how competent Paloma had been the entire evening, controlling her reaction to seeing her friends dead, rising to the new demands of questioning and sorting witnesses. She reminded herself she was trusting Hala's judgement over her own right now.

"That's right, stay calm." Hala squeezed Rocío's shoulders. "First of all, we didn't have any other options. Second, you needed to be the one to talk to Isis. Neither Paloma nor I could have managed that conversation. Paloma did as good a job as anyone. Do you think you could have stopped the ministrx of wreck if he wanted to leave?"

Rocío pictured the big florid man, and the rage drained out of her, leaving her limp. "No."

"Villalta should have sent their chief; that's about the only authority that might have kept everyone here, and I'm not even sure a rural chief would have been able to."

"Probably not," Rocío admitted.

"You need to fix your head with regard to Paloma."

"Okay. You're right. I know you're right."

"She admires you, Chío. Ask her why she wants to be an advocate, and fix your relationship with her."

Díaz had said the same thing. Now Hala was saying it. *Am I that wrong?* The thought made her feel like a cold hand had closed around her heart.

"But not right now," Rocío said tiredly. They'd been up most of last night and would probably be up most of tonight. Once that wouldn't have been a problem, but age made it wear on her much more. Tomorrow would be soon enough to make a new plan, and once she had one, she would feel better and she'd fix things.

"Soon, Rocío."

"I know. Can we talk about murder instead?"

"That is not a healthy reaction, just so you know." Hala drummed her fingers on Rocío's shoulder. "But yes, we have to talk about murder. I spoke with Isis's spouses. I know we weren't considering them as suspects in Prokofiev's disappearance, but these murders change everything. I suppose we could have unconnected cases of abduction and double homicide, but it seems rather coincidental. Tano and Jacinta seem to like Prokofiev and are worried about how Isis is handling his disappearance, but that could be a façade. Are either of them good enough actors to hide the kind of rage it would take to dump two bodies in their own garden?"

"Jacinta was an actress but she's never struck me as the jealous type. You couldn't be and be married to Isis. But general jealousy and specific jealousy are very different things. If she felt threatened by Prokofiev in some way ..."

They contemplated that for a moment. "Neither of them had any magic residue on them," Hala said, meaning they hadn't used magic in the last twenty-four hours or so. "They agreed to the fast test. I talked to the majordomo and pinned down the movements of the staff throughout the day. The short story is that either the majordomo is lying, or this magic can hide people from sight when they are alive and moving, not just when they're dead and unmoving. Which would shed light on Prokofiev's disappearance, if they're connected. I didn't see any window of opportunity for someone to get those bodies there otherwise."

Rocío was still thinking about magic residue. "I suppose it's possible that the magic involved was invested in an object. Like getting your house lights charged and turning them on with a switch. No magic residue on you or even the charger, who may have done it weeks ago."

"Thank you for making our list of suspects even longer."

"Oh, come on. I'm surprised you're not more suspicious of them because they *don't* have magic residue on them. It's April. Three quarters of La Bene are using magic to warm up their coffee or tea."

"True." Hala's breath misted in the air, proving Rocío's point. Away from the heaters, the inside of the house was as cold as the outdoors. But Hala was a warm, comforting presence along Rocío's left side.

"Wait," Rocío said, realizing what Hala had said about magic. "You think the dogs were killed to fuel necromancy to hide Prokofiev's murder or abduction Monday night? And that's how the bodies here were concealed?" The memory of the de Herreras in the courtyard flashed into her mind again. She set aside the image again.

"Who knows? We're working in an almost-absolute lacuna of data, if you ignore the possible necromancy." Hala grimaced. "However, something else doesn't feel right."

"I know," Rocío said, thinking out loud. "If we're right about the sub-com connection—"

"Do you think we are?"

"Let's set that question aside for the moment. If we're right, we have the disgrace and arrest of the lieutenant governor. The public disgrace of María Paz's secret being published in *Oye*, if she hadn't stopped it. And the disappearance of Aleksandr Prokofiev and the theft of the master dance score, which should have undermined the show and has infuriated if not embarrassed Isis."

"Corpses are extreme, not disgraceful."

"True."

"Are we wrong about the sub-com connection?"

Rocío flipped her hands palm up, gesturing uncertainty. "We have the notes connecting Isis and María Paz. But being wrong feels like being right, up until the moment you realize you're wrong. What do you think?" She braced herself for questions about Isis's culpability. Rocío didn't think Isis was stupid enough to kill people in her own house, but convincing Hala of that could take time.

"I think we don't have Aleksandr Prokofiev's body."

"What?" Rocío asked.

"These are the first bodies. It's a break in the pattern." Hala straightened and turned to face Rocío. "Something has changed. I think this was a mistake."

"It's so elaborate, it can't have been," Rocío protested, trying to catch up.

"Not the staging—the murders. I want to look at the scene again. Where there's one mistake, there might be others."

And she left, which meant Rocío had to interview Hala's share of witnesses as well as her own.

Rocío found Isis's majordomo and got her cup of coffee. "I need another room. Isis …" Searching for the words to finish that sentence, she took a slug of coffee.

"Happened?"

"Is using the other one," Rocío finished diplomatically. The coffee and the anticipation of the interviews was waking her up.

"The family dining room is not ideal, but it does have chairs and is close to the music room."

"That should be good."

The majordomo led the way, opened the door and turned on the lights, which, while very finely made, were more restrained in design than the chandeliers in the larger dining room. "How are you …? You don't need me to …" She gestured, seeming more unsure than Rocío about what she meant.

"No, I'm going to talk to"—*check on*—"Paloma and have her send me witnesses. So that's all I need from you. No, wait, Huchim—do you know where Paco is?"

"Ensconced with one of our cooks in the dairy," Huchim said. "He fought with the Peneche against the Shekas up north and has seen

184

his share of ... When I checked on them, he was telling Paco how to deal with the nightmares he'll probably have."

"Good." One less thing to worry about right now.

Huchim stood in the doorway, still holding the doorknob. She looked more uncertain than Rocío had ever seen her in the fifteen years their association with Isis had overlapped.

"You want to say something, but you're torn between your discretion as Isis's employee and being a good citizen," Rocío guessed.

Huchim leaned towards Rocío slightly but still didn't speak.

Rocío weighed the need to give information to get information. "Someone moved those bodies here, from somewhere else, to target Isis or someone in her family. Whatever you tell me can only help her, not hurt her."

"I don't like to say ..." Huchim bit her lip and then said in a rush, "It's just, two of the maids are Ka, and they were in the garden most of the morning, and the Ka have death shamans and all that. They do things with dead bodies. Do you think it has anything to do with that?"

"Tell me which ones, and I'll look into it," Rocío said gently. Huchim was a Ya surname. Four hundred years ago Villalta had been Yaxmihán, and old enmities died hard, passed down in sayings, place names and folk wisdom. But Rocío would still check.

Huchim gave Rocío two names, watched while Rocío recorded them in her notebook, and fled like she had committed a heinous crime. Rocío suspected the two maids were Ka the same way Huchim was Ya, which was to say they had a mixture of Benerex and Ka cultural heritage. But it would be good to look into Ka death magic. And Ya shamanism, which also had strong ties to ancestors, even past death.

Because that would be better than necromancy. Anything would be.

CHAPTER 13

"I'm just going to ask you a few questions, Gumersinda," Rocío said.

Gumersinda de Herrera Nuñes was Ministrx O'Higgins's older assistant, the one with darker brown hair. The soft lights and rich dark woods of the room flattered her, though she would have been attractive in any setting. Her rigid posture did not. She sat at the edge of a chair at an angle to Rocío, the barely contained nervous energy coming off her taking up as much space as an additional person.

"I'm recording our conversation. Is that okay?" Rocío asked, trying to make Gumersinda comfortable enough to answer questions instead of fleeing the room.

"Of course it's okay. This is a murder investigation, isn't it?"

"Thank you. What—"

"It is, isn't it? It's Martine and Loeis, isn't it?"

"What time did you arrive at Isis's house?" Rocío asked over her.

Gumersinda seemed to consider whether to keep asking, nodded to herself as if she had extracted an answer and said, "A little before two, for the meeting."

"Alone or with other people?"

"With Críspula de Herrera Carmona."

Rocío scribbled a note to herself.

"What are you writing? I thought you were recording this?"

Gumersinda leaned forward as if to snatch the pad from Rocío's hands, a belligerent note entering her voice.

There were any number of reasons someone might react poorly to being questioned during a murder investigation, such as grief, not just guilt. Shock took different forms. "I'm just writing your answers. It's easier than going through the recording later."

"Oh." Gumersinda subsided back into her chair.

"Did you see anything unusual tonight? Anything that strikes you as strange now?"

"No. It was just a party. A good party, before this."

"No one who shouldn't be here? Anyone acting strange?"

"No."

"How about before the party, at the meeting?"

"It was strange because Ministrx Soler is on house arrest, but nothing ..." She gestured vaguely. "Nothing else."

"Are you and Señorx Juan Pablo Ricci close?"

"You saw us at Ministrx O'Higgins's house. Do you think we're close?"

"I think you work closely together."

"Okay, yes," Gumersinda said. "So?"

"So what is he like?"

"Why are you asking me this? What does that have to do with ..." Gumersinda waved her arm in the direction of the patio.

"To answer your question, the victims are Martine and Loeis Carter de Herrera."

Gumersinda sucked in a breath and looked down.

"You're related to them, aren't you?"

"They're my cousins. Who would do this to them?"

"That's what I need to find out. How closely related are you?"

"Our mothers are cousins."

"And you're related to Ministrx O'Higgins and Ministrx Montenegro?"

"You think this has something to do with them?"

"I just need a feel for who's related to whom."

Gumersinda nodded, seeming to accept that. "He's my uncle, and Sofía Montenegro is a cousin on my mother's side."

"And what about Juan Pablo Ricci? Is he also related to them?"

"Also a cousin on his mother's side," Gumersinda said.

"How did he get along with Martine and Loeis?"

Gumersinda considered her for a long time. "Is he going to know what I said?"

"No, this is confidential between you and me."

Twisting her fingers together, Gumersinda said, "The same way he gets along with everyone he thinks can help his career. Their mother is one of Ministrx O'Higgins's favorites. He's the soul of decency with them."

"And with people he doesn't think can help his career?"

"If you're lucky, he ignores you."

"And if you're not?"

"You saw. He always finds your vulnerable spots, and then he presses. Says things."

"Just says things? Or is he violent, too?"

"You don't understand."

When she didn't say anything more, Rocío said, "Words can leave scars, sometimes deeper ones than those caused by physical harm. I just need to know if he's ever hit you or anyone else."

"No." Gumersinda sucked on her lower lip. "Look, if you're thinking he did this ... I'm not saying he isn't mean enough, but he'd never do anything to jeopardize his career, and Ministrx O'Higgins *is* his career."

"What if he thought he could get away with it?"

Gumersinda crossed her ankles and pulled her elbows tight against her sides. A shielding response, indicating her discomfort with the question. "Would he murder someone, you mean? I don't ..."

Rocío gave her a minute to fill in the rest. When she didn't, Rocío asked, "What upsets him, do you think?"

"A lot of things. People who don't know their place."

"You?"

"More Críspula."

"Who else? Any of the ministrx on the sub-com?"

Gumersinda measured Rocío, the corners of her lips tucked tight.

"Ministrx Soler," she said finally. "She gets his goat without even trying. And when she's on a rampage …"

"Did Ministrx Soler vote for him to take the position of third secretary?"

"No."

"Who else voted against him?"

"Ministrx Belli."

"Do you think he might be taking revenge on Ministrx Soler?"

Gumersinda shook her head. "Not like this. I can see why you'd think that … but I don't think … not like this. Please stop asking me these questions."

"Okay, Gumersinda, thank you for being honest with me. I have to ask you a few more questions, about Martine and Loeis." She waited for the other woman to nod. "This is going to be hard."

The camera Hala had used was the kind that produced instant pictures by magic without the need for an actual magicker. She took the photos out of her pad.

"I'm going to show you photos of your cousins. They don't show their injuries. I'd like to know if you notice anything unusual about their appearance." Rocío handed her the photos.

Gumersinda tucked a lock of hair behind her ear and bent over them for a long time. When she looked up, her thick dark eyebrows were furrowed. "No," she said flatly. "But I don't understand who would do this to them." She handed the pictures back.

"I will do my best to figure that out."

"No, I mean, who would do this to both of them? If it were Loeis only, I would say look at the pato players. Loeis played rough, and horses and people got injured." Pato, a game played by two teams on horseback, whose aim was to score by getting the pato, a ball with handles, through a ring, was notoriously dangerous, both on and off the field.

"Martine is just as aggressive in business," Gumersinda said. "If it were only her, I'd say maybe she got a jump on a competitor or locked someone out of a deal. But their lives don't overlap. They're almost entirely separate."

"Except for family," Rocío suggested. "Maybe not Juan Pablo, but someone else?"

Gumersinda's hands twitched minutely and stilled. "No."

"Someone attacking your family?"

"It's possible," Gumersinda said. "Our families are prominent in politics and business. It's a fact of life that people want what we have."

"Were Martine and Loeis involved in politics?"

"Who isn't? But if you mean were they political staffers or anything like that, no."

"Was there a disagreement in the family, maybe?" Rocío asked.

"A disagreement?" she scoffed. "That would make someone to do this? I don't think so." But she kept her hands pressed against her thighs to control their trembling.

"Is there anything else you want to tell me?" Sometimes that kind of open-ended question worked.

"No ... no."

And sometimes it didn't. "You can go, then," Rocío said, purposefully nonchalant, and tucked the photos into her pad.

"That's it?" Gumersinda asked.

"For now. Of course, I'll have to talk to everyone. Martine and Loeis's parents." Three of them, according to Isis. "Your parents." No reaction. "Do you have siblings?"

"Yes, two."

"Your siblings. Ministrx O'Higgins. Juan Pablo." No reaction. "Would you tell your cousin Críspula to come in?"

There it was—the tremor in Gumersinda's hands before she flattened them against her legs to hide it. Why did that upset her? Did she think Juan Pablo was a bully and Críspula was a convenient, safe target, and that a bully might escalate from petty meanness to worse actions, and Críspula might be willing to say things to a community justice advocate that Gumersinda wasn't? Or was it something else?

"If you think of anything, no matter how small, contact me at Miraflores CJC." Rocío waited. "You can tell me. I just want to find the person who hurt Loeis and Martine."

"Críspula is very upset, you know," Gumersinda said slowly. "I should stay with her. While you talk to her."

"Is she upset because she knows something?"

"No. She saw them—she was standing right there." Unlike most politicians, Gumersinda lied badly. Her political career would probably never advance beyond her position as a staff member if she didn't change.

"Did she tell you something you're not telling me?"

"No. Why are you badgering me? We don't know anything."

"Then my interview with her will be as brief as yours."

"I should stay."

"You can't." Rocío didn't soften the refusal, trying to provoke the young woman into a fuller reaction. "Procedure."

Gumersinda stood but kept her hand on the back of her chair.

"Is there something you want to tell me about Críspula?"

"You're taking this the wrong way."

"About her and Juan Pablo? I saw the way he treated her at Ministrx O'Higgins's house."

After another breath, Gumersinda clenched her fists and walked away, her posture rigid once more.

Rocío scratched a note to talk to her again and then flipped to a blank page, waiting to see what would happen.

The door creaked open. Críspula poked her head around the frame. "Hello," she said huskily.

"Come in, take a seat," Rocío invited, softening her own voice to match. "I know this has been a tough night for you. I only have a few questions."

"I thought ... maybe ... Paloma would be here."

"She's speaking with other people."

"I just ..." She collapsed into the chair, a handkerchief clutched in one hand. She bore very little resemblance to the well-groomed young woman Rocío had encountered only that morning. Her eyes were red and glassy, and her face seemed to sag with grief, adding years to her appearance. "I've always liked her," she whispered.

"This shouldn't be too hard, okay? I'm recording our conversation.

I need you to help us figure out who hurt your cousins. You saw it was them, right?"

Críspula's eyes filled with tears.

"Críspula? You saw Martine and Loeis?"

"Yes," she murmured. She cleared her throat and repeated it more firmly.

"Okay, do you remember what time you got to Isis's?"

"Around two."

"Who did you come with?"

"My cousin Gumersinda."

Rocío ran through her standard questions, asking whether Críspula had seen anyone or anything strange since arriving at Isis's house, but Críspula hadn't.

"Okay. What did you do after I saw you at Ministrx O'Higgins's house?" Rocío asked.

"We got ready for the sub-com meeting."

Rocío decided to approach the topic of Juan Pablo Ricci at an angle. "Ministrx O'Higgins seems like the kind of person who would mentor his staff. Do you like working for him?"

A microexpression passed over Críspula's face too fast for Rocío to interpret. Upset?

"He's under a lot of stress. I like working for him, but I liked it more before. He used to be more consistent." She nibbled her lip.

Rocío nodded. "Uh-huh?"

"He's been worried about something lately. Oh, I shouldn't say that—I don't really know. Gumersinda is more ambitious than me. Do you really want to hear this? I thought you were going to ask me about tonight. I didn't see anything."

"What do you think Ministrx O'Higgins is worried about?"

"The lieutenant governor, of course." She lowered her voice to a whisper. "Treason."

"Not anything more personal? Closer to home?"

"That is personal to Uncle William."

"Has someone threatened him?"

Críspula's eyes opened wide with surprise. "What?"

"Do you think Ministrx O'Higgins is worried because someone is threatening him?"

"He hasn't said anything like that."

"But what do you think, from your observations?"

Críspula's pupils flared as if Rocío had complimented her. Was she so starved for praise? "I think it's possible. But I think you should ask him."

"Okay. I will."

Críspula bit her lip and nodded.

"I'm going to show you some pictures. They're not gory. Take a look and tell me if they're who you think they are." Rocío placed the photos on the table next to Críspula, letting the corners click down and framing them with her hands.

Críspula hid her face in her handkerchief and shuddered a few sobs. "It's them. It's really them, isn't it? It's Martine and Loeis, and they're dead."

Rocío let her cry for a few minutes and then offered her a glass of water.

"What else is upsetting you?" Rocío asked. "It's not just that they're dead, is it?"

"Isn't that enough?" She swallowed and let one finger brush the edge of the photo of the man. It was harder to tell he was dead in black and white, but the shadow of pain on his face was still obvious.

"Críspula?" Rocío asked gently.

"Y-y-yes. There is something else. Gumersinda said not to tell you, that you would suspect us. But you wouldn't, would you?" She looked up pleadingly.

"What is it?"

"We had a fight, an argument, the four of us, the last time I saw them. And now I can't take it back, and I can't, I can't ..."

Rocío refilled the glass of water. Críspula pressed it against one cheek and then the other and put it down.

"When was this?" Rocío asked.

"On Tuesday. We had dinner with Uncle William. The ministrx, I mean."

"What was the fight about?"

Críspula shook her head.

"You have to tell me," Rocío said, injecting all the persuasion she could into her words. "I have to find out who did this to them. You can help me."

Críspula cried harder.

Rocío pinched the bridge of her nose. It had been a long day. She was tired, and there was so much to do before she could even think about snatching a few hours of sleep. She felt for Críspula and her pain, but she also needed answers from her.

She summoned up the voice of authority she used on the chaskis, the voice her parents' cook had used on her when she was a child. "I know you're feeling guilty that your last words to them were harsh ones, and you're grieving and probably angry, too, but I need your help. You can't make up *with* them, but you can make it up *to* them by telling me what you know so I can stop the person who hurt them." Rocío believed what she was saying, but even if she hadn't, she still would have said it. She had a murderer to catch.

"You can't tell their parents." Críspula's voice cracked. "Loeis was gambling on pato and losing. Martine took money from her mom's business to pay his debts. Gumersinda and I heard them arguing about it, and then we all had a big fight. And that's the last time I talked to them ..." Her voice trailed off into sobs.

Rocío considered this information. She didn't see how it could be connected to suspected necromancy, but that's what an investigation was for.

"Just a few more questions, and then you can go home. Do you know who Loeis owed money to?"

Críspula shook her head.

"Do you know who else might know about this?"

"No."

"Did Gumersinda tell you not to tell me anything else?"

"Just about the argument, I promise."

"What about Juan Pablo Ricci? Was he there for this argument?"

"Juan Pablo?" Críspula straightened up. "Why do you want to know about him? Why does everyone always want to know about him? I told you, it was just me and Gumersinda."

"You and Juan Pablo don't get along, do you?"

Críspula hunched forward again, her gaze on the floor. "You saw what he was like, didn't you?" she whispered. "He always gets what he wants, never mind anyone else."

"And he wanted the position of third secretary very badly, didn't he?"

"Yes."

"Enough to retaliate against the ministrx who didn't support his nomination?"

Críspula shook her head.

"Críspula?"

"I don't know anything about that. Just what I said before. I don't know why you're so interested in him." She slid down in her chair with her chin tucked to her chest, looking like a sulky teenager.

"Well, he's your competition, right?" Rocío asked in response to Críspula's body language.

Críspula perked up.

"You must know all his weaknesses, don't you? Drinking, gambling?"

"Some, but he's careful. He doesn't do anything Ministrx O'Higgins wouldn't like. He's really not that interesting."

"Does he play pato?"

"He watches, he wouldn't play," Críspula said scornfully. "He goes to the races sometimes with others just like him. I don't see what this has to do with Martine and Loeis."

"There's no way he could have overheard your argument?"

"No." Críspula frowned. "You should ask me more about Martine and Loeis."

"Do you know where they were earlier today?"

"Oh." Críspula bit her lip and looked fragile again. "At work, I would think." She started to cry. "I can't help you. I want to, but I just ..."

"Okay, Críspula, you've been a help. You can go home now," Rocío said.

"I ... I have?"

"We'll do everything we can to find out who did this to your cousins."

Críspula met Rocío's gaze for the first time during the interview, her eyes wide and wounded looking. "I believe you," she said softly.

After she left, Rocío tapped her pen against her teeth, thinking. Had there been something off about her conversations with both women? Or was Rocío's judgement impaired? Was she prejudiced against people like Gumersinda and Críspula and Paloma? How much was Rocío's upbringing informing—or hindering—her interactions with Benerex elite? Believing her judgement was clouded by her emotions was not a comfortable feeling.

Unfortunately Juan Pablo Ricci was next. Regarding him, she trusted her judgement.

She flipped her pen around and added to her earlier note to herself: *Have someone else interview Gumersinda and Críspula de Herrera again for a second opinion.*

Deciding what approach to take, Rocío evaluated Juan Pablo Ricci as he settled into the chair. His hair looked gilded in the soft light, and he had the look of a young man who knew exactly how attractive he was and used it and his youth to his advantage, especially with middle-aged women who could do something for him or his career. Rocío, sadly, did not fit in that category, in her estimation of his estimation. Case in point: although he sat neatly enough in his chair across from her, he somehow gave the impression of sprawling.

Usually Rocío preferred deflating egos rather than pandering to smugness, but this wasn't her personal life. There was a murderer to bring to justice. And in her experience, certainty of superiority led to carelessness and revelations.

"Thank you for meeting with me," Rocío said. "What do you think is going on here?"

"It's Ministrx Soler's lover, isn't it?" he said complacently, leaning back farther in his chair. "And probably some woman she caught him with."

Rocío blinked. "Her lover?" He couldn't mean the murder victims, could he?

"The one that's missing. I saw them last week, you know. Ministrx Soler and a man that wasn't either of her contract partners. Obviously. Kissing." He smirked expectantly, like he expected Rocío to rise to his bait as automatically as fog rolling into La Bene in June.

Rocío knew perfectly well that Isis's contract did not stipulate monogamy, as did Juan Pablo, she was sure. Betting on contract marriages—whether they would happen, whether they would be renewed, who would contract whom—was more popular than betting on horse races, and even the littlest details of those contracts were public knowledge. Though that didn't make it a respectable pastime.

"And?" Rocío pretended obliviousness, hiding her distaste, wanting to see where he was going with this.

"Did you hear what I said? She was kissing someone else."

"Oh! Do you know who it was?"

"That choreographer guy, the one who's missing. Obviously."

He was probably one of the ones who always bet on contract marriages exploding into litigation at their end.

"Where was this?"

"On La Quinta. By the shrine. Inside the grounds, closer to the stela than the street."

"Was that on Monday?" Rocío asked fake-idly.

"I said a week ago. Was Monday a week ago? No, it was not. I saw them last Thursday."

"I see. What about Monday? Did you see Ministrx Soler and her lover then? You could be a big help with our investigation ..." She let insinuation creep into her voice.

He leaned forward. "I'm sorry to tell you, Advocate, that Ministrx Soler was out of town on Monday."

She let the *Advocate* slide. "But since you're so observant, if you were in La Quinta on Monday, you might have seen something related to his disappearance."

"I didn't say I was in La Quinta on Monday. I wasn't. Aren't you a little off topic, Advocate? Shouldn't you be focusing on what happened here tonight?"

Rocío hid a sigh. "You're right, of course. What do you think—"

"I'll tell you what happened and help you get your investigation started. It's obvious. Ministrx Soler has a bad temper. She found out he was a philanderer and killed him and his lover right here. People don't just appear out of thin air."

She stared at him blankly. Martine and Loeis's identities couldn't still be a secret. The party guests had been gossiping in the music room for hours now without enough advocates to keep them all separate, and Paloma, Gumersinda and Críspula couldn't have been the only one to recognize them.

Is he trying to divert my attention from Prokofiev's abduction? It's a strange tactic, doomed to failure with the bodies right there.

Is this what I looked like to Hala when she said I was in denial? He's so certain, and he's so wrong.

It didn't mean he wasn't involved somehow. Or that he wasn't a bully. On the other hand, he might be merely a smug self-important man who did not believe his cousins were dead. If so, Rocío felt sorry for him. This part never got any easier.

"Señorx Ricci. I'm afraid that's not what happened. Didn't anyone tell you who they are, the two dead people?"

"Críspula told me some nonsense about it being our cousins, but she's wrong, it can't be." He read something in her expression and shifted uneasily in his chair. "What?"

"You didn't see the victims?" she asked carefully.

"I never saw their faces. Your partner didn't let me get close enough."

"I'm sorry. The victims have been identified as Martine and Loeis Carter de Herrera."

"No." His face stiffened.

"It would help if you confirmed it's them."

She slid two photographs across the table to him.

He looked at her another moment, apprehension clear on his face. "It can't be."

The denial of pain made a person hold still like that, but so did the decision to lie. And you could murder someone and still feel regret and pain and anger, as he clearly did. The regret could be for the loss. The things unsaid. Or things that couldn't be unsaid. Or it could be something more, something connected to the murders. Recognizing an emotion did not mean Rocío knew why someone had that emotion.

Juan Pablo's left hand was closer to the photo of Loeis than his right was to the one of Martine, and his eyes stayed focused on Loeis. She thought they had been close.

"It's them." The smug façade slid away, and he looked young and shocked and, for the first time, vulnerable. "Some of the others said … but I didn't believe them."

"They're your cousins?"

"Yes." Juan Pablo pulled himself up straighter and tried to set his face in a politician's mask. It didn't quite work, as his mouth and eyes were too pinched. "We went to the University together. I played pato with Loeis. We were friends."

"Can you think of anyone who may have wanted to hurt him?"

He shook his head in wobbly denial. "Hurt him?"

"He and Martine were murdered," Rocío said, moved to gentleness in spite of herself.

Murder was shocking, hard to grasp, upending everything people thought they knew. People didn't want to believe it had happened even when the photos stared them in the face. Juan Pablo could be dissimulating, but if he wasn't, Rocío found she didn't want to be the one to puncture his illusions about mortality and how the whole world loved him and his kind, as annoying as that attitude was.

He made a soft pained sound in his throat and looked at the picture again. "Are you sure? Maybe it was an accident."

Then again, maybe it wasn't so easily punctured. "Quite sure."

He winced away from her words.

"When is the last time you saw either of them?" she asked.

"Earlier this week. Tuesday. They came to dinner at the ministrx's house."

She noted he referred to it as the ministrx's house even though he also lived there. Most political staffers lived with their employers cum family members.

"Because they have connections to the Sub-Committee on Legal Affairs?"

"Because they're his cousins, and he likes to keep in touch with his family."

"Did they seem worried about anything?"

"No."

"Did they mention anyone threatening them?"

"No."

"Anyone hanging around who shouldn't?"

"Nothing like that. It was just a normal dinner. Loeis talked about horses. Martine talked about her job in her mother's business. We talked about our friends."

"Had they fallen out with anyone lately? Friends or family?"

"No. I told you, everything was normal. They were normal, and now they're ..." His face twisted, and then he clamped down on his emotions and pushed back from the table. "Stop asking me these questions. Please." His voice cracked.

"Have some water." Rocío made a show of flipping through her pad while he filled a glass and drank with quick sips that were like sobs. By the time he finished, his breathing had evened out. "I just need to ask you a few routine questions. What time did you get to Ministrx Soler's house today?"

"I don't know. Ask Críspula or Gumersinda. They keep track of that sort of thing."

"So you came with them?"

"No, I came with Ministrx O'Higgins." He straightened, as if the self-importance of that statement gave him strength.

"What's your best guess?"

"If I had to guess"—he made it sound like an undue burden—"just before two. For the meeting."

"Did you see anything amiss or unusual, either at the meeting or during the party?"

"Everyone was acting strange, but that's to be expected."

"What do you mean?"

"I can't really tell you the details ... confidential, you know. But the lieutenant governor's arrest and the accusations of treason are of great concern to everyone on the sub-com. A great many people are going to be questioned about their role in that." He tugged his shirt cuffs down, as if he would personally be cleaning house for the sub-com.

"Any of the ministrx on the sub-com?"

"I can't answer that question. Cempol knows."

"Do you get along with the ministrx?"

"Of course, I'm invaluable to them. Are we done? I'm sure I'm needed."

"I'm sure you are. If you could just let the advocate from Villalta know I said you can go, that will make it easier."

She folded a stick of gum into her mouth and watched him leave. Hala caught the door before it closed and came in.

"Well?" Hala asked, her voice vibrating with repressed energy.

Rocío eyed her narrowly. "His self-certainty makes it hard to tell anything. He dislikes Isis, that's for sure. I couldn't guess how far he'd take that dislike, and I didn't want to push too hard and spook him. But I doubt he killed the de Herreras." She paused, giving Hala a chance to share. When she didn't, Rocío asked, "It's all set up?"

"Advocate Cetz assigned one of her advocates to follow him. Anything he does in the next twenty-four hours, we'll know about."

"That's not all you came to say."

"The coroner said they were killed this morning, between twelve and sixteen hours ago."

Rocío checked her watch. Almost midnight. "So between eight a.m. and twelve p.m."

"More Villalta advocates have arrived. They can question everyone who's left. Advocate Cetz has everything under control here, and any forensic evidence requires careful analysis by the techs in a lab. Therefore, our course of action is clear."

"It is?"

"Yes." Hala gestured for Rocío to get up. "We need to return to the last place Eugenio Fernández killed and warn the people living there."

CHAPTER 14

THEY ARGUED ALL the way to the haunted castle.

"It's too obvious, Hala. A copycat killer is not going to make the original killer's lair his lair. I should be questioning the witnesses at Isis's house."

"The myth of the brilliant criminal mind is just a myth—you know that. Most often they're normal people trying to do right with incorrect tools when society has failed them. Then there are the desperate and damaged and those seeking relief. Often they don't think through their crimes because they result from flare-ups of emotion and no one ever taught them to follow the trail of their own thoughts, feelings and actions. If they aren't merely mentally deficient."

Rocío winced. Hala was tired if she was reverting to mental elitism. They all were. The cold coffee in the carriage hadn't done much to combat the strain of murder and the damp chill of the night. Paloma's eyes were glassy, and she hadn't said a word since they'd entered the carriage. She had also taken the unbelievable news that Hala and Rocío suspected necromancy, not imported magic, with an aplomb Rocío thought had more to do with emotional exhaustion and overload than anything else.

"Not okay," Rocío said.

Hala looked blank, and then her brain caught up with what her mouth had said, and she winced. "My apologies."

"None of those things apply here. Except that our killer is possibly damaged. And possibly seeking relief. This wasn't a desperate, unplanned murder committed in a welter of emotion. It was planned and orchestrated with—"

"Flare."

"I was going to say cunning and intelligence. And cruelty, to place them in the middle of the party and reveal them that way."

"The placement of the bodies was careful, yes," Hala said. "But is that what you think of the murders themselves?"

Rocío squeezed her eyes shut, picturing the gaping mouths of the wounds whether she wanted to or not. "No. That was rage."

"So we have uncareful murder and careful body disposal."

"Making it likely that Isis was targeted. I should be questioning the witnesses."

"Advocate Cetz has it under control. There were only a dozen people left to interview."

"But"—Paloma faltered under Hala's and Rocío's gazes—"but if someone is targeting the ministrx, why do it this way? Why murder two people she's not particularly close to and leave them at her house? Why them?"

"I suspect if we knew the answers to those questions, we'd know who the murderer is," Hala said.

"We don't know enough for it to make sense. And where is Aleksandr Prokofiev? Or his body? If any dead bodies were going to turn up in Isis's house, I would expect his."

Hala shook her head and stared at the darkness behind the window, no doubt running her own calculations. The carriage lurched through a particularly bad pothole, and Rocío slid to the edge of her seat. She settled back, bracing her feet against the opposite seat. Considering the road barely existed between the rural area of Villalta and the equally rural area of Roxal, Tomás was doing an excellent job driving the carriage.

"So you don't think Ministrx Soler killed them?" Paloma asked.

"All other arguments aside, I saw her face," Rocío said. "Shock, revulsion, horror … the murderer could feel all those things for various reasons, but she was saddened, too.”

“A murderer doesn’t have to be a monster,” Hala said. “She could murder and feel sad that it was a necessity, as she saw it in her mind.”

“You don’t think she did it, either,” Rocío said.

“I don’t form conclusions in advance of evidence, but”—Hala held up a finger—“but I’m convinced the murders did not take place in her house or on its grounds. For one thing, there is no place in the house private enough to torture and dismember two people while the staff prepared the house for a party with fifty guests. The staff were in and out of every room and outbuilding all day.”

“The only people to arrive before the ministrx were delivery people,” Paloma said. “Ice, chicha, wine. The foodstuffs were delivered earlier in the week.”

“And Ministrx Soler hasn’t left since returning to her home yesterday. Of course, the fact that the bodies were hidden from sight suggests that the murders could have been hidden from sight in a similar way, but the sheer complexity of such an undertaking makes it unlikely. The simpler explanation is that they were not killed at Ministrx Soler’s house,” Hala said.

“You don’t really know enough about necromancy to say that,” Rocío said.

Hala tilted her head in concession. “But we didn’t find blood, even using scent hounds from Villalta. It’s difficult to clean up so much blood so thoroughly.”

“So why are we going to the haunted castle?” Paloma asked tiredly. “I don’t understand what we’re doing. I know we sent Paco with messages, but shouldn’t we check on the other members of the sub-com? And why does it matter where Eugenio Fernández killed someone?”

“Do you know what the haunted castle is?” Hala asked.

“A tourist attraction?” Paloma said.

“Yes, but why is it a tourist attraction?”

“I don’t know. Why is it important?”

“In the normal course of things, it’s not. But before its current incarnation, it was the place where Eugenio Fernández killed at least eight people."

"Hala," Rocío said, "stop lecturing Paloma." Rocío turned to the younger woman. "Hala thinks someone is copying Eugenio Fernández Suárez. Using necromancy the way he did. Killing the way he killed. Maybe even killing where he killed."

Paloma still looked confused.

"The way Martine and Loeis were killed, the way their hands and feet were amputated—that's how Fernández killed people, to fuel his necromantic magic. I'm sorry, but we think someone killed your friends that way, and that he or she will keep killing." Rocío kept it simple and watched Paloma carefully, ready to offer comfort or a handkerchief or catch her if she launched into reactive violence. Though that seemed unlikely.

"Oh." Paloma merely folded her hands together and squeezed them tightly. She swallowed. "But I still don't understand why we're going to the haunted castle right now."

"Are you okay?" Hala asked.

"I'm ..." Paloma bit her lip. "Just, can you answer the question?"

Okay. If she wants to pretend everything is normal, we can do that. For a little while. "Hala thinks that if this killer is imitating Fernández in one way, they may be imitating him in other ways, such as making the castle their home base."

"And killing all its inhabitants," Hala said, exasperated.

"Thus taking us back to the beginning of this argument," Rocío said. "I think it's unlikely and possibly not as urgent as warning Oshinsky, Cempol and the other members of the sub-com that we suspect necromancy. We couldn't trust Paco with such sensitive information. The chaskis read all the messages."

"The CJC and Cempol are already aware of the threat to the ministrx, even if they don't know the exact nature of that threat," Hala said, "but no one is going to the castle to warn the people who live there. Or to see if they're still alive. There's a possibility the killer was already there. I doubt the forensics team will get anything from the crime scene at Soler's house. It was too contaminated. There were sheep on the back road. *Sheep.* This is a potentially uncontaminated scene, if we get there in time."

"If we *don't* get there in time," Rocío said.

"You know I hope they're alive."

"And that's why we're in the carriage," Rocío said.

"So you're not really arguing?" Paloma asked.

"Yes," Rocío said.

"No," Hala said. She raised an eyebrow at Rocío. "And we're all speaking the same language. Imagine if we weren't."

Rocío resorted to an obscene gesture, knowing it would make Hala laugh. Which it did. Paloma covered her mouth, slightly shocked, if Rocío judged correctly. "Sorry, Paloma. Yes, we're not arguing."

"No, we're not arguing," Hala hiccupped out.

"Shut up."

Unsurprisingly, no lights were on in the castle when they arrived. Hala's pocket watch read just after one a.m. The castle was a darker shape of walls and turrets against the night sky and the low moon, which was the color of lace stored for decades.

Hala and Rocío climbed out of the carriage, leaving Paloma sleeping. Rocío stretched her back, and Hala swung her left leg a few times to work out the stiffness. Tomás did horse things. He had stopped in front of the gate, a big iron thing in an old Ka wall. It was shut.

"Who lives here now?" Rocío asked quietly, trying to recall old gossip.

"An Intaa family. They've been here three years. They're still calling it Luken's Folly."

That name referred to the Iberex who had brought the castle to La Bene piece by piece from a mountain village on Iberon's northern border with Gal. He'd rebuilt it here, lost his fortune in the Iberon-Gal-Enkladt war, couldn't maintain the castle and committed suicide by hanging himself in the highest tower. To top it all off, his cousin found him and then broke his neck running down the stairs. In the confusion, no one thought to ask why he'd been screaming, and Luken's body wasn't discovered for another day. The property was truly untouchable after that; no one could afford it anyway, and it was left to crumble for about fifty years. That much was urban legend based in history. Rocío had ridden here on her bicycle with her brother and cousins as a kid, goading each other to sneak through the gates. She might be about to live a childhood dream. Unfortunately.

"When did Eugenio Fernández Suárez start squatting here?" Rocío asked.

Hala tried the gate without effect. "Best estimate is 332, based on the condition of the oldest body discovered."

"So who moves into a moldy castle where eight people have been murdered in a horrible fashion?"

"People who don't believe in ghosts." Hala took her lock picks from her pocket and knelt. Without looking at Rocío, she said, "What? That's a scientific statement."

"I didn't say anything."

"You didn't need to."

"You can't even see my face in the dark."

"Still didn't need to." Something clicked in the lock, and Hala leaned closer, presumably to hear better.

Tomás approached with the lamp and directed it over Hala's shoulder. "You shouldn't be doing that," he said.

"The Intaa don't believe in Benerex ghosts, only their own. The family gives tours and hosts haunted dinners. A surprising number of people like to be scared, or titillated, I suppose," Hala said.

"That's creepy. Are *you* going to stop her, Tomás?"

He grunted.

"I think that's the point," Hala said. "From all I've heard, the family seems remarkably well adjusted."

"Acknowledging the horrors contained in the horror of the soul," Rocío murmured.

"Chief Udinesi was concerned when they moved in, but having them here has actually cut down on vandalism and reports of ghosts." Hala twisted the bottom tool, and the lock clicked again. "Ah, that's it." The gate creaked open under her hand.

"Why do you know that about the chief of Roxal? That sounds like something I would know."

"Personal interest."

"Did either of you hear what I said?" Tomás asked. "Aside from the illegality of breaking and entering, if there's a murderer around, you shouldn't just leave the gate unlocked."

"That lock wasn't keeping anyone safe," Hala said. "Especially if the murderer is already inside."

"Chief Udinesi was responding to ghost reports?" Rocío asked. "Why wasn't the University ... never mind. What's your plan? You do have one, don't you?"

Hala extracted a vial from a thigh pocket. It held a suspiciously yellow liquid. "If there are dogs and they're male, this'll distract them."

Rocío prioritized her many questions. "And if they're not?"

"I have darts dipped in Somon."

"Dare I ask what is in that vial that only affects male dogs?"

"Urine from female dogs in estrus."

Tomás made a choked noise.

"In es—seres celestiales, you carry that around with you?" Rocío raised her hands in disbelief. "No, don't answer that. Fine. We get past the dogs, what then?"

"We reconnoiter. Peer in windows. See if everything looks normal."

"Because that's easy to tell about a haunted castle in the dark. Are you sure this isn't my plan?"

"It is lacking in some details. But if the murderer is here, I want to catch them. And if the family is here, I want to warn them."

Rocío could tell from Hala's voice that she was going to do this, come heavy wind or high seas, and she was sure Hala could tell she would go along with her, whether she thought it was wise or not.

"I'll be right back," Hala said and walked into the dark.

"You're not going to stop her, are you?" Tomás raised the lamp so he could look at her face.

"She's very goal oriented sometimes," Rocío said.

He muttered something she couldn't hear. He added, "At least don't involve Paloma."

Rocío started to pace, trying to keep warm and to think. Did her reluctance to wake Paloma stem from good motivations or bad, and did it matter?

"You and Hala have been detectives for years," Tomás said. "If there's trouble over this, you can weather it better than she can."

"Do you think she'll be a good advocate?" Rocío asked, realizing the question was impolitic only after she asked it.

"I think she deserves the chance to try."

As Tomás, an abandoned street child, had deserved a chance with the CJC? Interesting that even with such different backgrounds, he saw something of himself in Paloma.

"No," Rocío said. "I'm not going to wake her."

"Good. I need to check the horses." He took the lantern with him, and Rocío opened her eyes wide, trying to hurry her vision into adjusting to the dark.

Hala reappeared and waved Rocío through the gate. As she closed it behind her, it creaked again, too appropriately spooky in the night. Their footsteps crunched on the gravel drive, and insects chirped, a reassurance that, though it was easy to imagine everything was dead in the dark, the world was alive around them and a necromancer was probably not waiting to jump out at them. Probably. The smells of moist earth, sheep manure and pasture wafted from the fields to either side; Rocío wasn't sure how the sheep contributed to the haunted castle effect, though the structure loomed convincingly over the ragged geometries of hedges and flower beds.

Rocío only had time for an impression of a dilapidated silhouette before two moving blurs barreled out of the hedges, frantically barking.

"Um, Hala."

"I see them." Hala raised a blowpipe to her mouth. *Pfffft. Thunk.*

The first dog yelped. Then the second. They stumbled forward a few more steps and emerged from the shadow of the hedge.

Something was wrong.

They were a lot smaller than Rocío had expected guard dogs to be. And those barks had been higher pitched.

The dogs slowed and toppled over and lay still.

"Oh, no, no, no." Hala fumbled with a pocket. "Antagonist. Antagonist."

Rocío loped over and bent to examine them. Floppy ears, silky coats. *Tiny* bodies. She straightened to stare incredulously at Hala. "Did you just paralyze two papillon puppies?" Only one of the cutest breeds of dog in existence and definitely not guard dogs. Though she supposed it would still hurt if they bit.

Preparing a syringe, Hala knelt beside them. She injected one and then the other before collapsing to a sitting position. "I didn't *know*; it's too dark to see them well. And I didn't paralyze them, I sedated them."

Rocío sat to put her hand on the warm little bodies. Their ribs expanded and contracted as their lungs pumped.

"They'll recover now that I've injected them with a counteracting agent. That was too high a dose for such small dogs." Hala rubbed her hands over her face.

Rocío slumped to the ground, suddenly feeling the exhaustion of the last few days and the gray miasma that always clogged her senses after witnessing the aftermath of a violent death. "Oh, Hala."

"I know," she whispered tightly. "I think I must be more unsettled than I realized to have made such a mistake."

Rocío leaned her shoulder into Hala's and rubbed her back. She breathed in and breathed out, trying to capture a sense of calm. The chill from the ground seeped through her pants.

"Maybe this was not the best plan," Hala said at last.

"Hello?" a man called. "If that's you again, Antonio, I'm telling the advocates this time."

Rocío scrambled to her feet, Hala a beat behind her. *Well, some-one's here and not dead.*

The man seemed to materialize out of the darkness. He was very tall and big-boned, wearing only a towel around his hips.

"Not Antonio," Rocío said. "We're—"

"What did you do to my dogs? Did you—"

"They'll wake up in approximately fifty-five minutes. I—"

"Señorx—"

"What did you do to my dogs?" he roared, gathering them into his arms.

"Señorx," Rocío said, "we're detectives from the CJC. Your dogs are just sedated. They will fully recover." She didn't look at Hala. *They'd better.*

"We were concerned for your safety," Hala said.

His whole posture spoke of disbelief.

Rocío talked faster. "And we had some concerns that someone had murdered you and your family."

Hala clicked her tongue in disapproval.

"Is this some sort of prank? I know Virgilio; you're not from Roxal CJC."

"We're from Miraflores CJC, not Roxal."

"I want to see identification."

Rocío and Hala offered their ID booklets.

He opened Rocío's and squinted at it, but while he might have been able to see her photo in this light, he certainly couldn't see the small gray type.

"You'd better come inside." He cradled the puppies closer to his chest and led Rocío and Hala up the hill.

Rocío balked at the doorway. The lintel sagged, and the gap between it and the top of the doors looked big enough to climb through. The rest of the castle was in similar shape: moss covered, with stones missing from its façade, and was that a tree growing out of one of the windows? One of the turrets seemed determinedly crooked. She rubbed her eyes—still crooked.

The doors creaked as loudly as the gate as he pulled them open. Inside, an old-fashioned candle lantern hung from a hook in the wall, throwing more shadows than illumination. Dust puffed up under their feet. The plaster was stained and peeling where it wasn't covered by moldering tapestries. Just as Rocío was starting to wonder if this was their killer—puppies notwithstanding—the man pushed aside one of the tapestries, revealing a modern-looking door and behind it a living area that was obviously not meant for visitors.

Rocío's shoulders relaxed a bit as she took in the whitewashed walls, the electrified lights, the clean carpet and the comfortable, intact furniture. The man put the puppies—even more adorable now that Rocío could see them clearly, their large silky ears flopped halfway over their white, brown and black faces—on a chair with teeth marks on the arms before turning to examine Rocío and Hala.

Rocío examined him in turn. He was big in his bones, dark skinned and clean-shaven, his features similar to those of Yoru immigrants but with a more pointed chin and a higher-bridged nose than they characteristically had. Whether the difference was his individual physiognomy or an ethnic subgroup's variation was impossible to determine without further data, as Hala would say. He didn't have any distinguishing marks, and his towel was from Nadal, an exclusive and expensive clothier. Nadal linens were the only linens Rocío's mother would allow in her house.

He held up one ID booklet and then the other, comparing the photos to their faces, and then read through all the pages detailing their employment in the CJC, their physical descriptions, their oath of office to serve the community and La Bene's Citizen's Bill of Rights. Finally he grunted and handed them back.

"You may be who you say you are, but you still either broke the lock on my gate or climbed my walls to come here. You are unaccompanied by the local authorities, and you have shown me no papers to say you have the right to do these things here, which is not in Miraflores." His speech, while fluent, flowed and paused in a way typical of someone who had learned Benerex later in life. Rocío had not heard those specific patterns before. "And you have some absurd story about danger. Explain."

Coming from a man who made his living off a murder castle, that was a bit rich. "Two people were killed today," Rocío said.

"We have reason to believe the killer has been here," Hala said rapidly, as if he might not notice the enormity of what she was saying if she said it fast enough. "You and your family could be in danger. We need to search the building, question your family and staff, and check for evidence. Have you had any disturbances recently? You thought someone named Antonio was on the grounds—who is that?"

"And yet I understand that the detectives of community justice centers still follow procedures, even when it is murder."

"What about your family and their safety? Your staff?" Rocío asked.

"My family is asleep in their beds. As are my staff. The danger you are looking for isn't here."

"How many in your family?" Rocío asked.

He glowered at her. "My spouse, our two children, her sister, my sister and her spouse and their one child, my mother and her sister, and two cousins on my father's side."

"Twelve people." A small household for La Bene. "How old are the cousins?"

"They are both in their early twenties."

"How many staff members?"

"Those are all the questions I'm going to answer until you come back with Virgilio. *If* my dogs have recovered, I will talk to you then."

"They will," Hala said. "I assure you."

"What is your name, señorx?" Rocío asked. Hala shifted, no doubt uncomfortable with Rocío admitting they had charged in without even knowing the names of the castle's inhabitants.

"Anozie Ilozumba Castillo."

Castillo, or castle, for his home. "Thank you, Señorx Castillo. Please make sure everyone is here tomorrow—later today, I mean. They may have seen something they didn't realize was significant at the time, and it would be very helpful if they were all available to speak to the advocates who come."

"You really think a murderer was here?" he asked, rubbing his hand over his head, showing uncertainty for the first time.

"We believe they either have been here or will come," Rocío said, holding eye contact and leaning forward. "You need to warn your family. You should consider removing them from danger right now. You could leave your home for a short while, stay somewhere else. This person is extremely dangerous."

He held her gaze, and Rocío saw uncertainty there. "I will think about what you have said."

"If anything—anything at all—happens, send for Roxal CJC. I

hope that Detective Haddad and I will be able to return with the other advocates. But if we can't, here are our cards."

She held them out, and he accepted them automatically. She let her hand brush his and concentrated her limited magic skills. It was harder when she couldn't say the focusing words out loud, but she didn't want him to know she was checking for magic use. What she found wouldn't be admissible to an adjudicator like the official swabs were, but at least it gave her a baseline to judge his honesty when they questioned him later.

Her hand tingled. He'd used magic recently, though she couldn't tell more than that.

He asked them to wait a moment and left the room. Hala ostentatiously stuck her hands in her hip pockets and rocked on her feet but did not conduct any sort of search. Which would be illegal. And ill-advised at that point.

He returned in a dark red silk robe with a padlock in one hand.

Hala opened her mouth, and Rocío glared at her. She mouthed, "Do not say anything." He escorted them silently to the gate, which he closed firmly behind them.

Rocío turned her gaze on her partner.

Hala rubbed the back of her neck. "I need a coffee."

"You need some sleep, and so do I."

"Sorry." Hala opened the carriage door and nudged Tomás awake.

"Did you find anything?" he mumbled, rubbing his eyes.

"The Castillo family, alive and well."

He grunted and climbed onto the driver's bench. "The only place we're going is back to the CJC." He tried to glare at them, but his eyes were puffy from sleep, so it wasn't very intimidating.

"We know," Rocío said.

It felt almost warm inside the carriage. Paloma was curled in one corner with a blanket over her head and another over her legs. She stirred but didn't wake as the carriage jerked into motion. Rocío wrapped herself in a blanket.

"That was a mistake," Hala said.

"You don't say." Rocío leaned her head back. "But I'm glad to hear you say it all the same."

They'd had a few rocky years at the beginning of their partnership while they negotiated what was appropriate behavior before, during and after a mistake. Hala always apologized now, and Rocío thought she herself had gained a certain ... flexibility of mind regarding Hala's approach to life and restorative justice (which did not usually stray this far into dubious territory).

"We should have knocked on the door," Hala said.

"Sometimes the simplest way is the best," Rocío agreed.

"I did so want to test the urine theory."

"Test?" Rocío said, sitting up straight and glaring at her. "Hala, they could have been mastiffs instead of papillons!"

"It worked in the lab."

"You *promised* not to test these things when I'm there." She kicked Hala's seat. Hala just smirked, but Paloma groaned and ducked her head farther into her blanket. "Piérdalo, did I wake the baby advocate?" Rocío asked, her internal filter apparently having taken the nap she really, really wanted. Though it would be one less energy drain if Hala was right and she didn't have to guard against Paloma.

"Rocío," Hala said, half in reprimand, half an echo of Rocío's own incredulity.

"Seres celestiales, I know. I know I shouldn't call her that. She's just so, I don't know, earnest and considered."

Traits that would make a good advocate, if Rocío didn't see Paloma in a warped mirror held up by her parents.

"So you wish she were more like me," Hala said. "Admit it, habibti —you love me just the way I am."

"Fine, I love you just the way you are. And she's not a baby. It was wrong of me to say so. She did good today. She didn't hear me, and we salvaged something from tonight, so it wasn't a complete disaster. Let's just hope none of the mistakes tomorrow are ours."

CHAPTER 15

Even though it was almost three a.m., the Miraflores CJC was
blazing with lights. Rocío got Paloma, who bore a striking resemblance to a sleep-drugged two-year-old, headed towards the crash
room downstairs to get some more rest and then joined Hala and
Oshinsky in the briefing room.

"Why wasn't I given backup, Chief?" Hala demanded. Her hair
was sticking straight up where she'd been running her fingers
through it.

Reflexively Rocío licked her fingers and rubbed the spot she knew
from long experience looked like it was balding when she slept in
carriages, which she was not, thank you very much.

Oshinsky's whole body was drooping with weariness, from her
eyes to her shoulders, except her hands, which were locked tightly at
her waist. Something was wrong.

"Hala," Rocío said.

"There's been a murder," Oshinsky said. "Murders."

"I know," Hala said, just shy of shouting. "That's why I needed
backup. Fifty guests. Twenty staff. The Villalta medical coroner."

"No, there've been several more murders. Here. Isabella Corona
Costurerx and Mizn bin Selasa Jardín de los fieles. Isabella Corona
was Ministrx O'Higgins's longtime cook, and I don't have to tell you
Mizn bin Selasa was employed by the Bellis."

"What?" Hala asked.

Rocío sank into the nearest chair, sucking air through her teeth. Everyone knew of Mizn bin Selasa.

"Who?" Hala asked.

Okay, maybe not everyone. "He just won the Günneh prize for the garden he created for the Bellis. It's as beautiful as Ravela Liu's choreography for *Angharad's Ride*," Rocío said, naming her favorite dance.

"Oh. Oh no."

Hala's comprehension of what that loss meant, even if she didn't appreciate the form, saved her from getting kicked. By Rocío. Hard.

"Don't tell me—the hands and feet?" Hala asked with a lack of proper grammar unusual for her.

"Amputated and missing," Oshinsky said.

"The murders are connected, then." Hala shoved a chair out of her way, the legs screeching on the wooden floor, and started to pace.

"There's more. Isabella Corona and Mizn bin Selasa were disemboweled."

Rocío's knees went weak. If she hadn't already been sitting, she would have fallen. She propped her head on her hands and breathed deeply, in and out. *Could we have prevented this if we'd told everyone our suspicions? It seemed so unlikely. We* wanted *it to be unlikely.* "Hala ..."

"Cempol is involved," Oshinsky said grimly. "And not just because of the ministrx. Cempol is saying the most outrageous things, throwing suspicions around—" She checked herself, pressing her lips tightly together.

"Hala," Rocío said. "We should have—"

"After the battle everyone is a general," Hala snapped. "We did what we thought was right at the time. That's the only thing anyone can ever do." She ran her hands through her hair again, and Rocío knew she was feeling the same mix of guilt and dread, no matter what she said.

"What are you talking about?" Oshinsky demanded quietly. It felt like she was shouting. Rocío winced in anticipation.

"Cempol is saying it's necromancy, aren't they?" Hala asked.

"They are." Oshinsky grabbed Hala's arm and held her in place.

"And how do you know that?" Her blue-eyed glare was always disconcerting.

"We broke into the University vault of forbidden books." Hala meet her glare head-on.

"Because we had the same suspicions," Rocío said, "and we needed more information. But it wasn't conclusive, so we didn't bring it to you. We would have eventually."

"Since when has something needed to be conclusive? And breaking and entering? Breaking your oath of office? And then telling me about it? That's grounds for dismissal."

"That's not the point right now," Hala said. "We need to compare these murders."

"Chief, it seemed ridiculous." Rocío gestured helplessly. "Like we were dredging up childhood nightmares and inserting them into an investigation. Would you have believed us? You don't even believe Cempol, not entirely."

Oshinsky released Hala, folded her arms, and stared at Rocío for several long seconds. "We are not done, merely postponing this conversation. Tell me about your murders."

As Hala recounted the events of the evening, Oshinsky pressed her lips together so hard they almost disappeared, but she didn't interrupt. Their break-in at the haunted castle sounded even worse in Hala's concise summary.

"I see," Oshinsky said, and she sounded like she had stepped back from the shaky edge of rage. "The Cempol coroner gave a similar preliminary time of death for Isabella Corona and Mizn bin Selasa. They were hit over the head before ... the torture. The coroner said both the vivisection and amputation were performed while they were still alive. Or at least they were alive when it started." Her voice rasped on the last word.

"But they weren't stabbed?" Rocío asked. Work came first, before feelings of relief that Oshinsky wasn't going to take them off the case or guilt about past decisions she couldn't change. She'd wallow later.

"No. There was also more blood at the scene than could be attributed to their deaths."

"Blood typing should show whether it matches the de Herreras," Hala said.

"It may. The scene is quite messy. The bodies were found in a garden shed at the back of Ministrx O'Higgins's property during a search for the person who attacked him."

"Attacked him?" Rocío asked, her voice rising. "What happened?"

"I don't know. Cempol has restricted access to him. What I do know is that he was attacked between midnight and one a.m. in his house, and he's in the hospital with serious injuries. It's not clear whether he is conscious or able to answer questions."

"That's just enough time for Juan Pablo Ricci to have returned home. The advocate following him might have seen something," Rocío said.

"Ricci lives with Ministrx O'Higgins." Hala started to pace again. "Did Ministrx O'Higgins identify his attacker?"

"I don't know."

Rocío her face, trying to think. "So we have four murders, possibly all committed on Ministrx O'Higgins's property. The de Herreras were family. You said Isabella Corona was his cook. But Mizn bin Selasa was María Paz Belli's celebrity gardener. Why was he at Ministrx O'Higgins's house?"

"We don't have an answer to that yet," Oshinsky said. She looked like she wanted to pace but Hala was taking up all the room.

"Those poor people and their families." Not that anyone who would torture and kill would worry about who else they were hurting.

"This seems to indicate that someone is indeed targeting the members of the sub-com," Hala said. "Though this is a rapid escalation. It's likely something triggered this new stage. I only wish I could believe it was something we had done."

"Hala," Oshinsky said in a strained voice.

Hala frowned at her. "You know what I meant. You make similar statements. Last week—"

"That was not a quadruple murder," Oshinsky said. "Just don't say things like that where anyone else can hear."

"I wouldn't."

"Getting back on topic," Rocío said, "why is Cempol stonewalling us?"

Oshinsky swore again, tipping her head back and staring at the ceiling. Or, no—staring at Maurata's office, if she could see through several floors.

"Oh no," Rocío said. "What did he do?"

"The usual. Pissed off Dhavale by telling him how to do his job. Dhavale will allow you two to interview Ministrx O'Higgins, I assume because of your murders, but only when they say so, and only with a Cempol liaison present."

"Okay." The full weight of the day came crashing down on Rocío. She yawned, eyes watering. "But not now, right? Then there's nothing else we can do tonight."

"Don't think I've forgotten your ill-considered actions," Oshinsky said.

"No, Chief."

"No, Chief."

"I want you back at the haunted—at Luken's Folly tomorrow. Where you will proceed with *care*."

"Yes, Chief."

"Yes, Chief."

Rocío opened blurry eyes to find Paloma standing over her with a flashlight pointed at her. "What? What time is it?" It was always dark in the CJC's crash room, and at least one person was still snoring. Knowing the next day was going to start way too soon, she had stumbled down here after their conversation with Oshinsky, grabbed a bunk and passed out rather than returning home. "Is it time to go?"

She propped herself up on an elbow, turned on the table lamp and took in the other woman's appearance. First, she looked entirely too fresh and neat after the night they'd had, and she was wearing clean clothes. *Youth.* Rocío pushed away the flash of resentment. Second, Paloma's pupils were dilated, which could be the dim lighting, but her face was a rigid mask of non-expression so strong it was an expression. Plus her feet were planted far apart, and her free hand was in a fist. Rocío was going to go with rage.

"Why didn't you wake me up?" Paloma asked, her lips barely moving.

"When?" Rocío asked, though she had a very good idea of what Paloma meant. *I'm finally trying to make the right decisions for the right reasons, and now she's mad at me.* She sat up and rubbed sleep out of her eyes, feeling at a decided disadvantage.

"At the haunted castle. You shut me out. You don't trust me."

"Paloma, that's not what happened. What Hala and I did was not exactly by the regulations," Rocío said. "We were protecting you."

"You don't have to."

"Actually—"

"You don't. At the very least you should have let me decide for myself."

"Hala and I have been detectives for years. We have leeway you don't."

"You say you were protecting me, but you just don't think I can be a good advocate." Paloma dropped the flashlight on the table. The snoring stopped. It started again.

"That's not true," Rocío protested weakly. It was hard enough convincing herself Paloma would make a good advocate. She wasn't ready to convince Paloma that she was convinced. "As your trainer, it's my job to—"

"I don't need your protection." Paloma jutted her chin out. "I need you to teach me how to do this job and tell me things."

"Paloma—"

"You knew about the necromancy and didn't tell me that, either."

"It was just a theory—there wasn't anything to tell until we found the bodies, and then we told you right away." At least Rocío was on surer ground here. "We didn't even tell the chief."

"Well, here's what you need to know: the advocate following Juan Pablo lost him," Paloma said, and stalked away.

"Wait!"

Paloma didn't stop.

Rocío flopped onto her back. *What a way to start the day.*

"Do you think she's mad at me, too?" Hala asked from the next bed.

"I don't know, Hala," Rocío ground out.

Had Paloma heard Rocío call her a baby advocate last night? *No. Maybe. Piérdalo. What perfect timing.*

CHAPTER 16

"Have you seen any of these people before?" Rocío asked Anozie Ilozumba Castillo. They sat at a long wooden table in the modern non-haunted kitchen of the haunted castle with Anozie, his family and Chief Virgilio Udinesi Montalbán from Roxal CJC.

Rocío set out the photographs of everyone she and Hala had interacted with over the last few days, from María Paz Belli to Ministrx O'Higgins to Shen and Emma, glad that they had found non-gory photos of the victims. The photo of Aleksandr Prokofiev caught on the table's rough surface and flipped over. Rocío reversed it and smoothed her hand over the scarred wood. It was obviously used for cooking preparation as well as eating, and the Castillo family had relaxed a little as they sat. Rocío had asked Paloma, Hala and the forensic techs who were combing the rest of the castle for evidence to stay out of the kitchen while she spoke to the family. Paloma, however, had refused to leave Rocío's side, saying only, "I'm supposed to be learning from you." Rocío had let her stay as a very badly needed and grudgingly accepted peace offering.

Rocío examined the family as they examined the photos. Anozie was so fully covered by a robe that the bare chest and legs of last night might have been a mirage. His sister, his spouse and her sister were slighter but just as tall as Anozie, with hard, capable hands, their arms crossed over their chests and their faces stiff and expressionless. Their head wraps were of block-printed indigo cotton, and their dresses, of satin-weave alpaca wool, had a closer cut than was common in La Bene and had to be homemade, but impeccably so. The mother and aunt were dressed just as well, one in an Iberex-style wool suit with a fitted jacket and vest and wide-cut breeches and the other in a robe similar to Anozie's, except in saffron rather than madder red.

The beads all the women wore around their waists were an interesting cultural contrast to the more familiar clothing. The sister's spouse and the two cousins, also male as far as Rocío could tell, were attired in a similar variety, though one cousin's clothes were of lesser quality. The gold hoops in his ear were not, so Rocío concluded idiosyncrasy of dress rather than different treatment. None of the children were present.

When no one spoke Rocío nudged Chief Udinesi with her elbow. He was a big shaggy-headed man who talked and moved like molasses.

"Come now," he coaxed. "I've explained the difference between community justice officials and the policía you were used to before. Haven't you called me about the kids trespassing? And haven't they been sent home safe to their mothers? Some of them have even done community service for you to pay for the windows and locks they broke. You might be able to tell Detective Rocío something that helps her find the person who has murdered four people."

Nine shuttered pairs of eyes stared back.

Unless they'd been living under a rock, at least one of them must have recognized the picture of Lieutenant Governor Sabato. *This isn't working.*

"Will you give me the tour you do for visitors?" Rocío asked.

"Why?" Anozie asked.

"So I can get a feel for the place. And I was on stage for several years. In the chorus and as an actress. I appreciate a good act, and from your scenery—the castle, I mean—I can tell you've worked hard to create a good performance."

Anozie's sister-in-law, Ijeawele, sat forward. "What were you in?"

Ah, yes—a fellow theater aficionado. It was unlikely that not one of them had caught the Benerex affection for theater or music. Comedy or horror? Or ... *The Necromancer Dies Last.* Do you know it?"

Rocío felt Paloma's legs shift. She would bet Paloma had locked her ankles; Rocío had to resist that automatic defensive posture herself.

"Do I *know* it?" Ijeawele threw a look at Anozie's mother and controlled the excited rise of her voice. "We studied it when we set up the tours. Who did you play?"

"Domenica. The necromancer's—"

"—unsuspecting spouse and last victim."

"I always wanted to be the Ya priestess, but I wasn't old enough, and then I left the stage. Now I get to unmask the bad guys for real. Though generally we try for rehabilitation rather than sending people to the Ka for punishment."

"I heard players think the show is cursed. Like this castle."

"They do. It's hard not to. Things happen that don't when you perform other plays. I got locked in the prop room before our opening performance."

"Why is that a curse?" asked Golibe, the cousin with the gold hoops.

"I tripped over one of the fake dead bodies and landed in the fake blood. Burst all the bags—they're made to burst like that. I was covered in it when they found me ten minutes before the show. Maeve O'Riordan gave me her costume from *Mi Hermana*, and we went on and performed without any prop blood."

"Maeve O'Riordan? She's magnificent." Ijeawele clasped her hands in front of her chest, her eyes shining. "You performed with her?"

"Yes. She was the other lead. She's a very kind person."

"Brother," Ijeawele said to Anozie, "we should do the tour. She will appreciate it."

"I would, very much."

Anozie's mother pursed her lips. "It is better in the dark."

Rocío let her silence challenge the Castillo family's professional pride. Virgilio shifted as if he might speak. She squeezed his arm under the table, and he settled.

"Very well," Anozie's mother said. "Ijeawele will practice on you."

Ijeawele bit her lower lip, but her cheeks crinkled with the smile she tried to hide.

～

"A long time ago, far away from here, a man named Luken Iturburua became very rich building ships. But being rich was not enough. He decided he would do something that had never been done before: he would take apart his castle piece by piece and take it as far away as the world was wide ..."

Ijeawele led them through the castle, gesturing and unfurling a story of a man who couldn't admit he had made a mistake. The staged areas looked even more dilapidated and creepy after the homey kitchen.

As Rocío had hoped, the entire family trailed after Ijeawele, covertly watching Rocío's and Paloma's reactions, although when they reached the stairs to the tower where Luken had hanged himself, Anozie's mother stayed at the bottom. Rocío could see why; it was a long climb. Anozie's mother rejoined them, with Anozie's young daughter, at the bottom where Luken's cousin had broken his neck.

As they walked, the ghost story moved forward through time, through the castle's abandonment and its haunted reputation to Eugenio Fernández's occupation and atrocities. CJC techs looked up, puzzled expressions on their faces as Ijeawele's story briefly pulled them out of the fifth century, with its fingerprint dust and magic detectors, to the fourth century. Rocío followed Ijeawele and her family through an abandoned dining room with a candelabra adorned with cobwebs and into Fernández's killing room. Corpses littered the tables, their internal organs exposed and intestines trailing to the floor. Their hands and feet were amputated and missing. Rocío's stomach clenched, and Virgilio sucked in a pained breath.

On second glance, the corpses' faces held the waxed vacancy of dolls, cousin to the waxed vacancy of death. *I'm never going to look at a doll in the same way again.* The organs looked disturbingly real.

Ijeawele's words caught Rocío's attention. "They say it stormed the night Eugenio Fernández Suarez discovered the secret of becoming a necromancer, as if the Earth and the elements were crying out against his depraved acts," Ijeawele stage-whispered. "He had killed three times already and spied on the Ka shamans who practiced natural magic, part of the cycle of life and death, not divided from it, as Eugenio Fernández Suárez wished to be."

Virgilio leaned in. Even the cousins and the sister were not immune, caught up in her story.

"He took up the skull of his first victim, the young man who had offended him outside the Bank of La Bene. He took up a file and scraped scraped scraped at the bone, catching the bone dust in a silver cup sacred to the Ka, which he had stolen. Into a mortar he placed a handful of needles from the monkey puzzle tree, picked in the rain and smelling of pine.

"Needles from a monkey puzzle tree, as any child of La Bene knows, are poisonous, but Eugenio Fernández Suárez knew they also symbolized longevity to the Ka, which is why they are planted outside their temples and the places mummies are made.

"He added marigold petals, those flowers even the dead can smell, which represent the fragility of life, and he used his pestle and crushed and crushed the golden petals and the needles until they made a sticky paste and the clean smells of life fought the smells of death and blood and stone in the room."

Rocío listened with growing incredulity. Was this recent immigrant from the other side of the world telling a secret hidden in La Bene for centuries—for good reason? Or was it theatrics? She looked around, hoping Yaco was in the room. He wasn't, but Paloma looked sick, and Virgilio was shaking his head. She stepped closer to him.

"He added the paste to the silver cup and he added blood from his latest victim, the older woman who had offended him in the market. He said the prayer that the Ka shamans say over the bodies of their dead.

"He drank from the cup.

"He turned his magic on his heart.

"He fell down, a great pain blooming in his chest like a many-petaled marigold, but his heart did not stop its beating.

"Again he turned his magic on his heart. *Zzzt. Zzzt. Zzzt.*

"His heart stopped.

"He died.

"But his assistant, whose name has been willfully lost to history, turned on the machine doctors had invented to save lives and sent one last shock to Eugenio Fernández Suárez's heart. And it began to pump. He had died in truth and come back, bringing with him a dread magic that only he could wield.

"And that is how Eugenio Fernández Suárez became a necromancer.

"When next he killed, he used the pain and death of his victim to summon a magic unseen in the world until then. He spied on those he believed had wronged him and laid traps for them."

As Ijeawele continued recounting his depravities, Rocío blanked all expression from her face, glad of her theater training. The recipe, stripped of its dramatic trappings, sounded too credible. Virgilio began to stutter a protest, and she leaned close to whisper in his ear. "Later. We need their goodwill."

A glance at Paloma showed she had her hand over her mouth. Virgilio shook his head, but his brains weren't made of molasses, and he didn't speak.

The rest of the tour was a blur, though Rocío clapped at the end without consciously hearing the cue. Virgilio's hands stayed clenched and didn't relax until they entered, of all things, a gift shop. Hala was planted in front of several old photographs hanging on the wall.

"Is this Fernández?" Hala asked.

"There are only three known photos of him," Golibe answered, "and we have originals of two. This is him with his father and sister. This one was taken outside the Academia de música, before the earthquake shook it down and they rebuilt it. And this one was taken after his trial and published in the newspapers to prove he was dead. The original is in the Government Archives." The last photograph showed Fernández on a metal table, head tilted at an unnatural angle to show his neck was broken and to display the ligatures from hanging.

"They can't ... how could they ..." Virgilio asked Rocío in a low voice.

"They're still new to La Bene," she whispered back. "If they don't believe in our ghosts, why would they believe in necromancy? It's just a ghost story to them."

The tendons in his neck were rigid, and his pulse beat visibly at its base. "But how can they ..." he swallowed. "Would you talk to them?"

They both knew he meant more than just talking. *Seres celestiales, if I could run away from necromantic murder, I would.* But Rocío at least had an entire CJC working with her. Virgilio had only two advocates.

"Yes. I'll do it."

"Speaking of photos," Virgilio said loudly to Golibe, clearing his throat, "I promised the señorx I'd be back in time for tea."

"Ijeawele, you were magnificent," Rocío said, turning to the other woman. "I was sweating with nerves. I can't even imagine what it would be like to do your tour in the dark."

Ijeawele inclined her head regally to Rocío, one stage diva to another, and then grinned. "Mother says I give her the chills even though I've been doing it for years."

"Detective Haddad," one of the techs called from the doorway, "Señorx Tuz wants you."

"Excuse me," Hala said.

"Come." Anozie's mother gestured to the kitchen. "We mustn't keep Virgilio's señorx waiting."

The atmosphere as they all crowded around the table again was very different. Ijeawele was still smiling, and Anozie's daughter Eke sat on her mother's lap, eyes big, sucking on the palm candy Rocío had given her with her mother's permission. And Anozie was willing to talk.

"This one," Anozie said, putting his thumb on the photo of the lieutenant governor.

"Did you see him here?" Rocío couldn't picture that.

"Na. I mean in the elections." The others made various motions of agreement.

"These two came on a tour." He picked out the Prokofiev brothers.

"When was that?" Rocío asked, hiding her surprise.

"The beginning of January," Ndidi, Anozie's spouse, said. "I remember because it was so hot and they were suffering, so pale and sweating. We made them sit in the dairy with sweet tea and ice."

"They sang me a song," Eke said. "I didn't understand the words, but they said it was about a mother who loved her daughter very much."

"Anyone else?"

Anozie indicated no. The others as well, except Golibe, who frowned at the photos.

"Yes," Eke said. Her mother clutched her with surprise, and Eke squirmed. "She was here." She lay across the table to tap the photo of Críspula de Herrera Carmona.

"Are you sure, my love?" Ndidi asked, looking at Rocío and Paloma. Rocío smoothed the surprise from her face and hoped Paloma was doing the same. *Críspula de Herrera? It could be a coincidence.* But Rocío didn't believe it was. *Could she be an accomplice of some kind? A duped one?*

"Nuncle, don't you remember? It was the day I passed my swimming test and I interrupted the tour on accident, and some of the guests got mad but you didn't."

"Did this woman get mad?" Rocío asked.

"No. She thought I was funny, but I didn't care. I had to take the test three times, but I passed."

"Was she with someone else?"

"I didn't see," Eke said.

"Señorx Castillo?"

"I don't remember, but so many people come through, and"—he shrugged apologetically—"I'm still learning to tell the Benerex apart. They look very similar to each other."

"How about you?" Rocío asked Golibe.

Frowning, he picked up the photo. "Eke's right. I didn't remember for sure until she said that. I think she was here by herself. A lot of people come alone because their friends are too scared. Should I have … is she dangerous?"

"I don't know yet. When was this?"

"March sixth," Eke said, sitting up straighter. "Does that help?"

"It does, very much. Thank you, Eke. Thank you, everyone, for your help. The techs should be done soon. Then we'll—"

Yaco burst into the room, startling the aunt, who clutched her chest. "Sorry! Rocío, you're done, aren't you? You have to look at this," he said, the words rushing out. "We took photos of all the mirrors in the house and just got the first batch developed. I was showing Hala, and she recognized someone. She said you needed to see right away."

He thrust a stack of photographic paper at her. The photos had the greasy feel of the special sheets used by magickers to photograph reflective surfaces. Sometimes if the tech was good, the photos captured images that had been reflected previously in the mirrors or bronze plaques or silver teapots, as the case might be.

The top photo confirmed Eke's identification: a blurred black-and-white image of Críspula, her profile within an ornately framed oval mirror.

"Everyone else in that mirror is a family member." Yaco flipped through the stack almost too quickly to see, but Críspula was the only visitor, that was clear. "She shouldn't have been back there, am I right?"

Rocío read aloud the label in the upper right-hand corner. "Back corridor, east. What's there?"

"Nothing," Anozie said.

"Storerooms," Ndidi said. They both looked uneasy.

"Is there any reason a guest would be back there?"

"No."

Rocío's pulse was pounding. *Probably not a coincidence.* Críspula de Herrera. Close to O'Higgins and, through him, every member of the sub-com. Close enough to know, close enough to hate. Was she hiding hatred behind those smooth cheeks and perfectly coiffed hair?

"I'd like to see it. Yaco?"

"The techs are there now."

She stood. The Castillo family stood, too, and she said, "It would be better if only one or two of you came." She waited to see who they would choose.

"We'll go," Ndidi said, wrapping her fingers around Anozie's biceps. He patted her hand.

"I should go," Eke said. "It's the señorx I said, isn't it?" Her mother hushed her.

"Would you take us there?" Rocío asked the Castillos.

Ndidi led. As they passed through the castle's dining room, Rocío motioned for two advocates to follow. "Keep everyone else out of the corridor when we get there, okay?"

Yaco fell into step with Rocío and Paloma. "I heard from the Villalta CJC coroner," he said very softly. That was the coroner who had examined the bodies at Isis's house. "Cempol let him see their report, and the murders are a match, down to the saw that was used and the time of death."

Rocío sucked in a breath. "Time of death?"

"Yeah? What—"

"What time did they say?" She knew; she just needed him to say it, to confirm it.

"Between eight and eleven a.m. Friday morning," Yaco said obediently.

"Ancestros perdidos, diosas de mis madres y seres celestiales." *Between eight and ten, more like. Because by ten thirty, I was standing in Ministrx O'Higgins's black-and-white foyer, and Críspula de Herrera Carmona smiled and simpered at us, and either she is innocent or she is the coolest, most calculating murderer I've ever come across.* "Paloma!"

"Yes?"

"We can't wait for more confirmation," Rocío said. "I need you to go to Oshinsky now. Tell her Críspula de Herrera Carmona is our main suspect. Get our driver to take you."

"You're trying to get rid of me again." Paloma set her jaw.

Yaco misstepped and then steadfastly studied his feet.

Clearly the peace offering had not been enough. Like, say, an honest conversation about their relationship might have been.

"This is not the time, Paloma. Oshinsky has to find Críspula de

Herrera as soon as possible—but she needs to know to look. You have to tell her."

"No." Two spots of red burned on Paloma's cheeks like she had a fever. "A chaski can tell her."

"Seres celestiales, have you been listening? I can't send a chaski with this information; they read all the messages. I need someone I trust."

"That's not me."

"Paloma." Rocío stopped and blocked the other woman's way. "I am telling you, as your supervisor, that this is the most important thing right now, and you are going to do it." Even as she said it, Rocío knew she should have started with *I trust you. Piérdalo.* Habits were hard to change. "I do trust you; that's why I want you to do this."

Paloma's chin quivered. Rocío didn't know if she should expect tears or shouting. Her throat worked, and then she whirled and ran back the way they'd come.

Ancestros perdidos, I didn't say to tell Oshinsky about the recipe. She'll remember, Rocío reassured herself. *She's smart.*

"Is everything, ah, okay?" Ndidi asked.

"I sent her on an errand," Rocío said. "She's new. We're still adjusting to each other."

"Oh. I thought maybe you were talking about the models," Ndidi said, clearly assuming the role of hostess in an effort to restore normalcy. That is, if normalcy involved fake eviscerated corpses in the living room. "I don't like them either. We hired an artisan model maker. Usually he does anatomical models for medical schools. We had to pay him a lot because of the disturbing subject matter."

"They're the most popular exhibit," Anozie said in a subdued voice.

In the last room, a moldering tapestry on a rod was swung away from the wall, revealing a well-maintained door in keeping with the renovated areas of the castle. On the other side, electric lights lit another hallway and the charge boxes inelegantly fixed to the stone.

"Is this door usually locked?"

"No. We keep the guests moving with a guide in front and a guide at the rear to keep people from wandering off," Anozie said. "They kept walking into our living quarters when we first started the tours. Those doors have locks now, but most people assume there aren't any other rooms behind this one because of the tapestry and the windows."

The farther they walked down the hallway, the more clutter appeared: a sewing machine, a scrimshaw statue of a whale, a broken table with a matching upside-down chair and an oval mirror on top of it.

"That's the mirror," Yaco said, confirming the yellow evidence tag on one corner.

I'm surprised they got such a good image off it; it's so dusty.

At the end of the hall, another open door revealed a packed storeroom. More jumbled furniture lined one wall, and shovels, rakes and hoes hung neatly along the other, next to what looked like an exterior door. Boxes, crates, baskets and even an urn were stacked every which way. Two techs crouched in the middle, one dusting an empty hatbox for prints, the other scraping something into an evidence bag. Yaco tilted his chin; Rocío interpreted the gesture to mean something magic had been detected where the techs stood.

"What about that one, is it kept locked?" Rocío asked, pointing to the exterior door.

"Yes. We've had some trespassers and kids trying to scare each other," Anozie said.

"What was in the box?"

"Ndidi," Anozie said miserably.

Ndidi avoided her eyes. "We were trying to get rid of it. We've called every government office, hospital and school we could think of. We even asked a Ka priest if the Ka would take it."

An uncomfortable wild suspicion was forming in Rocío's mind. There were very few reasons anyone in La Bene, especially an Intaa family, would need a Ka priest, and they all had to do with death.

"What exactly is missing?" Rocío asked, dreading the answer.

"Eugenio Fernández Suárez's head," Anozie said in a rush.

CHAPTER 17

"SERES celestiales y las diosas de mis madres," Rocío swore. "That's bad."

"Why are you swearing?" Yaco asked. "Besides an evil necromancer's head loose in the world, I mean."

"Because—"

"It's done," Paloma said from the doorway.

Rocío knew she was upset and shouldn't take it out on Paloma, and she yelled anyway. "What are you doing here? I gave you a job."

"I asked our driver to deliver the message," Paloma said, her chin jutting out. "There was no need for both of us to go. You trust him, right?"

Just a moment to think, is that too much to ask? Rocío closed her eyes. What she wanted was to cover them, but she was the leader, she had to look like the leader, and a leader did not cover her eyes. She opened them again. *Now is not the time to yell at her or fix this. Or attempt to.*

"I trust him. But Paloma, we have to talk about this later," Rocío said as calmly as she could.

Paloma looked like she had been braced for a fight and didn't know what to do when it wasn't offered. At least she wasn't yelling. "Why do you all look like the plague ships just docked in the harbor?" she asked.

"Someone stole Eugenio Fernández Suárez's head," Ndidi said helpfully. "But I don't understand why this is a bad thing. Why would anyone steal his head?"

"What?" Paloma said. "You're telling tourists how to become necromancers using people's bones, and you had his head and *lost* it?"

"Paloma," Rocío said.

"What?" Yaco shouted.

"It's just a story!" Anozie said.

"Like other people's ghosts?" Paloma asked.

"Paloma!"

"Yes, like that!"

"Like electricity?"

Ndidi's head jerked back like she had been slapped. Anozie put his arm around her shoulder.

"What are you talking about?" Yaco demanded.

Paloma spoke over him. "Curses are real in Iberon."

"Paloma!"

"Fairies are real in Enkladt. Electricity and ghosts are real in La Bene."

"Paloma! Stop talking now, or I will have to put a formal reprimand in your file!" Rocío roared. But it was too late.

"No," Ndidi whispered. "You're saying necromancers are real, and a necromancer killed four people, and we helped it happen?"

"Can someone tell me what you're talking about?" Yaco said. The techs had frozen in place. Anozie and Ndidi huddled into each other, their expressions tight.

"Yes," Paloma said.

"No!" Rocío said. "Let's all calm down, please. We know exactly what we knew before, which is that someone is copying Eugenio Fernández Suárez's murders and has an unhealthy obsession with the man. But we also have a suspect, and Miraflores CJC will be arresting her very soon, so we all need to stay calm and not spread rumors, which can lead to panic." She glared at Paloma. "Yaco, I will fill you in later."

"But you said, 'That's bad,'" Eke piped up from the doorway. The two advocates whom Rocío had asked to keep the area clear were now inside, looking sheepish.

Rocío glared at them, too. "Can't anyone do what I tell them?"

"Is that lady doing bad magic?"

"Eke!" Anozie swept the child into his arms. "You aren't supposed to be here."

"Eke," Rocío said, "I'm very good at my job, and I'm going to stop the lady, but you have to promise not to tell anyone about this. Your mother and father have to make the same promise. Do you understand, Señorx Castillo? Good. Now, can one of you take Eke away?"

Rocío wanted to send Paloma away, too, preferably to get Hala, because they needed some rational thought in this room. But she suspected the other woman wouldn't obey that order, and she wasn't going to push Paloma down the path of public defiance again. *Because help me, ancestors, I did enough to get her on that path in the first place.* Oh, Paloma was responsible for her own behavior, but Rocío hadn't exactly fostered a supportive working environment for the younger woman. And she remembered a certain incident in her own past in the theater that had involved a lot of screaming at a director. Rocío had been younger than Paloma then, but some of the pressures on her had been similar.

"Paloma, help the techs finish up. Consider it a lesson on the chain of evidence. You," Rocío said, pointing to the first advocate, "go get Detective Haddad, and you," pointing to the other, "keep everyone else out of here."

"I want to staaaaaaay," Eke cried as her father carried her out of the room.

"When is the last time you saw the … skull?" Rocío asked Ndidi.

"And how did it get here in the first place?" Yaco asked.

"It's not a skull, really—more like a mummified head." Ndidi shrugged. "We found it in the old midden when we dug it up to install a septic tank. The workers found all sorts of things—old Ka coins, Ya arrowheads, bottles, a children's doll—but when they found the head they were very upset. I thought you people had some kind of death religion! How am I supposed to know what is real here and what is not? I thought this was a good place, no one cursing this one and that one, but now I don't know. We didn't even know what the head was at first." She hugged herself around the stomach, and her beads clacked softly.

"But how did it get in the midden?" Yaco asked.

"I don't know. I—"

Hala frog-marched the cousin with the gold hoops into the room. "They have Eugenio Fernández's head," she announced. She took in their horrified expressions, the empty hatbox, big enough for a human head, and the two techs still crouched on the floor, unmoving. "Are you telling me they *had* Eugenio Fernández's head and they *lost it*?"

"Please let go of Golibe. He can tell you. He was in charge of getting rid of it. I'll explain la—" Ndidi began to say.

"Señorx Castillo, please. The fewer people who know about this the better," Rocío said.

"Oh. Oh. Golibe, it's very serious business," Ndidi said. "Tell them about the head."

"I was trying." He shook off Hala's hold.

Hala let him and folded her arms across her chest.

"What I was trying to say was that we didn't know whose head it was when we found it; we just thought Benerex have some strange customs. And it seemed like it was an insult, putting it in a midden— that's got to be a universal insult? Unless it's some kind of fertility thing. But then why the head? Um, anyway, when we were setting up the castle, I went to the Government Archives to find newspapers that covered Fernández's trial. That's where I found that photo in a box of newspapers, and underneath was a folder." He looked at Ndidi again, who urged him on. "Right. Well. It was stamped confidential, but it was the public part of the Archives, so I looked." He breathed in and out hard and met Hala's eyes.

"I was looking for that folder," Hala growled. "Perdidos careless clerks. No, you're not going to get in trouble for looking. Just tell us what it said."

"The recipe was in there, and a lot more."

"What recipe?" Yaco and Hala asked.

"I'll tell you later," Rocío said, holding up her hand. "Let him talk."

"The newspaper said Fernández was hanged and burned, but the papers in the folder said his spouse was from a prominent family. She'd married against their advice, but during the trial she left her husband and returned to her them. Her family begged the adjudicator to not dishonor them by burning the body because of their grandson. I didn't understand that part." He looked around like he hoped someone would explain and shrugged when no one did. "The adjudicator compromised, and after Eugenio Fernández Suárez was hanged, he was also beheaded, and the adjudicator ordered that the head be buried separately from the body.

"All that time Eugenio Fernández's mother was sick, and they hadn't told her what they'd done. When she found out, she was appalled. She petitioned the adjudicator, saying her son's body should be burned and his memory erased from La Bene's history. But the adjudicator said he'd already ruled and refused. So somehow she got his head 'and gave him the burial he deserved if he couldn't be burned.' That's a quote. She and the head disappeared, and she was reported to be with relatives in Sacsayhuaman Ka. Apparently the adjudicators thought it was ..." He seemed to realize what he was saying, connecting the questions about the recipe and the concern over the missing skull. "Um, they thought the Ka Empire was probably far enough away that it would be safe." He swallowed. "But when we found a head in the midden, we thought maybe she thought he belonged here, with his victims ..."

"Shitted on by all and sundry for eternity," Rocío murmured.

"And so we decided it had to be his. We didn't think ... I've been visiting every government office I could think of, trying to get rid of it," he said, pleading. "We didn't know it was dangerous."

"Including the Ministry of External Affairs?" Rocío asked.

"Uh." Tensing, he looked longingly at the door, met Hala's eyes and flinched. "I think so. I think that's where ... I saw the woman. In the picture. The one Eke pointed to. I talked to her," he finished with a rush, his voice high.

"You didn't say that in the kitchen," Rocío said.

"You said she was dangerous!" He backed into a stack of boxes. "I was afraid. Eke was there. I couldn't say anything in front of her!"

"Detectives!" Ndidi marched in front of her cousin, her hands on her hips. "You said you are not like the police in our home country, but you are scaring him. And me. Is this how you act?"

"He lied," Yaco snapped.

"Golibe, Ndidi, we didn't mean to scare you," Rocio said. "We're just very concerned about what's happening. Not just for your safety, but for the safety of a great many people."

"It's okay, Ndidi." Golibe stepped out of her shelter and put his arm around her shoulders, though he kept a wary distance from everyone else.

"You're brave to speak to us," Rocío said, letting them hear the genuine admiration she felt. They had braved a new place, a strange culture and unfamiliar laws and customs to start a new life, and they were responding to an intimidating authority in the best way they could. "So, you're saying you spoke to Críspula de Herrera in the ministrx's offices in the House of Refugees, and then soon after she came here for a tour?"

"Yes." He nodded once firmly.

"When did you go to the Ministry of External Affairs?"

"In February. Late February, I think. I can check, I have a list."

"Is there anything else you haven't told us?" Rocío asked.

"No. That's all I know."

"Detectives, I think you don't need us anymore," Ndidi said, pulling Golibe towards the door.

"Just one more question and you can go," Hala said. "Did the papers you found say anything about where the rest of his body was?"

"They said the adjudicator took charge of it."

"Did they say who that was?"

"Yes?"

Hala waited a beat. "Did they say what the adjudicator's name was?"

"Oh. Yes. Patricio Montenegro O'Higgins."

Montenegro. Oh no.

They were gathered in the gift shop for a few minutes of private conversation, but given the events of the last hour, they were taking care to speak quietly. Paloma stood slightly apart, looking guilty. *Good.* And mutinous. Rocío stifled a sigh. *Not good.* Now that she had managed to sabotage the relationship, she was perversely more determined to save it.

"So, Patricio Montenegro O'Higgins entombed the rest of Fernández's body in the crypt in his cellars?" Hala said to Rocío. "For safekeeping?"

"Well, it *was* safe," Rocío said, her stomach registering doubt of that statement. "For over a century ... until Críspula stole it?"

"I should have seen it," Hala said.

"Críspula stole Eugenio Fernández's body?" Yaco asked, bushy eyebrows raised.

"We both should have seen it. It looked like a crypt," Rocío said. "And then Yaco told us someone had stolen a coffin."

"I'm standing right here, talking," Yaco said. "Are you saying Críspula stole Eugenio Fernández's body? That's strange, right? But not ... terrible? Not that there's any good reason to steal a necromancer's body. Why are you looking at me like that?" He stepped back.

"Because the Castillo family has been telling everyone how to become a necromancer, and, surprising no one, you need a dead body. Presumably a dead necromancer's body is even better."

"I really wish you hadn't told me that," Yaco said faintly.

"I told you that empty room was a crime," Hala said.

"Oh, good, focus on the important stuff."

"That's the recipe you wouldn't let anyone talk about?" Hala asked.

"Yes." Rocío quickly filled Yaco in on the whole necromancy thing and recited the Castillos' recipe for making new necromancers.

Yaco reached for the counter to support himself and knocked a tray of key chains with hanged men on them to the floor. "You're kidding me, right?"

Rocío wasn't sure if he meant the key chains or the magic. The day was starting to feel surreal, and the death and necromancy souvenirs weren't helping. "You tell me. Is it gobbledygook or not?"

"It sounds entirely too plausible." Yaco frowned. "It's completely outside my area of expertise—or, you know, anyone's, since it's illegal to study necromancy—but monkey puzzle tree needles are used in some kinds of Ka healing magic. And marigolds are obvious. Of course, the Ka would never eat their dead; that would be sacrilegious, not to mention disgusting. This is not good." He drew himself together with a visible effort. "The Castillos have to stop telling everyone who visits how to become a necromancer."

"Believe me, I already spoke to them. They're curtailing the tour extensively. More emphasis on Luken's Folly and general haunted castle, less Fernández and no recipe."

"But why?" Paloma demanded abruptly. "Why would Críspula need *his* head and *his* body if she already had the recipe? What difference would it make?"

"I have another question," Rocío said. "If she had the head and the secret to becoming a necromancer sometime in March, why did she need his body in April?

"I think we need an expert," Yaco said. "I'm a forensics magicker. The only things I know about necromancy are the things you know."

"Um," Rocío said noncommittally. "Hala? You haven't said anything for a while."

"Look at this." Hala strode over to the wall of photos. "What do you see?" She pressed her thumb to the frame of the family portrait.

The picture had the brownish tint, stiff poses and stern visages of early photographs, though that could be disposition or merely the effort of holding still long enough. Fernández's sister hadn't managed it. Her round-cheeked face was blurred as she leaned slightly away from Eugenio with his sharper, thinner face. One of her socks had slipped down almost to her ankle. She looked about twelve, Fernández about twenty. He would start his murder spree within the year. Their father's hand was clamped tightly on Fernández's shoulder. They were posed in front of a light-colored building with iron railings and bushy shrubs on the balconies above their heads.

"I didn't know he had a sister." Squinting, Yaco leaned closer to the picture. "Imagine living with the knowledge that your brother was a monster."

"She didn't have to." Hala pointed to a handwritten card below the photo.

"Look at this, Paloma." Rocío gestured her closer, trying to get her out of her aloof distance. Paloma didn't move. "Year of La Bene 328," Rocío read aloud. *I'm going to salvage this relationship if it's the last thing I do.* "Eugenio Fernández López—that's the father—deceased 340; Eugenio Fernández Suárez, deceased 335. Oh—Flora Fernández Suárez, deceased 328." Rocío felt pity for the little girl, even though the many years between them rendered it an even more useless emotion than usual.

"The same year the photo was taken," Paloma said in a subdued voice.

"I see a reason why Fernández's mother might have been ready to believe the worst of her son," Hala said.

"Is Flora on the list of his victims?" Paloma asked.

"She's on my list, now," Hala said. "What I think is that we're not going to get any more answers here."

Outside, the techs loaded their equipment into the carriages. One of the horses neighed and stamped while the driver checked her harness. Yaco's assistants descended on him as soon as he stepped out of the castle. Hala strode into the middle of the drive while Paloma stubbornly trailed behind. Rocío wavered between the two, but she had to go after Hala. *Piérdalo.*

"Hala, wait," she called.

"We don't have time."

"I have questions. Important ones."

"Ask in the carriage."

"I can't—"

"Where is our carriage?"

"That's what I'm trying to tell you. Tomás took the message about Críspula to Oshinsky. We'll have to share."

Hala pivoted and strode towards Yaco's carriage and into his cloud of assistants. One was saying, "About that magic residue—I think if we add the cofactor for—"

"We're going with you," Hala said.

"What? Oh, I don't think there's room." Yaco gestured at the techs.

"We're down a carriage," Rocío said.

"I'll sit with the driver." Paloma suited action to words.

"Paloma, you don't—" Rocío said.

Hala pushed Rocío towards the carriage. "You can't talk to her here anyway; too many people. Let her cool off."

"I don't think she's going to. I think she heard me call her a baby." Rocío sat, letting her head drop back, and then had to scoot over as three more techs piled in.

"Oof," Hala grunted.

"Sorry, Detective," the techs chorused.

From Hala's wry smile, Rocío knew the exclamation had been directed at her and was not the result of a stray elbow.

"You'll figure it out," Hala said under her breath. "I'll help."

"Detective Haddad? You think you'll figure it out in time to stop her from whatever she's doing?" Viernes, Yaco's youngest assistant, asked, misinterpreting the comment.

Everyone stopped talking and waited for Hala to answer.

"I know *we* will figure it out." Hala leaned forward. "That's what we do. Right, Yaco?"

"Yes." Yaco nodded once sharply.

Rocío studied the techs and assistants. *Whatever she's doing?* Why not just say *murdering people*? Unless ...

The carriage jolted into motion, and they all swayed against each other.

"Detective Díaz?" Viernes asked. "You've talked to the suspect, right? You don't think she's making an army of necromancers, do you? We'd have noticed by now if that's what she was doing, wouldn't we?"

Everyone stared at Rocío. Even Hala. Even Yaco, evil spirits take him. Rocío refrained from any of the melodramatic gestures she'd used on the stage. She *refrained*.

Whatever I say is going to set the tone for what comes next. Calm. I need to be calm.

Rocío glared at the tech who'd been in the storeroom. "That wasn't supposed to leave the room." *Not calm enough. What do I say to them?*

"It wasn't me! It wasn't. I didn't tell them. They already knew." He pushed back into the seat, hands raised in denial.

Rocío transferred her glare to Yaco.

"Everyone knew before me," Yaco said, waving his hands in a don't-look-at-me gesture, and Rocío decided how to handle the situation.

"Well, I'm sorry I wasn't quick enough with the necromantic gossip, Yaco. Next time I'll be sure you're the first to know."

It was a poor joke, but it broke the tension a little.

"I don't believe she's making an army of necromancers," Rocío said seriously. "Everyone she has attacked is someone she knows well —people she works with every day or is related to. That feels personal. She's settling a score of some kind." She paused, wondering why Juan Pablo hadn't been one of the first victims.

She manipulated me, she realized. In her sympathy for Críspula's situation with Juan Pablo, Rocío had forgotten who else was good with body language: victims. Their safety depended on reading other people's and controlling their own. Knowing when someone was angry and avoiding them or soothing them and being able to appear contrite or unobtrusive could keep an abuser from attacking. And being a victim didn't mean she couldn't also victimize others.

Rocío shelved the thought for later examination and surveyed her anxious audience. "You don't use an army for that. You want to see your victims' faces. We can use that, and we will use it to protect the people she's targeting and restore justice in La Bene."

Viernes loosened her death grip on the edge of her seat, and the other techs showed similar signs of relaxing.

Hala said, "Unless she has a grudge against all of La Bene," and they all tensed up again.

"Not helping, Hala." Rocío had to get them thinking, acting, or they'd stew in fears of magic and murder and riots and the breakdown of order Eugenio Fernández had inflicted on the city. "What do you think she wants his body for?" she asked the techs and magickers. She didn't mention her own suspicions, wanting to see if they got to the same place on their own. "Come on, if you're talking about it, you're theorizing. That's what you do, why you work for the CJC. This isn't any different from any other case in that way." *Don't contradict me, Hala.*

"Is she related to him?" Viernes asked tentatively.

"That's something to check." Rocío added it to her growing mental list.

"Could she want to adopt him as an ancestor?" one of the techs suggested.

"Maybe he's a kind of talisman?"

"That's an awful lot of work just for a talisman."

"Is she a strong magicker? Maybe she needs him somehow if she isn't."

"How would that work?"

"I don't know."

"Is she Ka? Does she practice mummy veneration?"

"Not in La Bene," another tech said. "It would go wrong."

"Maybe that's the point."

"Detective Díaz said it was personal. That wouldn't be personal."

"What if she's using B theory—"

"That's a heresy!"

"And necromancy isn't?" Viernes asked.

"No, it's a good question," Yaco said. "Hala what do you think?"

"I think Rocío has something to say," Hala answered.

Rocío squirmed at the thought of voicing her own personal fear aloud. She had wanted to ask Hala about it in private. The techs fell quiet in anticipation.

"What if she's using the body to talk to him?" Rocío asked reluctantly.

Everyone stared at her in horrified disbelief. Well, not everyone. Not Hala.

"But he's not her ancestor, is he?" Viernes asked. "So she shouldn't be able to talk to him, right? I mean, I can only talk to my own ancestors. And only shamans can use mummies to talk to other people's ancestors in the Ka Empire, right? So she can't. Can she?"

Hala grimaced. "I suspect that is why the adjudicator in Fernández's case wanted to burn the body. The whole point is we don't know. This isn't the Ka Empire, and there's a reason burial or cremation is required by law here."

The reason was that early Iberex burial practices, like crypts under the family home, had sometimes gone horribly wrong once they were transported to La Bene. Or necromancers might teach new students from beyond the grave, apparently. Rocío shuddered.

"As she went to so much trouble to retrieve it, we need to assume it's important and treat it as such," Hala said.

"I liked it better when I didn't know what was going on," Yaco said.

"Me too," Rocío said. "I'm afraid Fernández might be teaching Críspula necromancy in a much more direct way than we thought."

CHAPTER 18

As soon as Rocío stepped into the Miraflores CJC, she knew that she would not be allowed to pursue her eminently sensible plan to interview family members to see if they had any idea what had sent Críspula de Herrera Carmona, privileged daughter of wealth, assistant to one of the most powerful people in La Bene, on a killing spree.

Clearly her plan was going to be displaced by some piece of bureaucratic one-upmanship. She knew this because Oshinsky was at the front desk, flanked by a tenth-level magicker from Cempol, four stolid Miraflores advocates and Officer Smith. Furthermore, Oshinsky's professional mask flickered with relief when she spotted Rocío and Hala and then returned to neutrality.

Rocío stopped, Hala stopped, and Paloma and the techs and Yaco's assistants all stuttered to a stop, too. Not that Rocío blamed them for wanting to know what was going on. Even if she was jealous they were going to escape whatever bureaucratic nonsense was about to fall on her own head. Yaco was the only one who kept walking, but Oshinsky's words stopped him, too.

"Tuz, don't go. Everyone, this is Magicker Huaripani." Oshinsky nodded at the tall woman with graying hair. She wore an old but well-kept Iberex suit in yellow and orange wool and a Cempol/University magicker badge around her neck. "And Officer Ann Smith, also from Cempol. Haddad, Díaz, Faro and Tuz, stay. The rest of you I'll meet in the lab when I'm done here. We have a lot of work to do."

The techs and the assistants shuffled into motion, Viernes craning her head over her shoulder until she walked into the door-frame and had to look where she was going.

Magicker Huaripani, the other Díaz and Zhou, another competent, quiet Miraflores advocate, nodded in greeting. Smith didn't.

Oshinsky led them into the briefing room and closed the door. A picture of Críspula had been pinned to the board in the front with NECROMANCY? written in block letters below it.

"Thanks to the efforts of my advocates, we now have a suspect." Oshinsky gestured at the board. "And we believe she is copying the infamous methods of Eugenio Fernández Suárez, including necromancy."

At least Paloma had sent the message in its entirety. Thank the seres celestiales Oshinsky now knew as much as they did. Almost. They still had to tell her about Fernández's head. And the various theories Yaco's team had come up with.

Oshinsky swept them all with her gaze. "I don't have to tell you how serious this is or that this information cannot be shared outside Miraflores CJC or Cempol. Haddad, Díaz Rossi, Faro, Díaz Matides and Zhou, you're going with Magicker Huaripani to the House of Refugees."

There could be only one reason to send a Cempol magicker, trained in esoteric magic theory, to the city's seat of government, where all the political staffers and ministers had their offices.

But there was no good reason, in Rocío's opinion, that she and Hala should trail after the magicker. This was bureaucratic reasoning, and it was going to stop Rocío from doing *her* job so that she could be seen to be doing *a* job. And see Magicker Huaripani doing her job. Which Rocío really would rather not, since a lot of magic was probably necessary to apprehend a necromancer. She'd rather leave that to the experts. Bureaucracy made her head hurt.

"Chief, can I talk to you alone?" Rocío asked.

"You have two minutes. Tuz, you get to choose if you want to go or not. Magicker Huaripani will brief the rest of you on the way."

Rocío didn't miss the slight emphasis on *you* and revised what she was going to say while Oshinsky herded the others out the door. Especially as "alone" included not only Hala, which she was used to, but Paloma, which meant she had to set a good example. But just what kind of good example? A deference-to-the-chief example? Or a don't-send-me-out-on-suicide-missions-when-my skills-could-be-better-put-to-use-interviewing-people example? Or a this-is-how-we-play-nicely-with-others-even-when-we're-upset example? She decided to mix them all.

"Why, Chief?" Rocío asked as Oshinsky closed the door again. "You know we'd be of more use talking to Críspula's family and coworkers. We might be able to get information that helps us avoid a showdown with her that could be, uh, detrimental to public health and safety."

"I know it, and you know it. But as of this afternoon, Cempol is calling the shots," Oshinsky said neutrally. "Those interviews are going to have to wait." She held up a forestalling hand. "And before you ask me if the ministrx have been warned, Officer Smith assured me that they have and that eventually we'll have access to the reports on those interviews."

Rocío was sure that underneath her façade, Oshinsky was furious, but she was so controlled that most observers would never know. *For our benefit,* Rocío realized. Oshinsky was controlling her stage presence to indicate how her subordinates were expected to act.

I knew that, didn't I? But I didn't like adding Paloma to the team. It wasn't just suspicion; it was fear. I like my relationship with Hala the way it is, and Paloma, through no fault of her own, interferes with that. She wanted to smack herself in the head. *Hala is probably right about me being prejudiced against her, but I was also resentful, and my body language has been telling Paloma that all along, giving her the wrong clues about how to act. Which means Paloma's bad behavior is partly my fault.* Rocío sighed.

Ironic, really, that I spent the first ten years of my professional life learning to emote every feeling I had, and I'm going to spend the next ten learning to hide them again.

She pulled her attention back to Oshinsky. Internal epiphanies could wait.

"Maurata has supported Cempol's request. Since you identified the suspect, he wants you to liaise in the field with them. He wants you to identify her personally."

"Anyone with a photograph could do that," Rocío said, even though everyone in the room knew that. There was no arguing with Maurata and his brand of limited thinking, but she kept talking anyway. "This is ridiculous. We should be talking to Críspula's family. Especially that cousin of hers, Juan Pablo Ricci." *What kind of example am I setting now? A don't-take-bad-orders-without-bringing-them-to-the-attention-of-your-boss example, or is this just insubordination? Paloma is learning that one on her own.*

Oshinsky cleared her throat. "Juan Pablo Ricci is still missing."

"Chief, the Villalta advocate—" Hala said.

"Other advocates are pursuing the matter. Your objections are noted, but you have your assignment. Try to get a handle on what's going on. Discreetly. Haddad, Faro, anything you want to get off your chests?"

"I agree with Rocío," Hala said. "For the record."

This relationship isn't going to fix itself. "Chief, Paloma got you the information about the necromancy and the suspect's identity," Rocío said, trying to be the trainer—no, mentor—she should have been all along. "She"—*mostly, under stressful circumstances that I helped create*—"has been doing a good job." Only after she spoke did she realize Paloma might see it as an effort to preempt her own complaints and not as Rocío giving credit where it was due.

"Well done, Paloma," Oshinsky said. "I told you you had the makings of an advocate."

Paloma opened her mouth and looked at Rocío. For a moment she thought Paloma was going to ask to be assigned to someone else, and she didn't know how she felt about it. Relieved. Guilty. Annoyed. Embarrassed. Definitely embarrassed.

But all Paloma said was, "Thank you, Chief."

Hala tipped an approving smile at Rocío.

"Where was I?" Oshinsky rubbed her forehead. "Two of our

forensic magickers returned to the crime scene at Ministrx O'Higgins's. All the insects and small animals in the garden were dead. It looks very likely that she's using necromancy."

"Chief?" Hala hesitated. "Necromancy could explain the blackmail. Fernández used it to discover secrets. Maybe Crispula is using it the same way."

"You mean she might know we're coming?" Rocío asked, horrified.

Hala shrugged.

Oshinsky pressed her lips together in concern. "All the more reason to be careful. Don't take chances. I have confidence in you." She lightly clapped Paloma on the back. Paloma flushed with pride, and Rocío filed the gesture away for future use.

"A team left for de Herrera's family home with Cempol's other tenth-level magicker just before you got here. Is there anything they need to know that wasn't in your report?"

"Paloma?" Rocío asked, turning so she faced Paloma fully, her stance open and loose to communicate trust.

Paloma failed to mirror her, keeping her torso towards Oshinsky. Who had been her boss for years. "Yes," she said, chin up, "de Herrera has Fernández's head. And possibly his entire body."

Oshinsky cursed in her native language. "Tell Magicker Huaripani. Maybe she can make sense of it. I'll add it to my report. Keep up the good work tonight."

Oshinsky led them back to the hall and the others. "I don't have to tell you how serious this is or that Miraflores and Cempol are hoping for a quick, clean resolution. That's mostly on Magicker Huaripani, as she's the expert, so she's in charge, but the rest of you know what to do. Good luck."

Huaripani led them outside. Rocío kept an eye on Paloma, who was sticking to the other side of Hala. Going into a dangerous situation with this kind of conflict in the team was a bad idea. Maybe Hala could talk to her? Paloma seemed to like her a lot. Rocío felt her cheeks heat at the thought and then checked herself.

Jealousy? I'm jealous when I didn't even want to be her trainer? Sometimes I get very tired of the merry-go-round of emotions in my head. I'm forty-three, and I've had several years of therapy—you'd think I'd be more in control.

Regardless of her emotions, asking Hala to speak to Paloma about Rocío's mistakes would be cowardly, not to mention probably ineffectual.

The Cempol truck looked like it should be making farm deliveries, not carrying elite operatives. When Magicker Huaripani opened the back doors, Rocío half expected crates of chickens or cauliflower, but instead padded benches lined the three sides with strongboxes underneath them. Everything was neat and new.

As they climbed in, Rocío asked Yaco about the hard leather case he carried. He turned it so she could see the words stamped on it —CAUTION: MAGIC DAMPENER—then snugged the case against the strongboxes and propped his feet on it. Huaripani stowed hers in the strongbox beneath the bench with more care.

"It's a prototype that stores an all-purpose magic depression field. It has performed well in the lab, but we hadn't progressed to field tests yet," Magicker Huaripani said.

Rocío and Hala exchanged glances. The automobile was a prototype, and it had almost killed them once by exploding, on top of stalling and brake and steering failures.

"Oh," Hala said with a distinct lack of enthusiasm. Then again, they had borrowed the auto anyway to drive to the beach and then the University, so who were they to judge the magicker's toys?

"We thought it was an opportune time to see how it functions in real-life situations."

In other words, we might die anyway, so let's test the thing, because it's got to be better than nothing in a death match with a necromancer, and if it blows up, it'll probably take her, too.

Yaco peered dubiously between his feet.

"I shouldn't depend on it, though. It's slow and omnidirectional. You should all carry matches, as it will affect all magic deployed in the area, including lights and any magic you attempt."

She indicated the storage area under Paloma's seat, and Paloma dutifully handed out the matches and short candles she found inside.

"So you decided to come with us," Rocío said to Yaco to get her mind off the truck and the machinery that wanted to kill her.

"You *chose* this group?" Smith asked. "Magicker Huaripani, why did you let Oshinsky send us to the House of Refugees? You outrank her."

"That's Deputy Chief Oshinsky to you," Hala said sharply.

Rocío agreed with the sentiment. It was one thing for Miraflores advocates to call her Oshinsky, but another thing entirely to hear it out of Smith's mouth.

"Magicker Huaripani?"

"Why don't you ask Deputy Chief Oshinsky, since she's coordinating this effort?"

Smith half stood, realized Huaripani wasn't going to wait, and sat. "I don't understand you people," she muttered.

Díaz snorted. Zhou spread his legs, crowding Smith. Rocío was pretty sure Smith elbowed Zhou in the ribs, but Zhou didn't even flinch.

Huaripani knocked on the window separating them from the cab, and they lurched into motion. Rocío grabbed the hand strap above her head and braced herself. So much for her hopes that the truck would operate smoothly. *Prototypes beneath me, prototypes all around me.*

"I won't be able to replicate what Magicker Huaripani does, but it's not every day you get to see a tenth leveler take on a necromancer," Yaco said.

Rocío raised an eyebrow at him.

"Or ever, really."

"I thought you had more sense than that," Rocío said.

"I did, too. So." Yaco cleared his throat. "How likely do you think it is that she's at the House of Refugees?"

"Sitting in the ministrx's office waiting for us, you mean?"

It was the carriage and the techs all over again, with everyone staring at her, waiting for her answer. She'd become the de facto expert on Críspula because she'd spoken to the woman twice. Okay, one of those had been an interview.

Rocío thought back over her impressions. "She's levelheaded. We saw her right after the Carters were murdered, and she didn't turn a hair. She's smart. The best education money can buy, and assistant to a very powerful man. Politics runs in that family along with their blood. She wants something, and I don't think she's done. I don't think she's at the House of Refugees."

She was pretty sure Yaco's sigh was one of relief.

"Unless what she wants is there. Magicker Huaripani, do we know where the sub-com members are?"

"Ministrx O'Higgins is still in the hospital, both because of his physical condition and because it's easier to guard him there. Ministrx Montenegro and Belli are at their homes, and Ministrx Soler is of course still under house arrest. Ministrx Valdivia is at Cempol's headquarters. She's, ah, discussing some topics with her spouse.

"However, do not let yourselves become complacent. We don't know what de Herrera capable of. We don't know if she has actually replicated Fernández's methods, which mostly concerned conceal-ment and the discovery of secrets, presumably by speaking to the dead, or if she has created something new with abilities we know nothing about."

"Magicker Huaripani," Hala said, "if de Herrera also abducted Aleksandr Prokofiev, as seems likely, do you think there are so few witnesses because she did it using necromancy? And is there some way to use that to trace him?"

Magicker Huaripani steepled her fingers and tapped them against her lips. "Magicker Tuz, are you using the Bernabé-Caswallawn-Fumagalli-Quiroga test?"

For the next few minutes, Huaripani, Yaco and Hala tossed around a flurry of technical terms that Rocío couldn't follow. There was a reason she was only a proficient magic user.

Hala swore. "I wish I'd thought to ask this before we left the CJC."

"Magicker Huaripani, does that mean there is something you can do to trace Prokofiev?" Rocío asked.

Huaripani gestured for Yaco to speak.

"Yes, I can modify my original tests on the magic residue we found, but it will take several hours to set up and run."

"You could send Smith with a message," Paloma said sweetly, "since she's so eager to go back to the CJC."

Rocío winced. *That was aimed at me, as much as at Smith. Oh, I don't want to be in the same category as Smith for anything.*

"You—"

The truck juddered to a stop, and they all slid toward the cab, cursing. Rocío and Yaco knocked heads, and Smith wound up on the floor, red faced and incoherent. Zhou might have looked a little smug.

Well, at least I temporarily forgot my fear of automobiles, Rocío thought.

"We're here," Huaripani said unnecessarily.

The House of Refugees would have dominated any other plaza, but in the Plaza de la ciudad, which was as big as three pato fields side by side, it was merely very large and imposing. Although four of the five sides of the plaza were lined with buildings, the only structure that could attempt to rival it was the stone amphitheater at the opposite end, which was currently gaudy with caution tape for the construction of the seasonal ice rink. Their truck was the only vehicle in the plaza, and pedestrians cast curious looks at Rocío's group as they detoured around it.

About ten years ago renovations had married a modern glass entrance pavilion to the traditional Ka building of massive stones and inward-leaning walls. At the time, Rocío had thought it an unstable marriage contract that wouldn't last past the ink drying, but now she was kind of fond of it as a symbol of the new La Bene, the fusion of modern and ancient.

Tonight the House of Refugees looked like the perfect set for a massacre, but Rocío wasn't being pessimistic or anything.

Its lights blazed, illuminating the people inside as if with spotlights. Business was booming at the café, the couches in the lobby area were full and it looked like a dance troupe was performing on a low stage on one side. There were at least a hundred people visible, and the rooms and courtyards within routinely held hundreds more.

"Magicker Huaripani, why hasn't the building been evacuated?" Rocío couldn't keep the horrified tone out of her voice.

Magicker Huaripani huffed in exasperation. "Cempol didn't want to create a panic."

"With all due respect, Magicker—" Hala began.

"You shouldn't question Cempol's decisions," Smith said.

"It's not ideal. I know." Magicker Huaripani cut the air with her hand. "But this is what we have to work with. If we find the suspect, we will contain her quickly, discreetly and without loss of life. That is your mandate tonight."

At least Magicker Huaripani sounded confident that she *could* counteract Críspula's magic. Usually a tenth-level magicker would be more than enough, but this was not a usual situation.

"I think Cempol has been talking to Maurata," Yaco muttered, low enough that Huaripani could pretend she hadn't heard. If Smith did, she didn't get that it was an insult.

"We'll go to Ministrx O'Higgins's office first. If the suspect is not there, we will use a standard search pattern to move through the House. We will stay together. Any questions?"

"Why is our team so small?" Smith asked.

The other Díaz rolled his eyes, and Zhou stared at Smith like she was an insect he wanted to stomp on.

Is she really going to make Huaripani say that the magicker is the contralto and the rest of us are soubrette sopranos? At best we might be able to hurl our bodies at Críspula to give Huaripani a chance to take her down.

Rocío surveyed the team, mentally slotting them into different roles. Smith would definitely die first, charging in heroically-recklessly. Had Yaco cast himself as the dramatic hero, or maybe the tragic hero, by choosing to accompany them? Or was this a farce?

"Cempol made the decision. Are you questioning that? Any more questions related to the matter at hand?" Magicker Huaripani asked, clearly communicating they'd better not have any. "Good, let's go."

Inside they threaded their way through the crowd at a pace calculated to cover ground while not panicking anyone who noticed they were justice officials. They skirted the café, which smelled of garlic and onions frying in olive oil. Rocío's stomach grumbled. The patrons at the white-clothed tables dined on rissoles, sopa de cação, salada de polvo and the café's famous egg tarts. Rocío couldn't remember the last time she'd had one. Or when she'd last had a meal at all, come to think of it.

"Rocío," her mother called.

Rocío jerked, trying to spot her.

"Detective Díaz, this is not a social outing," Huaripani said.

"It's my mother, Magicker."

"Ah. Make it quick and be discreet."

"Do you know how to be discreet?" Díaz sneered.

Ignoring him, Rocío let the others draw ahead. Hala and then Paloma slowed, too, so that they weren't quite with Rocío but neither were they part of Huaripani's group. She wasn't sure if they were trying to protect her or just making sure she could find them again. And then her mother descended on her, in an impeccable white robe with triangles of blue embroidery that must have cost a fortune. Analicía pressed one cheek and then the other to Rocío's, and perfume stung Rocío's nose. Something with musk tonight.

"Darling, are you here for Teresa and Mateo's signing? How good of you. They'll be so pleased you could attend their wedding ceremony. Did you remember a gift? I—"

"Mother—"

"—know you didn't, so I got them an engraved clock and said it was from you, too. It was made by ..."

Analicía prattled on. She was annoying and shallow, and she was Rocío's mother, and a necromancer who had killed at least four people already was possibly in the building. *I have to tell her.* "Mother, you should—"

"Tell them to hurry," Hala cut in, and Rocío realized why Hala had hung back—to save Rocío's ass *and* her mother's. A rush of gratitude warmed her. "The meteorologists are predicting a freak thunderstorm and flash floods. You're going to Constanza's afterwards aren't you?" Hala named a fashionable banquet hall. "You know how Avenida lagunilla floods. You don't want to miss the dancing or ruin your clothes."

"Oh, Hala, thank you—you always have such *topical* information. Darling, I really must go." Analicía dashed off.

"That's your mother?" Paloma asked.

"Yes." Rocío felt a little dizzy. It was either relief or her mother's perfume, which was going to cling to her for the rest of the night. "You saved me. And my mother." She wanted to hug Hala but contented herself with hooking her arm through her friend's. Impulsively, wanting to share the good feeling around, she did the same with Paloma and steered them after Huaripani.

"She's your mother." Hala squeezed Rocío's arm.

"You were going to warn her," Paloma said. She didn't sound accusing, just a bit befuddled.

"I sometimes talk before I think. It gets me in trouble a lot." Rocío glanced sidelong at Paloma, who was still staring after Analicía.

"She didn't even listen to you."

"No, she didn't, did she?"

"Isn't she going to … I don't know, be upset when it doesn't rain?"

"You know those meteorologists." Hala waved her free hand airily. "It's hardly a real science."

They caught up to the rest of the group at the back of the lobby. As usual, several individuals and small groups were gawking at the Frida mural depicting the founding of La Bene and the end of the wars between the Ka and Ya Empires. Magicker Huaripani stood below the scene most people called "The Betrayal," with a haggard Patricia O'Higgins surrounded by ragged refugees and Ka and Ya warriors in the distance. Rocío wished Huaripani had chosen a less ominous scene, like "The Calming of the Waters" or "The Triumph," even. When courting optimism, why not be as ambitious as possible?

Logistically it made sense, however. The House of Refugees was actually four buildings centered around a large courtyard. Three of those buildings had smaller courtyards of their own. The building directly behind the lobby held the actual parliament chamber instead, surrounded by ministries and offices that spilled into the north building, on the left. Ministrx O'Higgins's office was in that building, and this was the leftmost door out of the lobby.

Rocío shook out her hands and made an effort to relax her muscles. Hala patted her pockets, her own preparatory routine, and the others went through their own rituals. Paloma was breathing rapidly, her arms pressed stiffly to her sides. Rocío knew that look: rookie nerves.

"Hey. Paloma." Rocío stepped closer and lowered her voice. "Take a few deep breaths." Rocío took a few of her own, exaggerating the rise and fall of her chest and abdomen, knowing Paloma's instinct would be to copy her. "Adrenaline can make you react more quickly and with more strength, but you don't want it to narrow your vision or your thinking too much, okay? Keep breathing deeply so you can use your brain, so your body doesn't take over. I know you've done the courses, but it's different when it's real. It's okay to be nervous."

Paloma nodded, and the skin around her eyes relaxed a little as she breathed deeply. "Thank you."

"Ready, everyone?" Huaripani asked. "Tuz, you identified the suspect in the photo, right? Will you recognize her in person? Okay, then you're next in line. Be ready to duck. Everyone else, stay behind us."

Díaz and Zhou exchanged incredulous glances and then shrugged.

"They do have a plan," Rocío said to them. "I understood that much from what they were saying in the truck." Díaz and Zhou looked about as reassured as Rocío felt saying it.

Huaripani strode through the building with the assurance of someone who had been there many times before, cutting through the corner of the main courtyard and into the north building. This late in the evening, most of the overhead lights were out, and most of the desks were unoccupied, but here and there light pooled on a desk and glinted off hairpins and tupus.

A group of young staffers gathered around a teakettle looked up as Rocío's group passed them. Their whispers made Paloma's shoulders tense again. Rocío clapped her on the shoulder and said softly, "They really do have a plan, you know."

And then the shiny plaque with Ministrx O'Higgins's name on it came into view. The door to his office was closed with no light showing under it. Huaripani touched the back of her left hand to it, her forehead creasing in concentration, and then stepped backed.

"No magic on the door. I don't think she's in there, but let's be cautious."

She knelt and unpacked her magic dampener, which looked like a tarnished globe orrery with too many rings, and gestured to Yaco to watch.

"How far should I stand back to protect my flashlight?" Hala asked.

"About three meters," Huaripani said.

"So theoretically, any magic at the far end of the office could be unaffected?"

"Correct." Huaripani pushed the machine closer to the door, and Hala moved outside its theoretical reach. "But everyone should stand well back. A few of the early prototypes overheated and burst violently, although that hasn't happened for a while."

Paloma gaped at her and then hurried to put a desk between her and the dampener.

"Just like the perdido automobile." Rocío checked that everyone else had moved back before standing next to Paloma.

"I'll just stand right here," Díaz said from behind Rocío. Her lips twisted in answer, but she didn't turn to look.

Huaripani pushed up from her knees and turned two of the knobs on the magic dampener, and the smallest ring began to spin, and then the next one out, in the opposite direction, and the next, until all of them were in motion. She sprinted behind another desk.

"We wait until—" The light above their heads went out. The dampener beeped, and a red light started flashing. "That's encouraging. But it's still best to be cautious." Huaripani moved to one side of the door.

Rocío positioned herself where she could see over Huaripani's shoulder, and Hala came up next to her. Huaripani twisted the doorknob and flung the door open. The office light sparked on and then burned out. A cloud of gray smoke and an overpowering skunk odor rolled out. Rocío coughed. Huaripani retreated, her eyes watering. Zhou gagged and backed up even more.

Hala pulled her flashlight from one of her pockets. It clicked on. "Hmm, less than three meters."

Díaz and Zhou exchanged a glance again, and Smith glared at them.

Hala swept the room with its beam. "Empty." She trained the light on a broken glass capsule close to the doorsill. "A stink bomb."

"You should know," Rocío muttered.

"It looks like it fell from the lintel when you opened the door, Magicker."

Huaripani stooped and prodded the broken glass with a pencil, then leaned closer to touch it with her fingers. "No magic that I can sense."

"No," Yaco said, running his hand around the door frame.

"Are you sure?" Smith asked, and for once Rocío couldn't blame her.

"A stink bomb is strangely childish," Hala said, "coming from someone who has dismembered two people."

"Hey, what are you doing to Ministrx O'Higgins's office?" One of the staffers marched up, his face wrinkled with disgust. "Security is on its way. What is that smell?"

"If you were concerned enough to call them, you should have waited for them," Zhou said. Díaz shifted to block the staffer's view of the office. At least he was making himself useful?

"Cempol." Smith thrust her ID booklet in the staffer's face, making him fall back a step.

"Smith, some discretion, please," Huaripani said.

Smith pocketed her badge as if that would undo her action.

"Oh. Do you ... is Ministrx O'Higgins okay? I mean, he's not ..."

"He's recovering," Huaripani said. "Did you see anyone go into his office today?"

The staffer gestured vaguely. "His assistants—"

"Both of them?"

"Yes? Yes. But not together. And his spouse, who was picking up some of his things. She didn't look too good. And security was with her. And the cleaners came at five, like they usually do."

"Do you remember what time the assistants were here?"

"Um, late morning or early afternoon. I don't remember exactly."

"Were the cleaners the last ones in the office?"

"As far as I know. Except they wouldn't do anything that smelled like *that*."

"No one is saying they did. Go tell security who we are and that we need them to keep everyone out of the ministrx's office."

He trotted away, clamping a hand over his nose.

"I don't know what to think about this," Huaripani said. "It's not what I was expecting."

Smith's lip curled. Díaz shook his head.

Rocío propped her hip on the nearest desk, dislocating a cheap figurine, and patted Paloma's arm. The adrenaline was running out of her, and she felt tired at the thought that she'd have to go through the cycle of hyperawareness and letdown who knew how many times before the evening was over.

CHAPTER 19

I FEEL like I'm trapped in a bad amateur play.

The search had taken on the feeling of unconnected vignettes in Rocío's mind: the three girls in a passionate clinch in one of the ministrx's offices who turned offended glares on the intruders, causing Smith to blush an amazing shade of pink and flee in acute embarrassment; the chaskis racing armadillos, of all things, in the courtyard of the north building; Díaz sniping; and the leaky sink in the restroom that Huaripani checked as if it were part of a plot to drown La Bene. Maybe it was—Rocío was losing her sense of perspective. Ironic, really, as she was currently staring at a scale model of Cerro dex poeta Akhmatova, the mountain to the northwest of the city, that was inexplicably on display in the main courtyard. Huaripani had told everyone to take a break before they moved on to the west and south buildings. Rocío needed a few minutes to stare vacantly into the air, not modeling as an example of anything.

Is the mountain trying to tell me something? She snorted. *I'm taking this amateur play idea too seriously.* She turned around, and there was Paloma, also studying the model. A few meters behind her, Hala made a *go on* gesture.

I don't want to. She fiddled with a pin in her hair. *Coward. Just pretend you're going onstage.*

"Do you know what this is about?" Rocío waved at the model.

"They found gold. Some people want to mine it," Paloma said.

"You don't think they should?"

"My family are devotees of the ser celestial of the mountain."

That ser celestial was a Ya deity of the mountain, poets and grass; Paloma must have more Ya in her than Rocío had thought.

"The city has asked my family to build the temple to propitiate the ser. I don't know what we'll decide."

"Oh." *Do this right, Rocío.* "Paloma?" She turned to face the other woman and raised her hands slightly, the vulnerable palms up. She kept her voice gentle. "I think you heard me say something about you I shouldn't have said."

Paloma's eyelids flickered.

Oh yeah, she did. "I'm sorry. I shouldn't have called you a baby, end of story."

Paloma's lips tightened.

"I didn't mean that you act like a baby at all. You're one of the most talented staff members at the CJC, and you will make a great detective." Rocío put her belief into her voice. "But—and this is not an excuse, it's an explanation—it's just, once you hit thirty-five or so, everyone younger than you starts to look uniformly young."

"I'm *twenty-seven*."

"Really young. It's an unfortunate side effect of getting older. I didn't mean to insult you, and it wasn't a comment on your abilities."

"Oh, so you didn't mean the parts about me being earnest and considered, either?"

"Are either of those qualities you don't want?"

"The way you said them, yes."

Rocío propped her foot on the low barrier around the model. "When you started at the CJC, you saw the therapist, right?" The question was a rhetorical device, as all incoming staff saw the therapist.

"Yes."

"And she told you that self-care was important, because we see terrible things. Sometimes we help the community heal and set new things growing, but that doesn't take away the cost to us of witnessing the terrible parts. Right?"

"Yes."

"And as Oshinsky's assistant, you started seeing that human behaviors repeat themselves and most people are not self reflective. They don't listen, and they either assume they know more than you or that you know everything, sometimes in the same sentence. It gets tiring. Right?"

"... Yes."

"And sometimes you see people as sets of behaviors you've seen a thousand times before, and that's wrong, but you react on it and know you could have done better and resolve to do better next time, right?"

Paloma eyed her suspiciously. "How are you getting me to agree with you when I don't want to agree with you?"

"The thing is, I haven't been fair to you, and I'm sorry. I was suspicious when the chief said you wanted to be an advocate." Rocío paused, turning over what she wanted to say next, how she wanted to say it.

"You thought I wanted Chief Maurata's job."

Rocío sucked in a breath, not that she was surprised. "Yes. I thought you might have picked up on that after this morning." She studied the dusty toe of her boot. "My parents ... I've been wrestling with some feelings that have nothing to do with you, but I took them out on you anyway."

"Your parents think I want Chief Maurata's job. Mine do, too. I let them think that. It makes it easier." Paloma said it as if she had said that woolen hats were best for winter.

It wasn't a skill Rocío had ever had with her parents. And if she had, she wouldn't have had those years on stage. What she regretted was not giving Paloma the chance to prove who she was, not who Paloma's parents were or who Rocío's parents were.

"My parents suggested I help you get that job."

"Oh. I wouldn't do that to Oshinsky."

Of course Paloma had her own loyalties to Oshinsky. If Rocío had been thinking clearly, she'd have remembered that.

"That suggestion made my already-bad behavior towards you worse. What I'm saying is, I'm sorry. I'll do better. Being earnest and

266

considered are good traits in an advocate. I'd like to start over as your mentor, if you'll let me."

"I want to be an advocate because—"

"You don't owe me an explanation. I owed you an apology. If, one day, you want to tell me, of your own free will, then I would like to hear it."

"I—"

"Let's go," Officer Smith called, and clapped her hands.

Rocío raised her eyebrows and Paloma stuck out her tongue, but since Smith was standing next to Huaripani, who didn't contradict her, Rocío moved to the door. Paloma fell into step beside her, their strides matching. A good sign they were moving in the right direction. Literally.

"What is wrong with her?" Paloma whispered, and Rocío was suddenly glad of Smith, who at least could be a common enemy.

"A terminal case of Enkladt. And no, you can't repeat that to anyone."

"Not even Hala?"

"Not even Hala."

Paloma flashed her an incredulous look.

"She would scold me." Which was true, but hadn't stopped Rocío before. But it was past time she tried to build a relationship with Paloma, and Rocío would use every trick she knew to do so. She couldn't let Oshinsky down. And she couldn't let herself down.

"Hmm."

Paloma didn't suddenly link arms with Rocío, but at least she seemed to be thinking about what Rocío had said.

Lightning flashed as they followed the garden path to the edge of the courtyard. Rocío wasn't the only one to jump and scan the sky. Thunder followed a few seconds later.

"Did you really check the weather report?" Paloma asked Hala.

"I always check the weather report when I'm with a high-level magicker. Electrical storms can have unpredictable effects on their magic because of the similarity between—"

"Stop talking. Everyone is skittish enough as it is," Rocío said, nodding at the others.

"It's common knowledge. Are you saying people shouldn't be prepared?"

"Actually it isn't common knowledge. I didn't know that," Paloma said.

"And in this case it isn't going to help anyone be prepared, it's going to make us all worry about what Críspula might be doing right now."

A coati appeared out of the flower beds. Smith jumped and then glared at everyone. Díaz snickered.

"Case in point," Rocío said in a low voice to Hala.

The coati sauntered into the middle of the path, stood upright on its back legs, its long striped tail swishing in the greenery, and examined them with its inquisitive dark eyes.

"People feed them," Zhou said, holding out an egg tart. The coati snatched it and turned away to devour it. Díaz shook his head at Zhou.

"I can't believe you wasted an egg tart on a coati," Rocío said.

Zhou held out his empty hands, and the coati scurried up a tree, agile as a monkey, its gray coat blending in with the darkness under the leaves.

"Let's go, people," Smith said.

"I can speak for myself," Huaripani said mildly, swinging open the heavy door that separated the courtyard from the west building. She gestured them inside. It was quiet and dark compared to the courtyard.

"Did they really predict a storm tonight?" Paloma whispered to Hala.

"No, that was just a coincidence," Hala whispered back.

After another two hours of searching, everyone had spooked at least once, and no one was laughing anymore; they were all drooping with weariness and too many adrenaline rushes in too short a time. One hour ago, when Huaripani had handed her case containing the magic dampener to Smith, Rocío had known the magicker did not expect to find Críspula in the House of Refugees. But that had not stopped Huaripani from executing their mandate with precision or making Yaco practice with the dampener he carried before finally looping back to the lobby. No one had seen Críspula other than the staffers outside Ministrx O'Higgins's office, and she didn't seem to have an evil villain lair set up in the cisterns or the kitchens. Wearily, Rocío dug her fingers into her lower back, trying to relieve the ache that had set in.

"All right, everyone," Huaripani said. "We knew this was a long shot. It may feel like we didn't accomplish anything, but we all know that eliminating possibilities is important. You did a good job."

"I told you she wouldn't be here," Smith said without actually looking at anyone. "And that we didn't have enough people to find her if she were."

Huaripani ignored this stunning piece of illogic. "Go home. Get some rest. Smith, you're liaising with Miraflores tomorrow. I—"

"Permission to leave, Magicker Huaripani," Smith said.

"Granted."

Smith thrust the dampener she carried at Huaripani and stomped off. Rocío didn't know her well enough, thank the seres celestiales, to know if that was hurt pride or a thwarted desire to tackle someone. It must be exhausting going through life that unhappy, but then Rocío had never understood her parents, either.

"Well. As I was saying, I can have the driver drop you off at the CJC."

"No thanks." Rocío raised her hands, palms out.

"I'm hungry and I want an egg tart," Yaco said in a loud, forced voice. "Anyone want to join me?" With both hands, he clutched the other dampener behind his back, like a kid inexpertly trying to hide a toy.

Rocío hid a wince. "Sure."

"I'll go with you, Magicker," Zhou said.

Díaz gave him a look of mingled horror and respect. Zhou shrugged. Díaz sketched a salute and walked with Huaripani and Zhou to the exit, leaving Yaco, Rocío, Hala and Paloma to choose one of the many empty tables at the café. Rocío picked one close to the freestanding kitchen/serving center/cashier station.

They had barely settled into their chairs when a waitress appeared and said, "I saw you come in, Rocío, and I saved you some egg tarts."

"Zoe, you're a wonder." Rocío rose and exchanged kisses. "I heard your sets for *Xica* are even more wondrous than usual. I have tickets for next week."

Yaco pulled out a chair and slumped into it. "I can't believe you talked me into this."

"I'll get those egg tarts," Zoe said and absented herself.

"Any problems?" Rocío asked.

"You mean besides the fact that I bribed a Cempol officer to keep this?" He tapped the dampener's case with his toe. "I'm going to lose my job." He rubbed his forehead.

There had been plenty of time between peering inside every office, maintenance closet and meeting room for Hala to convince Yaco they needed to search Ministrx O'Higgins's office without Cempol oversight, though it seemed he still wasn't completely convinced.

"You bribed her?" Paloma asked. Her tone of voice was remarkably similar to the incredulous look Díaz had just given Zhou.

Good thing I don't subscribe to a binary theory of sanity, because I'm not sure we'd come out on the sane side of that line.

"How?" Hala asked.

Yaco groaned. "I brought up my mother. Now I have to explain this to *her*."

"Oh, I see," Hala said.

"See what?" Paloma asked.

"She's the executive assistant to the dean of the University, and they're assigning offices in the new research building. It's much nicer than the building where Magicker Huaripani has her office now ..."

"And we thank you and your mother for it," Rocío said.

"This is not a good idea."

"They're not telling us everything, Yaco."

Zoe reappeared with the egg tarts, slid them onto the table and disappeared.

"Cempol? Of course not." Yaco grabbed an egg tart.

"How do you know?" Paloma asked. "Why are you all so sure?"

"You know it when you see it?" Yaco said around a mouthful of crumbs, quoting a famous adjudication.

"That was said about porn, and that adjudication was overturned." Rocío rotated her egg tart a quarter turn. "The reports they gave us on Isabella Corona and Mizn bin Selasa didn't contain any speculation."

"And Huaripani left out one of the calculations Yaco will need to readjust his tests, didn't she?" Hala asked him.

"Yes, and I should be running those tests right now so that we have the results in time to be of help. You know there are only three tenth-level magickers in La Bene and I'm not one of them, right?" He licked his finger and pressed it to a flake of crust.

"The dampener is just a precaution. We just want to see inside Ministrx O'Higgins's office. We don't expect Críspula to be there." Rocío finally bit into her egg tart. *Delicious.* Creamy and crispy in just the right way.

"And yet you asked me to stay."

"Hala? Would you tell him?"

"I agree that it's highly unlikely de Herrera is in the building or in Ministrx O'Higgins's office. I wouldn't expose Paloma to such a situation, as she is not a fully trained advocate yet."

"Hmm." Yaco rubbed his ear.

"To answer your question, Paloma," Rocío said, "many little things adding up to one big conclusion. Seeing them comes with experience, and that's why Yaco is here, because he can't unsee them, right, Yaco?"

"You are so annoying," he grumbled.

"Because you know we're right and you want the same things we do," Rocío said. "To find Aleksandr Prokofiev alive and stop Críspula de Herrera from killing anyone else."

"Argh. Fine. *Fine.* But I'm eating the last egg tart."

Yellow security tape festooned the closed door of Ministrx O'Higgins's office. On closer inspection the end of one piece was tucked between the door and the jamb, as if someone had held it in place while closing the door from the inside.

Yaco gave Rocío a look that clearly said *Are we really doing this?* but unpacked the magic dampener and positioned it against the wall. He fiddled with the knobs and then sprinted a safe distance away. Rocío held her breath. For a moment nothing happened and then the rings spun into motion. And spun.

"It didn't take this long before," Paloma whispered.

"That might mean there's more magic to counteract." Yaco looked at the overhead light, which hadn't been replaced, and around as if hoping for another obvious source of magic. Hala crossed her arms, her flashlight ready.

The dampener beeped, sounding as loud as an alarm in the almost-empty building. Paloma jumped. The red light flashed, in a reassuringly steady rhythm.

"I guess it worked." Yaco looked up and noticed everyone staring at him. "Uh-uh, no. I'm not opening the door. This wasn't my idea. Besides, I already turned on the undependable exploding magic machine. Someone else risk themself this time."

"Fine." Rocío motioned everyone back. Copying Huaripani's move from earlier in the night, she stood to the side and flung the door open. The smell of lemons, hot wax and muted skunk stink rolled out. It was dark. "We know you're in there," she said.

Hala scowled at Rocío, not amused.

"We know you're out there," Isis called back.

Rocío mouthed, "Isis?" and Hala shook her head as if to say *Are you really surprised?*

On the other hand, that was not the response Isis would make if she were warning them she was being held hostage by a well-bred necromancer.

"Detective Díaz?" Ministrx Montenegro asked.

"Are you under duress, Ministrx?" Hala asked.

"No. But I'd also say no if I were under duress. Could you turn the lights back on?"

Hala snorted. From a distance she pointed her flashlight into the room and then indicated it was safe. Rocío picked up the magic dampener, reasoning that its field would move with it. She stepped into the room and to the side.

The flashlight beam picked out Ministrx Montenegro and María Paz Belli at the desk, which was strewn with piles of folders. On one side Isis perched on top of a filing cabinet with a datebook in her hand, and on the other Ministrx Valdivia leaned against the wall with a notebook and pen.

Críspula de Herrera was notably absent.

Rocío put the dampener on the desk, the centermost point of the room. Críspula did not flash into sight. Still, Rocío motioned for the ministrx to move back and checked under the desk.

"It's clear," Rocío called to the others. "Thank you, Ministrx. Yaco, if I turn this off, will the lights come back?"

"We might as well try it." Yaco powered off the machine. For maybe three breaths nothing happened, and then the lights flickered back on and everyone squinted. Hala and Paloma crowded in and closed the door behind them.

"What are you doing here, Ministrx?" Hala asked.

"We're hiding," Isis said scornfully. "Cowering in fear."

So Cempol had told them about Críspula's necromancy. A surprisingly pragmatic decision on their part, considering the ministrx were the main targets.

"You're supposed to be home, Isis. On *house arrest*," Rocío said.

"Yes, because it's so safe there," Isis said.

"We're not hiding." María Paz rubbed her forehead. "We're looking for answers. There must be a reason Críspula is doing this, and if we can find out what it is, maybe we can stop it. Stop her."

Ana Valdivia gave her a pitying look.

María Paz's hair was scraped back in a utilitarian bun and there were dark shadows under her eyes. And while Ministrx Montenegro did not look as bad, there was something off about her appearance. After a moment Rocío realized that the pin holding Ministrx

Montenegro's shawl in place was backwards, the decorated side turned inward and the plain back turned out. This was not a woman who normally went out with her jewelry askew.

Isis looked much the same as always—in other words, furious—and Ministrx Valdivia ... well, Rocío wasn't sure how the woman had ever stopped disappearing into the woodwork long enough to get elected.

"So they told you," Rocío said.

"Yes." Ministrx Montenegro bit the word off.

"Ministrx Montenegro, have there been any more disturbances in your house?" Hala asked.

"No. We have a temporary wardstone in place now until a permanent one is ready. We also employed guards. Why are you asking me specifically?" She swept the advocates with her gaze and then narrowed her eyes at Hala. "You found out something about that room."

"And you didn't?"

"I found the house plans, but the only label on the room was an adjudicator's seal belonging to Patricio Montenegro O'Higgins."

"We believe it's probable that Críspula de Herrera stole Eugenio Fernández Suárez's body from your family crypts. How this will affect her ability to perform necromancy ... is ... unclear." Hala faltered on the last words as shock and disbelief grew on the ministrx's faces.

They stared at Hala, mouths open. Ministrx Valdivia dropped her pen, the click as it hit the tile floor loud in the silence. Then all the ministrx started shouting.

"What?!" Isis drowned out everyone else. "What are you talking about? Necromancy?! Are you crazy?"

"Cempol *didn't* tell you," Rocío said. "Of course they didn't." She pinched the bridge of her nose and considered if there was any way to make it sound less horrible. There wasn't. She raised her voice to cut through their noise. "We have reason to believe that Críspula de Herrera is practicing necromancy."

"They told us she was a *suspect*," Ministrx Montenegro said.

María Paz slid her hands over her eyes. Isis jumped from her seat, dropping the datebook, grabbed Rocío and shook her. "What has she done to Sasha? She's killed him, hasn't she?"

"Isis. Isis, stop." Rocío broke Isis's grip on her arms and held her in a double thumb lock, and Isis didn't even notice; she kept leaning forward into Rocío's hold. "We don't know anything more about Sasha."

Isis's eyes focused on Rocío's. Rocío waited for her to pull back a little and then let go.

Isis pulled at her hair and groaned. Then she whirled and kicked the filing cabinet. The dull thud made Ministrx Valdivia jump.

"Isis," Ministrx Montenegro said tiredly, like she'd said it too many times already that night, "control yourself."

Ministrx Valdivia rubbed her hand over her mouth. "This is all my fault."

"Nonsense," Ministrx Montenegro said. "Did you kill four people—"

"That we know of," Isis said.

"—and attack William? No, you did not."

"But if I hadn't confronted her ..." Ministrx Valdivia sagged against the wall and covered her eyes.

"Then we wouldn't know the extent of what she's done," María Paz said, patting Ministrx Valdivia's arm.

"Can we focus, here?" Isis demanded. "They just said Críspula is practicing necromancy and you're worried you hurt her feelings."

"I agree with Isis," Hala said, "in principle. You seem to know something about Críspula's activities but were ignorant of the necromancy, is that correct?"

"Yes, I think it's time we shared information," Ministrx Montenegro said.

"Paloma, can you take notes?" Rocío asked. She commandeered a large notepad from a stack on the shelf and handed it to Paloma, who looked relieved to have something to do.

"Hala, you don't need me for this," Yaco said. "I need to get back to the lab to run those tests."

"Of course."

He hesitated and glanced at the dampener. "I should really take this. I promised Magicker Huaripani nothing would happen to it. You're not going to, uh, do anything ...?"

"It's fine," Rocío said. "Take the perdido thing."

He grabbed it and ran out the door.

Hala cleared her throat. "I would like to start with Ministrx Valdivia. What do you mean you confronted Críspula?"

Ana Valdivia wrapped her arms around herself. "I had to know if it was true about Luka."

The lieutenant governor's arrest for treason felt as if it had happened weeks ago, not just four days ago on Tuesday, when all of this had started.

"Cempol took all his papers from the house, so I came here. Because he was accused of selling secrets to La Bene's enemies, I thought I might find something in the records of the Committee on Legal Affairs and External Relations. It's the parent body for the sub-com, so I have access," she said almost apologetically.

"Did you find anything?" Rocío asked, unable to resist the tangent.

"Oh, yes. He's guilty." She laughed painfully. "Everything they said about him in the papers is true. But I found something else, too. Críspula embezzled money."

"Money?" Paloma said. "Why would she ... surely she has money. That doesn't make sense."

"How much money?" Hala asked.

"About two thousand pesos."

Rocío and Hala traded looks. That was very close to the amount Señorx Legionnaire had spent refurbishing his club and financing his version of *La Ingenue*. Coincidence?

"She was very clever about it. At first it looked like Juan Pablo Ricci was responsible, but a clerk at the Central Bank owed me a favor ..." She shrugged. "Everyone feels very sorry for me these days. So I confronted Críspula."

"When was this?" Rocío asked.

"On Thursday morning. At first she tried to blame Juan Pablo, and then she cried and said it was for a friend. She made it sound like she was helping Loeis Carter de Herrera pay a gambling debt without ever saying so directly. I realize that now, but she was very convincing. I told her if she put the money back by the end of the week I wouldn't say anything. More fool me," she said bitterly.

"You should have told us," María Paz said. "We have a fiduciary duty to the sub-com."

"I was going to tell you at the sub-com meeting yesterday, but she swore she had returned the money right before she left for Isis's house. And then everything happened, and now we're here." She waved a hand around.

"So you shared this information with your colleagues and that's when you all decided to come here?" Hala asked.

"No," Ministrx Montenegro said. "Cempol notified us this afternoon that Críspula was a suspect in the attack on William. We agreed that the sub-com's files might contain information Cempol hadn't found and arranged to meet here. Then Ana told us about the embezzlement."

"I did tell Cempol," Ministrx Valdivia said.

"Have you found anything that gives you an idea of why she's doing this?" Rocío asked.

Isis muttered something about Críspula's feelings that everyone chose to ignore.

"Did you know she sent me a note? Anonymously, I mean," Ministrx Valdivia said. "I told Cempol, but ..."

"But they didn't tell us," Hala said.

"What did it say? Does Cempol have it?" Rocío asked.

"Yes, they have it. It said, 'Are you humiliated like you humiliated me?'"

"Do you know what she meant? How Críspula was humiliated?" Rocío asked.

"That's what we were trying to find out," María Paz said.

"Humiliation is part of politics," Ministrx Valdivia said. "Who knows what petty pinprick among the many was too much for her? There's nothing here that tells us what's driving her to do what she's done."

"Did you really think she'd leave a note about her motivations in

William's office?" Isis asked, her nostrils flaring. "She's too smart for that."

"I meant the missing files don't have anything in common except for the obvious, the sub-com. We don't have enough information," Ministrx Valdivia said, seemingly unruffled this time by Isis's display of temper.

"We have to do something," María Paz said. "We might find something no one else would notice. And you know it, Isis. You've risked breaking house arrest to be here, so stop being so disagreeable and be useful."

"Everyone stop talking," Hala said. "What is this about missing files? Ministrx Montenegro, please."

"Some of the personnel files are missing. So are the files on the final meetings for the armistice agreement, the convict exchange program with the Ka Empire, the bid proposals for expanding the embassy in Kooja Ya, and the travel permits for 446 to 448."

"Why those files?" Hala asked.

"If we knew, don't you think we'd have told you already?" Isis snapped.

"What Isis is trying to say is that we have not been able to pinpoint any reason Críspula would be interested in those files. We aren't even sure she took them. I believe we were reaching an agreement that it would be best to bring in the auditors and let them conduct an investigation," Ministrx Montenegro said.

"Maybe that's what she wants," Ministrx Valdivia muttered.

"I don't have anything to hide," Ministrx Montenegro said, her spine and her words stiff.

"Neither do I," Isis said, her chin jutting out.

"Nor I," María Paz said.

"Ana?" Ministrx Montenegro asked.

Ministrx Valdivia turned a notebook over and over in her hands. "I didn't think I had anything to hide, either."

María Paz patted her shoulder. "You don't. You're not responsible for his actions. Or hers."

Ministrx Valdivia huffed out a dry little laugh.

"Excuse me, Detective Haddad, but I believe we need to pursue this," Ministrx Montenegro said. "Are we in agreement? We will call the auditors?"

"I second the motion," Isis said.

"Fine," Ministrx Valdivia said.

"Then we are agreed. I'll talk to the Office of Internal Oversight tomorrow."

"Back to your impressions of Críspula de Herrera," Hala said.

Isis and Ministrx Montenegro exchanged a glance. Isis opened her hands as if relinquishing something to Ministrx Montenegro.

Ministrx Montenegro's voice shook when she spoke. "She dared to go to Isis's house. She sat with us in our meeting, as if she hadn't killed Martine and Loeis. She sat beside William and me with their blood on her hands." The tendons in Ministrx Montenegro's neck tightened as she grasped Isis's hand. If justice were a matter of will, Ministrx Montenegro's rage would have swept Críspula from the face of the Earth already. But it wasn't, and this mess was Rocío's job to take care of.

"I don't know what she wants. I don't know why she's doing this," Ministrx Montenegro said. "I feel like I don't know anything about her at all."

CHAPTER 20

Sunday morning started with the news that four sets of hands and feet had been discovered when Cempol drained the pond in Ministrx O'Higgins's garden and went downhill from there.

Piotr Prokofiev showed up at the CJC, shaking and pale, demanding to see his brother's hands. Rocío sent him to Cempol with Espinoza and cursed Isis, who had to have told him about the hands and feet, because their discovery was not common knowledge yet. Rocío didn't know whether to hope he could identify the hands or not. Juan Pablo was still missing, with no leads and no witnesses, and the information the ministrx had given them last night might be helpful someday, if the auditors found a connection between the missing files. They needed something now. Críspula could be anywhere, doing who knows what.

Plus Rocío had chosen sex with Khaled over sufficient sleep, a decision that had seemed therapeutic and cathartic at the time, but one she regretted now. Sort of. The memory of the kindness in his caresses might get her through another day thinking about Aleksandr Prokofiev's disappearance and the reality that Críspula equaled necromancer better than sleep would.

"All the fish were dead," Hala said quietly, sitting on the edge of Rocío's desk and rousing her out of her thoughts. Paloma hovered behind Hala uncertainly, and Rocío motioned her closer.

"What?" Rocío asked, trying to find her place in the conversation. "Oh. In Ministrx O'Higgins's pond?"

"Where the hands and feet were found," Hala said in an even lower voice. "They found dead birds, insects, tuco-tucos, even a cavy and a nutria. Nothing alive within three meters of the gardener's shed."

"I guess the plays got that right." Rocío pushed papers around on her desk.

"The techs managed to isolate enough blood to confirm that it's likely all four victims were killed there," Hala said.

Paloma looked queasy. "So she really murdered them and then a few hours later talked to us as if nothing had happened?"

Rocío hesitated, wondering if she should answer with the truth, but then she remembered what had happened last time she tried to protect Paloma.

"I think it's worse than that," Rocío murmured. She pulled two pieces of paper out of the stack in front of her. She pointed to a memo. "This is Críspula's handwriting." She pointed to the other paper. "And this is the note Cempol received saying that Ministrx O'Higgins wanted to meet with us. Cempol sent it over."

Paloma clapped her hand over her mouth. "They match," she whispered.

"Forensics says they match?" Hala asked.

"They do. And so do the notes Isis and María Paz received. What's more, Yaco told me this morning that the ink on the threatening note to Isis is the same as on the one to María Paz."

"So it really was her." Paloma groped for a chair and dropped into it. "I mean, I know we thought it was her, but it really was her. And she ... what, was gloating? How could she?"

Rocío and Hala looked at each other over Paloma's head.

"It's a question we ask ourselves a lot," Rocío said. "La Bene is small. We help people we know, and we arrest them, too. Sometimes the signs are there, and sometimes they're not."

"You know what's really frustrating?" Hala raked her hands through her hair. "I can't tell if she's calculating or reckless. Did she set out to murder four people and lure Cempol and the CJC to her door so she could gloat, or was this a chain of events that got out of hand?"

"The ministrx didn't know either," Rocío said morosely.

Rocío, Hala and Paloma had questioned the ministrx for hours the night before, without much more to show for it. Everyone had thought Críspula was a nice young woman, struggling a bit in Juan Pablo's shadow while determining if politics was the right choice for her. In spite of the bullying, which Ministrx Montenegro had thought not too severe, none of them would have guessed at the violence within her.

Paloma stood up abruptly. "So what are we going to do?" she demanded. Two spots of red burned on her cheeks. "Why are we just sitting here?"

A few people turned their heads to stare.

"Where would you like to go?" Rocío asked gently.

"We should talk to Ministrx O'Higgins!"

"I'm working on that."

"Then we should talk to Gumersinda de Herrera. She must know something."

"She's sitting with Ministrx O'Higgins at the hospital, so if we get to talk to him, we'll be able to talk to her, too."

"Then we should be out looking for Críspula! To stop her."

"Cempol is doing that with the magickers. They're much better equipped to arrest her than we are." Rocío softened her voice. "A lot of being an advocate is knowing when to let other people do what they're best at. Sometimes we sit here at the CJC and search through statements and reports, looking for something we missed."

Paloma stared at her for a long moment and then closed her eyes, breathing deeply. The flush had faded from her cheeks when she opened them again. "I know. You're right. I just want to do something."

"We all do," Hala said. "This is—"

"Detective Haddad." Oshinsky waved them over. Officer Smith loomed next to her in the doorway. "You have an interview with Ministrx O'Higgins in forty-five minutes. Get going."

"For real this time?" Rocío asked.

"Commander Dhavale arranged it," Oshinsky said.

"I'll get our coats."

Oshinsky stopped Paloma with a hand on her arm. "Not you. Ministrx O'Higgins requested that only Hala and Rocío interview him. Is that right, Officer Smith?" She leveled a firm look at Smith.

Smith didn't waver. "Ministrx O'Higgins wants only experienced advocates."

Paloma glared at Smith and then transferred the look suspiciously to Rocío.

"I had nothing to do with this." Rocío lifted her hands helplessly. "Please find out if forensics has anything else for us. We'll fill you in when we get back."

Officer Smith accompanied them to the hospital, nipping in the bud any attempt to avoid her and Cempol's oversight. Rocío took the lead, as she usually did in these situations. Situations calling for snow jobs. She paused in the cream-and-blue-painted hallway before they reached Ministrx O'Higgins's room. Sounds were muffled and the air smelled of lemon cleaner.

"Officer Smith, we've been working together for days now, and we've never discussed official procedures for CJC advocates collaborating with a Cempol liaison," Rocío said, channeling her parents' accountant. His smooth manner always worked with them. "I'm sure you could tell me all about it. Perhaps we could go to the cafeteria? I'd love a cup of coffee."

She held out her arm for Smith to precede her. Smith didn't take her cue, so Rocío stepped closer, still babbling professional niceties about their offices working together, wishing for once she were a man, so the side crowding technique would be more effective. Women usually responded to this invasion of their personal space by retreating, and it should have been even more effective on an Enkladt refugee, whose personal space was culturally larger than a native Benerex's.

Alas, Smith was a rock, not a woman, and didn't move.

"You don't have time," Smith said, her hands clasped at mid-torso height as if she were in charge. "Your appointment with Ministrx O'Higgins is at ten thirty."

"Let's go in, then," Rocío said.

Smith looked at her pocket watch. "It's 10:26."

"The situation is rather urgent." Rocío tried not to clench her teeth. "Surely—"

"You can see the ministrx at ten thirty."

"Well, then, what can you tell us about his condition?"

"I'm not permitted to share the details of the investigation with you."

How was it possible that every word out of Smith's mouth was more pompous than the last?

If Rocío said anything, it would be beyond sarcastic. She settled for "Hmm?" Not that Smith needed Rocío's encouragement to keep spewing nonsense.

"You would need to apply to Commander Dhavale."

"Commander Dhavale is aware that we're here, as he arranged this interview, which you know, because you told us. I'm sure that indicates we should receive any information you have."

"I'm not aware of what Commander Dhavale is aware of."

"I see," Rocío said, changing tack. "Officer Smith, Detective Haddad and I have conducted almost twenty murder investigations. Our experience is at your disposal, but please, let us do the talking, in accordance with the regulations that bind Cempol and the CJCs."

"I see."

Rocío really didn't think she did, but she and Hala could work around Smith. After all, they had Maurata, and Smith was junior league in comparison.

"It's ten thirty." Hala nodded at the door. They waited for Smith to open it. She was exactly the type whose feathers would be ruffled if anyone else did it.

Unfortunately Smith didn't take the hint. Rocío hid a sigh, knocked and opened it herself. Predictably Smith bristled, drawing herself up taller and frowning.

Hala slipped between them, preempting whatever Smith was

about to say. "Thank you, Officer Smith. I'd appreciate your help here."

Rocío allowed herself to roll her eyes to relieve some of her exasperation and then followed them into the room.

O'Higgins was propped up in a bed the Hotel Grande wouldn't mind offering its guests. A bandage covered his right temple and a short wound on his cheek was sutured closed with black stitches. It looked like it had been caused by a ring or a weapon that punctured rather than sliced. His hands, resting on the white silk counterpane, were purple and swollen with cuts on the knuckles and ragged fingernails. Defensive wounds. Any other injuries were hidden under his long-sleeved shirt and the covers.

"I'd say good morning, but you look like you've had better," Hala said.

"I'm still alive," Ministrx O'Higgins said acerbically.

"You're right. Good morning."

"Although Cempol already spoke to you, it's standard practice for the local CJC not to read Cempol's report so we can form our own impressions and then compare them," Hala informed him.

"I know." His eyebrows crimped together. "I helped preserve those regulations five years ago. Get to the point."

"So you know I need to inform you of our procedures and that we will be recording this conversation." Hala placed the recorder on the empty bedside table. The other held a pitcher of water and a glass. Smith reached across Hala and placed a Cempol recorder closer to Ministrx O'Higgins, pushing Hala's out of the way. Hala lifted her eyebrows at Smith but didn't give her the satisfaction of breaking her intro chatter. "Detective Díaz and I will ask you some questions, and we'd like you to tell us in your own words what happened."

"Who else's words am I going to use?" he grumbled. His hands clenched on the counterpane and released before he spoke again. "My grandson woke me up, saying he had heard noises. I thought it was just a nightmare, but for some reason I made him stay in my room and I didn't wake my spouse, thank the seres celestiales. I heard a noise, like a crash, and went downstairs. The lights were on in my study.

"Crispula was there, papers all over the floor, furniture knocked over."

Rocío drew in a sharp breath, surprised.

"I thought she was drunk. We argued. Then she suddenly stopped speaking and looked past me. She looked so scared. Not like a little girl is scared, but like an adult, with knowledge in the fear. I turned around." He paled and sweat beaded on his upper lip. He breathed heavily and then began again, hesitantly. "There was someone in the doorway. It was hard to see him. Darkness seemed to hang about him. And little lights and a smell ..."

Rocío's chest constricted. Inexplicable lights, darkness and the smell of death. She had thought she had resigned herself to the idea that they were dealing with necromancy, but she realized now she'd been hoping Ministrx O'Higgins would tell them something that took necromancy off the table. *The human capacity for denial knows no bounds. I wonder if Hala has considered a paper on the topic.* Hala met her eyes, her expression dismayed.

"You didn't tell Cempol this. What kind of lights?" Smith leaned on his bed, the linens denting under her hands. O'Higgins flinched and then flushed.

Rocío pulled on Smith's shoulder, using the pressure to suggest the other woman should back off. "Officer Smith."

"Blue, like a spark from an electric wire." He stopped again.

"Please go on, Ministrx O'Higgins. We need to hear what you have to say," Hala said.

Just as he opened his mouth, Smith asked, "Where were the lights, exactly? High? Low? On something?"

Rocío really wished she could pinch the nerves in Smith's shoulder to shut her up. But that wasn't the way Rocío did things. *I really resent that she's making me think about committing violence so early in the morning.* She pressed down on Smith's shoulder. "Officer Smith."

"About waist height."

"Your waist?" Smith asked.

"Let's let Ministrx O'Higgins finish telling us what happened,"

Rocío said, "in accordance with CJC procedure, which we discussed earlier. Specific questions can wait."

"I—" Smith tested Rocío's grip.

"Shush." Rocío retreated a few steps, pulling Smith with her.

"Ministrx O'Higgins?" Hala asked.

He raised a trembling hand to his cheek. "Pass me the water," he said, trying for command but missing the mark and landing on querulous.

Not good. He wasn't the type to forgive others for seeing his weakness.

Hala poured him a glass of water, her movements brisk and impersonal, doing her best to block his view of Smith and Rocío.

O'Higgins's voice was steadier when he spoke again. "He seemed to move without moving and he was so tall." He grimaced. "I felt like I was picked up and thrown down. I don't remember much else. Just pain. "

"He—"

"Procedure, Smith," Rocío hissed. Smith shut up and Rocío let go.

O'Higgins didn't notice. He was looking into his memories and there was no doubt they weren't pleasant.

Rocío didn't think he had ever been assaulted before. He had that look in his eye. It was a terrible thing to feel all the edges of your body exposed, flinching from all the assaults that were suddenly possible when the body had felt inviolable before. To feel an attack might happen again at any moment, that you hadn't seen it coming the first time, and now you knew you could not stop it from happening again.

Rocío didn't think he would welcome her insights, so she merely said, "It won't always be this hard. It will get better. I've seen hundreds of people recover from something like this."

"Not like this."

"Like this," she said. "It will get better." He didn't believe her now, but that wasn't the point; the point was to plant the seed and let it grow along with his recovery. Others would tend and water it and help him recover.

"Can you describe the smell?" Hala asked briskly.

"It smelled of death, like a slaughterhouse or worse."

Rocío's nose wrinkled in sympathetic remembrance. You never forgot that smell. She took a deep breath, but even the whiff of disinfectant was a reminder of death and catastrophic injuries. "Did you see what happened to Críspula?"

"No. I didn't." He struggled upright. "But you must see that what you're saying about her can't be true. I was attacked by someone else. It was a man, I tell you."

"Could you identify him if you saw him again?"

"No." He collapsed back into the pillows. "I couldn't see his face. I told you, it was dark. It was like when you go from bright sunlight to an indoor room and everything is just shapes."

"What made you certain it was a man?" Hala asked.

"The way he moved. Or stood. I don't know. It was a gut reaction."

"Could it have been Juan Pablo?"

"What are you saying?" He breathed deeply, his nostrils flaring.

"I'm asking questions to elicit information from you, nothing more," Hala said.

"You're wrong. They're good children. She's my sister's daughter. She's a good girl. Juan Pablo wasn't there. Neither of them could do the things you're accusing her of." His face flushed red, and his breath rasped in his throat.

"Don't worry about that now," Hala said.

"What did you and Críspula argue about?" Rocío asked.

"How much money she was spending."

He was a good liar. He controlled his eyes and his hands, but his feet twitched. Everyone always forgot to control their feet.

He gulped water and choked, his eyes tearing up. "I should have known Isabella wouldn't leave without notifying me. I should have done something to find her."

Oh, very good—cover the lie with another emotion.

Rocío opened her mouth to pursue the line of questioning, but Smith got there first.

"Ministrx O'Higgins, this may be hard." Smith fanned a stack of crime scene photos at him. Isabella Corona, butchered. Mizn bin Selasa, butchered. A close-up of an amputated wrist. "But we have—"

"Out. That's it, you're out." Rocío pushed Smith out of the room, glad to have a problem she could solve. "What is wrong with you?"

Ministrx O'Higgins gagged. Looking over her shoulder, Rocío saw Hala shove a bowl under his mouth. He vomited and gasped, clutching his ribs. Rocío turned to give him privacy. Smith stared. Rocío closed the door and seized Smith's elbow, her grip intentionally painfully tight. "Go get the nurse."

"I'm required to stay—"

"I have had enough," Rocío snapped, aware she needed to control herself better. "Get the nurse and when you come back, stand against the wall and keep your mouth shut."

"You can't talk to me like that."

Rocío counted to three before she spoke again. "Ministrx O'Higgins is in distress," she said, recovering her control with superhuman effort. She consciously relaxed her grip and searched for a tone of voice that would work on Smith: reasonable, slightly coaxing, deferring to the other's status, imagined or not. *Why isn't magic good for anything really useful? Like smiting petty bureaucrats.*

"He requires assistance—your assistance and a nurse's. You're in a position to help him. I'm sure he'll remember what you've done in the future."

That did it. She didn't have to punt Smith down the corridor; the infuriating woman practically lunged for the nurse's desk.

Think of the paperwork. If smiting bureaucrats were possible, there would be paperwork for it. Rocío rubbed her forehead, trying to smooth the tension there. When she looked up, Gumersinda was at the other end of the hall, looking lost.

A nurse bustled into the ministrx's room, Smith unfortunately dogging him. Through the open door, Rocío saw Hala help Ministrx O'Higgins sit up. Hala wordlessly handed him a cloth for his mouth. He seemed relieved not to be fussed over. Hala was certainly the right woman for that non-job.

He leaned back, wheezing. "Is … is … that a sedative?" He nodded to the syringe in the nurse's hand.

"It's to relax you. It will help with the nausea and the breathing," the nurse said.

"Wait." He turned to Hala. "The smell, the lights ... you know what they might mean."

The nurse huffed impatiently.

Hala waved the nurse back. "I know. We know."

He sagged against the pillow. "Ancestros protect us."

Smith looked from one to the other, her mouth open in confusion, but thank the seres celestiales, nothing came out of it.

"Detective, we cannot allow this, this perversion in our city." O'Higgins glared at her like glaring was a safety line in a rough sea. And then he turned gray, his eyes rolled back in his head and his breath rattled.

"That's enough," the nurse said. "You need to leave."

"What perversion?" Smith asked as Hala herded her into the hall. So much for her confusion keeping her quiet.

"More confirmation." Hala closed the door behind her.

"What is?" Smith asked.

Rocío shifted, and Smith automatically adjusted her stance to face her, which kept Smith's back firmly to Gumersinda.

Rocío gestured at Hala, who said with great pleasure, "I'm not permitted to share the details of the investigation with you. You'll have to apply to Commander Dhavale for that information."

Smith couldn't let that pass, which allowed Rocío to slip down the corridor and beckon Gumersinda out of sight.

CHAPTER 21

Up close, Gumersinda looked awful. Dark circles shadowed her eyes, and the skin on her face seemed looser. Like she'd just found out someone close to her was a murderer. Rocío was sorry to see the tautness of youth and privilege gone, though she had resented it only days ago. She didn't wish this experience on anyone.

"Gumersinda," Rocío said softly and then waited, giving the younger woman time to say whatever was burning her tongue.

"I lied." Gumersinda's voice was husky and strained.

Rocío controlled her reaction. "That's okay. You can tell me the truth now."

Gumersinda swallowed. "You see ... Críspula went to Ministrx Soler's early, on her own, on Friday. She told me she didn't want to go in the carriage with Juan Pablo, that she needed to get away from him for a while, and that I needed to lie about it because she didn't want anyone to know how bad his bullying had gotten." She started talking faster, the words tripping over each other. "But she didn't kill anyone. She couldn't. I mean, yes, Juan Pablo is horrible to her, but he's not dead, is he? That's got to prove something. And Loeis and Martine were her friends, why would she hurt them? So it really couldn't be her, you have to see that." Gumersinda clutched Rocío's wrist and squeezed, as if not sure what was real anymore.

Rocío hated the way people's crimes left gaping holes in the lives of those around them. Their friends and loved ones were left trying to darn them like drunk spiders spinning inadequate webs.

Truth is better than lies. She had to believe that, because it was the only way she knew to help people like Gumersinda, the ones who had to pick up the pieces. She chose the truth that might help both Gumersinda and herself; she had the weight on her shoulders of so many more people who needed help. *This is for Aleksandr Prokofiev,* she reminded herself. She took Gumersinda's hand. "Gumersinda, did you know Juan Pablo is missing? Do you know where he is? We're worried about him, about his safety."

"M-missing?" Gumersinda's eyes widened with new fear, and her fingers tightened around Rocío's wrist.

"Since Saturday night."

"No. I thought he was out, that he was gambling, out with his friends. It's what he usually does when the ministrx doesn't need us. He's just, she couldn't …"

"Have you seen Críspula since the party at Ministrx Soler's?"

"We went home together. I went to bed. I haven't seen her since then. I didn't wake up the next morning until Cempol arrived. But Ministrx O'Higgins said a man attacked him. It couldn't have been her."

"We have a lot of evidence that suggests Críspula is at least involved in blackmailing and threatening other ministrx, and there are clear links between her and the murders."

"No, it can't be." Gumersinda started crying.

Rocío felt bad for this young woman, loyal to Críspula and betrayed by her with all the rest. But that didn't stop the pricking of instinct, which made her ask, "Gumersinda, is there something else you want to tell me?"

"Yes." She sniffled, wiping tears off her face, and straightened her shoulders, putting some distance between them. "I don't believe you, you know. That's why I'm telling you this. When you came to Ministrx O'Higgins's house on Friday morning and Críspula gave you those papers, I took something out. I asked her about it, and she got very angry, but I'm not dead, am I?"

"What was it?"

"It doesn't have anything to do with this. It was something that would make Ministrx O'Higgins look bad."

"Did it have something to do with the files missing from the sub-com's records?"

Gumersinda's face went blank.

"The personnel files? The armistice agreement? The convict exchange program?"

Gumersinda twitched at that last item. *The convict exchange program? What does that have to do with anything?*

Rocío kept talking to keep Gumersinda from realizing what she'd revealed. "The embassy in Kooja Ya? Travel permits? Is that what they've been arguing about? Ministrx O'Higgins and Críspula?"

"I don't know."

Rocío asked variations on the question, but Gumersinda shook her head and refused to answer. "Okay. I really appreciate you telling me these things. I hear what you've been saying about Críspula's innocence." *Not that it changes my opinion.* "Just one more question. Did Críspula ever mention someone named Shen or Emma?"

Relief broke over Gumersinda's face at this easier question. "Oh, yes, they're theater friends. I met Emma once. She's very normal. Not a murderer or anything."

This kid is never going to survive in politics. Rocío hid her excitement.

Emma the anarchist, who had been convicted of mutilating rats and leaving them in the House of Refuges. Who was doing hard labor in the Ka Empire as part of the convict exchange program, and who was pals with Shen. It wasn't hard proof, but it was a possible connection between Críspula and the stolen dance score and Aleksandr Prokofiev. And had Emma even killed the rats, or were they Críspula's early experiments gone wrong ... or right?

"They have some kind of business deal going, don't they?" Rocío asked. Implying you already knew something was a tried-and-true method of getting information from someone.

"I don't know if you'd call it business. Críspula is backing a show they're in."

Rocío doubted that. Shen and Emma enjoyed the arts as much as anyone in La Bene, but they weren't interested in creating it. "Do you know what it's called?"

"No."

I can bring Shen into the CJC and question him. He'd already admitted he'd stolen the dance score; would he admit it if Críspula had paid him to do it?

"Okay, thank—"

"But I did hear her mention someone once who I think has something to do with the show," Gumersinda said.

Rocío linked her hands behind her back, waiting.

"Señorx Legionnaire."

Yes! Rocío squeezed her wrist hard where Gumersinda couldn't see it. She kept her expression lightly interested when what she wanted to do was bounce with excitement. After a few more minutes of chitchat, she managed to send Gumersinda home ignorant of how much she had revealed. Hala and Smith hadn't reappeared, so Rocío headed for the exit, planning her next steps.

Then she saw Magicker Huaripani at the hospital's exit. The excitement of Gumersinda's revelations still hummed in her body. *What's worked once can work again.* And the worry about what exactly Críspula was doing with Eugenio Fernández's body was an itch at the back of her mind she couldn't ignore any longer. She strolled up to the magicker.

"Gum?"

Surprisingly, Huaripani accepted a piece. They chewed in companionable silence for a minute. There was no one within earshot. "Nice day, isn't it?" Rocío said.

Last week's clouds had blown out to sea, and the sun glared brightly over everything. The temperature had gone up overnight, melting the ice that had delayed their arrival at Isis's house on Friday. The sun was warm on the top of Rocío's head.

"Yes. I can't stand the rain."

"Me neither. On such a sunny day it's hard to believe de Herrera is using Fernández's body to talk to him."

Huaripani sighed. "Indeed."

For a moment giddy exhilaration swept over Rocío. It had worked.

Then the dread kicked in, and she felt the bottom drop out of her stomach, like she'd just fallen several feet. *I knew it. Oh, ancestros, I didn't want to know it.*

"Wait, who told you that?" Huaripani turned on her, frowning.

Rocío tried to sound nonchalant, not nauseated. "You just did."

～

Rocío burst into the CJC, shouting for Espinoza, with Hala right behind her and Smith right behind Hala, still yapping for an explanation. Rocío had hustled them back to the CJC as fast as she could without stopping for explanations that wouldn't have been appropriate in public anyway.

"Espinoza, get someone to bring in Shen the anarchist. I have a connection between him, Críspula and Señorx Legionnaire. Piérdalo, let's bring in Señorx Legionnaire again, too. We have to see the chief."

Rocío left Espinoza calling names and the other advocates hurling questions at their backs and raced for the stairs, almost running into Yaco and Paloma at their foot.

"I know why she stole the body," Rocío said.

"I think I figured out a way to find Prokofiev," Yaco said.

"What?"

"What are you people talking about?" Smith asked.

"Upstairs," Hala said.

They piled into Oshinsky's office, the smell of hot beeswax and gardenia rolling over them. A larger-than-usual amount of candles and flowers graced Oshinsky's small altar, almost hiding the photographs. Rocío kissed her thumb to her own ancestors for their blessing.

"Chief," Rocío said, "Magicker Huaripani just confirmed Cempol believes Críspula is using Fernández's body to communicate with him. That means she has access to everything he knew. She's not just making up necromantic magic as she goes; she's being taught by its creator."

Paloma and Oshinsky stared at her in horrified disbelief.

"Ridiculous," Smith boomed. "There's no such thing as necromancy anymore."

"Go tell that to your superiors or stop speaking." Oshinsky rubbed her forehead. "Every time I think it can't get any worse ..."

"Uh, Chief?" Yaco said, ignoring Smith's sputtering complaints, "I have some good news—well, depending on your definition of good—and it's kind of urgent. And Cempol should know, so maybe Smith could, uh, go tell them?"

"Yaco, spit it out," Oshinsky said.

He cleared his throat. "So, ah, four of the ten tests I ran worked, and now we know that de Herrera's magic is incredibly strong. Unfortunately. Confirming, uh, what Rocío just said." He paused, maybe to let them all absorb that information, maybe to contemplate his own mortality. Or maybe it was just nerves. He was sweating.

"I thought you had good news?" Oshinsky asked.

"I object," Smith said. "These tests were not cleared with Cempol. They are unorthodox and suspect and—"

"Officer Smith, please shut up, or I will have you ejected from my office," Oshinsky said.

Smith snapped her mouth shut.

Yaco cleared his throat again. "Yes, the, um, good news. We can use the physical test results to lead you—us—to Aleksandr Prokofiev. Probably. Or at least to the residue of any magic he has performed in the last twenty-four hours or so. That's not precise. Nothing about this is precise."

"Oh, well done, Yaco," Hala breathed. Rocío clapped him on the shoulder a little harder than she intended in her enthusiasm, and he rocked on his feet.

"Yaco." Oshinsky banged her hands on her desk and stood up. "This changes everything. Good. This is good. We need—"

"Uh, Chief." He ran a hand through his hair. "There's one more thing you should know. I don't think this effect will last very much longer. A few hours at most. The magic is fueled by the physical residue we found, like a fire fueled by wood. When the wood burns up, there's no more fire. I wasn't aware this would be the case when I initiated the test. I therefore recommend that we notify Cempol—I mean, someone with decision-making power—of my findings right away and that both their tenth-level magickers be, um, deployed to apprehend Críspula."

"Thank you, Yaco. Excellent work in challenging circumstances. I don't think you could be expected to know beforehand the parameters of a test that you essentially just invented," Oshinsky said.

"Thank you, Chief."

"Paloma, would you call one of the chaskis in? Cempol needs to be informed right away."

Paloma opened the door and squeaked in surprise. Maurata loomed on the other side. He pushed into the office, and Paloma fell back a step, out of his way. "Chief Maurata."

"I hear you have a way of finding this woman who's disrupting the city," he rumbled.

Behind him, the lab tech Viernes mouthed, "I'm sorry."

Maurata advanced, crowding Rocío and Hala out of the way. Paloma dodged around him and scooted a chair back to make more room.

"Yes, Chief," Oshinsky said. "I was just about to come see you. I'm about to notify Cempol that their assistance is needed."

"Nonsense. You have a Cempol liaison right here."

"Chief, we need a Cempol magicker and backup."

"This is urgent, Oshinsky. I expect more from you. Are you sending Haddad and Rossi? Go to it, then."

"Chief, with all due respect, we need at least one high-level magicker."

"Are you saying Tuco here isn't good enough?"

Yaco grimaced at his mangled name. At least Rossi was one of Rocío's surnames.

"You shouldn't talk like that in front of him," Maurata said.

"No, Chief, just that de Herrera is very dangerous, and Cempol has instructed us to not engage her, especially not without their presence."

"You have a Cempol liaison, and this woman is a menace. Make your people do their jobs." He turned his back on Oshinsky and faced Yaco. "I want you to go now."

Yaco's lips moved, but he didn't say anything.

"That's an order, Oshinsky, Tuco. I expect you to follow it." He left.

"Chief." Yaco gestured helplessly.

Oshinsky held up a finger. "This is what you're going to do. You are going to see where the test takes you, very slowly. You will take every precaution. If you identify a building where you believe Prokofiev is located, you will inform me, stay out of sight and wait for a Cempol magicker to arrive. Understood? Paloma, it's my opinion that the chief's orders didn't apply to you, so you get to decide whether you go with the others."

"Of course I'm going. We're going to find Aleksandr Prokofiev!"

Oshinsky looked like she wanted to caution against that hope but instead kept the words to herself. She met Rocío's gaze, her expression like that of a mother sending her child out into the world to find what hope and hurt came to them.

Yaco's beaker led them to the Plaza de la ciudad.

At first Rocío thought they were going to the House of Refugees, and her heart sank, because they weren't going to find Prokofiev there; they had gone over every centimeter of that building. But Yaco detoured around it, leading them across the plaza, through a crowd of people listening to a guitarist, past a cart giving off the lovely smell of fresh crepes with nut paste and an artist chalking a fractal design on the big paving stones. The rumors of necromancy must still be contained, or the artist would have been painting slogans and skulls and inducing panic. Rocío grimaced. *Small comfort.*

Yaco slowed as they approached the westernmost point of the plaza and the amphitheater. The stage, now hidden under the ice rink and the temporary buildings housing the café and everything else needed to make the rink a fun winter destination, was level with the plaza, while the tiers of stone seats were built into the base of Cerro de la democracia, the first of the foothills that eventually climbed into the Cordillera del sur. Only a few groups of people sat high in the seats, cupping warm beverages and enjoying the view of the plaza and the city.

Yaco led the group in a complete circuit around the stage, checking the beaker frequently, and then stopped at the KEEP OUT, UNDER CONSTRUCTION sign.

"In there."

Hala folded her arms. Paloma let a frown slide across her face, and Smith pursed her lips. Rocío tilted her head back to consider the site. The yellow caution tape marking the construction area fluttered in the breeze, and the sun reflected off the glass windows of the café, making it impossible to see inside. The rink itself was hidden behind a temporary blue barrier.

"How does this keep getting stranger?" Rocío said.

"It is close to the House of Refugees," Paloma said. "And you have to walk through Parque Dolores to get here from La Valle."

"But they're opening next week," Rocío said. "There should be workers all over the place."

"Maybe it's too warm?" Yaco asked.

"Where did Haddad go?" Smith asked suspiciously.

"Oh!" Rocío threw up her hands, suddenly exasperated that everyone was acting exactly as they always did. "The situation only wanted that. You"—she pointed at Smith—"go to Cempol and tell them again that we need Magickers Huaripani and Chuquisengo right away. Paloma, go with her and send a tube to the chief to tell her where we are. Yaco, you and the dampener stay with me."

Yaco had said it was as good an opportunity as any to return it to Magicker Huaripani, and no one had argued. No one had said out loud that it could be the only shield they had against Crispula's magic, but they were all thinking it.

"What are you going to do?" Smith asked.

"I'm going to confer with Magicker Tuz about how much time we have before that beaker becomes useless. Go!"

Paloma hooked her arm through Smith's and pulled her away. Unfortunately Cempol and the attached tube office were on the north side of the plaza, not too far from the House of Refugees, and

Smith wouldn't be out of Rocío's sight for anywhere near long enough.

"Did you see where Hala went?" Yaco asked quietly.

"Yes." She waved a hand at a maintenance shed. "Hopefully she'll come back with useful information, though she could have said something before just wandering away. *Do* you have any idea of how long we have?"

"I've been doing calculations based on how quickly the residue seems to be burning up. So yeah. About two hours. Maybe a little less."

"Great. Surely two hours is enough time for the magickers to get here."

He cocked his head at her.

"I'm trying to be optimistic."

"About bureaucracy? Has that ever worked before?"

"Yes! Maybe ... once?"

CHAPTER 22

Paloma reported back forty-five minutes later that her message had been sent and received. Smith was still at Cempol, arguing their case and actually making herself useful for once. Unfortunately the office was practically deserted, and Commander Dhavale hadn't informed the officer in charge that Smith had clearance to send messages to him or the magickers.

"Did Smith talk to Commander Dhavale's secretary?" Rocío asked.

"No! She has some very strange ideas about how things work. I finally sent a tube to the secretary telling her what's going on. The tubist at least had a sense of humor about sending a tube to an office literally meters from her own. I thought I'd better catch you up. I can go back."

"Let's give them a few more minutes to sort themselves out."

Paloma looked around like she thought Críspula might jump out at them from behind the nearest group of people. "Has anything happened here?"

"We climbed the amphitheater to look down into the work area," Rocío said. "We didn't see anyone about."

"And we talked to a bunch of the people up there," Yaco said, "but no one has seen any movement. I don't think the residue test is working the way I thought it was."

"I'm not sure I agree, Yaco," Rocío said. "The rink is a soupy, half-frozen mess. It's supposed to open in three days, so why isn't anyone working? There's definitely something wrong here."

On cue, Smith stomped up to them. But Hala also appeared from around the corner of the rink.

"You first, Officer Smith. What happened?" Rocío asked.

Smith growled and pounded her fists on her thighs. "I got the message out, finally, but they're at Luken's Folly. That stupid ... it's going to take at least an hour and a half for them to get here. I had to send a chaski on a horse!"

"Okay, deep breaths," Rocío said in spite of the worry clenching her stomach to the size of a peach pit. Any delay could cost Aleksandr Prokofiev his life. If he was still alive.

Smith snarled at Rocío and turned her back, hopefully fighting for control.

"Hala, do you have good news for us?" Rocío asked.

"Yes and no. I've been talking to the facilities manager for the amphitheater."

"I didn't even know there was a facilities manager," Paloma said.

"The amphitheater is connected to the city's water and sewer systems. They supply water for the ice rink and the buildings, and the waste from the toilets and the kitchen goes into the sewer.

"The manager said that the rink company got a stop-work order on Wednesday that cited a fault in the cooling system. Work stopped, but there was someone on-site on Wednesday and Thursday, because the plumbing systems were active. The manager thought it was magickers fixing the cooling mechanism, but since Thursday evening there hasn't been any activity, and the workers haven't returned."

"So there's no one in there," Paloma said.

"And hasn't been since Thursday." *We're not even close to Prokofiev.* Rocío folded a piece of gum into her mouth. "Yaco, how much time is left?"

"Less than an hour. I really thought the test was working."

"Hala?" Rocío asked.

"I believe it's unlikely de Herrera is in that building or that we will be exposing ourselves to undue risk if we enter. I looked at Yaco's calculations and his test should work, so it's possible that Prokofiev is in there or was in there. Either way, there could be important evidence inside. I think we should go in, but I will not force anyone."

Everyone nodded except Smith, who still had her back turned.

"Officer Smith?"

Smith said something unintelligible.

"Officer, time is still of the essence, even if Aleksandr Prokofiev is no longer in the area."

"Which orders do I follow?" Smith mumbled to the ground. She spun around and advanced on Hala. "I'm not supposed to approach de Herrera without at least one Cempol magicker, but I'm also not supposed to let you go off and do whatever you want. Can't you just wait?"

"That's not possible," Hala said with commendable gentleness. Rocío wasn't sure she could've managed it. "Prokofiev could be in there, hurt or dying. Didn't your training cover what to do in this type of situation?"

"No!"

"Then you will have to use your judgement."

"My judgement?" Smith paced away.

Rocío took that as her answer. "Everyone else ready?" she asked. "Let's go."

"It makes sense if you think about it," Yaco said brightly. "It's a good place for a magicker to hide. None of our magic tools will work here; there's too much ambient magic. The detector would most likely point at the batteries for the rink, while the dampener—"

Smith whirled around and glared at Hala, blocking her way. "Regulation three twenty-five of the city code requires community justice officials and advocates to find the owner and request permission to enter their property."

"Regulation three twenty-five, paragraph nine, subsection b," Hala said, "advocates may enter when they have reasonable suspicion that a life or lives may be endangered and the advocates' actions could mitigate that danger. It also addresses threats to the public welfare, all of which apply. It won't do, Officer Smith. You have to decide."

"You didn't consider—"

"I am not arguing with you." Hala unhooked the caution tape, creating an opening. Smith set her mouth and stepped out of the way.

Yaco pointed towards the café, but Hala led them past the ticket booth and the skate rental room for a quick look through the windows. Smith trailed behind them, grumbling under her breath. Both buildings were empty of everything except furniture still wrapped in movers' padding, which looked undisturbed. The smell of feet seemed to hang outside the skate room, but Rocío knew it was just a fancy thrown up by her overactive brain. Children shouted on the plaza, and everyone jumped.

Yaco turned towards the café. A corner of the cheerful orange-and-white-striped awning flapped in the breeze where it hadn't been retracted all the way. Terrace tables were bundled against the wall, and neither Críspula nor Prokofiev was huddled beneath them. Rocío snorted softly at her ridiculous thought.

Hala nodded sharply. The plan they had worked out as they followed Yaco's beaker had called for Rocío to go first with the dampener, but the place practically hummed with magic, making it useless. If, against all expectations, Críspula was here, Rocío could turn it on and throw it at her in the hopes it would explode as it overloaded.

Hala motioned for the others to stay back and approached the door. Rocío went to a window at the end. Cupping her hand against the pane, she squinted inside. On one side there was a counter and an empty display case. The rest of the large room was full of chairs upended on tables, like a forest of modern sculpture. There were no people or signs that anyone had been there recently.

Hala eased the door open. Rocío signaled for the others to follow. If they were wrong and Críspula was here, the bottleneck at the door would provide her with an opportunity to strike at them. It felt like tiny ants were crawling over Rocío's skin. *Funny how I never felt that sensation before going onstage.* Of course, most of the dangers onstage were psychological rather than physical. The adrenaline was similar, though. She entered the room last, leaving the door open. They stood, listening. Yaco cocked his head. Paloma squinted and turned in a slow circle.

Hala consulted them with a glance, and everyone shook their heads or shrugged to show they hadn't heard anything. She pointed at the door to the kitchen, and they threaded their way through the furniture.

At the back of the room, one chair stood askew in front of a table.

Rocío hissed for the others' attention. They stopped to listen again. Rocío held her breath and strained her ears. Hala peered through the small window in the door to the kitchen. For a long moment she didn't move, and then she signaled that it was clear. She pushed through the door. Rocío followed on her heels.

The smell of burnt tomatoes and grease assaulted Rocío's nose, and she scanned for the source. Opposite her was a gleaming stainless steel counter dividing the room in half, and beyond it a door that had to lead outside.

The wall on the right was lined with empty shelves, and on the left was a range with an industrial-sized pot sitting lopsided on a burner not intended to hold something that large. When she checked, food was crusted in the bottom of the pot and on the counter next to it. Rocío hovered her hand over it and, when she didn't feel any heat, touched the side. "Cold," she whispered. A touch test confirmed that the stove was also cold.

"Look at this," Yaco said quietly, his voice strained. Rocío followed his gaze to the gleaming stainless steel counter. From this angle she could see that one edge was pitted and black and slightly depressed.

"Is that ...?" Smith took a few steps closer. "Is that blood?" she asked faintly and swallowed hard.

Yes, now that Rocío looked closely, there were a few spots of blood on the counter, though not enough to warrant Smith's reaction. She couldn't have become an officer if she was one of those people who fainted at the sight of blood, could she?

Rocío moved around the end of the counter and saw what had captured Smith's attention. "Seres celestiales. Smith, step back."

Dried blood crusted the sealed-cork floor in a stain as long as Rocío's arm. Smith seemed frozen in place.

"Smith. Step back. If you don't, I'm going to touch you on the shoulder, and by whatever spirits you hold dear, you will not jump forward into the blood."

Smith shuffled backwards towards Rocío.

"Good. You're doing good, Officer Smith. I'm going to take your arm now."

Rocío held Smith firmly in place and bent sideways to peer under the counter. The stain kept going for at least half the width of it. "Let's go." She walked Smith to the door to the seating area.

"It's a lot of blood, isn't it?" Paloma asked. "Does this mean he's dead? Or is that someone else's blood?"

Rocío didn't like either answer.

Smith's pallor had given way to a splotchy blush.

"Stay there until you're feeling better," Hala said. "You look like you're going to throw up. This is a crime scene; you will not contaminate it. Use your coat if you have to."

"I'm not in your chain of command."

"I'm aware of that, but I was hoping common sense would kick in."

"Advocates, please." Rocío moved to block their view of each other. "Let's do what we came here to do." She thought Smith was embarrassed for once, and Hala's reaction wasn't helping. Smith's mouth snapped closed so hard Rocío heard her teeth click.

Yaco frowned at his beaker and then pointed to the wall with shelves.

"Paloma, would you please make sure that no one surprises us from the back door?" Hala asked. "Officer Smith, would you do the same for the interior door? Thank you."

Smith leaned against the wall with her arms folded but did as Hala asked.

"There's a pantry or something here. I don't see how you open it." Yaco felt along the wall. He pressed a panel and then jumped back as the door slid sideways, and the smell of stale sweat wafted out. "This is it," he said flatly.

Rocío stepped forward to look inside. It was in all respects a normal pantry, except for the narrow mattress crammed under the lowest shelves. A light blanket was crumpled at its foot.

"That's grim." Yaco leaned over Rocío's shoulder.

"But as of Thursday afternoon he was alive," Rocío said. "Probably."

"That blood, though …" Paloma said.

"He climbed the shelves." Hala pointed to the left. A shelf in the middle had buckled under his weight. Just below the ceiling was a vent. Its grill was crumpled at the bottom.

"That's a desperate man who thought that vent was large enough to try," Yaco said.

"Maybe he thought he could shout for help." Rocío shuddered.

"We need a forensics team." Hala stepped inside the pantry and stooped to examine the floor. A tile squeaked under her knee.

"A Cempol forensics team," Smith called.

Rocío winced at how loud she sounded.

"Or I'll register a complaint with Commander Dhavale and with your boss."

"Yaco, step out for a moment, would you?" Rocío asked. "I'm going to close the door, and I'd rather not be locked inside."

"Yes, *Detective* Díaz," Yaco said with a dirty look in Smith's direction. He closed Hala and Rocío in.

"You know," Rocío said quietly, examining the inside of the door, "I think some of that obnoxiousness is because she's young and uncertain and trying to prove herself. Though even without that, I think she'd be self-righteously officious."

"Look at you—now that you've committed to Paloma, you're extending your mentoring skills to Cempol fledglings."

"Shut up. It's analyze her or spank her like a spoiled child. Not that spanking is okay."

The metal door seemed standard, with a frame for a clipboard and a handle that should have prevented anyone from being locked inside. A bunch of scratches radiated around it.

"Look out for whatever he used to try to force the door open. Metal, probably."

Hala grunted in acknowledgement and gently spread the blanket open. Rocío tried the door. As expected, it didn't open. "Yaco!" She thumped on it. After a pause that stretched too long, it opened.

"Whew. I was rapidly developing claustrophobia." An unsettling insight into what it might have been like for Aleksandr Prokofiev to be locked in here for several days.

Yaco grimaced in agreement and returned to the counter, kneeling to get a better look at the floor. Paloma asked him something; she looked composed and was handling the blood as well as she'd handled the dead bodies at Isis's.

Rocío stepped into the middle of the pantry. A tile squeaked under her foot. "Kidnapped late on Monday or early Tuesday, held we don't know where until sometime on Wednesday. Presumably held here until Thursday, but gone now. Why keep moving him? Why keep him alive when she's killed so many other people?"

"We didn't see the bodies in Isis's garden until de Herrera wanted us to. Maybe she's confident she can hide him," Hala said.

"You don't think he's here still?" Rocío asked, alarmed. She raised her voice to call, "Paloma, can you bring me the dampener?"

"What was she doing on Thursday?" Hala asked.

"Living a normal life on the surface. Going to work. Getting ready to murder and poison people."

"But not Prokofiev? Why?"

Paloma stepped into the doorway with the dampener. "Where should I put it?"

"As close to the mattress as possible," Hala said, kneeling. Paloma crouched next to her, and another tile squeaked under her knee, definitely a C note.

"I thought Russo and Daughters did these temporary entertainment buildings. Shoddy construction isn't like them," Hala said.

Rocío barely heard her. The first tile had also squeaked in tune, and the second, too. How likely was that? Three faulty but tuned tiles in the room where an artist who made his life with music had been held captive?

Paloma murmured something and reached for the knob on the dampener.

"Stop!" Rocío yelled. "Don't turn it on!"

Paloma lost her balance and fell back into a seated position.

"Help me look for more tiles that squeak."

They found seventeen. Hala dropped evidence flags to mark them (of course she had evidence flags in her pocket) and kept out of Rocío's way as she retraced her steps from the far wall to the door. She hit only three tiles. Prokofiev was tall. If he walked normally, he would step on even fewer.

"Am I leaping to conclusions, or do these notes have a Rus flavor to them?"

There had been a craze for Rus music and dancers last year, possibly prompting the Prokofiev brothers' decision to come to La Bene. From the doorway, Rocío measured the room with her eyes again. A man dancing in the Rus style, with its quick gliding steps, might hit all seventeen tiles.

Rocío closed her eyes, blocking out Smith, who had left her post to peer into the pantry skeptically, Paloma's surprised expression and Hala's hopeful one. Rocío shook out her shoulders, picturing the dancers at the summer festival. They'd been wearing black and red, both the women and the men in clothes that swirled as they turned. Yes, that was it. They had started on the left foot.

She opened her eyes and danced.

Thirteen tiles sang on her first try.

"That's definitely a tune," Hala said.

Paloma gaped at her. "That's amazing. How are you doing that?"

"Once again proving a life in the arts isn't a waste," Rocío said absently.

"We almost destroyed it," Paloma marveled. "The dampener might have wiped it out."

"How did he do it?" Yaco nudged a tile with his finger, making it sound. "I've never seen Benerex magic applied this way." He put his cheek flat on the floor and squinted at the tile while rocking it back and forth. "Oh, I think I see."

Something wasn't right. The sense picture the notes made in Rocío's head went from home to away. Most music went the other way—away to home. From the wall to the door. She danced in the other direction and hit fifteen tiles. It was definitely a tune. A song she knew. She repeated her steps, faster this time. Yes.

"I know that," Hala said. "What is it?"

"A Rus folk song that was popular last year, 'Mi'ja.' It's about a woman locking her daughter in a tower to protect her from her husband."

"Typical victim punishing. Why not do something about the husband?" Yaco asked.

"She does, but first she makes sure her daughter is safe in—"

"—the tower at the height of the city," Smith said. "La Torre de los ancestros is right here, and it's the highest tower in La Bene. That's where she took him. He found out and left a clue. We have to act now before she moves him again." Her face was alight with excitement and the zealotry of someone who sees herself as a savior.

"Smith, I think—" Rocío said.

"No time. Come on—we need to tell Commander Dhavale." She bounded away, almost knocking down Yaco.

"Smith, wait," Hala called.

"Commander Dhavale might be here already. I have to catch him."

She wrenched open the back door and plunged outside.

"At least we know de Herrera is not the kind to leave booby traps," Hala said.

Paloma looked sick. "I didn't even think of that."

"Plenty of time to get suspicious and cynical," Yaco told her.

"Well, we were hoping she'd just go away," Rocío said.

"I'm done." Yaco patted his satchel. "I have a sample of the blood. Forensics will have to do the rest."

"Rocío?" Hala asked.

"Yes, I'm done."

"We'd better catch up to Smith before she goes off and single-handedly bungles the rescue," Hala said.

"Hmm? Oh, I don't think that will happen."

"This is Smith we're talking about," Hala said.

"I'm pretty sure she's on the wrong trail."

"What do you mean, she's on the wrong trail?" Hala asked.

"Those are the lyrics in Benerex. They're different in Rus. By the time the Prokofiev brothers arrived in La Bene, 'Mi'ja' wasn't the number-one song anymore, it was ... never mind. They probably never heard the Benerex version. The song isn't about a tower at all, it's about a lighthouse."

CHAPTER 23

"I THOUGHT you said Smith couldn't mess this up," Hala said.

"I underestimated her skills."

Rocío, Hala and Paloma sat on Hala's desk, as far away from the fatuously beaming, puffed-up Smith as possible while still being able to watch the farce play out. Almost every Miraflores advocate was crowded into the aisles between desks, rarely used helmets cradled in the crooks of their arms, faces apprehensive or resolutely blank, awaiting the resolution of the ... discussion ... between Maurata and Oshinsky on the stairs. The occasional word spiked the air.

"... Cempol!" Maurata said.

"... seasoned detectives ..." Oshinsky countered.

"... Cempol!" Maurata shrieked.

Several people flinched and then tried to pretend they hadn't. Smith's lips moved as she counted advocates. Her attitude struck Rocío as possessive, as if Smith were envisioning leading them into battle. Kids these days. Except this kid was sending everyone on a wild goose chase while Críspula did who knows what.

"... orders ..." Maurata said.

Paloma blew out an exasperated breath.

Right, not kids. I'm not thinking of them as kids. Young adults? Except Rocío's anger grew bigger when she thought of Smith as an adult and not an impetuous youngster craving approval. *Adults crave approval, too*, she argued with herself. *Look at me. And no, I'm totally not thinking about this to avoid thinking about this slow-motion disaster.*

"Oh no, Oshinsky is signaling you," Hala said.

"What do you mean, me?" Rocío asked.

"I'm not the Rus folklore expert." Hala nudged her hard, and Rocío had to turn the fall off the desk into a walk towards the chiefs. *Give me patience*, she prayed to her ancestors as she climbed the steps.

"Detective Díaz, would you please tell Chief Maurata what you told me?"

"Yes, Chief. After our discovery, we stopped to consult a Rus expert about the original lyrics of 'Mi'ja.' The expert also knew the date of the Prokofiev brothers' arrival in La Bene."

In fact the expert was Piotr Prokofiev, but Maurata would quibble, so Maurata didn't need to know that.

"He confirmed that the lyrics in Rus refer to a lighthouse, not simply a high tower. Moreover, the Prokofiev brothers arrived in La Bene well after the popularity of 'Mi'ja.' They wouldn't know the translated version."

She hesitated, wondering how to say the next part without eliciting a knee-jerk reaction from him. "Respectfully, señorx jefe, the information from Cempol came from Officer Smith. She is young and eager, and in this case she has jumped to a conclusion that is incorrect." Maurata continued to look mulishly convinced of his course of action. "She is mistaken." Rocío gripped her wrist behind her back to keep in everything else she wanted to shout at him. "Señorx jefe, La Torre de los ancestros cannot be the correct location."

"I don't understand all this. The song says tower, so it must be the tower."

"Chief, the Benerex version says that because our word for tower fits the music while our word for lighthouse does not."

"That's ridiculous," he said, sticking his chin out. "A word is a word."

Rocío tried to control her expression as she looked at Oshinsky. Behind Maurata's back, Oshinsky spread her fingers in a tight little gesture of exasperation that no one else would be able to see.

"Cempol says the objective is the tower, so that's where we're going."

"Reo, that came from the Cempol liaison, who didn't have all the facts before reporting in. Officer Smith," Oshinsky called, "could you come here?"

Smith bounced up the stairs. "Yes, Deputy Chief Oshinsky?"

"Detective Díaz, would you explain to Officer Smith what you just explained to us?"

"Of course." Rocío kept her explanation short, aware of Maurata fuming over her head.

Smith turned gray and closed her eyes. They snapped open a mere second later, and she said, "Chief Maurata, it seems that my information was incomplete. I would have to advocate for further dialogue with Cempol before any action is taken."

"I don't understand this."

"She's saying she doesn't believe the tower is the correct objective now that she has more information," Oshinsky said, her voice hard-edged.

"No. Cempol says the tower, so it must be the tower."

"Chief, that was *this* Cempol officer, who is now saying something different."

"A word is a word, and I've made my decision. I don't appreciate you trying to interfere. Advocates," he said, raising his voice.

Oshinsky made an aborted gesture like she wanted to clap a hand over his mouth. Smith's mouth dropped open.

Oh no. Rocío hadn't believed even Maurata could reach this level of pigheaded misguidedness. *Why don't I ever learn?*

"Advocates, we have a difficult task ahead of you, but I have confidence you will prevail. And if you die, we will remember your names."

"Chief," Oshinsky croaked.

The advocates shifted and exchanged glances. Someone whispered loudly, "He can't even remember our names while we're alive."

"Quite right," Maurata said, so intent on himself, as always, that he didn't even hear the whispers. "Deputy Chief Oshinsky will lead this rescue and apprehension mission, and she will be issuing firearms for the duration. Good luck. My thoughts are with you, and may the seres celestiales look kindly on our endeavors." He nodded benevolently and hurried up the steps.

"Señorx Advocates." Oshinsky's voice boomed through the office, and immediately everyone stopped shuffling and turned their attention on her. "No one is dying today. The request form in triplicate allowing civil servants to die on duty has not crossed my desk."

"You'd have to do the report in quadruplicate now," Espinoza called, and everyone laughed a little too hard.

"Just so. And you know that I have refused to institute the quadruplicate forms at least until next Monday. Therefore the government has not given you permission to die.

"However, Chief Maurata was right about one thing."

That was as close to publicly condemning Maurata as Rocío had ever heard Oshinsky come.

"I will be issuing firearms to everyone. If you have not kept your firearms certification up to date—and that does have to be done in triplicate—you will not be able to support your coworkers. I hope that is not the case for anyone here." She raised her hands. "We have two objectives: neutralize de Herrera and anyone working with her, and rescue Aleksandr Prokofiev.

"We will be working with two tenth-level magickers from Cempol. They will be responsible for neutralizing de Herrera's magical abilities. We are responsible for providing them support in any way they order and for not interfering with their efforts. Any questions?"

"Are you coming with us, Chief?" Espinoza asked.

"Coming with you? Espinoza, you're all coming with me." The laughter sounded like relief. Rocío mentally cursed Maurata again.

"Pérez is distributing the firearms. Hop to it, Señorx," Oshinsky ordered. "Officer Smith, if you would give us a moment."

She waited for Smith to descend the stairs, all of the bounce crushed out of her. Rocío almost felt sorry for her. Almost.

"My hands are tied on this, Rocío," Oshinsky said softly. "I can't go against the chief and Cempol. You and Hala have Díaz and Yaco and my permission to go to the lighthouse."

"Chief, a *necromancer*." Rocío threw her hands up, not even taking pleasure in the dramatic gesture. "We need—I don't even know what we need, because no one has done this before."

"I'm not sending you on a suicide mission. Check it out. See what there is to see. Take pictures. Get me some kind of proof in case I can't convince Cempol, but I'm hoping we'll be right behind you. I sent Fede to Commander Dhavale's secretary before I spoke to Chief Maurata. I had a feeling this would happen."

Everyone knew the secretary ran Cempol as much as Dhavale did, and Fede was her nephew. If anyone could get Cempol pointed in the right direction, it was the secretary.

"But the gears of bureaucracy grind slowly and often in the absolutely fucking wrong direction. Do not get yourselves killed."

Rocío squeezed her face between her hands and then took a deep breath. "Okay, Chief."

"I trust your judgement. And Hala's." Oshinsky nodded at Hala across the room. She was staring at the ceiling, talking soundlessly to herself. Probably in Ebeya, which was the language she always used when coming up with an improbable solution to an impossible situation. Rocío tried to take some hope from that.

"I'm going to try to get this debacle on wheels turned in the right direction, but you can't count on our immediate support. And one other thing ..."

Rocío paused with her hand on the rail and the bad feeling in her stomach climbing up her throat.

"I'm afraid Smith is going to have to go with you."

"We need a plan," Hala said.

Rocío, Paloma and Yaco nodded. The other Díaz stood with his arms crossed, clearly unhappy, though he hadn't yet shared what exactly was making him feel that way: the suicide aspects of their mission, or just the company. Rocío was sure he'd tell them eventually.

Unfortunately, Smith was sharing. Again. Her voice echoed off the walls of the now eerily empty CJC. "We shouldn't be doing this without Cempol."

"You are Cempol, Smith," Rocío said.

"Not all of it," Smith muttered.

"Then you shouldn't have gone over Detectives Haddad's and Díaz's heads." Paloma put her hands on her hips and frowned at Smith, reminding Rocío why she liked Paloma. It was a good sensation, even amidst this mess.

"I have to agree," Yaco said, though he didn't clarify which part he was agreeing with.

"In any case, we're not doing it without Cempol. We're just going to be a little ahead of them," Rocío said.

"Oshinsky said reconnaissance, and that's what we're going to do." Hala swept them with her gaze.

"You can't do that without Cempol, either." Smith tried to crowd Hala. Hala didn't budge and met Smith's outraged glare with her own cool one.

Rocío picked through the bag she kept ready for stakeouts. "You're perfectly welcome to go urge Commander Dhavale to hurry up and meet us there, as Cempol wouldn't be going to the wrong place if it weren't for you."

Smith deflated like punctured balloon, though Rocío didn't think that would last long.

"But we need a plan for a worst-case scenario," Rocío explained again. *Thermos, empty. Binoculars, mittens, dried fruit. Bullets.*

"My intention is to avoid putting us in such a situation," Hala said, "but just in case."

"Unlike some other people," Yaco said under his breath.

"Mateo," Hala said to the other Díaz, "you need to know that the Cempol magickers think it's quite possible de Herrera is able to communicate with Fernández because she has his body. That means she's not a novice—it's likely she has access to all his expertise."

"At magic that causes death and pain," Yaco pointed out helpfully.

"Are you kidding?" Díaz's sputtered. "This is not a time to develop a sense of humor, Hala."

"I'm not kidding."

He groaned and rubbed his hand over his face. "Well, I always thought I would go out in a blaze of glory."

"No one is dying." Rocío stared at him until he shrugged.

Paloma looked a little pale around the edges. Smith looked ... eager, confirming Rocío's belief that she had hero fantasies.

"Which is why we need a plan," Hala said.

"I still have the Cempol dampener." Yaco pointed to the machine on the next desk over. "That might protect us a little. If we can get it working in time. And if we manage to get it close to her, preferably between her and us. It's really not a good idea for us to get close to her, though."

"Oshinsky will come through." Rocío tied her bag closed and rested her hands on top. "I have an idea. Part of an idea. It's something my nonna used to tell me—that the Ya had a way to protect themselves against ghosts, and that people in La Bene used it during the Ghost Years. Yaco, do you know anything about that?"

"Oh. Oh. Oh." He ran his hands through his hair and pulled on it, then turned his back to them and muttered to himself.

Smith rolled her eyes and opened her mouth, likely to say something awful. Everyone glared at her, even Díaz.

"Yes." He spun around and pointed at Rocío. "Your nonna was a genius. We need a placenta. Human if possible, cat, dog, goat, whatever, if not. As fresh as possible."

Smith opened and closed her mouth, but nothing came out. It was clichéd, but she looked like a carp. There was very little pleasure in this situation, so Rocío would take it where she found it.

"Rocío?" Hala asked.

"Yes, I can get a human placenta, Hala. Without harming anyone," she assured Paloma, who was going past white and into green. "It's going to be okay."

"Also a dozen eggs, chaste tree berries—we have those in the big first aid kit—and ... needles from a monkey puzzle tree. Yes, that's it." He nodded decisively to himself and looked up. "What? Monkey puzzle trees are an important part of Ya and Ka magic. We'll make—"

"Explanations later," Hala said. "Yaco, what will this do?"

"Hopefully give us some protection against necromancy if, ancestros protect us, we wind up face-to-face with her."

Smith wrinkled her nose. "That can't work; it's not real magic."

"It's not magic like we're used to thinking of magic." Yaco gestured broadly. "It's a remnant of when La Bene was Ya. It's sympathetic magic, like the way putting your ancestors' favorite foods on their altar makes it easier to talk to ..." He trailed off at her slightly revolted expression. "Oh, you don't, I forgot you're ... you weren't born in La Bene, were you."

"I don't do that." Smith drew back, as if he'd suggested she marry her brother.

"I didn't think you could actually get more offensive." Rocío jerked open the drawer where Hala kept her stakeout bag and dropped it on the top of the desk.

Díaz tucked his hands into his armpits as if restraining himself from decking Smith.

"What?" Smith asked.

"You just managed to offend everyone here."

Smith just looked blank.

"By suggesting our religious practices are repugnant."

Smith opened her mouth, and Rocío could tell she was going to continue to be offensive.

"We're not arguing over the nature of magic or religion, Smith," Hala said. "As I was saying, if it comes to a confrontation with de Herrera, our best hope is to keep her talking and distracted while we wait for Cempol. That's Rocío's job."

"Hala." Rocío put up a hand to stop her. "She's not going to want to talk to me. She lied to me. You're going to have to do it."

"No. For what I'm planning, I need her attention off of me."

"That leaves me." Díaz checked his holster.

"Um." Hala stroked her chin.

"What? I can talk."

"Without enraging her into killing us all?" Hala nodded to his hand on his gun. He dropped his hand, glaring.

"Actually ..." Rocío paused, suddenly doubting her judgement. She'd been wrong about Paloma. *What if I'm wrong about Críspula?*

"Rocío?"

She steadied herself on the trust she saw in Hala's eyes. "I think she's going to want to talk to Paloma. And I think we should let her."

"Me?" Paloma squeaked.

"What?" Yaco asked.

"Now, that's just irresponsible." Díaz stabbed a finger at Rocío. "She's not even an advocate, hasn't been out from behind a desk for an entire week yet."

"I think Críspula has an attachment to Paloma, and we need to use every tool we have." Rocío faced Paloma. "If you think you can. If not, I don't think you should come, because you'll draw her attention no matter what."

"I barely know her," Paloma protested.

"But she's engaged with you every time we've seen her, and she's asked about you when you weren't there."

"She has?" Paloma looked like she'd taken a bite of papaya and wasn't sure it was okay to eat. Papaya got that slightly vomity taste when it was off.

"She talked to you at Ministrx O'Higgins's house, and she asked about you when I interviewed her at Isis's house."

Rocío watched Paloma. She saw fear, and determination, and earnestness and eagerness and sincerity, all good traits for an advocate, now that Rocío could see past the distorted mirror of her prejudices.

"I haven't given you a lot of reasons to trust me, Advocate Faro. But you kept your cool at Isis's house when we saw the bodies. You did a good job interviewing witnesses and sorting them out. You've combed through garbage and stood up to me when I pushed you down. I believe you can talk to Críspula. But this is your decision. Only you can make it. You know who you are and what you're capable of, or you wouldn't have fought so hard to be an advocate."

Paloma smiled slightly at the title, pulling her shoulders back and standing up straighter.

"Very touching," Díaz said sarcastically. "Hala, are you going to allow this? She's not even trained. She should stay here."

"Let's hear what Paloma has to say."

"I can do this," Paloma said firmly.

Hala hesitated. "Rocío, are you sure about this?"

"That Críspula won't talk to me? Yes. That Paloma can talk to her? Yes. That if we face Críspula, we'll probably all be killed? Yes. But you knew that already, Paloma, didn't you?"

Paloma crossed her arms. "Advocates serve. That's what we do. In a perfect world, we wouldn't have to do this, but right now there's no one else who can. I can do this. I want to do this."

"Rocío is manipulating her!" Díaz said.

"Everything is manipulation. If you think the oath of office isn't a manipulation of your emotions, you're naive."

Díaz sputtered at Rocío. Even Hala looked a bit taken aback.

"Paloma's right. We serve. There's no one else right now. And she's had all the training she needs for this kind of conflict. I know. I had it, too, in my parents' house. She's an adult. She's made her decision, just as we all have." Not that that would lighten the guilt one bit if Paloma got killed during this little outing.

Hala ran her hand through her hair, looking uncertain. "Rocío, could Críspula just want to kill Paloma?"

"I don't think she wants to kill her. I think she wants Paloma to justify what she's done."

"You're staking her life on that observation," Hala said.

"I know."

"Okay, Paloma. You're coming."

Paloma's expression wavered between elation and dread. Rocío tucked an extra package of jerky in her bag for her.

"You can't be serious!" Díaz exploded.

"If all goes to plan, these preparations will be unnecessary. Cempol should be right behind us," Hala said.

"And if it doesn't?" Yaco asked. "What are we going to do then?"

"I have an idea about that. Yaco, do you have one hundred milliliters of powdered aluminum, iron oxide and glycerin?"

"Thermite? Hala—"

"Do you?"

"Yes." He drew the word out reluctantly.

"I'll need eggs for this, too. Officer Smith, go buy, beg or steal two dozen eggs—the fresher, the better."

"I won't—"

Hala glared at Smith, who for once stopped talking. So she did have a smidgeon of survival instinct in her.

"I'll buy them," she said sullenly.

"I don't care what you do as long as you get them. Díaz, get a bag of weapons ready. You're our best shot. And get me five of those blown egg ornaments that people hang in their windows in spring."

"What color do you want?"

"Very funny. Yaco, I'll need your smallest funnel."

"Hala—"

"Shush. And gloves. Here's what I think we should do."

She told them her plan.

CHAPTER 24

"Remind me one more time how a man like Maurata gets to be chief?" Rocío asked so she wouldn't ask "Where is Cempol?" again.

She was crouched behind a boulder clutching her binoculars and trying to get them to focus on the lighthouse. The wind off the ocean was cutting through her jacket, and she was shivering so hard the focus wheels kept jerking past the point of sharpness. The lighthouse was bright and white and still, about fifty meters away past a rippling boulder field. It stood at the pointy end of the triangular headland, which dropped away directly behind it; there was another drop less than half a meter to Rocío's left. Behind her group was a stand of eucalyptus trees and the road where they'd left the automobile.

The clouds racing overhead made Rocío feel a little dizzy, like she was at the prow of a ship plowing into the ocean. Or maybe it was fear and frustration and the waiting and the endless shush of the waves crashing at the base of the cliff. In the last hour they'd seen no sign that Críspula was in the lighthouse. Neither had they seen any signs that anyone else was in the lighthouse, which, according to Hala, was staffed full-time with three keepers. The headland wasn't called Punta Mala for no reason; even with the lighthouse, several ships wrecked on this stretch of coast every year. So yeah, the lack of visible keepers was a point of data suggesting Críspula was there.

"Political favors," Hala said, answering Rocío's question about Maurata. "And nepotism. His father's family was instrumental in—"

"You shouldn't talk about your chief that way," Smith said.

Did the woman ever get the stick out of her ass? Unbelievable.

"Can we focus on the matter at hand?" Yaco asked. "Are we going to stay here and wait for Cempol, or are we going to leave before this necromancer blasts these rocks and us into tomorrow?"

"Can a necromancer do that?" Díaz asked.

"I don't believe she's here," Smith said.

"No, she can't," Rocío said.

"Probably," Hala said.

"Maybe," Yaco said at the same time.

"What?" Rocío glared at Hala and Yaco.

"Necromancy isn't just about revealing the hidden." Yaco scrunched down further behind his rock. "It also accelerates decay. So she could crumble the rocks under us and drop us into the sea. Probably."

"I know how I know that, but how do you know that?" Hala leaned on her elbow to see Yaco.

"I've been doing some reading. Since we went to the haunted castle."

"What kind of reading?" Hala sounded outraged that he had managed to find information she hadn't.

"Not all nepotism is bad," Yaco muttered. "I talked to my mother, and she talked to an archivist at the University's legal library. She let me read the journals of the magickers who examined the haunted castle and the other places Fernández used necromancy."

"And you didn't *share*?"

"The journals were *chained* to the *wall*."

"More books chained to the wall," Rocío said. "We didn't see those."

"You what?" Yaco asked.

"What about your notes?" Hala asked. "Were they chained to the wall, too?"

"It wasn't that useful! Besides, I saw you talking to Magicker Huaripani. If anyone knows what to do with a rogue necromancer, it's her. Wait, that's redundant, isn't it? Can you have a non-rogue necromancer?"

"Focus, people," Rocío said. "We're supposed to be gathering intel on the vengeful copycat of the archfiend architect of necromancy, who may or may not be in that lighthouse. We have one fifth-level magicker, Díaz's mystery bag, two pairs of binoculars, and Fede's coffee, which Yaco stole. Again."

"Yeah, that's helpful," Yaco said.

"You forgot the thermite in those blown egg ornaments," Hala pointed out.

"And the placenta," Paloma said valiantly.

"It's not a mystery to me." Díaz patted the bag next to him.

"Fine, and a bunch of bickering advocates who won't focus on the extremely serious situation we're facing, *and* thermite and eggs *and* various pieces of equipment, which are part of a last-ditch plan *we will not use* because Cempol *will* arrive. Hala, what is your assessment, please?"

"She started it," Yaco said. Rocío glared at him.

Smith hunched her shoulders. "I don't understand you people."

"I think it's unlikely that we'll get more confirmation that de Herrera is here besides the absence of the lighthouse keepers," Hala said. "On a normal day I think they would clean the light, come outside, etc. Let the horses out for exercise."

There were no conveyances in sight, but there was a barn to the right of the lighthouse big enough to shelter a carriage and two horses.

"I doubt they all decided to abandon their post. Is it possible the detector is reacting to the magic maintaining the light?"

Yaco had made Paloma stop using the magic detector about half an hour ago because all it did was point southwest at the lighthouse and drain Paloma's energy.

"Possible," Yaco said, "though I would expect a more constant reading if that were the case."

"Any sign of Oshinsky and Cempol?" Hala asked.

"I was trying not to ask that." Rocío swept her binoculars up the red, empty road. "No. Where are you, Oshinsky?"

"We should—"

"I think you were wrong, *Detective* Haddad, and I was right," Smith said. "She's not here and I'll prove it to you."

She stood up and waved her arms at the lighthouse.

"Officer Smith, get down," Hala ordered.

"Not until you say we're going to La Torre de los ancestros, the tallest building in La Bene. Where I said we should go. They're all *there* saving them, and we're *here*."

"You are out of—Mother of the Holy Ones."

Black smoke erupted from the top of the lighthouse and within two breaths engulfed it. The smoke clung to the lantern room, completely obscuring the glass panes and the narrow balcony that surrounded it, pulsing and changing in density and darkness. It wasn't actually smoke, unless there was an invisible barrier keeping it in place, as its edges stayed firm and coherent, not shredding in the stiff wind. A tiny hole pierced it, and then another and another, letting through the blue of the sky behind it. Rocío blinked, and the holes became lights like malevolent stars, sending a shiver through her. The longer she looked, the more lights she saw sparking in the smoke, cold, pale blue lights that seemed to make the morning darker.

Díaz tackled Smith, dropping them both into the dirt. "Stay down." He disentangled himself from her and glared. She glared back. Blood and dirt smeared one cheek.

"O'Higgins said he saw lights that seemed to give off darkness instead of light." Rocío's voice sounded distant even to herself. *Shit, shit, shit.*

"Can I use your binoculars?" Smith asked Rocío, sitting up.

"No. Haven't you done enough? Hala, we need to get out of here."

Smith grabbed the binoculars and turned back to the lighthouse.

"Hey, you—"

"There's a hostage and he's bleeding." Smith pointed to the top of the lighthouse.

"Perdidos ancestros," Yaco swore viciously. "This time she's right."

Rocío snatched back her binoculars. "I don't ..." The black cloud was spooking her, *piérdalo para siempre*, and it was larger than before.

"At the top, on the balcony, in the cloud," Smith said.

Rocío spotted him. He was weirdly hard to see, and adjusting the focus just made him blurrier. Crimson stained his white shirt, though—that was unmistakable. "*Piérdate.*" She barely bit back *Smith*. She handed the binoculars to Hala. "Do we have descriptions of the lighthouse keepers?"

"One is missing an arm, and this man has all his limbs. The descriptions of the others are not useful at this distance," Hala said. "Everyone, get your gear. We're leaving."

"We can't abandon him." Smith crossed her arms.

"We're not abandoning him. We're following orders to observe, report and return with sufficient resources to make a rescue feasible."

"We didn't get orders to abandon people."

"Smith, take a deep breath and think this through," Rocío said, realizing a little deep breathing of her own wouldn't be amiss.

Paloma copied her and looked a little less freaked out. Díaz adjusted his mystery bag on his shoulder, and Rocío guessed he wished they were somewhere else as much as she did.

"We don't know what de Herrera is capable of and our orders were not to do anything reckless like confront the necromancer in a location of her choosing without the right tools or people." *Or stand up and announce our presence.*

"You and your deep breathing." Smith obstinately kept breathing at her own rapid pace. "That's a *person* up there. Who you want to abandon."

"Officer Smith, this is not a discussion," Hala barked. "We are leaving right now."

"You can't make me." Smith puffed up, trying to look bigger, which was kind of hard because they were all crouched behind boulders, trying not to present a target.

"Get your head down." Paloma tugged on Smith's arm. "What are you, twelve?" That would have been deeply funny in different circumstances.

Yaco groaned and rubbed his head with the hand holding the binoculars.

"I don't think this is the time." Paloma patted Smith's shoulder.

Smith shrugged her off.

Hala raised her eyebrows at Rocío, clearly asking if Rocío had a better way to handle the walking, talking interpersonal problem that was Smith. Díaz reached for Smith's arm.

Smith kicked him in the stomach, shoved Paloma away, and bolted up the road towards the lighthouse.

Díaz folded, his face contorted in pain and his mouth open for air.

"No!" Yaco shouted, lunging for Smith. She evaded him and ran out of the shelter of the rocks. Yaco stopped short, his hands over his mouth.

"Smith, get back here!" Hala shouted.

"Seres celestiales." Rocío crawled to Díaz.

The sound of gunshots cracked through the air.

"Smith's down," Yaco said. "Shit."

Right at that moment, Rocío could not bring herself to care. Díaz choked and curled into a ball, wheezing as his diaphragm started working again to pump air into his lungs.

"It's okay, Mateo, the worst is over. Don't fight it." She pressed her fingers to the pulse in his wrist, checked her watch and started counting.

"Is Smith dead?" Hala asked.

Lots of suppressed emotion in that sentence, oh yes. Rocío savagely repressed her own. "It's high, but that's expected," she told Díaz. She wiped the sweat from his forehead with her sleeve.

"She moved her arm!" Yaco shouted and then dropped his voice. "She's not dead."

"Which window did the shot come from?" Hala asked.

"I didn't see," Yaco said.

"Me neither," Paloma said in a small voice. Her hands were clamped around her opposite forearms, and her face pale, but she wasn't panicking. You never knew, when it came right down to it, who would panic and who would stay calm, and it was always a relief to find out.

Díaz's color was better, and his breathing was calming. He twisted his hand to grab Rocío's.

"You're doing good, Díaz. You too, Paloma." The corners of Paloma's lips hitched upwards in acknowledgement. Rocío turned back to Díaz. "I want to check your abdomen."

"I'll be okay," he rasped.

"Good. I'm still checking. Does this hurt?" She palpated his abdomen, watching him closely.

"It's sore. That's all."

He didn't show any signs of severe pain, and she moved up to his chest to check for rib fractures. "How about here?"

"No." He exhaled with relief.

"Your pulse is dropping, too. Which is good, because it would hurt Oshinsky to demote me after I kicked Smith's ass into next Tuesday."

"She's shot," he said.

"Yeah. I *suppose* that's punishment enough."

"I'm glad to hear you talking, Díaz." The corners of Hala's eyes crinkled at the irony of that statement. "Are you physically able to help with a rescue?"

Rocío met Hala's eyes and saw the same determination she felt. It should have been a relief that her personal dislike of Smith wasn't affecting her decisions, but her dread was too great. She swallowed. She couldn't even wish for Smith's descendants to forget her. The situation was too dire. *Seres celestiales protect us.*

"Yes." Díaz levered himself into a sitting position.

"Are you willing to do this?" Hala asked everyone.

Díaz's and Yaco's faces were grim with agreement. Paloma set her lips, but Rocío read uncertainty there.

"Paloma, you can drive, correct?" Hala asked.

Paloma nodded.

"If you agree, I'd like you to get the automobile when I give the signal and get as close to Smith as you can. We'll be covering you."

Paloma's face hardened with resolution and she nodded again, more sharply.

"Okay. Honk the horn when you can't get any closer. Díaz," Hala said, "how many—"

Another crack broke the air. It didn't sound like a gunshot. Rocío looked around wildly. Nothing seemed to change, and then the boulders they were hiding behind flattened, and the rock under her feet vibrated and began to slide slowly towards the ocean.

"Move!"

She scooped up the dampener with one hand, shoved Paloma with the other and lunged forward. For one breathless moment she slid backward even as her feet ran forward. Paloma reached the next set of boulders and turned, arms outstretched. Rocío jumped and grabbed one of Paloma's arms. Paloma hauled her forward. The ground stayed firm under her feet.

Yaco slammed into her and the three of them fell. Rocío dropped the dampener, twisting to avoid Paloma. She slammed into the ground with her forearms and saved her head from smashing into a pointy rock. Yaco landed on top of her and her head bounced off the rock after all. "Ow, ow."

"Sorry, I'm sorry." Yaco rolled off her but stayed low behind the much smaller boulders remaining between them and the lighthouse.

Rocío half sat up. All her pieces seemed to be attached. "Paloma?"

"It's just an abrasion," Paloma said, examining the blood on her left arm.

"Hala?" Díaz asked.

Rocío twisted and looked over her shoulder.

Hala wiped blood off her forehead, examined her fingers and gingerly probed the cut. "Can one of you bandage this for me?" She pulled a folded bandage from one of her pockets.

Rocío shook her head in disbelief. Seven years, and she still couldn't believe the amount of stuff Hala carried. Paloma scooted forward to help.

Rocío crawled to the dampener. The case was scuffed but not dented. When she opened it, the machine seemed unharmed, all the rings still round and attached to each other.

"Smith is still alive," Yaco reported from where he lay among the boulders. He'd managed to hold on to his binoculars. "She's breathing. I don't see the hostage anymore and I still can't see anyone in the lighthouse."

"They can see us," Rocío said grimly.

"The road is gone," Hala said.

Rocío turned. A ten-meter section was gone like a bite in a cake, including the shelf of rock they'd been crouching on and a large chunk of the road. Waves pounded loudly against the new shoreline like they were trying to map the shape of it. The automobile and most of their gear was on the other side of the newly formed ravine. "Great. There goes our quick getaway. That's all we need. We might be able to drive around on the rocks, but it'll be slow and we'll be exposed."

"Whichever way we go, we'll be exposed," Hala said.

"We're still going to try to get Smith, though, aren't we?" Yaco asked.

"Díaz?"

He unzipped his bag and removed metal pieces that he quickly assembled with no wasted motions.

"A grenade launcher?" Yaco asked, his voice squeaking. "What about the lighthouse keepers? Prokofiev? You can't—"

"No." Díaz pulled out three canisters.

"Smoke bombs," Hala said, the bandage a white slash over her dark skin. Paloma turned a bloody scrap of bandage over in her hands, shrugged and pinned it to the ground with a rock.

"I hate my life," Rocío said. "Why do I feel like I'm ten? Smoke bombs and stink bombs and haunted castles. What's next? Fart cushions?"

"We should be so lucky," Paloma said unsteadily. "Should I still go for the automobile?"

"If de Herrera can do that to the cliff, what can she do to the automobile?" Hala asked.

"That thing isn't stable at the best of times," Rocío exclaimed. "Paloma, do not go for the auto."

"That's ... a good point," Yaco said. "I'm a fifth-level forensics magicker, Hala. I can't do miracles."

Hala rubbed her forehead, encountered the bandage and dropped her hands. "I know. This is what we're going to do. Díaz will fire two smoke bombs. Rocío, will you recover Smith? Good. The rest of us will cover you with gunfire. We will retreat to that white eucalyptus tree." She pointed to a slim tree to the left of the new ravine and the automobile. "The terrain flattens out there and we'll have the cover of the trees while we run to the road where it loops around."

They need to make flesh-colored bandages. Hala's basically wearing a giant shoot-me-in-the head sign. "Hala, do you have a hat?"

"No. Are we ready?"

"Wait." Rocío squinted at the lighthouse. The door at the bottom opened and a man walked out stiffly with both hands in the air. The sunlight glinted on his blond hair.

"Hello?" he shouted, his voice cracking.

"Juan Pablo?" Paloma said. "Oh no."

"Juan Pablo Ricci?" Rocío asked. "The missing Juan Pablo, third secretary to the sub-com? Diosas de mis madres."

"Is he a hostage or a coconspirator?" Yaco asked.

"She'll kill you all," Juan Pablo called, "if you move." His voice wobbled and his arms shook. "She k-killed the lighthouse keeper. You saw what she did to the road."

"What's going on, Juan Pablo?" Rocío shouted.

"She's possessed, talking to herself. She has—" He cried out and fell back against the doorjamb. "She says to stop talking and come here now, or she'll kill me and the others."

"Okay, we're coming. Do you hear that, Críspula?" Hala shouted. "Do you see anyone with him?" she demanded in a lower voice.

"No," Yaco said, lowering the binoculars.

"The needle is pointing at him." Paloma was crouched over the magic detector. "Or the lighthouse. Not that it wasn't before, because of the black cloud thing, but it kind of jiggled around first."

Rocío patted Paloma's shoulder, took the magic detector away from her and shut it off.

"I think Punta Mala just became Punta Peor," Yaco said.

"Not funny," Díaz said.

Rocío clapped a hand to her forehead. "Like no one's ever heard that joke before. Points for trying though."

"Now!" Juan Pablo shouted. "Please."

"Hala?" Yaco asked.

"She says she thought better of you and she doesn't want to kill Aleksandr Prokofiev, but if that's not enough—" Juan Pablo staggered and went down on one knee.

A eucalyptus tree three meters from the one Hala had pointed out disintegrated. First the trunk imploded in slow motion, then the branches and then the leaves. For a moment, brown and green dust hung in the air like a tree ghost, and then it blew away. Part of the cliff and a section of the road slid down into the sea.

"Sutayta Al-Mahamali," Hala swore to the mother of poetry and mathematics. "We're going to have to go in there, we're going to have to use guns and we're going to have to use my plan. You all know what to do. Use your judgement. Yaco, do what you can. Rocío, leave Smith. Maybe de Herrera will forget about her. Paloma, stay close."

"Please," Juan Pablo yelled. The terrified pleading in his voice made Rocío's stomach feel like it was climbing up her esophagus.

"None of that," she muttered to herself, swallowing hard. "We're coming," she shouted. "We're standing up. Críspula, don't shoot." She checked her gun and replaced it in the holster. She wanted both hands free for now. She stood up and held her breath. No one shot her.

Díaz slung his bag over one shoulder and the big weapon over the other so that it was mostly hidden by his body. Holding his pistol alongside his leg, he stood. Rocío started breathing again, mostly because she had to.

"We're walking to you," Hala called to Juan Pablo. She motioned Paloma into the center of the group, Rocío behind her, and took her place at the front. Yaco took the back, and they walked forward slowly.

Juan Pablo sagged against the door.

The back of Rocío's neck itched with the certainty of an imminent attack. Hala's and Díaz's heads swiveled as they scanned the headland while Paloma stared straight ahead, her jaw set. Yaco muttered to himself, his voice shaky but his steps crunching steadily behind Rocío.

"You know this is what they tell you not to do in every training scenario you ever have as an advocate. Don't let yourself be taken hostage. Do not enter an enclosed place with a violent person, especially a building with only one exit."

"Yes, Yaco. Paloma, please note you should not do this," Rocío said, dividing her attention between the shadowed doorway and Smith.

"Noted," Paloma said, her voice strangled.

As they got closer, Rocío saw the regular movement of Smith's chest. Not that she didn't believe Yaco, but some things you needed to see for yourself. "Thank you, seres celestiales," Rocío said fervently. Blood stained the bottom right side of Smith's shirt where the protective vest stopped. She had managed to fold her shirt over the wound and stanch the bleeding.

"Officer Smith, it looks like the bullet passed through the edge of your left abdominal oblique muscle," Hala said. "It's not life-threatening if you control the bleeding and get medical care, though I'm sure it doesn't feel that way."

Sweat beaded on Smith's forehead and rolled down her temples into her hair. Her pupils were dilated and the whites visible all around. "No," she panted.

"I'm sorry, Officer Smith," Rocío said. "You'll be on your own for a while. Try to get help if you can. We're going into the lighthouse. She'll be distracted by us, and you'll have a chance to get away. Don't go straight back; part of the road is gone behind us. Take the automobile." Smith's eyes rolled back in her head. "Officer Smith, listen—we need Magicker Huaripani or Chuquisengo." *I wish I could give her more help.* "We're depending on you. Officer Smith?"

Smith grunted something.

"Keep walking," Hala said.

"Good luck, Officer Smith," Rocío said as she passed.

The walk seemed interminable, but the lighthouse grew bigger. As the details became clearer, the walls grew lines between the stones, the stones gained texture and Juan Pablo's face came into focus. He was crying, though whether if was from pain, relief or terror Rocío couldn't tell. Probably all three.

Half the pins were missing from his hair and it hung in dirty locks around his shoulders and over his face. Blood and dirt stained his shirt, and he had a bruise on his cheek. He looked like he'd had the insolence beaten out of him. It wasn't a good look. Brutality never was.

Rocío's jaw tensed and her steps firmed. Finally they were coming face-to-face with the woman who had caused so much pain.

"Hurry," Juan Pablo begged. His eyes widened as he noticed Paloma and he pushed himself to his feet. He kept his gaze on Hala's face, as if he needed it to be the only thing in the universe. A blush crept up his cheeks.

"Are you hurt?" Hala asked across the last two meters.

"Me? A little, not, not ..." He began crying harder.

"It's okay. We need your help, Juan Pablo. Can you tell me where she is?"

"Inside," he gasped between sobs.

"Where inside?" He didn't answer. "You're doing well. Juan Pablo, what floor is she on?"

He shook his head but showed six fingers without lifting his hands.

Moving slowly and keeping her hand in view, Hala reached for his shoulder. Shudders moved through him like a sine wave. And that was a very Hala comparison.

"We're here now," Hala said quietly. "How many people àre inside with her, Juan Pablo?"

He folded down his thumb and first finger on one hand and closed the other.

Three people. The two other lighthouse keepers and Aleksandr Prokofiev, probably. Unless he was counting himself?

"It's Cr[ispula, right? Your cousin?"

"I—I—I ..."

"Juan Pablo, look at me. You're doing really well."

"She'll hurt me," he cried, but he made a fist and rocked it like a head nodding. "You have to come." He lurched inside, favoring his left leg.

Hala exchanged a glance with Díaz. He nodded and stepped through the doorway, moving immediately to the right, gun raised. Hala followed a heartbeat behind him, her gun ready, and stepped to the left.

Rocío's throat closed up.

"There's no one here," Hala called.

Rocío stepped inside.

CHAPTER 25

THE GROUND FLOOR of the lighthouse was dim and lined with water barrels and little else. Rocío blinked rapidly to make her sight adjust more quickly. For the moment it felt warm out of the wind, and she opened her coat. On the left, only the lowest steps of a stone staircase were visible before it disappeared behind a shielding wall. Its loose spiral reminded Rocío of the stairs in the haunted castle, which had been engineered for defense. These hadn't, but they would work just as well for Críspula; she could easily pick them off as they emerged from the stairwell. All she had to do was wait.

Juan Pablo headed for the stairs, his legs stiff with fear.

"Are there any traps?" Hala whispered urgently. "On the next floor or any of them?"

He shook his head. "She is the trap." He missed a step, stumbled, righted himself and kept going.

"That's reassuring." Yaco put a hand on the wall to support himself.

Díaz straightened from examining the barrels and stared after Juan Pablo. "This is really bad."

"I've never seen anyone that afraid and still walking," Yaco said. "Do you think she's compelling him some way?"

"You're asking *us*?" Paloma whispered.

"Rocío." Hala jerked her head at the case Rocío still held.

Rocío knelt, extracted the dampener, set her teeth and turned it on. It stuttered and then whirred into motion, the rings whipping around smoothly. Hopefully that meant it hadn't been damaged when it fell. She wrapped her arms around it and stood. It was an awkward armful, the hard corners biting into the insides of her arms, the outside ring tall enough to sheer the skin off her chin if she didn't remember to keep it up.

Hala turned to the stairs. Díaz jostled in front of her and she yielded first place to him. Rocío could feel Paloma's breath on the back of her neck as they followed. Díaz disappeared around the curve of the stairs. Rocío braced herself for gunshots.

"It's clear," Díaz called softly.

By the time Rocío emerged on the next level, he and Juan Pablo were already out of sight again.

The metal barrels lining the walls on this level were labeled OIL and FLAMMABLE. Rocío winced. She hadn't stopped to think whether the lighthouse had converted to electricity. *Great, the likelihood of involuntary self-immolation just went up.* Rocío hurried after Hala.

The kitchen on the next floor was also empty.

Two plates had been abandoned on the table. The remains of chilaquiles with eggs and salsa verde were brown, crusted and crawling with ants. A teacup was overturned on the floor, dried tea spattered around it, and the lighthouse logbook lay next to it, stained brown, the pages bent.

They kept going. Rocío's thighs burned from the weight of the dampener, but her breathing wasn't strained like Yaco's behind her. Paloma was silent as a mouse. When they reached the fourth floor, the pantry, Hala stopped Díaz. If Críspula hadn't moved, she was two floors above them. Juan Pablo kept climbing.

Rocío deposited the dampener on the floor and shook out her arms. From the insulated pouch on his belt, Yaco extracted metal canisters the size of Rocío's fist and handed them out, keeping one for himself. Or two, since he still had Smith's. This was the plan they weren't supposed to need to use, but here they were, using it. *Please, Nonna, let this work.*

The canister was still cold when Rocío took it, and water vapor drifted out when she opened it. She hissed as she touched the cold watery paste to her cheek. She was the only one who made a face, but then only she had actually handled the placenta. It made it impossible to fool herself about what made the paste so red.

Rocío had been lucky; a doula friend had just come from a new mother's labor, and the mother had generously shared half the placenta. Rocío had cut it into small pieces and blended it with the eggs, chaste tree berries and monkey tree needles and then run a spark of magic through it. It hadn't smelled any more than fresh meat did, and it didn't smell now. The backup vials they carried weren't insulated and would be different, not to mention less efficacious.

"I can't believe we're really doing this," Rocío muttered.

Paloma paused with her fingers on her nose. "You don't think it will work?" she whispered.

Oops. "I meant the whole situation is ridiculous. I believe Yaco and my nonna." Rocío managed a grin. "If he says the life potential in the placenta and eggs will shield us from death magic and the dampener won't affect it, I'll rub it all over my body. Do you realize you did festival flowers?"

"I did?" Paloma started to rub away the flowers on her face.

"Don't, I think it's jaunty."

Paloma grinned, a little cramped grin, but her next movements weren't as stiff, so maybe that had helped. Rocío wished all the same they had managed to leave Paloma behind, but war and youth and all that. And maybe Rocío's trust in Paloma today would help make up for past days of distrust and have some good effect on future days. If they survived into any future days.

"Where are you? She's w-waiting. She doesn't like that." Juan Pablo slipped on the last stair as he came down and caught sight of their reddened faces.

Hala had painted squares on her cheeks and forehead and the backs of her hands. Díaz looked like he had run all ten fingers down his face, and Yaco had vaguely circular patches on his face and hands. Rocío wasn't sure what her own looked like, though she had automatically applied the paste the same way she would have applied greasepaint for the stage.

Hala holstered her gun. Díaz handed her a box from his duffel bag. She extracted the stiff little bag that held the egg ornaments and hung it carefully around her neck. Those were the most dangerous part of the plan, the part that made it more suicide mission than a real strategy. Hala moved stiffly but surely.

If they had to use Hala's plan ... Rocío really hoped they didn't have to. Maybe they were wrong about Fernández's body.

Last, Hala pulled on silk gloves and then wool ones over them. At least it was cold enough that they wouldn't draw attention.

"What are you doing?" Juan Pablo asked. His eyes moved from face to face and dropped to the dampener on the floor, still whirring away. Some of the fear eased out of his expression.

Is he comforted? *Seres celestiales, he thinks we have a plan. A good plan, a non-suicidal plan. The plan Cempol probably has.* She wasn't going to disabuse him of the notion, especially as it might be one of the last ones he ever had. *Too bad one of my last thoughts might be about him. Where is Cempol? Another great last thought. Come on, you know better than that. Negative thoughts, negative outcome.* Too bad the opposite wasn't assured.

"Go on," Hala urged him. "We're coming."

The next floor was a bedroom and noticeably narrower. One more to go. The hair on the back of Rocío's neck was trying to lift into orbit and the protective vest was chafing under her arms. Everyone's breath was strained now, and Rocío's heart seemed to hit the front of her chest with each beat.

I hate this. She didn't even know which part she hated most: the waiting for violence and probable death; the threat to her friends and strangers she was supposed to protect; the power an unscrupulous person could wield over another; or Smith lying in the dirt, possibly bleeding to death, cutting short her chances to grow out of her obnoxiousness. *All of it.*

Above them Juan Pablo yelped in pain. Díaz stopped on the stairs and they bunched up behind him. He pointed ahead, and Yaco tapped Rocío's arm and indicated the step above Díaz. Biting her lip, she eased the dampener into place.

"Don't hurt him, Críspula," Hala called.

"Come out and I won't," Críspula called back.

Her voice was rougher and deeper than Rocío remembered. And weirdly accented. The sibilants were harder and the vowels longer.

What is she playing at?

"I could have killed you as soon as you walked into the lighthouse, you know. That little wall won't protect you."

Juan Pablo grunted with pain. The dampener spun faster and began to emit a whining noise. Cracks popped across the floor, and the stair Díaz stood on fractured down the middle. He jumped to one side and glared at the dampener, looking betrayed. The walls groaned and dust sifted down. Rocío distributed her weight evenly, like she would on a boat, ready to jump or dodge.

"I can bring the whole building down. So come out NOW."

Was that her full strength? Or was that what she can do in spite of the dampener? Unfortunately Rocío didn't think Yaco would know, even if there were time to ask.

Díaz and Hala had a brief intense argument just by staring at each other, and then Hala sighed, and Díaz quickly stepped up and to the side.

"Ancestors." A long pause. "Literally."

Paloma blinked rapidly, her breath short and shallow. Rocío squeezed her shoulder and whispered, "Trust yourself and your instincts. Don't forget to breathe."

Paloma nodded and held her breath, but Rocío's attention was drawn to Hala as she stepped beyond the "protection" of the wall. Rocío braced herself; losing sight of her friend felt like a vise clamping around her heart. But apparently Hala didn't die either, and then it was Rocío's turn.

She saw Fernández's body first and froze.

The newspapers of the time were wrong, and the Castillos were right. This was not a skeleton, hastily decapitated and interred in a secret crypt. This was a fully mummified body.

Eugenio Fernández Suarez, murderer sixteen times over, necromancer, was seated awkwardly in the room's only chair, arms crossed over his chest and knees bent unnaturally close, as if he'd been folded into the burial posture reserved for criminals put to death and then crammed into a coffin. His body looked like that of an emaciated elder, the flesh sucked close to his bones with age, flaccid muscles and joints clearly outlined, the texture of his skin so perfectly preserved it seemed it would yield to the touch.

That is, if you wanted to touch it for some incomprehensible reason and risk your fingers and your soul, which Rocío didn't.

In contrast, his face was young, as full as it must have been in life, the lips plump, with flesh above the nasolabial lines and the eyelids closed over full sockets. It looked like he was sleeping, throwing doubt on the reports that he had been hanged. But. His skin was dark brown—the brown of dirt, as if soil had replaced skin and flesh atom by atom, like the petrified forest Rocío had seen once in the north. The skin had an almost grainy texture, as dry and hard and shiny as new leather. The hair was no longer separate strands but more an impression of hair across his skull.

It was true, though, that he had been decapitated and Críspula had stolen his skull.

Fernández's head was on the floor below his own feet.

CHAPTER 26

Críspula was adorned with death.

She stood on the low bed built into the wall and held Aleksandr Arkadyevich Prokofiev in front of her like a shield. He looked very much like his brother, Piotr, except even wanner and thinner. The knife in Críspula's hand dimpled the skin of his throat. The dried blood smearing his collarbones and the top of his shirt showed this was not restraint on Críspula's part but tactics.

A dead or fainting hostage was not a good shield, and he looked dangerously close to the latter. His eyes were glassy and not tracking, his expression despairing and blank at the same time and he seemed unaware of the blood collected in the scuffs on his boots or even the partly eviscerated body just beyond his toes.

The dead man curled around the gaping wound in his abdomen, a drying pool of blood coating him and the floor all around him. Rocío swallowed hard at the sight of the fleshy drying mounds of his organs and tried to look at his face instead, but it was turned towards the floor and covered by his dark hair. She didn't know the lighthouse keepers and wouldn't have recognized him, but she owed him witness as well as justice.

It was too late for him, even if we had entered the lighthouse when we first arrived.

One of his arms was outstretched in pleading, just touching the knee of Juan Pablo, who knelt next to Prokofiev. Fresh blood trailed down Juan Pablo's neck from a cut under his ear. Críspula's spread fingers clawed his shoulder possessively.

Rocío raised her gaze to Críspula's face. Her clean, full cheeks, elegant neck and elaborately coifed hair looked as they always had, newly made repulsive by awareness of her murderous actions. As well as by the blood drenching her.

The spray of blood across her yellow Folawiyo sweater was dark and dry, and the legs of her trousers had soaked up blood as well, as if she had knelt in a puddle of it, but there were no corresponding marks in the blood on the floor.

That's two dead lighthouse keepers, then. And the third? Was the man we saw on the balcony a trick to draw us in, or does he yet live? And who shot Smith, and where is that gun?

Thank the seres celestiales the room did not smell of death; the ocean wind blew straight through the two open windows and chilled the sweat on Rocío's body so that she had to suppress a shiver. She didn't want to draw Críspula's attention by moving. The woman's eyes were avid, and she drank in Juan Pablo's whimpers, Díaz's grimace of disgust. Her gaze faltered when she met Paloma's and darted to Rocío.

They had spread out, as they'd agreed. Yaco barely out of the stairwell, close to the dampener in case he needed to shut it off to perform magic. Hala next, in front of the mummy so she could slowly, slowly edge closer to it. Then Rocío and Paloma almost directly in front of Críspula, and then Díaz, farthest into the room.

"Look who's here, Juan Pablo. It's the mighty detective. Did you think she was going to save you? No one is going to save you. She's not smart enough. I lied to her face and she never knew."

The banality of it was steadying. Fear, superiority, revenge—these things never changed. Though it looked like this time she'd been right about Críspula. Sometimes she hated being right. She couldn't give Paloma an encouraging look, but she hoped the ones she had managed before were still present in her mind. They all needed Paloma to be strong.

Juan Pablo bent his head, hiding his expression. His Adam's apple convulsively bobbed up and down as he swallowed.

But there was still a chance Rocío could keep Críspula focused on her instead. She calculated her response: enough to goad, not enough to push Críspula into mayhem. With each interaction, each lie they had told each other, Rocío and Críspula had entered into a relationship. And fear, superiority and revenge led to predictable actions. Not necessarily the ones Rocío wanted to provoke, but Críspula was also a victim, and guilt, shame and love led to predictable actions, too. Plus every moment they kept her talking gave Cempol and their magickers more time to appear. And more time for Hala to get into position.

"You weren't lying about everything, though, were you? You didn't plan to kill Martine and Loeis," Rocío said lightly.

It was Críspula's turn to swallow hard.

"What happened?" Rocío asked. "You loved them, didn't you? That wasn't a lie. Did they suspect you? Or were they just in the wrong place at the wrong time? Why don't you tell the truth, now that you can?"

"It's *his* fault." Críspula kicked Juan Pablo in the back.

He whined with pain.

"Is it? Tell me about it," Rocío invited.

"I had to do it because of him." Críspula kicked him again, viciously, and he sprawled forward, his hand landing in the dead man's intestines. He squealed in disgusted horror and flung himself back, shaking blood and tissue off his hand.

Paloma mewled in distress, and then covered her mouth with her hand.

Críspula zeroed in on Paloma, reminding Rocío of leeches on the forest floor, impossibly stretched out against gravity, ready to jump to a new food source. Rocío didn't know how leeches chose whose blood to suck, but she thought Críspula had a predator's instinct for the weakest of the group. Most criminals who preyed on people did. Fear tightened around Rocío's heart again and she ground her teeth.

If I can just hold her attention, maybe Paloma won't have to talk to her at all. Just in case I'm wrong.

"What did he do?" Rocío asked urgently.

Críspula ignored her. "Don't pretend you haven't thought of it," she said to Paloma, pointing the knife at her and then sliding the flat of it across Prokofiev's chest like a caress.

Paloma jerked in shock and then froze.

"That older brother of yours—you've probably thought about slicing him open slowly, preferably with something not too sharp, haven't you? I know." Críspula smiled a cousin's smile at Paloma, the kind women shared over wine and gossip late at night. She sounded like an elite Benerex woman again, her voice light, her vowels quick.

Paloma's throat worked, and she looked at Rocío, her eyes wide and panicky and entreating.

"Críspula," Rocío said sharply. "How does it feel to be the abuser now? Do you feel the same power Juan Pablo felt?"

"Answer me!" Críspula demanded, still focused on Paloma.

Paloma shook her head wildly.

Rocío had been right about Críspula's fixation on Paloma. There was no escaping it. No false sense of safety to be found by keeping Críspula's attention off her. Now she needed to be right about Paloma's abilities. They all needed Paloma to be right about her own strengths.

"Don't answer her," Rocío said. *Come on, Paloma, talk.* "Críspula. I'm the one you want to talk to. Paloma can't help you."

"What are you doing here, Paloma, with these people?" Críspula asked, a sneer kinking her upper lip on the last words.

"You don't have to answer her, Paloma," Rocío said, trying to will Paloma out of her shock.

Paloma shook, long trembles that moved through her body from her head to her feet. Her throat and mouth worked but nothing came out except a strangled gasp.

"Señorx Críspula, you can talk to any of us," Díaz cajoled. "You don't want to talk to Paloma, she doesn't know what's what. And that's what happened to you, too, isn't it? You got in over your head. You didn't mean for this to happen. We can sort it out. Help you."

Díaz, I'm going to kill you. If there was a worse thing to say to a woman who felt ignored and overlooked, Rocío couldn't think of it.

Críspula's eyes narrowed. "You talk like you think I have to listen to you. I don't have to listen to you anymore. Don't you get that?"

"I—"

"Stop *talking*. I do the talking now. Give me your guns. All of you."

"Señorx Paloma," Díaz said.

"My title is Señorx de Herrera."

And she picked up the missing gun from the bedclothes and shot him.

Time seemed to slow.

Díaz reeled back. Blood sprayed from his head, his stunned expression turning into one of shock and pain.

Rocío locked her throat against the shout trying to claw its way out.

Díaz slumped into a sitting position on the floor and touched the side of his head. He looked up, astonishment taking over his expression again. He groaned. "You shot me."

Rocío sucked in a sharp breath, and time seemed to click into its normal progression.

"Piérdalo," Críspula said, shaking the gun. She aimed it at Díaz and cocked it.

Diosas de mis madres, let this work. Please don't let her kill me. Any of us.

"I should have listened to you, Díaz." Rocío stepped forward. "You said Paloma was too young. Just a baby. A stupid, overeager, inexperienced baby who would get people killed. Are you happy you were right?"

Paloma recoiled, appalled, her eyes filled with pain. Rocío hid her flinch and stared back at her levelly. *Come on, Paloma. Listen to what I'm saying and talk to her. You're the one she wants to talk to.*

Críspula swung the gun to point at Rocío.

Rocío kept her gaze on Paloma in spite of all her instincts shrieking at her to watch Críspula, address the threat, neutralize the situation. *Talk to Críspula. You need to act. You can do it.* Rocío tried to communicate that belief with her expression.

"I can kill her instead, Paloma," Críspula said. "I only missed because I had to shoot left-handed." She tilted the knife in her right hand, light flashing off the blade. "I won't miss this time. Or I could kill Juan Pablo. Show you how it's done. You'd like that,

Paloma, wouldn't you? I know you would. Just tell me so. You choose."

She jabbed the knife towards Juan Pablo and accidentally sliced Aleksandr's neck. He didn't even protest, just swayed on his feet, breathing heavily.

A shiver ran through Críspula and emotions chased each other across her face: pleasure, malice, anger. Fear.

Wait, fear?

The room darkened.

At first Rocío thought the sun had gone behind a cloud, but the room kept getting darker, the air thicker, as if smoke were filling it.

It was as if the black smoke they'd seen above the lighthouse was defying natural laws to stream down inside through the windows. Just as if. Not that there was anything natural about it, so it could do what it pleased. Again Rocío recalled Ministrx O'Higgins's words at the hospital. *Darkness seemed to hang about him. And little lights, and a smell.*

The fetor of a slaughterhouse rolled over her, so thick it seemed to have weight as it slid up her nose and into her throat: old blood, rotting organs, sweet rotting meat and pain. Her breath rasped as if she were inhaling smoke. Ministrx O'Higgins hadn't mentioned that.

Críspula still stood rigid, seemingly not doing anything, her gaze fixed on Fernández's body, and Rocío realized the dark miasma was billowing out from it like a noxious exhalation, as if the essence of death had entered the room. Pale blue lights danced around him like little holes cut into reality.

Run. Her thoughts gibbered. She felt frozen in place, her heart stumbling through its beats against the vise around it. Her eyesight blurred and her fingers and toes tingled before going numb. Her consciousness of her own body felt far away and foggy.

Críspula sliced Prokofiev again, this time in a deliberate and controlled way. He moaned and his knees buckled.

Her eyes rolled back in her head. "I showed them," she said, her voice deeper like a man's and vibrating and echoing as if she stood in a tiled room, the words twisting around that unfamiliar accent again.

A shadow grew behind her, a tall, attenuated man, the lights buzzing around him. Rocío could almost see a mouth moving as Críspula spoke, the darkness hardening into features, like someone standing in shadow just too deep to reveal more than a glimpse of him. The bright blue of the sky beyond the open windows seemed a thousand kilometers away.

"I showed them all, and now I'll show you, and you'll learn to cower before me."

The voice was like an echo of an old-timer's accent. Like the echo of an echo.

The shadow put its hand over Críspula's on the knife. Its other hand wrapped around her arm. Its mouth moved, the words inaudible to Rocío.

"Nnnnnnnnoooo!" Críspula shouted. She jerked back and forth as if she were resisting its grip. "They'll shoot us if you kill him. You promised we wouldn't kill him. He's going to make a dance for me! He promised and you promised!"

The gun slipped from her grip and landed on the bed, miraculously not discharging. Rocío felt like her numb feet were nailed to the floor. *I should get her gun.*

There's no way I'm getting closer.

The shadow's mouth moved again, and this time Rocío heard a whisper at the edge of hearing, the words too far away for comprehension. Not far in distance, but far the way Nonna's voice sounded now that she was dead. The whispering grew louder, pressing at her, scrabbling like a mouse at the floorboards, wanting to get in.

At the University, Hala had read from the adjudicator's book, and it had said, "The accused boasted that he could speak to all the dead, not just his own ancestors, and that there was a great clamoring in the afterlife."

They had asked why Críspula wanted Fernández's body. Maybe they should have asked why Fernández wanted Críspula to find his body.

Rocío was very afraid that the shadow before her was the man who had attacked Ministrx O'Higgins. Not a coconspirator. Not a man.

Fernández, more than a ghost and less than dead.

CHAPTER 27

"CRÍSPULA." Paloma's voice cracked. She clasped her hands behind her back and cleared her throat, then tried again, louder. "Críspula, I —I wanted to come. You asked what I was doing here. I wanted to see if it was true. That it was you doing all those things. I wasn't sure if I should believe it. But it was you. You did all that, Críspula."

Críspula groaned, a creaky, unnatural sound.

Was the shadowy figure growing less substantial? The whispers more muffled?

Paloma threw a panicked look at Rocío.

"Keep going," Rocío mouthed.

"How did you do it?" Paloma asked loudly. "Will you tell me how you did it? They don't tell me anything. They don't respect me. Just like they didn't respect you, Críspula. But now they do."

"Nnnnnnn." Críspula gagged on a guttural sound of pain. She seemed to physically tear her gaze away from Fernández's mummy, swaying into Prokofiev as she turned to look at Paloma.

The room brightened. The smoke thinned. The eerie lights blinked out one by one. A breeze swept through the room, raising goose bumps on Rocío's arms and chilling her nose. She coughed, and the smell scraped out of her throat and nose like a physical thing.

The shadow disappeared like a soap bubble. There one breath, gone the next.

No. Not gone. The darkness had retreated to surround Fernández's mummy in a dark halo.

"Don't do that," Críspula shouted. "That's not what we agreed." She smoothed the heel of her palm over the blood on Aleksandr's neck, slicking it over his skin, the knife quivering dangerously close to his ear. "I'm sorry," she crooned softly. He shivered.

Rocío had the impression that Fernández grimaced with frustration. His soul was in this room as much as his body, a ninth player on the stage and possibly the strongest. And he seemed just as monstrous as all the reports made him out to be. Though not even Hala had anticipated that Fernández was such an active participant in Críspula's murder spree. Rocío wanted to look at Hala to see what she thought of all this, but she didn't dare draw attention to her in any way.

"You have to *make* them respect you, Paloma," Críspula said. Her voice and posture were her own again, all that eerie attention back on Paloma.

Rocío drew a thick breath, her lurching heartbeat slowing.

"I want to know how," Paloma whispered, her body swaying forward, her eyes fastened on Críspula.

Críspula leaned forward, mirroring Paloma. "You don't have to obey their orders."

How long could Paloma keep this up? Where was Cempol, piérdalo? And what about the perdido dampener? Why wasn't it working? Until it did, they were a helpless audience to Paloma's conversation with Críspula. At least Críspula seemed to have forgotten about their guns again.

Rocío flicked a look at Díaz. He sat with one hand pressed to his temple, his blood wet and red against the duller, darker placenta smeared across his cheek. The other hand was braced against the floor, keeping him upright.

"They'll say they're protecting you but what they're doing is taking all the good stuff for themselves," Críspula said.

Paloma flinched and Críspula laughed. "They call you a baby, they treat you like a baby, like you don't have thoughts, don't have ambitions, like you don't have the competence to do the smallest littlest things."

Was the well of magic in Fernández's mummified body that deep, or was the dampener broken, making them wait for a beep that was never going to come?

"She's just like Ministrx Soler." Críspula sneered the words, jerking her head at Rocío. "Everyone always fawning over her. Why should she get everything she wants? Sasha likes me better. Don't you, Sasha?"

"I like you better," Aleksandr said woodenly. A muscle twitched next to his blood-smeared eye.

"You should get away from her," Críspula said, "like I got Sasha away from Ministrx Soler, may her ancestors forsake her."

"Can you help me?" Paloma stumbled over the words. "With that?"

Críspula barked out laughter and then seemed to choke on it. "Help you! No one helped me. You know whose help I needed? Whose help I expected? Who was supposed to be there for me? William O'Higgins!" Spittle sprayed from her mouth. "He's my uncle! And you know what he did? He accepted a bribe from this one." She jabbed her elbow into Juan Pablo.

Rocío flinched. Paloma flinched. Even Díaz flinched.

Rocío didn't think Paloma could do this much longer. Never mind the rest of them. One of them was going to pass out soon from pain or blood loss or sheer ongoing terror.

"He's done it before. I know. My perfect uncle isn't so perfect."

"I didn't," Juan Pablo whispered. "No bribes."

No, Rocío didn't think he had bribed O'Higgins. He was the type people just gave things to. The irony, of course, was that Críspula was, too, but in this case it seemed more had been given to Juan Pablo and Críspula didn't have the emotional maturity to cope.

Críspula hit him again. "Beg me to stop."

"Please. Stop." He cowered, a moan of pain spilling from him before he clamped his lips shut. She smiled and he forced himself upright again, shuddering with the effort.

Rocío trembled as she tried to suppress her reaction, though rage was a welcome alternative to terror. Was this the hatred of a victim turned by power into viciousness? Or was it something else, perhaps Fernández's influence? She made herself focus on Críspula's tirade, though it was the same blaming vitriol Rocío had heard from countless others. It was never their fault.

"He named Juan Pablo—just a cousin—the third secretary to the sub-com when that position was *mine*," Críspula ranted. "Everyone knew it was mine. I'm his niece! I did everything Uncle William asked and more. I did things before he even knew he wanted them. I worked for years for this and he promised it to me. He promised, and then he turned around and gave it to him, this useless whiner."

All this violence and pain because Críspula hadn't gotten the job she thought she deserved? Spoiled and ambitious, she was not prepared for a life that didn't hand her exactly what she wanted. And she was probably justified in her grudge against Juan Pablo, who also always got everything he wanted, even more so than Críspula. Rocío wished she were surprised, but entitlement wasn't rare.

"You understand, don't you, Paloma?" Críspula asked.

Paloma bit her lip.

Just say what she wants to hear, Rocío silently urged her.

"You could talk to the other members of the sub-com and tell them about the bribe," Paloma said haltingly. "I'm sure they'd reverse your uncle's decision. I'm sure Ministrx O'Higgins is very sorry now anyway."

"I don't need anyone's help. No one has ever helped me so now I'm helping myself."

Paloma's eyes widened. Rocío almost choked on the outrageousness of that claim.

Díaz scoffed, and Críspula's gaze jumped to him. Her grip loosened on Aleksandr, and he swayed. Críspula's hand jerked, almost as if she didn't have any control over it, and she sliced his shoulder open. (Of course, wasn't that what all abusers said, that they couldn't control themselves?)

Críspula gasped in shock and closed her hand over the wound, pressing down so hard that Aleksandr dropped to his knees.

"No! Stop. I'm in control here. It's what we agreed! We agreed!"

Her voice changed, twisting into the strange accent, growing deeper. Her shoulders reset in a posture not her own. She spasmed and was Críspula again. Was Críspula disappearing under the weight of Fernández's body language, Fernández's posture, Fernández's soul?

Rocío didn't want to know what would happen if she disappeared entirely. "Críspula!"

Hala was very close to Fernández's body, just waiting for the perdido dampener to beep.

Paloma looked helplessly at Rocío, seemingly at the end of her resourcefulness. She'd kept Críspula talking for longer than any of them had expected she'd need to.

Críspula jerked again and her hand sprang open, exposing the wound on Aleksandr's shoulder. She licked lips suddenly twisted in an expression her face had never worn before.

"Señorx de Herrera," Rocío said desperately, unsure what was going to come out of her mouth but sure she'd rather deal with Críspula than Fernández's incarnation. "I think you're upsetting Paloma. She's quite fond of the Prokofiev brothers' choreography. Piotr Prokofiev is waiting for his brother, Aleksandr here, to start working on a new dance. Did you know that? Isn't that what you want, a new dance?"

Críspula's eyes focused again, Fernández fading away, and she petted Aleksandr's hair, the knife waving above his head. "This is not my fault," she whined. "I didn't mean to hurt him. He's an artist."

"I can see that," Rocío said dryly. Críspula seemed to take her literally, some of the tension leaking out of her. *What else can I say to this powerful spoiled brat? How is* that *different from any other day in my life?*

"I just wanted him to see. That's all I wanted, for everyone to see *me*."

The dampener beeped three times.

"What—?" Críspula said, sounding lost.

Darkness fell abruptly, like all the shutters had slammed closed. Rocío's fingers and toes went numb, not even passing through tingling first.

"No!" Críspula shouted.

The not-lights clustered around Fernández's body, illuminating the grain of his cheeks, making it seem like his eyes were moving under their closed lids, looking at them. The rank stench surged back into the room, coating the inside of Rocío's mouth and throat. *What? How did the dampener make things* worse?

"Ahhhh." A man's sigh of pleasure seemed to fill the room. The skin on the back of Rocío's neck creeped. She searched wildly for the shadow, didn't find it.

"No. You don't know what you've done," Críspula said in a small voice. Wisps of smoke seeped out of her eyes and ears and mouth and formed a dark nimbus around her head. It thickened and blackened and twisted down the length of her body. "I was holding him back."

"I can't stand her either," Fernández said with Críspula's mouth. "I suppose I have to thank you before I kill you."

Rocío shuddered.

Críspula turned the knife on Prokofiev, too slowly, even accounting for the warped perceptions of Rocío's adrenaline rush.

Hala jumped forward. Rocío pulled her gun from its holster, her fingers almost too numb to feel it in her hand.

CHAPTER 28

JUAN PABLO SCREAMED, a release of pent-up pain and terror and fury, and lurched into Críspula, fouling Rocío's aim. He grappled for the knife, Fernández's shadow obscuring his face except where the pinpricks of light gleamed off the whites of his eyes, turning them a spectral blue.

"You stupid boy," Fernández shouted through Críspula's mouth.

Rocío stalked forward, stiff with terror. *No, no, no,* her mind gibbered. *Don't get close.*

From the corner of her eye, she saw Hala grab Fernández's head from the floor and wedge it into the space between the mummy's chest and thighs. She yanked the egg ornaments filled with thermite from the stiff little bag around her neck, her mouth shaping a desperate prayer. The yellow, blue, purple and white decorations stood out bright and cheery and incongruous in the dim room.

Hala crushed the first egg on the mummy, smearing the red thermite, gluey with glycerin, across his back. She slammed the second egg against the base of his spine and the third into his face. Eggshells and thermite clung to her gloves.

Díaz staggered to his feet, groping for the flare gun. He bent sharply and vomited, falling to one knee. He moaned and clutched his head, bright fresh blood showing through his fingers.

Paloma met Rocío's eyes across Díaz's back, her mouth parted in an *o*. Finally Rocío could tell what Paloma was thinking, and it seemed like Paloma read Rocío's thoughts in turn. As if they had coordinated it, Paloma spun and jumped onto Críspula's back. Rocío jammed her gun back into its holster, ran to Díaz and wrenched the flare gun from his hands. She wheeled to join Hala.

Hala heaved the mummy, chair and all, out the window. She stepped to the side.

Críspula screamed with rage.

Rocío fumbled with the gun. She could barely feel to cock it and had to look to make sure she had. *Don't drop it*, she prayed. She gripped it in both hands and positioned her numb finger on the trigger. She'd have one chance at this.

She leaned out until the windowsill cut into her stomach and aimed. Fernández was still wedged into the chair, spinning as he fell past the edge of the headland towards the ocean below. She watched for one more breath to get the timing right and pulled the trigger on the flare gun. There was a muffled pop and a spurt of flames. Smoke trailed behind the bulky cartridge as it flew through the air.

A heartbeat later Fernández's body jerked with the impact and spun faster. Críspula screamed again.

Rocío drew in one tense breath and then another, waiting. Then the thermite flared hot and yellow like a firecracker. With a thump and a whoosh, flames engulfed Fernández. Flaming body parts broke off and trailed behind like comets. The skull slipped free, a dark sphere wreathed in hot yellow flames.

"Yes." That had been one of the more tenuous parts of the dubious plan—whether the separated head would burn, too. But they couldn't have lit him on fire inside the lighthouse; thermite burned anything it clung to, including flesh, gloves and stone. Díaz had carried the flare gun for the same reason; one spark, and it would have been Hala blazing like a cremation pyre.

A wave crashed against the rocks at the cliff's base and the spume reached up for Fernández's body. The wave withdrew, and the ocean's surface smoothed into a wrinkled blue expanse. The body smashed through it. And shattered. And sank. And continued to burn, like those weird surrealist paintings by Varo of suns under the sea.

"It worked!" Rocío shouted and thrust herself back into the room. "Paloma—" The rest of the words died in her throat.

Críspula was prone on the floor, Paloma kneeling on one outstretched arm and Yaco on the other. Prokofiev was curled in a whimpering ball and Juan Pablo was backed against the bed, still breathing. But the dark miasma hung over them all, swirling sluggishly like disturbed sewage. Tiny points of not-light glowed in Críspula's eyes.

"No," Rocío whispered. The thermite was burning Fernández to the bone, she was sure of it.

But she still couldn't feel her fingers.

"They were my cousins," Críspula said softly. "I didn't want them to die just because they were annoying." She sucked in a harsh breath. "Something is wrong. I can't see."

"Yaco? Hala? What's going on?" Rocío wanted to look out the window and check that Fernández was still burning, but she knew he was. "Why didn't that work?"

"I don't know! I'm just a fifth-level magicker!"

Críspula bucked. Hala threw herself across her legs, the thermite-smeared gloves nowhere in evidence, thank the ancestros for small favors. The bloody knife was out of the way, too, stuck in a pillow on the bed. Paloma pressed down on Críspula's arm, her face set and white. Yaco bit his lip and cried out.

"I needed that body," Fernández said with Críspula's mouth. "I needed that! Now I'm trapped in here with her!"

Críspula banged her head against the floor, shouting wordlessly. She heaved violently, sending Paloma flying into Juan Pablo. He squealed and pushed back, and they fell on top of Críspula, the knife suddenly in his hand. Paloma grunted with pain and rolled to the side. Juan Pablo flailed, scrabbling wildly, and stabbed Críspula in the shoulder, whether on purpose or accidentally Rocío couldn't tell.

Críspula arched up and bit Juan Pablo's face.

He screamed and fell back, his hands covering his savaged cheek, the knife standing up in her shoulder. Críspula spat out the chunk of flesh. It sizzled when it hit the ground, and the black cloud followed it and spattered out like cold water hitting hot grease.

"Sere celestiales," Rocío swore.

Juan Pablo curled up, moaning with every breath.

Paloma lunged and pinned Críspula again, not particularly careful of the knife. Yaco braced his arm across her forehead and she snarled up at him.

On the stairs the dampener whined, the sound of a motor overloaded beyond its capacity. Yaco said, "It sounds like it's going to blow up. Stay back."

"Is that good or bad?" Díaz croaked. At some point he had crawled in front of Prokofiev, shielding him from … everything, Rocío supposed. He could be a good advocate, in spite of his personality.

Shielding. Inspiration struck.

"It could help," Yaco said uncertainly.

"Give me your vials of placenta." Rocío clumsily stripped the extra vial from her own belt.

She bit out the stopper and poured the bloody mess on Críspula's face, half expecting the possessed woman to go up in flames, but she just sputtered and wrenched away. The knife seemed to be slowing her down. Unless, like Rocío, her extremities were going numb.

"Quickly, the others."

Paloma shook as she handed hers over, and Rocío spared her a supportive smile, then pictured how ghastly it must look with the blood on her face and murmured, "You're doing good."

"The cold one is over there." Yaco motioned with his head.

Rocío knelt next to Críspula and gestured to him. He pinched Críspula's nose closed, smearing the bloody paste across her face and into her hair. Rocío squeezed the other woman's cheeks, forcing her mouth open, and poured. Then she slapped one hand over Críspula's mouth and stroked her throat with the other, trying to keep her motions professional and distant, not cruel. The dark cloud thinned.

Críspula swallowed and choked. She swallowed again. Lights danced over her skin.

The dampener whined at a higher pitch, stuttered, whined again. Exploded. Pieces of metal ricocheted into the room.

Críspula slumped. Yaco released her nose hastily. Her eyes

opened wide, pleading. The weird blue sparks there dimmed. Rocío lifted her hand and Críspula keened.

Rocío poured the last vial of placenta paste into that open mouth. Críspula gagged, swallowed and sucked in a breath, seeming to suck in the dark halo along with it. The darkness shredded, shrank, disappeared. Críspula went limp and stared up, unseeing.

They all waited. Rocío held her breath. She didn't hear the others breathing, either.

Finally, leaning over her, Rocío said, "Críspula de Herrera Carmona, I know you're in there." Half hope, half summons.

Críspula didn't react.

After a minute Rocío asked generally, "What do you think?"

"I can feel my toes," Yaco said.

"It smells like the ocean again," Paloma added.

Rocío took a deep breath and scratched her cheek, drying placenta paste flaking under her fingers. "Let's try sitting her up."

"Better take the knife out first," Paloma said coolly, gesturing to where it was still embedded in Críspula's shoulder.

The wound bled sluggishly when Hala pulled the knife out. She wrapped the wound with a bandage she conjured from a pocket, and they propped Críspula against the bed, unresisting.

"Is she dead?" Díaz called.

"No," Hala said.

"Is she in there?" Paloma asked. "Or is she … gone?"

"Leaving what?" Rocío asked, appalled.

"Críspula de Herrera Carmona, tell me about the files you took," Hala said briskly.

"Really?" Rocío protested. The smells of blood and drying placenta and burnt flesh furred her throat. She wanted to sit on the floor and rest, just for a minute, not revive Críspula. She didn't really care if she was lost to Fernández. She didn't.

"It might help. If Fer—he—doesn't know or care about them," Hala said. "Yaco?"

He shook his head violently but said, "Don't ask me. I don't know."

"You took those because your uncle is doing something illegal, isn't he?" Hala asked.

Críspula's eyes popped open.

Everyone jerked back.

Críspula laughed, a normal woman's laugh, though tinged with hysteria.

Rocío felt a bit hysterical herself and had to check her own urge to shriek. Or howl. Or cry.

"Yes." Críspula gasped. It was entirely her voice. "Yes. I showed him. I showed all of them, didn't I? He pretends to be so devoted, such a public servant. I knew what he was doing, and he still didn't choose me. How could he do that? How could he discount me like that? He has—"

A gunshot echoed through the room. Críspula jerked and screamed. Blood bloomed on her unbandaged shoulder. Her eyes closed, and she sagged to the side. Paloma and Yaco ducked away.

Rocío spun on her knees to face the door, drawing her own gun.

Smith slumped in the doorway, blood all down one side, a gun in her hand and a very satisfied expression on her face.

CHAPTER 29

"ARE YOU KIDDING ME?" Hala shouted.

Paloma jerked the sheet from the bed and wadded it against the gunshot wound. With her other hand, she checked Críspula's pulse. "She's not dead," she shouted. "I don't know how, but she's not dead."

Rocío concentrated on holstering her gun. Her hands shook with rage.

"What in the names of the most holy did you think you were doing?" Hala yelled at Smith.

"I shot her. I got her."

"Of all the ill-considered stupid stunts—you almost shot my advocates!"

"Give me your weapon," Rocío grated out. *I will stay calm,* she told herself, wrestling with adrenaline and not at all with misdirected homicidal urges.

But Smith opened her mouth to say something fatuous—Rocío just knew it—and she lost it and shouted in her face, "As soon as you're recovered, I'm going to kick your ass into next Tuesday, and I don't care if Oshinsky demotes me. You're as spoiled and reckless as de Herrera." She tore the gun from Smith's grasp.

Terrified relief that they weren't dead, that Aleksandr Prokofiev, Juan Pablo and Díaz weren't dead, and yes, that Smith and Críspula weren't dead—that no one was dead who wasn't supposed to be dead —propelled more words out of her than Rocío intended to say.

"You have been nothing but an impediment since this whole thing started. You're so full of yourself, you can't even see anyone around you, and you're a bigot and your own stupidity got you shot. Why can't you listen to anyone but yourself?!"

"I—" Smith said.

"Sit down and shut up!" Rocío roared.

Hala touched Rocío's arm. "That's enough."

Rocío allowed herself to be nudged away from Smith.

"She's shot, and we don't beat up anyone when they're shot," Hala said pointedly, looking at Smith.

"Unlike some people," Rocío said. "I am going to report you, Smith."

"I—"

"Do not talk right now, Officer Smith." Hala blocked Smith with her hand. "You're in a room full of angry, shocky people with guns, and I might change my mind about beating up people who are shot." She glared at Smith, who finally shut her mouth. "Sit."

Smith tried to outstare Hala and didn't last two seconds. She braced herself against the wall and slid down to a sitting position.

"She was restrained," Hala said. "You shot a prisoner who was already injured."

"No." Smith's head jerked back, and she blinked rapidly. "That's not ..." She looked around the room. "I shot a dangerous murderer."

"You shot a helpless prisoner," Hala said. "Think about that."

Rocío stalked away. "Where is Cempol?" she shouted.

"We need more than Cempol at this point," Hala said. "We need a medic. Several medics."

"Paloma," Rocío said in a slightly calmer voice, kneeling next to her, "you go. Take the automobile." She slid her hands on top of Paloma's and took over applying pressure to Críspula's wound as Paloma slid free.

Críspula opened her eyes.

"Ahh!" Rocío jerked and managed to keep the pressure on Críspula's shoulder. "Seres celestiales, woman. Don't you stop?"

"Paloma," Críspula whispered.

Paloma backed up a step.

"Ignore her," Rocío advised. "Yaco, can you tie her feet together since we can't secure her hands?"

"Paloma," Críspula rasped more loudly. "You'll help me, won't you? You understand. You can help explain ..."

"I'll help you, right to the adjudicator," Paloma said coldly.

Críspula blinked. "But you said—"

"I did my job as an advocate, and I said whatever I had to to keep your attention on me so Hala and Rocío could burn Fernández's body."

"But we're—"

Paloma talked over her. "We are *nothing* alike. I made myself bait, and you fell for it. And I've never thought about cutting up my brother like a piece of meat! Or killing dogs. I used to think you were just spoiled, but you're a horrible person who doesn't understand that other people are real. You're a monster."

"I'm not—"

"The company you keep doesn't lie."

Críspula closed her eyes and turned her face away.

"Paloma," Rocío said, drawing Paloma's gaze to her, "you did good today. You were perfect."

"Thank you, Detective." Paloma grinned with deserved pride. "I chose better teachers." She ran out of the room.

A little bit of warmth eased into Rocío. Something good had happened here amid all the ugliness and pain. She and Paloma had started over, had taken the first tentative steps into a working relationship and camaraderie. Together. Because without Paloma's goodwill, they would have foundered on the rocks Rocío had steered them onto. It was human nature to resist change, but it was also human nature to adapt and to make the best of a bad situation. And now the situation was not bad at all. Not at all.

She looked down at Críspula. Well, some parts weren't bad.

Yaco finished tying Críspula's ankles together, took the blanket from the bed and covered the dead lighthouse keeper. He approached Juan Pablo where he stood with his back against the wall and spoke softly without touching him. When Juan Pablo lifted his head, his hand cupped around his cheek, Yaco motioned towards the window.

Juan Pablo was shivering, and Rocío became aware of the cold seeping into her bones. She could feel every one of her cold fingers, though, and the bright normal sunlight showed just how exhausted and terrible they all looked, smeared with blood, placenta and dirt. Yaco pointed downwards, presumably at Fernández's still-burning body, talking earnestly.

I hope he burns for a good long time.

Díaz, a white bandage wrapped around his head and a blanket clamped under his arm, accepted a pitcher of water from Hala. Blood stained the right side of his shirt, but he had wiped the placenta off his face and looked less intimidating. Rocío's skin itched at the reminder of the mess on her own face.

Díaz shuffled over to Prokofiev, who sat slumped on the other side of the room. He wasn't shivering despite his light shirt and the multiple cuts Críspula had inflicted on him. "Señorx Prokofiev?" Díaz crouched slowly, not allowing his head to go lower than his torso, and arranged his supplies on the floor. He unfolded the blanket, revealing a stack of clean towels. "My name is Mateo. I want to put this blanket around you and clean your wounds. You're safe now, and your brother is waiting to see you."

Prokofiev closed his eyes and opened them again. He focused on Díaz, his Adam's apple bobbing as he swallowed. Sense and awareness seeped back into his face. And hope. His lips moved, shaping the word *Petya*. He let Díaz dab a towel against his neck.

Rocío hid a sigh of relief and tried to keep the pressure on Críspula's wound even, hard enough to keep the bleeding down but not so hard she was punishing the woman. Regardless of how much she wanted to.

How long would it take Paloma to get to the city with part of the road missing and the unreliable auto? How long to find help? Were Cempol and all of the Miraflores advocates still at the Torre de los ancestros in the city center?

Yaco closed the window, and the room gradually grew warmer.

Eventually Críspula's bleeding slowed, and Hala helped Rocío wrap the wound. Rocío sat back on her heels, shaking the cramp out of her hands.

The sound of many feet pounding on the stairs jerked Rocío out of her daze. Magicker Huaripani and a stocky, dark-haired man who had to be Magicker Chuquisengo swept into the room wearing breathing masks.

"Finally," Rocío said. *Wait, breathing masks?*

"Magicker," Hala said, "de Herrera is contained but could still be a threat."

Magicker Chuquisengo checked his forward motion. "The criminal is contained? Explain." His voice was muffled behind the heavy glass-and-metal mask.

Stealthy movement drew Rocío's eye in time for her to see Magicker Huaripani conceal a small crystal bottle behind her back.

Hala explained about burning Fernández's mummy, his continued presence in Críspula's body and the placenta paste. It sounded fantastic even to Rocío, and the magickers didn't bother to hide their incredulity.

They exchanged a glance, and Huaripani strode forward. Rocío got another look at the cut-crystal bottle. It was a lovely atomizer with a purple squeeze bulb and tassel that wouldn't have looked out of place on Rocío's mother's vanity. Huaripani raised it.

Rocío had a split second to think. Breathing masks. Something aerosolized. *They* had breathing masks. Cempol was always reckless and arrogant, but would they risk injuring everyone in this room to neutralize Críspula? *Yes, yes, they would. If I warn the others, I warn Críspula. But Prokofiev is injured. Whatever is in that bottle could worsen his shock.*

"Hold your breath!" she shouted. "Díaz, help Prokofiev!"

Huaripani wheeled to face Rocío, brandishing the bottle. Rocío held her breath and clapped her hand over her mouth and nose for good measure.

"What do you think you're doing?" Magicker Chuquisengo roared.

Rocío pointed with her free hand to Prokofiev—bloody, battered, slashed and listing sideways.

"Explain yourself," Magicker Chuquisengo demanded.

Rocío stole a quick glance at Críspula. The younger woman glared up, her lips pressed tight. It didn't look like she was breathing. Rocío gestured at the bottle Huaripani held.

For a moment it looked like Huaripani was going to spray the contents at Rocío, but then she growled and moved to stand over Críspula. "Everyone move back," she said, her voice tinny. "If you don't have masks I recommend you leave the room immediately."

Rocío stepped back, uncovering her mouth. "Prokofiev and Ricci are too injured to move."

"Give the kidnapping victim a mask," Huaripani said, evaluating the room with a glance. Críspula began to look desperate for air.

Chuquisengo handed a mask to Díaz, who helped Prokofiev into it.

"The rest of you will have to leave," Huaripani said.

"I don't—" Juan Pablo's voice cracked. He bit his lip and started again. "I want to see. What you do. So I know she can't—" He covered his mouth, his throat working.

Críspula sucked in an audible breath and pinched her lips together again. Huaripani cursed and glared at Rocío.

"The rest of you stand next to the window and hold your breath," Huaripani ordered.

Yaco opened the window, and the temperature in the room dropped. Rocío, Hala and Díaz joined him.

Together the magickers stooped over Críspula. Chuquisengo pinched Críspula's nose shut and covered her mouth. Her eyes rolled with panic. Rocío winced. It looked ... barbaric when they weren't fighting Críspula for their lives.

They waited. And waited, longer than Rocío would have. Críspula twisted against their hold, bending her head back.

"Now." Chuquisengo removed his hands.

Huaripani squeezed the bulb. Críspula wheezed in a breath along with whatever drug they had administered. She stared up at them, eyes rolling, the blue lights in them flickering to life again. A spark of electricity jumped over her skin and died. A moment later Críspula sighed and went completely limp.

Juan Pablo opened his mouth to speak. Huaripani gestured *no* sharply. "Wait for it to disperse out of the air," she said.

Huaripani consulted a watch. Rocío could hear the seconds ticking away. The magicker waited several long heartbeats before saying loudly, "She's under." She pulled her mask onto the top of her head, apparently so she could look down her nose at everyone.

"What is that?" Hala asked flatly.

"An admixture of Somon and Libertas, if you must know," Chuquisengo said.

Hala jerked with surprise. "That's irresponsible and—"

More footsteps pounded up the stairs. Only Prokofiev was too tired to startle.

Oshinsky and Commander Dhavale burst out of the stairwell, trailing a bunch of nervous-looking armed advocates and Cempol officers.

Rocío took a deep breath, the tightness in her chest finally easing. They could stop now and hand this over into competent, trusted hands. Let someone else take responsibility for a little while. She leaned against the wall, her knees suddenly weak with exhaustion. Her muscles ached. Her face itched. And she had a headache behind her right eye.

"Detective Haddad, what happened?" Oshinsky demanded. "You look like you've been bathing in blood. There's more blood and a melted machine on the stairs, and something is burning *underwater* off of Punta Mala."

"Where are the medics we asked for?" Hala pushed forward to stand in front of Oshinsky. "Aleksandr Prokofiev and Juan Pablo Ricci are wounded, as are Díaz and Officer Smith. The other blood isn't ours."

"Medics!" Commander Dhavale roared down the stairs, and the crowd shifted and scrambled to make way for the three medics.

"Críspula de Herrera is also in need of emergency medical services due to both a gunshot wound and an overdose of sedatives." Hala rounded on Chuquisengo. "The combination of Somon and

Libertas could kill her or cause permanent brain damage in her state. Not to mention whatever it might have done to the rest of us. It's not approved for human use."

"Other concerns had to take precedence." Chuquisengo rubbed at the dents the mask had left in his broad, dark cheeks. "It was the most efficacious method of removing her as a threat to the city. Brain damage was not my first concern."

"You were going to sedate everyone in this room without warning, including two injured victims." Hala glowered at him. "That was reckless in the extreme."

"You could all be suborned or infected. They could be coconspirators." Huaripani jerked her head at Prokofiev.

Hala snorted scornfully.

Two of the medics bustled around Críspula and Smith, while the third approached Prokofiev with a quiet word and his hands spread to show he wasn't a threat.

Hala turned her back on the magickers. "One of the lighthouse keepers is dead, Chief." She indicated the body on the floor. "We haven't found the other two."

Commander Dhavale named off five officers to search the lighthouse.

"Mateo, how badly wounded are you?" Oshinsky asked. "Wait." She turned back to Hala. "What did you mean, the medics you asked for?"

"The medics I sent Paloma for. Where is she? She deserves a commendation."

"What do you mean, where is she? Isn't she with you?"

Hala's hands dropped nervelessly by her sides. "We sent her to you."

"She's not with me." Oshinsky looked around as if Paloma were a misplaced pencil. "She's with you."

Rocío stared back at her. "Oh, seres celestiales. She took the auto. What if it blew up?"

Commander Dhavale roared for two more officers, whom he sent to look for Paloma. "They'll find her. She can't have gone far."

"They'd better," Rocío said. "She was a hero today."

~

After a long process of debriefing, explanations, recriminations (from Cempol) and arguments (by Oshinsky, on behalf of her advocates), hot soup (gratefully received), and the discovery of the dead bodies of the two missing lighthouse keepers (mournfully received), they were allowed to leave with only one more task assigned to Rocío and Hala.

They stopped at Rocío's apartment to clean up, change and quickly swallow down tacos al pastor and coffee. Rocío's collection of scrapes and cuts throbbed out of sync with each other now that the adrenaline was well and truly gone.

When they entered La Valle, a band was playing 'Paciencia' for the full cast of *La Ingenue*, with Piotr and La Zorra dancing aggressively at the center of the crowd, their every movement defiance of the lyrics that counseled resignation. Their legs entwined, unbraided, slid sinuously apart. He twirled her out with a snap; she demanded his return with a twist of her hand, and he went.

If Piotr was as good a choreographer as he was a dancer, *La Ingenue* must be astonishing.

As they stalked across the stage, Piotr caught sight of Rocío and Hala and froze. La Zorra followed the direction of his gaze and shouted something just as the singer's voice swelled with the force of the chorus. La Zorra stooped, wrenched off one high-heeled shoe and threw it at the double bass.

The thump of contact was inaudible, but the bassist drew his bow across his instrument with a screech and fouled the elbow of the bandoneónista to his left. The bandoneón screeched like an angry cat. The band squealed to a stop.

The bassist looked like he was on the verge of flinging himself on La Zorra, a measure of how much he treasured his instrument, when La Zorra bellowed, "The detectives are here for Petya," and everyone stopped and turned to the door.

"He's alive," Rocío announced. "We found him."

Piotr fainted. La Zorra caught him before he knocked his brains out on one of the strip lights. Rocío and Hala walked to the stage, the dancers moving out of their way and crowding up behind them.

Pepe whispered, "Is it true?" as they passed.

"Yes. I hope you have enough booze for a celebration."

"You are a miracle worker." He clutched his hands together in front of his face and kissed his thumbs. "Who took him?"

Rocío didn't see any reason not to tell him. The news of the kidnapping would be all over the city soon, though she thought the necromantic aspects would be suppressed as much as possible. "Críspula de Herrera. Ministrx O'Higgins's assistant. Do you know her?"

"Oh." A look of realization bloomed across his face. "*Oh*. She came here a few times. Including Monday night. I thought she had a crush on him."

"She didn't kill him when she had the chance, and she killed a lot of other people, so maybe she did like him," Rocío said.

"Seres celestiales spare me from that kind of attraction. And I thought theater people were strange. Go on, talk to him." Pepe waved at the stage.

The bandoneónista had donated her glass of water, and the violinist had donated his handkerchief so La Zorra could pat Piotr's face. The singer produced a pot of peppermint menthol balm to wave under his nose. All combined, they woke him. La Zorra helped him sit up.

"What did you say?" he croaked.

"He's alive," Rocío said, kneeling to look him in the eye, "though he's had a difficult time of it." She took his hands. "He's injured and weak from blood loss and lack of food. He looks bad, but he's going to recover. We can take you to him now. He's at the University Hospital."

Piotr leaped to his feet and then slumped into La Zorra's arms, looking green and weak-kneed. "Will you go with me?" he asked her.

"Silly man," she said, patting his cheek. "Of course I'm going with you."

"We should all go," the singer said, and was answered with enthusiastic agreement.

Rocío had a mental image of them all crowded into Aleksandr Prokofiev's hospital room and accidentally suffocating him with their affection.

"He's not able to see many visitors," Hala said loudly, as if she was thinking the same thing.

"You should stay and plan a welcome home party," Rocío said.

Hala muffled a snort of laughter.

Pepe waved his hands over his head. "Yes, we must have a party for my favorite choreographer."

Rocío sighed for the short memories of entertainers and led the procession out the door.

Aleksandr Prokofiev looked up from his hospital bed, apprehension tightening his features, and then recognition kicked in and he extended both hands to his brother. His smile rearranged the haggard lines of his face in a not-quite-pleasant way.

Piotr gasped. La Zorra pushed him in the direction of the bed, and he obligingly fell across it and grasped his brother's arms. They spoke in rapid Rus, tears on their faces, glowing with happiness and relief. The human capacity for recovery was not endless, but Rocío believed Aleksandr Prokofiev would achieve it, in spite of the wounds both physical and mental.

Rocío and Hala exchanged a smile. This moment made the terror and the stress worth it and pushed away their effects, leaving Rocío light-headed and suffused with warmth. It wouldn't last, but it was a feeling she could look back on when the remembered terror and exhaustion and worry returned and tried to convince her they were the only true emotions. No—there were reunions and happiness and the world returned to knowable and controllable size so people could go on with their lives, in this case literally making music and beauty. It was why Rocío did the work she did.

And there were friendships, old and new, with people who gave the gift of themselves to those around them. Life, like a theater troupe, never remained the same, and if you embraced those changes, wonderful things could happen: relationships that enriched your life and productions that brought joy to so many.

With unspoken agreement, Hala and Rocío turned to leave and

give the brothers their privacy, but La Zorra put a restraining hand on Rocío's arm.

"Thank you for bringing Sasha back. There will be much rejoicing in La Quinta, and probably someone will tell your story in art. Who knows? Dance, plays, songs!"

Hala grimaced, but Rocío quite liked the idea of a play about her. *Maybe I could star as myself.*

La Zorra raised her voice. "Petya, our friends need to go."

"Of course." He bounced up from the bed, took Hala by the shoulders and kissed both her cheeks, then repeated the actions with Rocío, who laughed at the surprised expression on Hala's face and kissed Piotr back.

He took one of Rocío's hands and one of Hala's. "Friends, yes. I am so apology for what I said when I first saw you. You brought my brother back, and I have poor words to say my thank yous." He paused and squeezed their hands. "So I will say them the better way, with dance. We will perform *La Ingenue* at the outdoor theater on La Quinta and dedicate it to you and Miraflores Community Justice Center."

Hala slanted a look at Rocío. Nope, neither of them was going to mention Cempol. Let Maurata and Commander Dhavale have a fit about it if they wanted.

"No thanks are needed, but they are greatly appreciated. We're happy to be able to return your brother to you," Rocío said.

"No, no, you cannot leave yet. My brother would like to take your hand," he said and insistently pulled them forward, only letting go to transfer their hands to his brothers'. "Sasha, this is Detectives Rocío and Hala."

"Thank you," Aleksandr said, holding on and not letting go. His voice was raspy and deeper than his brother's. "I felt like all was a fog and I would die. When she moved me from the ice skating rink to the lighthouse, I was in despair, and not even the light of the sun could bring me hope. But then you came, painted for war, and said my brother's name, and I felt hope spring up in me like dancer's high jump."

"You told us how to find you," Hala said. "Rocío found the song you left and knew what it meant."

"Ah." His eyes opened wide in surprise, and he collapsed back against the pillows.

"We wouldn't have found you without the clue you left for us," Rocío said.

When a victim knew that their efforts—their agency and actions—had led to their rescue or to locating the criminal, it helped them to heal, both physically and, more important, mentally. No one liked to feel helpless, and one of the best antidotes to victimization was reminding them they weren't, that they had contributed to their own rescue.

"I didn't think anyone would find it," Aleksandr said faintly.

The door banged open, and Isis charged in with her spouses behind her. "Sasha!" she bellowed.

Rocío squeezed Aleksandr's hand and made way for Isis. Rocío exchanged smiles with Isis's spouses and slipped out, Hala right behind her.

"I think he's going to be okay," Rocío said, searching in her pockets for a piece of gum. "Do you think we can find someone who will tell us how Díaz or Ministrx O'Higgins are doing? Or should we knock on Ministrx O'Higgins's door and ask him?" She gestured at the door in question. "It's right there."

"Díaz, maybe. I'm not sure I'm up to extracting information from the staff about the ministrx. We'll hear soon enough."

Hala must be tired if she didn't want to snoop. At the reminder, every strained muscle and cut demanded Rocío's attention. *I don't even remember pulling a muscle in my back. Getting old is the worst.* She was about to suggest the bathhouse and a massage when Oshinsky appeared at the end of the hallway and beckoned to them.

"Rocío, Hala," Oshinsky said. "There you are."

Rocío assessed the look on Oshinsky's face and braced herself for bad news. "Is it Díaz? Is his wound worse than we thought?"

"No. Díaz is fine. He and Officer Smith will make full recoveries, and Díaz should be back at work soon. Even de Herrera is expected to recover. From her wounds, at least.

"Magickers Chuquisengo and Huaripani are guarding her, even though she's sedated. They're taking your report seriously." Oshinsky interlaced her fingers and paused. "No. It's Paloma," she said heavily. "We found the automobile off the road about a kilometer from the lighthouse. It was in a ditch, which is why we didn't see it earlier. It looks as if there was an accident, but there's no sign of Paloma. Cempol has officers searching for her, and Advocate Espinoza is with them. As soon as more advocates are freed up from this de Herrera mess, I'll put them on it."

Rocío could barely speak for the pressure in her chest. "Chief, did it look like a bad crash?"

Hala's eyebrows furrowed, and she moved closer so Rocío could feel the warmth of her body along her side.

"No. The auto is barely damaged, and there was no blood at the scene. She's probably in some farmer's house getting her cuts cleaned up. We'll find her. And no, you may not join the search. The only thing you're doing today is recuperating."

"Is that what you call debriefings with Cempol?" Hala asked.

It was a poor joke, but it helped Rocío start breathing normally again. *They'll find her. They have to. She's smart. She's capable. She wouldn't be my mentee if she wasn't. Ha.*

"And that," Oshinsky said. "No avoiding Cempol."

"Thank you, Chief," Hala said.

Ministrx O'Higgins's door opened, and Ministrx Montenegro sailed out. "Deputy Chief Oshinsky. Detective Díaz, Detective Haddad. I hear we have you to thank for saving the city from Críspula."

"Yes," Oshinsky said.

"William's condition improved as soon as we received the news, so you have my thanks for that as well. They're discharging him in a few days." Ministrx Montenegro frowned. "Maybe he'd prefer to stay at my house for a few days.

"Commander Dhavale said Críspula was upset because we chose Juan Pablo as third secretary over her. Spoiled girl, thinking she didn't have to pay her dues like everyone else. If she'd just waited ..." Ministrx Montenegro fingered her tupu. "It's better to know now that her character is weak, but what a cost to pay for the knowledge. Juan Pablo is not in good shape."

Although the words were neutral, something about the way she said them made Rocío think the ministrx shared her opinion of Juan Pablo. And if that was the case, why hadn't she done anything about the situation under her nose before it descended into retaliation and murder?

"It seems he bullied her quite badly," Rocío said sharply, "and that she didn't have recourse in the people around her, who might have been expected to help her."

Ministrx Montenegro's head reared back. "Are you defending her?" she bit out.

"No. Not at all. I'm saying that it's hard to find the right path when no one points it out to you."

"She was a spoiled brat who blamed other people for her failures."

"Yes. But like many people who are bullied, she struck back eventually in a very harmful way. At the end, I think she realized it and was fighting Fernández as much as we were, although that might have been because he had invaded her body and taken control, not just of the magic but of the direction of events." Rocío shrugged. "I'm not saying she's not responsible for her actions, just that I can see how she got here."

"Detective Díaz's empathy makes her an extremely effective advocate," Oshinsky said.

"You indict your friends Isis and María Paz with this accusation," Ministrx Montenegro said.

"I'm not indicting or accusing anyone, just thinking out loud about the responsibilities we have to the people around us." *Paloma, where are you?*

Ministrx Montenegro bared her teeth in what some might mistake for a smile and turned to Oshinsky. "Deputy Chief, will you inform me of the funeral arrangements for the lighthouse keepers? The sub-com will do something for their families."

"Críspula," Hala said in the tone of someone who has just realized something.

Everyone turned to her, surprised.

"What about her?" Oshinsky asked.

"Ministrx Montenegro, would you say you had a good relationship with her, better than her relationship with Ministrx O'Higgins?" Hala asked.

"Not better than her relationship with her uncle." Ministrx Montenegro raised her eyebrows in confusion. "She's a distant cousin, and I saw her often because of the sub-com meetings, but we weren't close."

"But you're the only one she hasn't attacked personally, is that right?" Hala asked intently, her eyes never leaving Ministrx Montenegro's face. "You've told us everything?"

"No, no personal attacks. I don't know—"

Hala snapped her fingers, making Rocío jump more violently than she probably would have before the day's events. "Your house. She was the one who destroyed your wardstone. It's your house."

"What?"

"Oh no," Rocío said, catching up to Hala in that way that sometimes happened when one of them had a realization and somehow catalyzed the other into having the same insight.

"We never figured out de Herrera's revenge against you, ministrx," Hala said. "Why didn't I see it before? She used that lichen to destroy the subte tunnel and your wardstone to get Fernández's body. What if those aren't the only things she decided to destroy? I think you had better check the foundations of your house."

"No." The blood drained from Ministrx Montenegro's face.

Oshinsky supported her with a hand under her elbow. "Surely you would have seen the effects by now if she had used it on the house."

"I'm not sure about that," Hala said. "Foundations are quite substantial by design."

"I need to go." Ministrx Montenegro turned abruptly and hurried away.

"I don't know whether to hope you're right or wrong," Oshinsky said.

Hala ran her hands through her hair. "Me neither."

"Well, it's not your problem now. Go home. Yours aren't going to fall down on you." Oshinsky made shooing motions.

"We're going, Chief." Rocío's legs felt like rubber after that last revelation, and she linked her arm through Hala's. "Do you think your cousin is still experimenting with tagine? I could eat again. Especially if he has those cookies with poppy seeds."

"You know what this means, right?" Hala asked as they walked towards the exit. "Old Nico saved the city and prevented catastrophe by telling me about his empty subte room. He's never going to let us forget it."

"You're never going to let me forget it either, are you?"

"Nope."

Rocío bumped Hala's hip with her own, and Hala bumped back. "I really need a cookie. I'm going to need a lot of cookies."

Hala laughed as they joined the swirl of pedestrians on the crowded street. The autumn sun, high in the vaulted blue sky, warmed Rocío's shoulders, dispersing the shadows, for now.

EPILOGUE

Ministrx O'Higgins sat in a chair by Críspula's bed. The bruises and cuts on his face had healed, though his arm was still taped up and a cane leaned against the wall.

The bed was more like a pretty crystal coffin. Yaco had explained it, but Rocío hadn't listened past the confirmation that it would keep Críspula alive until Magicker Chuquisengo could figure out how to separate Fernández from her soul, psyche, personality matrix—whatever one believed in—without killing her. Rocío had overheard Chuquisengo tell Huaripani it could take the rest of his life to unravel the scientific/magical/spiritual conundrum. He'd sounded rhapsodic, solidifying Rocío's dislike for him.

Críspula had kept a datebook, the kind a good housekeeper or an aspiring politician might keep. Whom she had met and where, what interested them, what she had done each day. Wednesday, March 4, the day Juan Pablo had been chosen as third secretary, had been crossed out with a heavy hand, repeated strokes almost shredding the page. Two days later, an entry read, "Haunted Castle, found it."

From there the carefully penned notes became terser, sloppier. Social interactions disappeared, replaced with a catalogue of slights. One page in late March said, "Uncle William. Why?" Rocío couldn't guess how much of the disillusioned tone was in her imagination and how much was in the shakily drawn letters. The pages after that were blank or filled with the word *no* over and over.

So how much of the crime spree had been Críspula de Herrera, and how much had been Eugenio Fernández? And what was worse: if Críspula had been misguided and spoiled, was taken over by Fernández and was trapped with him forever in her body, or if she had been as close to evil as anyone Rocío had ever encountered, a murderous descendent in spirit of Fernández?

Rocío didn't like not knowing, but no one could know. The adjudicator had ruled Críspula incompetent to be judged for reasons of possession. And that had led to this room on the top floor of Ministrx O'Higgins's house and Críspula laid out like a corpse with sunlight shining in a thick bar across her dark hair and white shift. Dust motes danced in the air.

Hiding Fernández's body in a dark, forgotten crypt hadn't worked out so well. Would this be better? A small machine on the floor pumped air in and out of the casket. If you watched long enough you could see Críspula's chest inflate with breath, pause for too long and deflate again. Rocío had been there long enough to witness it many times over. So had Ministrx O'Higgins.

"It's the least I can do for her family," he said, breaking the silence. "They are well established, but this kind of care is beyond their means."

Rocío watched Críspula's face. She looked peaceful. The weird blue lights in her eyes were hidden behind her closed eyelids, and the leaded glass cover, secured with steel clasps and locks on each of the four sides, left any movement open to view. Just in case.

Earlier, Gumersinda de Herrera Nuñes, Críspula's cousin and Ministrx O'Higgins's other assistant, had stopped Rocío on her way up the stairs. She looked even worse than before. Her hair was dull like she hadn't been washing it, and her cheeks were chapped.

"Detective Díaz."

"Rocío," Rocío said, and waited. She could extend a helping hand, but the other woman had to take it.

"Rocío. How could she have done that? H-hurt so many people. I don't know who she is anymore, and I would have said a few weeks ago that I knew her best in the world. Do we ever know anyone?" She wiped her cheeks like she was wiping away tears even though she wasn't crying.

Rocío remembered the moment she had decided to leave her parents' home and the life they wanted for her. She had looked inside herself and realized she didn't know who she was, that the self was a fiction to tie up the spaces inside, like the spaces between the stars— black, deep and so wide—so that each person could live and function with the myth that they were one coherent personality and not become madmen or hermits contemplating the face of the divine. In those spaces were all the possibilities of what a person could do and be, good or bad, and everything in between, surprising even oneself.

"I don't know," Rocío said, examining this girl who was so like Críspula in family, in background, in schooling, and in so many more ways. They could have been twins, except Críspula had made decision after decision that led to murder and Gumersinda had made decisions that led her to wherever it was she was heading. "We don't even know ourselves. But knowing that we don't know, that's something that can help guide us."

She had tried to comfort Gumersinda in some small way, but she had no desire to offer comfort to Ministrx O'Higgins now.

"She was a good girl," he said. "Her parents had such hopes for her, like all parents do." When Rocío didn't respond, he asked, "Why are you here?"

"I feel ..." So many things. Sympathy. Compassion. Anger. Sorrow. Frustration. That Fernández had robbed Críspula of the chance to make own her choices, or make different choices, or make any choices at all. An adjudication at least gave a sense of closure, of all sides being heard, of the catharsis of speaking. This was just limbo.

"I've been where she was," Rocío said, "wanting something so badly and feeling stymied on all sides by people and events outside my control." She patted her pockets, searching for a piece of gum and covertly keeping an eye on him.

"But you turned to a life of justice and assisting others, not murder and kidnapping."

Rocío turned to look at him fully. She couldn't find any hint in his face of the incongruity between his statement and what she and Hala suspected of him. They had only those few words Críspula had spat at the end of their standoff in the lighthouse. Hala had been stomping around the CJC, terrifying the chaskis or immersed in the archives for days at a time, looking for connections between him and the convict exchange program with the Ka Empire. For anything that might have tipped a sheltered, spoiled woman into kidnapping and murder.

Or maybe she just had a murderer's heart. Rocío didn't know. Couldn't know.

"True." Rocío unwrapped a stick of gum and folded it into her mouth. "But at a vulnerable point in my life, I was lucky to have people around me who listened to me and gave me advice."

"We failed her," he said heavily. "I go over it again and again in my mind, wondering what moment turned her from a sweet young girl into a murderer."

"I think it was the secrets. About the lieutenant governor's treason. And maybe about other members of the sub-com. I think she found something she couldn't face. Do you know what it was?" she asked, studying his expression.

"No," he said.

Not a twitch of his eyes, hands or feet betrayed whether he told the truth or lied.

Hala leaned against the wall surrounding Ministrx O'Higgins's house with her face tilted towards the weak sun. It was the first unguarded moment Rocío had caught her in since Aleksandr's kidnapping and Paloma's subsequent disappearance. Lines of worry and exhaustion drew down the corners of Hala's closed eyes and mouth. Rocío hated to disturb her, but Hala straightened as the guard closed the gate.

Rocío thought of and discarded several comments. Instead she settled next to Hala so their shoulders touched. The sun warmed her skin, and she couldn't help wondering if Críspula could feel it in her attic crypt. Hala's warmth against her side was more solid and dependable.

"What's this?" Rocío flicked a finger against the brown paper bag in Hala's hands. Elegant script proclaimed it from Benito's. "I thought you reserved us a table?"

"What happened?" Hala asked tipping her head towards the house.

Rocío leaned harder into her and absently watched the pedestrians. "He was lying," she said finally. "I know he was lying, but I don't have the twitch of a finger to prove it."

"That's as we expected," Hala said. "We'll figure it out." She raised the bag and brightened her voice. "This is a chocolate eclair. And this is a lead." She displayed a slip of paper in her other hand.

"Paloma?" Rocío asked, already reaching for it.

"The very same."

"Then what are we waiting for?"

— THE END —

Subscribe to R. Morgan's awesome newsletter for exclusive bonus content, including a scene from Críspula's point of view in the lighthouse, the short story, "A Case of Fear," where Rocío and Hala investigate art vandalism at a newfangled thing called an "art gallery", and updates on upcoming books.

Sign up at www.rafmorgan.com.

CHARACTER LIST

Miraflores Community Justice Center

Rocío Díaz Rossi: a detective, nickname Chío
Hala Haddad Sosa: a detective
Reo Maurata Martínez: chief
Oshinsky bas Rifke: deputy chief
Paloma Faro Otxandabaratz: Oshinsky's assistant
Mateo Díaz Matides: a detective
Selma Espinoza Onyeneme: an advocate
Zhou: an advocate
Yaco Tuz: a fifth-level forensics magicker
Viernes: a junior forensics tech
Paco: a chaski
Khadija: a chaski
Tomás: driver

Miraflores neighborhood

Gustavo Zivai: third-level magicker at the tube office
Old Nico: superintendent of the Miraflores subway line
Señorx Romero: owner of Café Storia

Rocío Díaz Rossi's Family

Analicía Rossi Dey: Rocío's mother
Xavier Díaz Vargas: Rocío's father
Nonna Antonetta: Rocío's maternal grandmother, deceased
Miguel: Rocío's brother
Sebastián: Miguel's spouse

Hala Haddad Sosa's Family

Giaconda Sosa di Monica: Hala's mother
Tamim Haddad Khalil: Hala's father
Salwa Haddad Sosa: Hala's youngest sister
Khaled Haddad Nehme: Hala's cousin

Members of the government of the city of La Bene and their households

Carmen Soto Cruz: governor of La Bene

Luka Sabato Soto: lieutenant governor of La Bene, married to Ana Valdivia Áquila

Ana Valdivia Áquila: a ministrx, married to Luka Sabato Soto

Sofía Montenegro Dhavale: a ministrx
Verra Montenegro: her daughter
Alexa Singh: Sofía Montenegro's majordomo

María Paz Belli Chambi: a ministrx, nickname Maipa
Entienne Mīchuki Dufresne: her spouse
Mizn bin Selasa Jardín de los fieles: their gardener, winner of the Günneh prize

William O'Higgins Cruz: ministrx of external affairs
Críspula de Herrera Carmona: his assistant and niece

Gumersinda de Herrera Nuñes: his assistant and niece
Martine Carter de Herrera: his cousin
Loeis Carter de Herrera: his cousin
Juan Pablo Ricci Cartier: third secretary to the Sub-Committee on
Legal Affairs, his cousin
Isabella Corona Costurerx: William O'Higgins's cook

Isis Soler Ibáñez: a ministrx
Tano: her spouse
Jacinta: her spouse
Huchim: her majordomo

La Quinta neighborhood

René Sahakian Quispe: nickname Pepe, owner of La Valle bar/theater
venue
Aleksandr Arkadyevich Prokofiev: nickname Sasha, a choreographer
employed by Pepe, brother to Piotr, recent immigrant from Rus
Piotr Arkadyevich Prokofiev: nickname Petya, a choreographer
employed by Pepe, brother to Piotr, recent immigrant from Rus
La Zorra: a dancer
Señorx Legionnaire: owner of The Legionnaire club/venue
Shen: an anarchist
Emma: an anarchist

Central Municipal Police (Cempol)

Álvaro Dhavale Vizcaino: commander
Ann Smith: an officer, Enkladt refugee
Huaripani: a tenth-level magicker
Aapo Chuquisengo Camal: a tenth-level magicker

Roxal Community Justice Center

Virgilio Udinesi Montalbán: chief

Villalta Community Justice Center

Cetz: an advocate

The Haunted Castle

Anozie Ilozumba Castillo: owner, recent immigrant
Ndidi Castillo: Anozie's spouse
Ijeawele Castillo: Anozie's sister-in-law
Golibe: Anozie's cousin
Eke: Anozie's daughter

PLEASE LEAVE A REVIEW!

If you enjoyed this book, it would be fantastic if you would leave a review!

First of all, I want to know what you thought!

Second of all, honest reviews help bring a book to the attention of other readers and to retailers' algorithms that decide which books to show people. When people see books they might buy them! If they do that means I can keep writing new books for you to enjoy.

Please consider leaving a quick review (it doesn't have to be long) on the review page where you purchased this book or on Goodreads.

Thanks so much!

R. Morgan

AUTHOR'S NOTE

tldr;

I wanted to write a story that was something like this: If Phryne Fisher had a bestie in a very alternate Latin America with magic. AKA two older women best friends solve a mystery, lots of competence, no damsels.

The long version:

I love mystery books and cop shows.

One of the reasons I'm drawn to these types of stories is that there is almost always a happy ending. The bad guy is caught. Justice is served. The bad situation is resolved in favor of the good guys. So often in the world the bad guys get away, justice isn't served, the good guys suffer. So often in fiction, I'm leery of whether that happy ending is really a happy ending, or an ending that upholds all the things I see wrong with our society and policing in the United States.

Even before the events of 2020, I struggled with the sexism, objectification of women, racism, homophobia, police brutality and protagonist-centered morality (when everything, no matter how questionable, the hero does is right, because the hero does it) embedded in them.

Cornell West said, "Justice is what love looks like in public." That's what I want to write. The characters in my books practice a form of restorative justice that doesn't exist in our world, but I hope that one day could exist, where offenders are rehabilitated, not punished, and victims and the community have a direct say in that process, and where the appropriate services are provided by trained personnel (for example, mental health professionals providing services to help mentally ill people, rather than police shooting them), and the people with power take ethical actions because that is the right thing to do.

There is also no explicit sexual violence in my books, because I'm sick of being fed it, I never want to read it and I certainly don't want to write it. Women are equal and queerness is normal in my books, too, for the same reasons.

Another reason I love these types of stories is the relationships that grow between people in difficult circumstances. There usually is a team of people working together with interesting group dynamics. They work long hours, see terrible things and need to depend on each other. I love friendship stories and I wanted to write a buddy cop story, but where the buddies are two middle-aged women, something we rarely get in this genre, and who are not objectified sexually and are not vessels of female pain for consumption.

So sometime in the summer of 2017 (Northern Hemisphere time) episode 61 of the podcast 99% Percent Invisible, "A Series of Tubes," about pneumatic tubes, collided with my love of and frustrations with Miss Fisher's Murder Mysteries (books and TV show) and my love of and frustrations with steampunk, gaslamp, flintlock and all things fantasy that seem to always be set in Great Britain or some alternate world that looks a lot like Great Britain and the idea for this book started to be born.

But let me explain. No, there is too much. Let me sum up. (Sorrynotsorry about The Princess Bride joke):

1. Pneumatic tubes are cool

2. Phryne Fisher (author: Kerry Greenwood; Australian TV show, Miss Fisher's Murder Mysteries) is awesome but she would be even more awesome with a best girl friend who is her partner and equal (Jack in the TV series is all very well but I'm much less interested in

romance than I am in friendships and especially friendships between women)

3. I am so sick of Great Britain or Generic Europe being the setting for so many fantasy books. I especially have problems with books set during the period of Empire that do not grapple with the damage done by the colonialism, imperialism, slavery, genocide, and theft of people, ideas and goods that made it possible.

Through the magic of creativity, imagination, the subconscious or whatever you want to call it, Rocío Díaz Rossi and Hala Haddad Sosa jumped into my brain, jumped into a setting (someplace like Buenos Aires, Argentina, which was mentioned in the podcast episode, or Mexico City — more about that in a minute —), jumped into a time (a time with pneumatic tubes, obviously, and all that implies) and jumped into fantasy, which is one of my favorite genres to read and write. But it was just an idea still and some interesting characters, but there was no story around them. I let them sit in my head, developing.

Then a massive life change happened to me. There was a lot of crying and emotional exhaustion. There was also a promise to myself: when I got through this one awful month I would then get through the next awful months by writing about Rocío and Hala, and because I didn't have a plot for them I would just copy the plot of *The Death of the Necromancer* by Martha Wells, one of my favorite books and the one I read the most in 2017. It didn't matter if I copied someone else's plot because this was a project just for me, to keep my sanity intact. It turned out it didn't matter anyway because you cannot put Rocío and Hala into someone else's plot and expect it to go smoothly. You'll notice I said I started writing in 2017 and you're reading this in 2021 or later. It did not go smoothly, but it did soothe my heart and it gave me something to write while I recovered my equilibrium and figured out how to live this new life thrust on me. (If you haven't read *The Death of the Necromancer* by Martha Wells, it's a fantastic book and one of my favorites. You might like it if you liked this book. You might even find some small similarities and you might laugh at a few tributes in *The Adventures of*....)

Going back to setting now, Latin America has its own complicated history of empire, colonialism, imperialism, slavery, genocide, and theft of people, ideas and goods. Using it as inspiration is complicated, because I am a white USAian who has lived and worked in Latin America but I'm not from there. I hope I have been thoughtful, not harmful, inspired, not appropriative. I hope that I have created a book that does homage to another part of the world than Generic Europe Fantasy Setting and that it fulfills some of your desires for fantasy that's a little different from what you've read before. I want to be clear that my book does not take place in Latin America. The world I built is inspired by the languages, cultures, geographies and histories of Latin America but it is not meant to be a one-to-one representation of a real place. I wanted to write a story that looks at possibilities, and I have tried to write about a place without the racism of our world, without the imperialism of the United States, Spain or Great Britain, a world without sexism and without the kind of religious strife that is all too real right now. (I have probably failed. Our lives our steeped in all these things and it is hard work to free our imagination of them.)

I believe that fiction can be an escape but it can also help us to imagine a world that is better than the one we have now. In the history of the story world I created, there were no equivalents to European empires, from the Romans to the Spanish or the British; there were no plagues of small pox, measles or flu to devastate people living in the equivalents of the Americas; and there were no organized religions that are often instrumental in the subjugation of peoples, genders and other religions in our world. It was inspired by many things, not least the time I spent living in various places in Latin America.

Some specific inspirations:

Hala's mother Giaconda Sosa di Monica is totally inspired by Mercedes Sosa, an Argentine singer. The line in chapter 9 "...Perfecto distingo, lo negro del blanco..." is from "Gracias a la vida," written by Violetta Parra, a Chilean singer and song writer. You can listen to Mercedes Sosa's version in Spanish (my favorite), Mercedes Sosa and

Joan Baez with English subtitles and Violetta Parra singing "Volver a los 17" (my favorite of hers).

I listened to Astor Piazzolla's Libertango album on repeat for much of the writing of this book. Sometimes I listened to Django Reinhardt's Djangology album.

Some other songs I was thinking about when I made up song titles:
Facundo Cabral singing "No soy de aquí"
Juan D'Areinzo performing "Paciencia" in 1937, one of the first tangos
Serrat singing "Cantares," originally a poem by Antonio Machado
Alejandro Fernandez singing "Si tu te vas."

The magpie clock in chapter 6 is based on one of the most expensive clocks ever sold at auction, designed and manufactured by Patek Philppe.

The Ya calendar is the Maya calendar, because I couldn't invent anything so amazing and complicated. I used this calendar converter.

I watched Life in a Lighthouse, 1940's - Film 7383 way too many times trying to get the big confrontation in the lighthouse right.

And finally, in chapter 24, Hala swears by Sutayta Al-Mahamali, who was a real woman, born in 10th century Baghdad and who was an expert mathematician.

ACKNOWLEDGEMENTS

The year I started writing this book, 2017, was one of the worst years of my life (yes, even compared to 2020, the year I'm writing the acknowledgements). I wouldn't have made it through without Cari, Ignacio, Gökhan, Jill, Kamma, Katie, Natasha and Yuko. Thank you for your friendship, your love and your support.

I also wouldn't have made it through that year, when I couldn't read anything new, without Martha Wells' books, which I re-read in rotation all year with Katherine Addison's *The Goblin Emperor*. Thank you for writing such great books that hit all my narrative buttons, Martha Wells.

Casey Blair, Theresa B., Julie C., Marissa Lingen and Janice Smith gave me invaluable feedback on early and later drafts and helped me shape this book into the one you are holding in your hands. The beginning of this book was much more confusing before they read it. Jill Westwood, bless her, read it THREE times, and is my partner in crime, my cheerleader and one of my oldest friends. Alison Cherry saved me from all my typos and grammatical lazinesses, though you did copy edit out one of my favorite jokes, Alison. Don't worry, I put it back. Jenny Zemanek made another beautiful cover for me.

Thank you to my family, Mom, Dad, Katie and Aunt Sara, for believing in me, supporting me, shoving my books into people's hands and actually reading them. Did you know most family members of writers don't? I always knew you were special.

Thanks to everyone in the podcasting community and FB groups who have shared their knowledge freely and generously, you also helped me get here.

And in memory of John Pantuso, who formatted my first book in print. May you rest in peace.

EXCERPT FROM BETWEEN THE MOUNTAIN AND THE SEA

Chapter 1

"Ready?" Iyo asked his twin sister Issa. He tucked a stray lock of her tawny hair under the scarf to hide it. Today was one of the three days a year Issa had to face the invaders, and they were known for taking what they wanted.

"R—" Issa cleared her throat. "Ready." With her animal-gold eyes lowered and her hair hidden, all traces of the invader who had raped their grandmama during the Conquest of Olendara disappeared and she looked fully Olendaran, brown skin over sharp bones.

"I'll be there," Deeka, their seven-year-old neighbor said, curling her hand into Issa's.

"And me," Deego, her twin said.

"We'll take care of each other," Issa said and somehow managed to raise her chin while still looking down.

They crossed the Westing Bridge over the canal and joined the streams of Olendarans entering the market square to declare their taxes for the next season. Not even Deeka and Deego, starting their apprenticeship rotation as oyster divers today, were exempt, though they would barely earn enough to buy one family portion of rice this season. And after taxes, not even that. Iyo pushed away thoughts of their own earnings—reduced now that Mama and Uncle were so sick —and started to pay attention to his surroundings.

The old temple, as scarred and maimed as any living veteran of the invasion, still dominated the square in spite of the gouges in the blue stone façade where the invaders had hacked away the images of the Whale and Dolphin. Most of the arcades were bricked up with the warm yellow stone that looked so right in the rest of the city and like a forty-year-old wound here. There were only three entrances now, open and ready to swallow Olendarans. The closest was heavily guarded. It led to the caves below the old temple, once the holiest place in Olendara, where the ocean met the land and priests had asked for miracles from the Whale and the Dolphin. Or so the priests said. They were dungeons now and no miracles occurred there.

Wooden stalls closed up around them, narrowing the view to vendors and their wares, which was mostly fruit in this section. Papaya, salak, mango—the smell of durian rolled over them and Deego sneezed. We should talk, to blend in more, but I can't think of anything to say. Anything I can say here. A gold-skinned invader lounged against a stall piled with imported star melons. The tricolor braid and whistle pinned to his black and red vest swung as he straightened, frowning at Iyo. No, at Deeka, who was openly staring.

"Deeka, stop looking at him," Iyo hissed.

Issa pulled Deeka closer, and Iyo cut behind a row of bundled sugarcane that reached higher than their heads. On the other side, Issa led them the long way around, out of sight of the invader and his three-squad, while Iyo kept a watch behind. After a few turns, Iyo signaled that the invader hadn't followed and Issa stopped at Mama and Uncle's empty stall. One withered flower was caught between the counter and the upright, a reminder of normalcy. The cabinet underneath, where Uncle locked his spinning wheel, looked untampered with, due as much to the neighbors' care as the taxes to hold the spot. Mama should have been there, Uncle spinning coir at her side, watching the invaders who bought her flowers.

"What are we doing here?" Deego asked. "Are your mama and uncle better?"

Iyo winced.

"Of course they're not," Deeka said. She stuck her wet finger in his ear and made him shriek, a sound he cut off quickly. He looked around to see if anyone had noticed.

Everything they did was circumscribed by the invaders. Resentment flared, but Iyo pushed it down. If he thought about how much he hated them, he wouldn't be able to do the things he had to do.

"Don't fight here." Issa pulled the kids apart. "We're just stopping for a moment." She touched the dead flower but left it in place. "Iyo?"

"My line is even longer than I expected. I should go with you."

She made a rude noise. "And spend all day here? No. I'll find someone to walk over with," Issa said. In spite of the invaders' own laws against stealing women, it didn't stop them from harassing women, and Issa's unique coloring seemed to rouse an avaricious, animal-like response.

Iyo left Iss, Deego and Deeka in a line with only a few mothers and uncles and their apprentice-age children. His line, in contrast, snaked halfway down one side of the square and hooked to the right in front of the old temple before curling around the bell tower and ending at the table set up over the First Holy Well, which was capped, blocked and the centerpiece in the rite of seasonal humiliation.

The younger twins in front of him were arguing about the children's races tomorrow during the festivities. Later today the guilds would issue invitations to their apprentices to join as adults. Tomorrow, all seventeen year olds would be initiated into adulthood. His invitations and his initiation. For a moment, the old, familiar worry about what happened during initiation, while the rest of Olendara partied, pushed aside the newer, sharper worry about Mama and Uncle.

Tomorrow we'll be adults. It felt no more real than when he had thought 'next year we'll be adults' or 'in four years we'll be adults.' For the first time, he didn't know if he wanted to be an adult, not if it was anything like this last moon and a half.

The line crept forward. Worry for Mama and Uncle swept over the other worry, rearranging it like a wave over shale. A three-squad ambled by, two men white as raw fish, the third dark, their kilts the color of fresh-spilled blood. Their posture, swords and crossbows said they owned the plaza. Deego and Deeka's blind cousin Loira, who fed the Olendaran prisoners in the old temple, didn't get out of their way fast enough and they tripped her. One of Loira's other cousins caught her and earned a casual slap for spoiling the invaders' fun.

Iyo's hands curled into fists. The invaders moved on to the old man scrubbing sea parrot guano off one of their precious beast statues. A group of Belennite refugees walked by and blocked Iyo's view.

Another normal day.

Across the square, voices rumbled in upset. The twins in front of him stopped arguing, their shoulders tense. Iyo's neck prickled. The line was too bunched up for him to see anything. "What's happening?" he asked.

The girl behind him whispered, "Something at the new registration table."

Whale and Dolphin drown it, not today. Not Issa.

Deego darted out of the crowd. "Iyo! It's Issa. An invader—you have to help."

I shouldn't have left her alone. He pushed out of the line and grabbed a hammer from a cobbler's stall.

"No, boy, don't do that," the cobbler implored.

"Stay here," Iyo said to Deego.

Iyo ran. He dodged another snarling statue and the Olendarans who had stopped to stare. As he got closer, he could see Issa with a pale invader's fist wrapped around her hair, forcing her face up. A gold woman and a dark man watched. Issa's scarf was gone and her tawny eyes stared back at him unblinking. Did the invader understand her expression? Was he enjoying her fear?

<No,> Iss said loudly in their language. <I don't want to be your concubine.> Her voice cracked on the last word.

<You already belong to us. Anyone can see it.>

<Sir. Sir, I mean, Captain,> a merchant said, <you can ask, but you have to let her go now that she's said no. It's your law.>

<The law wasn't meant for ones like her,> the invader said.

The gold one smacked the merchant. The pale invader bent Iss's head back farther.

<I am Olendaran. The law does apply to me,> Issa said, her voice flat with fear.

Rage narrowed Iyo's vision. The invader wasn't going to let go, and the others weren't going to stop him. Iyo raised the hammer. Two small hands circled it and he jerked free. Deego threw himself at him, wrapping his arms around his waist, mashing the hammer into his side.

"Iyo, Iyo, Iyo," he yelled, drawing attention to them in the too-quiet market.

"Don't be stupid," a stranger said. "You know the penalty for using a weapon against them."

"Don't be stupid," Deego said. "Be smart. Please, Iyo. No weapons. No fighting. Your grandmama needs you to stay alive. Look at Deeka."

Deeka was perched precariously on top of a stack of large amphora that were probably full of oil—no, indigo dye by the stamp on their sides. Iyo sucked on the scar on his lip. He wanted to smash through the invaders and kill them all, but the kids were right. He wasn't thinking. The punishment for attacking an invader was death. With a weapon, torture before death.

Deeka mimed pushing the top amphora off. Iyo jerked his chin in agreement and dropped the hammer. She rocked back and forth on the pile. At first nothing seemed to move, but a great heave that tumbled her from her perch set them toppling. They bounced and rolled unevenly and hit the beast statue with the same accuracy she used with her slingshot on rodents. The amphora shattered. Blue dye drenched the statue from muzzle to rump. It looked offended.

Bystanders jumped back and murmured in dismay. Everyone except the invaders crowding Iss stared. Whale drown them. Iyo ducked behind two men and yelled in his best invader accent, <The statue—they're desecrating it.>

The pale invader looked away from Iss. She stomped on his toes and he reared back. She slid out of his grasp and along the edge of the table. Iyo bowled into the group, elbowing their ribs with more force than he would in a crowd of Olendarans. Even the little pain he caused was satisfying, and it opened enough space for Issa to run.

The pale invader grabbed at Iyo's elbow. He jerked free and kept running. A glance over his shoulder showed the invader running a few steps after them before his fellows called him back to deal with the more serious problem of the defaced statue. They had been bending their own laws and they knew it. Issa's appearance always had that effect on them.

His hands trembled with anger as he tapped Issa on the shoulder. They slowed to a walk, just two more Olendarans leaving the market. Issa pulled her second scarf from her belt and covered her hair. Her breath was uneven. Iyo didn't look at her; his anger might catch the wind again and fly. There were too many invaders tempting it.

When they reached the wide, stone bridge over Slow Turn Canal, Iyo pushed aside the other pedestrians to reach the railing and looked back. A buffer of empty space surrounded the blue statue and the dark-skinned invader next to it. But they didn't look like they were organizing a search to find Deeka. Iyo's hands trembled harder at the realization of just how much he'd allowed Deeka to risk. *I wasn't thinking.*

He leaned on the railing, and the chipped stone bit into his hands. "Do you see them?"

"They're fast... look."

Deeka waved from the steps of the Westing Bridge, and Deego was jumping along the row of boats tied up along the canal below her.

"I shouldn't have let them do that."

"You couldn't have stopped them and also helped me. They know their age protects them."

"Not as much as they think."

"Or as much as you thought either," Issa said. "Look, the invaders aren't whistling for reinforcements, just impressing everyone in sight into a clean-up gang."

"Drown it. I hope that's all it is." Nearby merchants produced baskets of water and the impressed Olendarans knelt to scrub the statue. "Did you get them registered?"

"No," Issa said. "Dora Dano will have to take them."

"I didn't pay either, drown them. You'll have to come back with me later."

"I know."

Deeka and Deego met at the entrance to Flower Street, hooked their arms over each other's shoulders and strutted out of sight, as proud as any rooster. Relief stole the last of Iyo's energy and he slumped against the railing.

"That's that." She slid a glance at him, and he saw the long scratch on the side of her face.

"Iss, I'm sor—"

"Nothing wrong with me." Which meant she didn't want to talk about it. She never did.

ABOUT THE AUTHOR

R. Morgan has prepared all her life to be a writer, though she didn't know it. Like that time she volunteered to protect sea turtles on a beach in Costa Rica and wound up with half her body in the nest at 3 am with a blue plastic bag under the turtle's butt to catch her eggs to relocate them so poachers couldn't find them. Or living in Bangkok, Thailand, which is where she is now for her day job. (She's from the USA, but she has also lived in Mexico, Costa Rica and Nicaragua.)

Mostly she has worked as a technical editor and a Spanish to English translator in the US, Mexico City, Lima, Moscow and Surabaya, but she has also worked as a dog walker (sometimes taking 11 dogs to the park at once, but usually only two or three), on bilingual websites in Bogotá and Montevideo, and in district court (criminal) and family court in the US as an advocate. She has been asked to interpret from Portuguese even though she doesn't speak Portuguese (it was an emergency) and gotten up at 4 am to edit a meeting report and ended her day at the Bolshoi Theater watching Russian ballet.

Her favorite things are long rambling walks, preferably under trees, but a city will do, the smell of rain and a good book. Her favorite poetry anthology is *Americans' Favorite Poems*, edited by Robert Pinsky and Maggie Dietz, and don't even ask her to pick a favorite book. She has too many.

She writes YA fantasy under the name Raf Morgan.

ALSO BY R. MORGAN

Writing as R. Morgan

Between the Mountain and the Sea

River of Lies: A Rocío and Hala novella

Writing YA fantasy as Raf Morgan

The Desert Wall

The Red Fortress (coming soon)

Edited by Raf Morgan

Swift the Chase: Scenes from 9 Fantastic Stories

www.ingramcontent.com/pod-product-compliance
Lightning Source LLC
Chambersburg PA
CBHW070815190726
48292CB00006B/2026